THE ROAD
OF DANGER

THE ROAD OF DANGER

THE REPUBLIC OF CINNABAR NAVY

DAVID DRAKE

TITAN BOOKS

The Road of Danger
Print edition ISBN: 9781785652356
E-book edition ISBN: 9781785652363

Published by Titan Books
A division of Titan Publishing Group Ltd
144 Southwark Street, London SE1 0UP

First Titan edition: October 2018
2 4 6 8 10 9 7 5 3 1

A CIP catalogue record for this title is available from the British Library.

Printed and bound in Great Britain by CPI Group UK Ltd.

What did you think of this book? We love to hear from our readers. Please email us at: readerfeedback@titanemail.com, or write to us at the above address.

To receive advance information, news, competitions, and exclusive offers online, please sign up for the Titan newsletter on our website:

www.titanbooks.com

To Scott Van Name
Who was much younger than I was
when he learned to appreciate Gaudi.

AUTHOR'S NOTE

I use both English and metric weights and measures in the RCN series to suggest the range of diversity which I believe would exist in a galaxy-spanning civilization. I do not, however, expect either actual system to be in use in three thousand years. Kilogram and inch (et cetera) should be taken as translations of future measurement systems, just as I've translated the spoken language.

Occasionally I think that I don't really have to say that in every RCN book. It's obvious, after all, isn't it? But there's a certain number of people to whom it isn't obvious. They'll write to "correct" me, and that gets on my nerves.

The plots of my RCN novels often come from classical history. Ordinarily that means something I've found in a Greek historian whom I've been reading in translation. In the present case, however, I resumed reading the Roman historian Livy in the original. I found my situation in the disruption which followed the Battle of Zama and the surrender of Carthage to end the Second Punic War.

One of the advantages in going back to primary—or at least ancient—sources is that the ancient historians mention things which modern histories ignore as trivial. They weren't trivial to the people living them, and to me they often do more to illuminate the life of the times than do ambassadors' speeches and the movements of armies.

Northern Italy at the end of the third century BC was a patchwork of Roman colonies and allies, Celtic tribes recently conquered by Rome, and independent tribes, mostly Celtic. A man calling himself Hamilcar and claiming to be a Carthaginian raised a rebellion against Rome. In the course of it he sacked cities and destroyed a Roman army sent against him.

Nobody was really sure where Hamilcar came from. Supposedly he was a straggler from one of the Carthaginian armies which passed through the region, but there was no agreement as to which army.

There are two perfectly believable accounts of his defeat and death. They can't both be true, which leads to the possibility that neither is true. All we know for certain is that Hamilcar disappears from the record and from history more generally.

The point that particularly interested me was that the Roman Senate reacted by sending an embassy to Carthage, demanding that the Carthaginians withdraw their citizen under terms of the peace treaty. This makes perfect legal sense, though appears absurd in any practical fashion.

Livy's account got me thinking about the problems that the envoys would have had. The Romans were going to Carthage with demands which weren't going to be greeted by their listeners with any enthusiasm.

They had it easier, however, than the Carthaginians who were presumably tasked to proceed to the chaos in Northern Italy and corral Hamilcar. Whatever the Carthaginian people thought of the situation, they were in no position in 200 BC to blow off a Roman ultimatum. There's no record of the Carthaginian response, but I believe they made at least some attempt to comply. Otherwise there *would* be more in the record.

I decided that I could find a story in that. This is the story I found.

—Dave Drake
david-drake.com

But if you come to a road where danger
Or guilt or anguish or shame's to share,
Be good to the lad that loves you true
And the soul that was born to die for you,
And whistle and I'll be there.
—A. E. Housman
More Poems, XXX

Chapter One

HOLM ON KRONSTADT

Captain Daniel Leary whistled cheerfully as he and Adele Mundy turned from Dock Street onto Harbor Esplanade, walking from the *Princess Cecile*'s berth toward the three-story pile of Macotta Regional Headquarters. Daniel had every right to be cheerful: he and his crew had brought the *Sissie* from Zenobia to Cinnabar in seventeen standard days, a run which would have stretched a dedicated courier vessel. They had then—with the necessary orders and authorizations—made the run from Cinnabar to Kronstadt in eleven days more.

The *Sissie*'s fast sailing meant that Admiral Cox could get his battleships to Tattersall in plenty of time to prevent the invasion which would otherwise lead to renewed war between Cinnabar and the Alliance. Neither superpower could resume the conflict without collapse: forty years of nearly constant warfare had strained both societies to the breaking point. In a very real sense, preventing war over Tattersall meant preventing the end of galactic civilization.

Not a bad job for a fighting corvette. Pretty bloody good, in fact.

"That's 'The Handsome Cabin Boy,' isn't it?" asked Officer Adele Mundy. "The tune, I mean."

"Ah!" said Daniel with a touch of embarrassment; he hadn't been paying attention to what he was whistling. "Not really the thing to bring into an admiral's office, you mean? And quite right, too."

"If I had meant that...," Adele said. She didn't sound angry, but she was perhaps a trifle more tart than she would have been with a friend if they hadn't just completed a brutally hard run through the Matrix. "I would have said that. I was simply checking my recollection."

She pursed her lips as she considered, then added, "I don't think anyone who could identify the music would be seriously offended by the lyrics. Although the record suggests that Admiral Cox doesn't need much reason to lose his temper. No reason at all, in fact."

Daniel laughed, but he waited to respond until a pair of heavy trucks had passed, their ducted fans howling. The vehicles carried small arms which had been stored in the base armory while the ships of the Macotta Squadron were in harbor.

As soon as the *Sissie* reached Kronstadt orbit, Daniel— through the agency of Signals Officer Mundy—had transmitted the orders he carried to the regional headquarters. Admiral Cox wasn't waiting for the chip copy to arrive before he began preparing to lift his squadron off.

"Cox does have a reputation for being, ah, testy," Daniel said. "That probably has something to do with why he's here in the Macotta Region when his record would justify a much more central command."

Navy House politics weren't the sort of things a captain would normally discuss with a junior warrant officer, but Adele's rank and position were more or less accidental. She was a trained librarian with—in Daniel's opinion—an unequalled ability to sort and correlate information. If necessary, Daniel would have classed her as a supernumerary clerk, but because Adele could handle ordinary communications duties, she was signals officer of the *Princess Cecile* according to the records of the Republic of Cinnabar Navy.

Three blue-and-white vans stencilled SHORE PATROL over broad vertical stripes tore past; the middle vehicle was even ringing its alarm bell. Adele followed them with her eyes, frowning slightly. "What are they doing?" she asked.

"Carrying spacers picked up on the Strip to their vessels," Daniel said. "I'm sure that the wording of the recall order justifies it, but there's no operational reason for that—"

He nodded after the speeding vans.

"—since it's going to be forty-eight hours minimum before the majority of the squadron can lift off."

Coughing slightly, Daniel added, "I've found that people who enlist in the Shore Patrol like to drive fast. And also to club real spacers who may have had a little to drink."

He kept his voice neutral, but the situation irritated him. The Shore Patrol performed a necessary function, but fighting spacers—which Daniel Leary was by any standard—tended to hold the members of the base permanent parties in contempt. That contempt was doubled for members of the Shore Patrol, the portion of the permanent party whom spacers on liberty were most likely to meet.

"I see," said Adele. From her tone, she probably did.

Daniel shivered in a gust of wind. In part to change the subject, he said, "If I'd appreciated just how strong a breeze came off the water at this time of day, I'd have worn something over my Whites. I don't have anything aboard the *Sissie* that's suitable for greeting admirals, but I guess I could've dumped my watch coat onto his secretary's desk before I went through to his office."

He'd noticed the local temperature from the bridge when the *Sissie* landed, but it hadn't struck him as a matter of concern. While he was growing up on the Bantry estate, he'd thought nothing of standing on the seawall during a winter storm. *I'd have been wearing a lizardskin jacket, though, or at least a poncho over my shirt.*

Today Daniel wore his first-class dress uniform, since he was reporting to the Macotta Regional Commandant. Anything less would be viewed as an insult, even though technically his second-class uniform—his Grays—would be proper. As he had said, Admiral Cox had the reputation of not needing an excuse to tear a strip off a subordinate.

"We've been aboard the *Sissie* so long," Adele said, "that I'd forgotten how the wind cuts too. At least it's not sleeting, and we don't have to sleep in it."

She glanced toward him with a raised eyebrow. "At least I hope we won't have to sleep in it," she said. "Poverty provided me with many experiences which I would prefer not to revisit."

Daniel hoped Adele was being ironic, but it was just as easy to treat the comment as serious—as it might be. He said, "I don't think we'll be sleeping in a doorway tonight, but I may have Hogg bring us heavy coats before we walk back to the *Sissie*."

They'd reached the line of bollards that protected the front of the regional headquarters. The two guards at the main entrance wore battledress, and today their submachine guns weren't for show. Unsmilingly, they watched Daniel and Adele approach; the alert must have made everyone on the base a little more jumpy than normal.

Adele shrugged. "I did think that Admiral Cox might have sent a vehicle for us," she said. "Or his Operations Section, at any rate, but perhaps they're too busy dealing with their new orders to worry about courtesy toward the officer who brought those orders."

Adele *did* wear her Grays. They weren't tailored as closely to her trim body as they might have been, so that the personal data unit along her right thigh and the pistol in the left pocket of her tunic were less obtrusive. There wouldn't be a problem about that: formally, Signals Officer Mundy was a junior warrant officer on the corvette *Princess Cecile*, accompanying her commanding officer. As such she was beneath the notice of an admiral in the Republic of Cinnabar Navy. Informally...

Daniel wasn't sure that his friend even owned a set of Whites. When Adele deemed that a situation required formality, she wore civilian garments of the highest quality. By birth Adele was Lady Mundy of Chatsworth, head of one of the oldest and once most powerful families in the Republic. When she chose to make a point of it, no one doubted that the Mundys retained a great deal of power.

The headquarters building was of yellow stone, not brick as Daniel had thought when he started down the esplanade. The corners, and the cornices above the windows on each of the three floors, were of a slightly darker stone than the walls. In all, very skilled workmanship had gone into a building which nonetheless had no more grace than a prison.

Three officers wearing utilities but saucer hats with gold braid came out of the door in a hurry; one clutched a briefcase to her chest. A light truck with six seats in back pulled up beyond the bollards. They got into the vehicle and rode off. The tires of spun beryllium netting sang on the pavement.

"Captain Daniel Leary, just landed in the *Princess Cecile*," Daniel said to the Marine sergeant who seemed the senior man; both guards had relaxed when the strangers sauntered close enough to be seen as harmless by even the most paranoid observer. "Here to report to the regional commander."

"It's to the right just inside the door," the sergeant said, gesturing. "But we got a flap on here, so don't be surprised if some clerk checks you in."

Daniel nodded pleasantly. It wasn't the proper way to address a senior officer, but Marines weren't in the same chain of command as spacers until you got up to the Navy Board—which was a very long distance from Kronstadt. The other guard pulled open the door for them, though the gesture was marred when two more officers came out, talking in excitement and taking only as much notice of Daniel and Adele as they did the line of bollards.

The lobby must have been larger originally. A splendid crystal chandelier hung in line with the door, but a waist-high counter now stood a full ten feet out from where the right-hand wall must have been.

A clerk under the eye of a senior warrant officer acted as gatekeeper to the several officers who wanted to get through. Beyond the counter were six consoles occupied by clerks.

Across the bullpen was a closed door marked ADMIRAL AARON J COX in raised gold letters. The door of the office beside it was open; the commander seated at the desk there wore utilities. It was unlikely that a regional headquarters operated on a combat footing normally, so she must have changed out of her dress uniform as a result of the signal from the *Princess Cecile*.

The commander got up when she saw Daniel enter and approach the counter. Instead of greeting him, she tapped on the admiral's door and stuck her head in. After what must have been a few words, she turned and called across the room, "You're Captain Leary?"

Yes, which makes me your superior officer, Daniel thought. Aloud he said pleasantly, "Yes, Commander. My aide and I are bringing orders from Navy House."

Adele held the thin document case in her right hand; she didn't gesture to call attention to it. Her face was absolutely expressionless, but Daniel could feel anger beat off her like heat from an oven.

With luck, Admiral Cox would ignore Adele during the coming interview. With even greater luck, neither Cox nor his aide would manage to push her further. Daniel had the greatest respect for his friend's self-control, but he knew very well what she was controlling.

"Come on through, then," the commander said. "The admiral has decided he can give you a minute. Casseli, let them both in."

The warrant officer lifted the flap. The three officers on this side of the counter watched the visitors with greater or lesser irritation.

Adele smiled slightly to Daniel as she stepped through. "I'm reminding myself that there are fewer than twenty present," she said in her quiet, cultured voice. "So there's really no problem I can't surmount, is there?"

Daniel guffawed. The commander—the name on her tunic was Ruffin—glared at him.

I wonder what she'd say, Daniel thought, *if she knew that Adele meant she had only twenty rounds in her pistol's magazine? Of course, she normally double-taps each target....*

Admiral Cox's office had high windows with mythological figures—Daniel wasn't sure what mythology—molded onto the columns separating them; the pattern continued, though at reduced scale, along the frieze just below the coffered ceiling. The furniture was equally sumptuous, which made the admiral's mottled gray-on-gray utilities seem even more out of place. The regional command seemed to be at pains to demonstrate how fully alert they were, but changing uniforms wouldn't have been one of Daniel's operational priorities.

Daniel took two paces into the room and saluted—badly. He was stiff with chill, and he'd never been any good at ceremony. "Captain Leary reporting with dispatches from Navy House, sir!" he said.

The admiral's return salute was perfunctory to the point

of being insulting. He said, "They're the same as what you signalled down, I take it?"

"Yes, sir," Daniel said. Adele was offering the case—to him, not to Admiral Cox. "I had been warned that time was of the essence, so we took that shortcut to save the hour or so before we could get the *Sissie*—the ship, that is—down and open her up."

"Navy House was quite right," Cox said, as though the decision had been made on Cinnabar instead of on the *Sissie*'s bridge. He was a squat man whose hair was cut so short that it was almost shaved; he looked pointedly fit. "Hand them to Ruffin, then, and I'll give you *your* orders."

"Sir!" Daniel said. He took the chip carrier from Adele, who hadn't moved, and gave it to the smirking Commander Ruffin.

"Indeed I will, Captain," the admiral said. His smile was that of a man who is looking at the opponent he has just knocked to the floor, judging just where to put the boot in.

Adele Mundy liked information—"lived for information" might be a better description of her attitude—but she had learned early that she preferred to get her information secondhand. Life didn't always give her what she wanted, but she had tricks for dealing with uncomfortable realities.

At present, for example, she was imagining that, while seated at her console on the bridge of the *Princess Cecile*, she was viewing the admiral's office in hologram. That way she could treat what was being said simply as data, as information with no emotional weight.

For Adele to display emotion here would compromise her

mission and would—more important—embarrass her friend Daniel. She therefore avoided emotion.

"Maybe you think I don't know why your noble friends at Navy House sent the information by your yacht instead of a proper courier ship?" Cox said. His face was growing red and he gripped the edges of his desk hard enough to mottle his knuckles. "Is that it, Leary?"

The phrase "noble friends" settled Adele's data into a self-consistent whole. Cox's father had been a power-room technician and a member of a craft association which provided education for the qualified children of associates. Cox had excelled in astrogation training; then, at a time of great need during the Landsmarck War thirty years ago, he had transferred from merchant service to the RCN.

That Cox had risen from those beginnings to the rank of admiral was wholly due to his own effort and abilities. It wasn't surprising that he felt hostile to a highly regarded captain who was also the son of Speaker Leary—one of the most powerful and most feared members of the Senate. Cox had no way of knowing that Daniel had at age sixteen broken permanently with his father by enlisting in the Naval Academy.

"Sir," Daniel said carefully. He would have probably have preferred to remain silent—there was nothing useful he could say, after all—but Cox's phrasing didn't permit him that option. "I believe the Board may have taken into account that the *Princess Cecile* was fully worked up, having just made a run from Zenobia. I honestly don't believe that a courier— the *Themis* was on call—which hadn't been in the Matrix for thirty days could have bettered our time from Xenos."

Adele wondered if commissioned officers could be charged with Dumb Insolence or if the offense was only applied to enlisted spacers. She would like to look up the answer with her personal data unit.

She would like *very* much to escape into her personal data unit.

"I'm supposed to believe that it was all for practical reasons?" Cox said in a hectoring voice. The design inlaid on his wooden desktop showed men with spears—and one woman—fighting a giant boar. It was very nice work. "That your father didn't have dinner with Admiral Hartsfield and say that his son should be sent to the Macotta Region to burnish his hero image?"

"Sir," said Daniel stiffly. His eyes were focused out the window over the admiral's shoulder. "I truly don't believe that my father has any connection with the Navy Board. I myself haven't spoken with him for years."

For a ship to make a quick passage between stars, it had to remain in the Matrix and take advantage of variations in time-space constants varied from one bubble universe to the next. Most vessels returned to the sidereal universe frequently, in part to check their astrogation by star sightings but also because humans do not *belong* outside the sidereal universe. The pressure of alienness weighed on crews, affecting some people more than others but affecting everyone to a degree.

Daniel had spent nearly all the past month in the Matrix, and most of that time out on the *Sissie*'s hull. That had allowed him to judge every nuance of energy gradients and adjust his course to make the quickest possible passage.

It was discourteous for Cox to abuse a man who had just undergone that strain. It was dangerous to do so in front of the man's friend, who had undergone the same strain and who had killed more people in the past few years than even her own fine mind could remember.

Admiral Cox drew his head back slightly and pursed his lips. The new expression wasn't welcoming, but Adele found it an improvement on the angry glare which he had worn until now.

"Well, that doesn't matter," Cox said gruffly. "The orders say that you're to put yourself and your ship under my command during the operation. That's correct, isn't it?"

Perhaps he had recognized how unjust he had been. And perhaps he had considered some of the stories he'd heard about Officer Mundy.

Daniel took a needed breath. "Yes, sir!" he said brightly. "If I may say so, I believe Officer Mundy's—"

He nodded toward Adele with a smile.

"—information-gathering skills—"

"That's enough, Leary," Cox snapped, returning the atmosphere in the office to the icy rage of moments before. "I've heard about your tame spy...."

He made a dismissive gesture toward Adele. His eyes followed his hand for a moment but as quickly slid away from Adele's still expression. She had been sure that her face was expressionless, but apparently she had been wrong about that.

Where did he get the idea that I'm tame?

"Anyway, I've heard about her," Cox said more quietly, looking at Daniel and then to the holographic display skewed toward him from the right side of his desk. "In my judgment, my regional Naval Intelligence Detachment is quite capable of sweeping up these supposed plotters on Tattersall without help from outside. I'm therefore—"

Commander Ruffin was grinning.

"—going to assign you and your corvette to a matter of great diplomatic concern, Leary. I'm sending you to Sunbright in the Funnel Cluster to remove the Cinnabar citizen who's reported to be leading a revolt there. Ruffin will give you the details."

"Sir?" said Daniel, more in surprise than protest. "Sunbright is an Alliance base, isn't it? Why—"

Cox slammed his left palm down on the desk. Papers and small objects jumped; Adele noticed that the display became an unfocused blur for a moment. *Even a ground installation should be better insulated against shock than that.*

"I said, Ruffin will take care of you!" Cox said. Less harshly, he continued, "Ruffin, brief them in your office and then get back here. We've got a lot of work to do on this Tattersall business."

"Sir," said Daniel. He saluted and turned to the door, reaching it before Commander Ruffin did.

Adele followed. She decided to feel amused, though she didn't allow the smile to reach her lips.

She had started to pull out her data unit when Cox referred to Sunbright. That would have been not only discourteous but even an offense against discipline, likely to cause trouble for Daniel as well as herself. She had therefore controlled her reflex.

But that restraint made it all the harder to avoid using the other tool which Adele used to keep the universe at bay. It would have been even more troublesome to have drawn her pistol to shoot dead the regional commandant and his aide.

Chapter Two

HOLM ON KRONSTADT

Daniel supposed that he should have waited for Commander Ruffin to usher them into her office, but she was behind Adele, and Daniel *really* wanted to get his friend out of the admiral's presence before something happened. He was thinking tactically, not what he'd expected when they entered the headquarters building.

An RCN officer must always be ready to deal with a crisis. Daniel grinned.

He swung Ruffin's door back and waved Adele through with a flourish. Ruffin, close behind Adele, stiffened with irritated surprise.

Daniel's grin broadened and he repeated the gesture. "After you, please, Commander," he said.

Ruffin paused, then stepped through without looking at Daniel until she had reached her desk and sat down behind it. He closed the door behind him, standing with his back against the jamb. Adele was already seated at one of the severely functional chairs in front of the desk. The data unit was live on her lap.

Adele served Cinnabar not only in uniform but also as an agent of the Republic's intelligence service. Daniel knew of the association and had even met—socially—Mistress Bernis Sand, who directed those operations.

Daniel was a patriot as well as an RCN officer, and he would help his friend Adele in any fashion that she requested. That said, the whole idea of spying struck him as grubby and unpleasant. He accepted that it was necessary, and he had used information which Adele provided without looking too closely at how she had come by it; but the admiral's reference to "your tame spy" had filled Daniel with as much disgust as anger.

He could only guess how Adele had reacted to the gibe. That guess, however, was the reason Daniel had been in such a hurry to get his friend out of the admiral's office.

Ruffin's desk and console were RCN standard, no different from the units in the outer office; the three chairs and the filing cabinet for hard copy were equally utilitarian. The multi-paned window, however, was framed by pillars of gorgeous wood which had been turned in spiral patterns.

Daniel had to restrain himself from walking over to examine the orange and black grain more closely. *Is the wood local?*

Instead of speaking immediately, Ruffin brought her console display live and began sorting information with a touch pad. It wasn't clear whether she was being deliberately insulting or was just flustered.

Cheerfully, Daniel said, "I wonder, Commander? Did you originate the plan to send us to Sunbright or did Admiral Cox devise it on his own?"

Ruffin looked up with a furious expression. "Your arrival allows the Macotta Squadron to concentrate on the crisis on Tattersall!" she said. "Instead of sending elements off to the Funnel Cluster on what isn't properly an RCN matter anyway."

She cleared her throat. "Now if you'll sit down," she said, "we'll proceed with the briefing."

"I believe I'll stand, Commander," Daniel said. There were advantages to being fobbed off on an aide of lower rank. "I think I'll absorb information better this way."

Daniel had very little personal experience of bullying. As a boy he'd grown up with his mother on Bantry, the family estate on the west coast, while his father spent his time in Xenos, ruthlessly pursuing money, power, and bimbos. Hogg, now Captain Leary's personal servant, had been the child's minder and male role model.

Daniel thought back to those days with a wry grin. He had been what his mother described as a high-spirited boy; others had found harsher terms. Nobody was going to bully the young squire, but neither were the sons of freeborn tenants going to be pushed around by a pipsqueak kid.

Therefore Daniel had had the living daylights whaled out of him more than once. He gained respect on the estate because he kept getting up; but he kept getting knocked down again too, until Hogg decided it was time to end each fight by hauling his charge off to be cleaned up to the degree possible.

Goodness knows how Hogg explained the damage to Mistress Leary, but fortunately she spent most of her life in a gentle reverie. She probably hadn't paid much attention to her son's cuts and bruises.

At the Academy, the system itself was designed to crush cadets into RCN discipline. That, like the give-and-take of Bantry, was simply part of life. Occasionally someone would be singled out for personal attention, but not Daniel: he didn't behave like a victim; his father, estranged or not, was powerful and famously ruthless, and Hogg, while his deportment lacked a good deal of what was expected of an officer's servant, projected the cheerful air of a man who had garroted rabbits and was more than willing to garrote men who tried to harm his master.

Cox and his flunky, however, were using RCN authority to display their pique rather than to serve the Republic. Daniel would obey the lawful orders of a superior officer—but when the superior officer was a prick abusing his authority, a Leary of Bantry didn't roll onto his back and wave his legs in the air. And as for the prick's lower-ranking toady...

Daniel grinned. His native good humor made the expression a great deal more cheerful than it might have been on another man's face. *Let alone on Adele's...*

Ruffin flushed angrily to see the smile, though the gods alone knew how she was interpreting it. She said, "Sunbright is an Alliance world in the Funnel Group, which to the Alliance is a separate administrative unit from the Forty Stars. They're both part of the Macotta Region to us, to Cinnabar, so that's why Xenos has handed this nonsense to us. The External Bureau has! This has *nothing* properly to do with the RCN."

The outburst proved Commander Ruffin was capable of umbrage at someone other than the captain and the signals officer of the *Princess Cecile*. As for who properly should have been handling a given duty, however…the External Bureau was the Republic's diplomatic hand, and the RCN was the sword which gave point to the Republic's diplomacy. If the diplomats chose to offer a job to the armed service, Daniel's feeling was, "So much the better!"

A starship vented steam in a shriek that only slowly tapered back to silence. Daniel instinctively glanced out the window behind Ruffin, but the back of the building here faced away from the harbor. Chances were that one of the squadron had built up calcium in a cooling line, and the pre-liftoff test had nearly burst the tubing before a technician managed to open a valve.

"Four years ago," Ruffin said, "a rebellion broke out on Sunbright. They grow rice on the planet, a fancy variety and quite valuable, but the planet hadn't attracted much attention. Five years ago, however, Fleet Central on Pleasaunce decided it was a good location for a staging base in case we tried to threaten Alliance holdings in the Funnel."

"Was there any chance of that?" Daniel said, drawn back into professional speculation as his personal irritation cooled.

Ruffin's snort showed that what Daniel remembered of the region was correct. "Bugger all!" the commander said. "Xenos keeps us starved for parts and crews here in the Macotta, and as for the ships—"

She threw up her hands. "The *Warhol* is old, and the *Schelling* was launched when my grandfather was in service. I don't think there's an older battleship in the RCN. *We're* no threat to the Funnel."

She cleared her throat and added, "Though we can see off that cruiser squadron from Madison easily enough. They're

Marie Class and haven't been first-line ships for a generation."

"How does a rebellion on Sunbright become an RCN problem, then?" Daniel prodded gently. Out of the corner of his eye he saw the flickering of the control wands which Adele preferred to other input methods. She had doubtless called up all the available information on the situation and could have briefed Daniel with a few quick, crisp sentences.

Though it would be informative to see how Ruffin framed the data. Often you learned as much from how people told you things as you did from the content.

"Well...," said Ruffin, glaring at her own display. "Well, the rebel leader uses the name Freedom, but he claims to be a Cinnabar citizen and to have backing from the Republic. This was fine during the war, of course, but since the Truce of Amiens..."

Ruffin grimaced and cupped her empty hands upward.

"Anyway, Pleasaunce complained to Xenos," she said, "and Xenos handed the whole business here to the Macotta Regional Headquarters. Without any extra resources, I might add!"

Brightening, she added, "Until you arrived, that is. You let us get on with the real crisis and still satisfy those pansies in the External Bureau."

"I see," said Daniel. He expected he would see a great deal more as soon as he and Adele could talk freely outside Macotta Headquarters. Her wands had continued to flicker without slowing since the moment she had seated herself in a corner of Ruffin's office. "Do you here in the region have any suggestions about how to carry out the task?"

"Any way you please, Captain!" Ruffin said. She stabbed an index finger into her virtual keyboard and straightened with an air of accomplishment. "According to your reputation, you're quite the miracle worker. Perhaps you can work another one here. Whether you do or not, that reputation is just the sort of window dressing that we need to get Xenos off our backs while we fix Tattersall."

She gestured to her display; from Daniel's side of the desk, the hologram was a blur of color which averaged to gray. "I've sent all the information we have to your ship, the *Princess*. You can access it at your leisure. I don't have anything else to add."

"Then we'll leave you to your business," Daniel said. Out of common politeness, he tried to keep the disgust out of his voice.

He nodded, then turned and opened the office door; Adele had put her data unit away in the thigh pocket a tailor had added to her second-class uniform.

Adele will certainly have something to add.

"I'd like to sit for a moment before we return to the *Princess Cecile*," Adele said as she and Daniel left the outer office. "The benches around the fountain in front of the building should do."

In her own ears the words sounded like those of a prissy academic. Which of course she was, but the fact didn't usually irritate her so much.

"Right," said Daniel with a smile and a nod. "You know, it seemed nippy as we were walking up the avenue, but now the breeze feels like a good thing. Our reception warmed me considerably."

He really did seem to be in a good humor, though how that could be after the interviews with Cox and Ruffin was beyond

Adele's imagination. Daniel saw the world just as clearly as she did, but somehow he managed to put a positive gloss on the same bleak expanse of arrogance, incompetence, and greed.

Adele walked around the fountain and settled, facing back toward the headquarters building. The statue of the cherub in the center would spout water straight up in the air through its trumpet when the fountain was operating, but the pool had been drained for the winter.

The circular bench was cracked, seriously enough that Adele moved the width of her buttocks to the right. That in turn meant that the line from her to the cherub no longer extended through the building's main door. The lack of symmetry made her momentarily furious.

She smiled suddenly. Daniel said, "Adele?"

"Admiral Cox made me angrier than I realized," Adele said, looking at her friend. She felt the smile still quivering on her lips; it wasn't a feeling she was familiar with. "I'm still angry, it appears. That's reasonable, but planning to shoot the head off a statue because it's in the wrong place—"

She indicated the cherub, deliberately using her left hand: her gun hand.

"—is as foolish as the admiral himself."

Daniel looked from Adele to the statue—it was dull gray metal, probably lead—and then back to the tunic pocket where Adele kept her pistol. "I suggest you use a heavier weapon," he said. "Or I suppose we could move closer?"

Adele kept silent for a moment. Then she said, her voice as dry as Daniel's own, "Thank you. I'll continue to review my options."

She cleared her throat and went on. "The Macotta

Region remained quiet during most of the war. The regional squadrons are small compared to the volume for which they're responsible, and both Cox and his opposite numbers are more concerned about being out of position if the enemy attacked than they were of attacking the enemy. But seven years ago, Captain Baines swept through the Funnel with a fast-cruiser squadron drawn from the Cinnabar Home Fleet."

"Right," said Daniel. "A stunt, really. Baines did quite a lot of damage to shipping, but it wasn't significant because *nothing* in the Funnel is significant. He stressed all his ships and lost the *Grey* in a landing accident because her thrusters had limed up."

He shrugged. "I gather it was good for morale, though," he said. "On Cinnabar itself, that is. I don't think there was a single regional commander who didn't think he had a better use for a couple of Baines' eight cruisers than to send them off to the back of beyond."

"Yes," said Adele. "In any case, there's a rumor that Freedom is an officer from Baines' squadron, left behind either by accident or deliberately to rouse a rebellion. *That* is why the Alliance demanded that we repatriate our citizen and probably why Xenos tasked the RCN rather than the governor's office."

She remembered Daniel's raid on the Pleasaunce Home System in the ancient *Ladouceur*. Because of Adele's training, she had initially believed in factors she could tabulate: tonnage, missiles, cannon, date of construction. Experience had taught her that personnel, not hardware, won battles.

"I don't recall Commander Ruffin mentioning that this rebel is an RCN officer," Daniel said thoughtfully.

"It's possible that she considers the possibility as ridiculous as I do," Adele said. She saw no need to keep the contempt out of her voice. Besides, she supposed she would have been just as tart if the commander were part of the discussion. "More likely, she's as clueless as the people on Pleasaunce and Xenos who accepted the unfounded rumor to begin with. Other than the fact that Captain Baines passed within approximately thirty light-years of Sunbright some three years before the rebellion started, there's no connection."

"Then there's no way to track the fellow?" Daniel said. "I thought that if he really were one of Baines' officers, you could... Well, I've seen what you can do with a database. And Sunbright's population is probably under a million, isn't it?"

"Eight hundred and ninety-three thousand," Adele replied absently—from memory; she didn't have to break into the stream of data crossing her display. "Though I'd expect that figure to be low. Sunbright didn't really have a central government until the Alliance imposed one while the base was under construction, and most of the existing population regards the new officials as an occupying force."

She looked up from her display and met Daniel's eyes. She realized that she felt *good*. "Daniel," she said, "I think this will really be a challenge. I'm rather excited about the prospect. Shall we get back to the *Sissie*? I'd like to talk this over with Cory and Cazelet. That is—if you don't mind?"

Strictly speaking, Adele had no authority over commissioned officers—Cory was a lieutenant—or even a midshipman like Cazelet. Both men had an instinct for information gathering, which on-the-job training with Adele had honed to a fine edge.

As a practical matter, everyone aboard the *Princess Cecile* jumped when Adele forgot herself and said, "Jump!" She tried to hold to RCN proprieties, though—when that didn't interfere with her accomplishing the task before her.

"Yes, of course," said Daniel, rising. While at rest he looked pudgy, but he didn't need to use his arms to help lift himself from the uncomfortably deep bench. "Ah—I realize it isn't properly our concern anymore, but do you think the local Naval Intelligence section will be able to handle the business on Tattersall?"

"Yes, of course," Adele said—more curtly than she intended. Her mind was on the next several stages in the process of locating Freedom and getting him off Sunbright. "When two RCN battleships appear over the planet, the plotters will fall all over themselves to inform on their friends before their friends inform on them. That's what happened when the Three Circles Conspiracy unravelled, you'll remember."

That's what happened when your father unravelled the Three Circles Conspiracy, she thought. *And in the process of doing so wiped out the Mundy family—with the exception of the elder daughter, Adele, who was studying off-planet.*

"I bow to your expertise," Daniel said mildly.

Adele felt her lips form a tight smile again. Hunting down Freedom was a proper task for a person of her skills, so she would do it. But she hadn't forgotten Admiral Cox and his aide, either. They had behaved discourteously to fellow RCN officers.

And one of those officers was Mundy of Chatsworth, who was no longer a helpless orphan.

Chapter Three

HOLM ON KRONSTADT

The vehicle Hogg had found for them was a surface car with friction drive—a roller on a single central strut—but an air-cushion suspension. Adele, in the backseat with Daniel, didn't know what the advantage or claimed advantage was over vectored thrust like the armored personnel carriers which had become familiar to her, but no doubt there was one.

"It rides very smoothly," Daniel said approvingly but perhaps with a touch of wonder.

Adele sniffed. Hogg had a remarkable facility for finding vehicles, but they never rode smoothly when he drove them. This car had the logo of the Macotta Regional Authority on its front doors. She doubted that Hogg had simply stolen it, but anything was possible with that old poacher.

"And just in case you was wondering how this happened to show up," Hogg said, patting the fascia plate with his left hand; they swerved toward but not quite into a heavy truck speeding along the other lane of Dock Street with a load of frozen sheep carcasses. "We're testing her for the repair depot, and it's all open and aboveboard."

"I'm glad to hear that, Hogg," Daniel said, smiling but definitely sounding as though he meant the words. "And I'm also glad not to have to walk back from headquarters."

We were apparently all thinking the same thing, Adele realized. *Well, by now we know one another well enough to be able to predict certain responses.*

"Ah," said Hogg, this time without turning his head toward his master in the backseat. "Your liquor cabinet's short of a couple bottles of that apple brandy you picked up on Armagnac. There wasn't time enough to get into a poker game, but I can find something to replace the booze by tomorrow morning, I figure."

Adele's personal data unit balanced on her lap while she sorted the information which she had trolled in squadron headquarters. She shifted to a cultural database with her control wands, then said, "The local liquor is plum brandy. There appear to be better brands and worse ones, but from commentaries I've found, I think absolute alcohol from the Power Room would be a better choice than the low end of the spectrum."

She scrolled farther down and added, "In fact, I think paint stripper would be a better choice than the low end."

"Perhaps Hogg and I could arrange a taste test," said Tovera, the first words she had spoken since she arrived beside Hogg. "I'm sure there's paint stripper we could requisition from squadron stores. Or—"

She paused. Tovera was short, slim, and colorless, a less memorable person to look at than even her mistress.

"—perhaps I could get it by killing the supply clerk and everyone else in the warehouse."

Hogg guffawed. "Spoiled for choice, aren't we?" he said.

Daniel grinned also, but Adele noticed that the humor had taken a moment to replace a perfectly blank expression. Tovera was an intelligent sociopath. She had neither conscience nor emotions, but a strong sense of self-preservation made up for those absences.

Tovera had learned to make jokes by studying how normal human beings created humor. Similarly, she functioned in society generally by copying the behavior of those whose judgment she trusted.

Tovera trusted Adele. If Adele told her to slaughter everyone in a warehouse—or anywhere else—the only question Tovera might ask was whether her mistress had any preference for the method she used.

"I'm sure," Adele said in the present silence, "that if I *do* ask Tovera to wipe out a nursery school, I'll have a very good reason for it."

The men laughed, and Tovera smiled with appreciation.

Hogg thrust the steering yoke hard to the left, sliding neatly between the tail and nose of a pair of heavy trucks in the oncoming lane. Adele blinked. A stranger might have thought that it was a skilled though dangerous maneuver; she had enough experience of Hogg's driving to know that he'd simply ignored other traffic.

They had pulled onto the quay separating the last two slips—31 and 32—in the Kronstadt Naval Basin. They sped past a squadron repair ship—which was undergoing repair herself; all twelve of her High Drive motors were lined up beside her on the concrete—and pulled to a halt beside the corvette—and sometimes private yacht—*Princess Cecile*.

"Welcome home, boys and girls!" Hogg said. He gestured toward the ship with the air of a conjurer.

The *Sissie* lay on her side like a fat, twelve-hundred-tonne cigar. Within, the corvette had five decks parallel to her axis; the bridge was on A—the topmost—Level in the bow, and the Battle Direction Center with its parallel controls and personnel was at the stern end of the corridor.

At present the dorsal turret, near the bow with two 4-inch plasma cannon, was raised to provide more internal volume. The ventral turret, offset toward the stern, was underwater and therefore out of sight.

Adele put her personal data unit away and got out. Instead of going to the catwalk immediately, she stood for a moment looking toward the *Princess Cecile* over the car's roof.

Adele had first seen the corvette cruising slowly above Kostroma City, launching skyrockets and Roman candles from her open hatches as part of the Founder's Day festivities. Then the vessel was merely an object: large, noisy, and unpleasantly bright to look at. Adele now knew that to save spectators' eyesight, the *Sissie*'s thruster nozzles had been flared to reduce the intensity of her plasma exhaust, but at the time the light had seemed to stab through her slitted eyelids.

Since then, Adele had spent almost as much time on or about the corvette as she had away from it. With Daniel as captain, they had fought battleships, entered enemy bases, and travelled to the edges of the human universe.

At various times the ship's rigging had been burned off, it had lost the outriggers on which it floated following a water landing, and portions of its hull had been melted, dented, or holed. After each battle the rebuilt *Princess Cecile* had arisen as solid as before, ready to take her captain and crew to the next crisis.

Hogg was joking, but the *Princess Cecile* really was more of a home than Adele had ever had on land.

"Hey, Six?" called a Power Room tech, one of the four spacers in the guard detail at the head of the boarding bridge. "They've got a real flap on here. Every bloody ship in the harbor's working up her thrusters and taking stores aboard."

Adele instinctively reached for her data unit to check the name of the speaker, a squat, androgynous woman who was cradling a submachine gun. Her face was familiar, but Adele didn't connect names and faces very well.

Daniel grinned and said, "As well they should be, Damion. Thanks to the fast run that you on the ship side and the riggers both made possible, the Macotta Squadron is able to lift in time to prevent another war."

Adele's lips twisted wryly. Though she wasn't good with flesh-and-blood people, she'd never had a problem keeping authors and their respective documents straight.

The boarding bridge was a twenty-foot aluminum catwalk extending from the concrete quay to the *Princess Cecile*'s starboard outrigger. There it met the ship's boarding ramp—the main entry hatch in its fully lowered position.

Three pontoons supported the catwalk. It was wide enough for two people to walk abreast, but Adele knew that Daniel in the lead and Tovera following closely behind were both ready to grab her if she started to topple into the water.

Hogg, at the rear of the short procession, swam like a fish. He would drag Adele up from the bottom of the slip if that were required...and would dive down again after her data unit if it somehow had slipped out of its pocket. Every member of the *Sissie*'s crew knew that Adele would rather be stripped naked than to lose her data unit.

"I was thinking, master," Hogg called. "If you weren't going to need the car right away, this might be a good time for me to top off the liquor cabinet."

Daniel turned and stepped aside for Adele as he reached the ramp. "Officer Mundy?" he asked, raising an eyebrow. She hadn't spoken of the course of action she had planned while sorting data from the headquarters' computers.

Adele stepped onto the ramp. It was thick steel and seemed as solid as the continent itself after the queasy flexing of the catwalk.

"I'm sorry, Hogg," she said over her shoulder. She spoke loud enough for Daniel to hear, but the question was really the servant's. "Captain Leary and I will be going into town as soon as he's changed out of his Whites and I've briefed Cory and Cazelet. We're going to visit Bernhard Sattler, the merchant who acts as honorary consul for the Alliance on Kronstadt. I hope that Sattler will give us information that will help with the mission we've been assigned."

And whether or not Sattler is consciously helpful, I expect that the data I draw from his files will prove useful.

* * *

Daniel had changed into a second-class uniform—gray with black piping—because that was the proper garb for visiting a civilian of no particular importance, but it was also a great deal more comfortable than his Dress Whites. At this point Adele was in charge because she had a plan; he was following her orders. He was pleased that she had ordered him to wear his Grays, though.

He wasn't sure why Tovera was driving while Hogg sat beside her in the front seat; presumably it was something the two of them had worked out. Hogg liked to drive, but nobody—his master included—wanted to ride with him a second time. Driving gave Hogg great pleasure, though, and Daniel loved as well as valued the man. Hogg was his servant, certainly; but he was also Daniel's father in the non-biological sense.

"Kronstadt doesn't have formal diplomatic representation with the Alliance," Adele said, her eyes on the display she was manipulating. Daniel didn't imagine that what she was looking at had anything to do with what she was saying: the ride to Sattler's warehouse was simply an opportunity to give him background while she delved much deeper herself. "An honorary consul is a private citizen with an Alliance connection of some sort. He helps Alliance citizens who are having problems. Our External Bureau calls the equivalent official a consular agent."

"He helps spacers who've been rolled and missed their ships?" Daniel said. "That sort of thing?"

Adele shrugged without, Daniel noticed, affecting the way her control wands moved. She claimed the angle and position of the wands provided her with quicker, subtler control of her holographic display than any other form of input device.

Daniel believed her, but the only other people he had seen using wands were Adele's protégés Cazelet and Cory. From their expressions as they struggled, they didn't get the results Adele did.

"Yes, usually spacers," she said toward the blur of light that coalesced at the point where her own eyes focused, "but it can be any Alliance citizen who's been robbed or has some other kind of legal problem. From information in the regional computers, I believe I can find a great deal more in Master Sattler's own files."

Tovera swung the car so wide around dining tables outside a restaurant that Daniel was afraid that they would scrape the front of the shop on the opposite side of the street of segmented paving blocks. Buildings in this older section of Holm—along the river, the original starship harbor—were faced with pastel stucco. Enough of the covering had flaked off to show that the walls beneath were brick or stone, definitely not things to drive into with a plastic-bodied vehicle.

About the best thing one could say about Tovera's driving was that her collisions were likely to be at much slower speeds than those of Hogg. She was mechanically overcautious instead displaying Hogg's incompetent verve.

Daniel coughed to clear his throat. Something must have showed in his expression, because Adele glanced toward him and said, "I expected to face danger in the RCN. I hadn't appreciated how much of it would involve riding in vehicles which my shipmates were driving."

They had reached a warehouse building with double doors

along the front. Tovera pulled the car to a halt abruptly enough to tilt the bow forward. The air-cushion suspension damped the jolt better than Daniel had expected when he braced his hands against the seat ahead of him.

Before he could speak, however, the car hopped forward another twenty feet, putting them about as far beyond the pedestrian door in the center of the facade as they had been short of it on the first try. It looked as though Tovera was trying to shift into reverse.

"Stop!" Daniel said. "That is, thank you, Tovera, but this is quite good enough."

He slid his door back—it telescoped into the rear body-shell—and got out of the car before Tovera could back up anyway. He was fairly certain that she wouldn't take direct orders from anyone but Adele, and he wouldn't have wanted to bet that even Adele could be sure her order would be obeyed.

Tovera was a pale monster. She was a frequently useful monster, but a monster nonetheless.

The legend painted in bright orange letters above the doors of the building was BERNHARD SATTLER AND COMPANY. Tovera had disadvantages as a driver, but her navigation was consistently flawless.

Adele walked around the car to join Daniel. She carried her data unit in her right hand instead of putting it away in its pocket. Tovera followed; Hogg already stood beside the office door.

"Both of you wait in the street," Adele said crisply to the servants. "You'll attract too much attention."

"I—" Tovera said. She held her attaché case before her,

closed but unlatched; inside was a small submachine gun.

"I won't have you jeopardizing the task by turning this into a procession," Adele said. She didn't raise her voice, but the words snapped out. "Anything beyond Captain Leary and his aide will make them wonder."

She glanced at Daniel, who had been waiting for direction. He noticed to his own amusement that his hands were crossed behind his back as though he were At Ease before a superior officer.

"Captain," Adele said. She nodded to the door.

Daniel, smiling faintly, entered the offices of Bernhard Sattler and Company. Rank didn't have to be formal to be real, and *he* had no doubt as to who was in charge here. It wasn't him.

A clerk looked up from her console on the other side of a wide wooden counter. Another female clerk was talking with animation to a pair of warehousemen wearing leather bandoliers from which tools hung. From the door to the left came the sound of a heavy load clattering along an overhead track.

"I'm Captain Leary," Daniel said, pitching his voice to be brusque but short of threatening. "I'm here to speak with the honorary consul on RCN business, and I'm in a hurry."

All four employees were now looking at him—and not at Adele, as he had intended. The clerk at the console flicked a glance at the frosted glass panel in the wall but returned to Daniel and said, "Ah—may I tell him your business? He's pretty busy and I—"

"I am an RCN officer on a Cinnabar possession," Daniel said, speaking a hair louder but not shouting yet. "I have RCN business with a resident alien here, and I'm *about* to stop asking politely."

The clerk's jaw dropped, giving her the expression of a gaffed fish. The workmen turned and strode into the warehouse area without looking back. The clerk at the counter started toward the glass door, but it opened before she'd taken a full stride.

The burly man who strode out was beardless and nearly bald, but his full moustache met fluffy sideburns. He made a quick bow toward Daniel and said, "Sir, will you come through, please? I am Bernhard Sattler, and I am at your service."

The clerks got in each other's way as they hopped to lift the gate in the counter. Daniel nodded to them as he stepped through; Adele followed, as silent as a shadow.

Sattler waited to close the office door behind them, then seated himself behind a desk of gray metal with an engine-turned surface. He smiled wryly at Daniel and said, "They're really good girls, you know; my nieces, both of them. But they were born on Kronstadt, and they don't appreciate the subtleties of my being a naturalized citizen who was born on Bryce."

"No harm done," said Daniel. He appreciated the delicacy with which the merchant had claimed to be a Cinnabar citizen, not a resident alien. They both knew that it was a distinction without a difference when dealing with an RCN officer on a Cinnabar regional capital.

The office was windowless, but large holographic cityscapes gave depth to three walls. The shelves on all sides contained a mixture of hardware and paper—loose, in binders, and as books. Some of the hardware could be samples of warehouse stock, but the lengths of worn chain and greasy pulleys might better be on a scrap pile.

Daniel grinned. The room reminded him of the days he

had spent as a child in his Uncle Stacy's office at Bergen and Associates' Shipyard. Commander Stacy Bergen had been the finest astrogator in the RCN, then or now. Daniel's high reputation for slipping through the Matrix in the swiftest and most efficient fashion rested on the training he had received from his uncle before he even dreamed of joining the RCN.

Sattler opened a drawer. Without looking down, he said to Daniel, "If I didn't think it would insult you, Captain, I would offer you a drink."

Daniel didn't move, didn't even breathe out for a moment. Then he let a slow smile expand across his face.

"I've drunk some of the worst rotgut ever brewed in a barracks," he said. "I don't guess anything you've got in that drawer has the chops to insult *me*."

Sattler laughed from deep in his chest and brought out a fat, double-tapered bottle covered by an upturned glass. He set the glass on the desktop, then paused with the bottle lifted. Nodding toward Adele, he said, "Will your aide ... ?"

Daniel followed his eyes. Adele sat on one of three straight wooden chairs, engrossed in her display. The edge of her seat had been whittled into a procession of cherubs buggering one another, apparently the whimsy of someone with a jackknife and a great deal of raw talent.

"She will not," Daniel said dismissively. He took the glass and the chair on the other end from Adele's; it hadn't been embellished, but one leg was enough shorter than the other three to click on the floor when he moved.

Sattler drank directly from the bottle, watching Daniel as he did so. He lowered the bottle and said, "Angels' Tears,

Captain. A Bryce specialty, as you may know."

Daniel took a reasonable sip but held it in his mouth for a moment before he swallowed. The straw-colored liquor tasted like wood smoke, but it was as smooth as anything he'd drunk of such high alcohol content: it must run at least 150 proof.

"Very good," Daniel said. He took three more swallows to lower the contents of the glass by half, then leaned back in his chair. He said, "Tell me about the Sunbright Rebellion, Master Sattler. Who's backing it?"

Sattler set the bottle on his desk. "Officially," he said, "interloping traders who bring in weapons and take out loads of rice. You know Sunbright rice?"

Daniel shrugged. "I know of it," he said. "It's valuable, I gather."

"Yes," the merchant agreed, "but it is delicious beyond even its present high price. As it's exported farther and farther from Sunbright, the demand will continue to rise, and so will the price."

Daniel shrugged again. "You said, 'officially,'" he said. "And the truth?"

"Clan chiefs on Cremona," Sattler said. "Maybe half a dozen out of thirty-odd, all told. Cremona's in the Funnel, but it's independent. As a matter of fact, it's *so* independent that it hasn't been worth the Alliance's time to take the place over, tempting though I'm sure the idea has looked even before now. The only way to get all the clans to cooperate is to bring in off-planet troops for *everybody* on Cremona to shoot at."

"There's no government?" Daniel said, crossing his ankle over his knee as he sipped his liquor. He wondered what it had been distilled from.

Sattler drank also, then said, "Not one that anybody pays any attention to unless they feel like it. There's even an army, but it's barefoot boys and riffraff who'd sell their equipment for a drink—if they had any equipment. The larger clans have private armies that aren't as much of a joke, though."

Daniel nodded. "And no joke at all if you're trying to move through a city," he said. "I can see why the Alliance wouldn't make the investment, though I suspect the regional government has been pushing for it. And has been overruled from Pleasaunce."

It was a real pleasure to deal with a man like Sattler, who was willing to be honest when he was sure that he was talking to someone who wanted the truth—and that his listener wasn't going to be easily fooled.

"I shouldn't wonder," Sattler said. "Nobody in the Funnel government has taken me into their confidence, but that's what *I'd* be saying in their place. There's pirates operating out of Cremona too, though they mostly don't pick on Alliance or Cinnabar-flagged ships."

He held the bottle out and raised an eyebrow. Daniel looked at his glass—an ounce remaining—and shook his head. "I didn't get off on the best foot with Admiral Cox this morning," he said, telling the truth but lying by implication. "The last I need is him claiming that I was drunk while on duty."

Daniel had needed to drink with the merchant to set the right tone for the interview, but he'd done that. Four ounces, even of strong liquor, wasn't going to put him under the table or even give him a real buzz, but more wouldn't improve his job performance.

Sattler thumped the bottle down and said, "It's not just

Cremona, though. Now, before I explain this, you have to understand something. To Cinnabar, the Forty Stars and the Funnel are both ruled—administered, if you're delicate about words—"

"I'm not," said Daniel as he emptied his glass.

"Right," said Sattler. "They're ruled from here and called the Macotta Region. To the Alliance they've got separate governments until you get up to the Seventeenth Diocese on Port Sanlouis. Admiral Jeletsky has the Forty Stars Squadron on Madison. He doesn't care what happens in the Funnel, and neither does Governor Braun. In fact, if their administrative rivals are having trouble on Sunbright, they both figure that they're twice to the good. And that's why—"

He slapped his desktop with the fingers of his left hand. The bottle jumped.

"—quite a lot of the weapons going to the rebels come from Madison. Most of the smuggled rice is sold there too, with no questions asked. You see?"

Daniel grimaced. "All right," he said. "I've seen things not a lot different on Cinnabar protectorates. I can believe it, well enough. But what about this 'Freedom' I hear about, the dashing rebel leader?"

"Now there you got me," Sattler said, glowering. He looked at the wall, then grunted and rapped a control with an index finger like a mallet.

Flickers at the corners of Daniel's eyes drew his attention: the three holographic wall displays had switched from cityscapes to images of a woman half Sattler's age with a pair of six-year-old boys.

The previous scenes had meant nothing to Daniel, but the fact that Sattler had changed them certainly did. With only minimal information to go on, Daniel would have made an even-money bet that the images were from the merchant's home world, Bryce, and that he had realized they weren't the most politic decorations to be flaunting to an RCN officer.

Sattler would have known better than to call attention to the images, however, if he hadn't punished the bottle pretty heavily. Though he seemed calm enough, Daniel's sudden arrival must have been a shock to his system.

"Don't worry about it," Daniel said, staring down into his tented fingers. "Unless you're lying to me, in which case you have worse problems than what you put on your walls."

The merchant sat still-faced for a moment, then barked a laugh. "You've given me no reason to lie," he said. "But sorry for acting like a prat."

Sattler cleared his throat, then switched two of the displays back to streetscapes; the woman and children continued to beam from behind his chair. "I don't know who Freedom is or if he's one person," he said. "There's some who say he must be several people, a junta speaking through one throat. Anyway, he knows things—knows things and knew things. The first attacks, the start of the rebellion, hit every government arms stockpile on Sunbright before they had anything like real security."

"The rebels would have to be very organized to carry off the timing for that," Daniel said, frowning. He looked at the glass in his hand. "People on Cremona wouldn't be able to do it. Nobody off-planet could have."

Sattler nodded. "And this Freedom was putting out feelers for exchanging rice for equipment at least three months before the shooting started," he said. "Placing orders on condition of rice being delivered at the time agreed. There's enough small traders that some of them were willing to chance that the deal would come through. With guns from security-force warehouses in rebel hands, the customs and excise inspectors out in the farms had to run for the cities or have their brains blown out, so there was plenty of rice to trade for more guns and equipment."

"You say 'small traders,'" Daniel said. "Do you mean from Cremona, or ...?"

He was afraid the answer was going to be, "From Kronstadt and other Cinnabar worlds." Which would sooner or later mean war.

"Cremona, sure," Sattler said, "but it's more than that. They stage through Cremona mostly because it's a short jump to Sunbright. But it can be anybody who's got a ship of five hundred or a thousand tonnes and is looking for quick cash."

"Which is *every*body who's got a small tramp freighter," Daniel said with a laugh. He let his expression return to neutrally pleasant. He said, "So, you think that Freedom really is somebody—or somebodies?"

Sattler nodded. He touched the bottle but didn't lift it again. He cocked his head to the side and said, "Look, Captain, you don't need to lecture me about what my place is with you in the room, but—look, you talked about you being 'on duty.' If you told me just what that duty was, I might be able to help more."

Daniel pursed his lips. He didn't look toward Adele, but he could see out of the corner of his eye that she was still focused on her display. Sattler was paying no more attention to her than he was to the saucer hat which Dan had tossed on the desk when he sat down.

"The Alliance requests that we remove Freedom from Sunbright because he's a Cinnabar citizen," Daniel said. "Admiral Cox has delegated that duty to me. Frankly, I wouldn't have been surprised to learn that it was a complete fool's errand. As I said, the admiral and I didn't get off on the right foot."

Sattler tapped the desk three times while staring into the middle distance. He straightened in his chair and picked up the bottle.

"Give me your bloody glass," he said. Daniel handed it over for another four ounces.

Sattler drank from the bottle, then lowered it and said in a harsh voice, "I'm a trader, you know that. I've got ships as well as this—"

He waved generally with his left hand.

"—and other stuff. Before the last war I had six ships."

Daniel sipped and nodded. He didn't interrupt.

"Other shippers in the region laid up their hulls right away," Sattler said. "There's more pirates than patrols in the Macotta even when things are peaceful, and in a war the pirates all claim to be privateers. I left my ships out because I'm from Bryce. I had to prove that I'm a good Cinnabar citizen. When the third ship got taken, I grounded the three I still had. It was worth that to me not to have questions asked."

Daniel nodded again as Sattler drank.

"We've got peace again," the merchant said, his voice roughened further by the liquor. "My ships are out. I'm making money."

He leaned forward and said, "I'm making money out of the revolt on Sunbright. I guess you figured that?"

"Yes," Daniel said; he sipped. Sattler was a successful businessman, and the biggest business in this region must be the rebellion on Sunbright.

"But I don't want war again," Sattler said. "The business might survive, but it might not, and if things got bad enough—well, I've seen mobs, and I don't want to be facing one. The security police are bad enough. If I could help you find Freedom, I would. But I can't."

Adele shut down her data unit and straightened. Daniel emptied his glass, set it on the desk, and got up. Grinning at the merchant, he said, "Well, Master Sattler, I believe you. Which is a pity, because I'd certainly welcome a shortcut to the goal I've been set. Good day to you and—"

He nodded to the woman and children on the left wall.

"—your family. I'm going to ponder what seems at present to be an intractable problem."

Adele fell in behind him as he walked into the outer office. Neither niece noticed the visitors were leaving until Daniel had lifted the gate in the counter himself. The girls stared in frozen horror despite Daniel's pleasant smile to each of them.

"Where to, young master?" asked Hogg, standing at the back of the car; Tovera was at the front.

Daniel smiled faintly. The words were a challenge of sorts—to Adele, who had slapped both servants down without hesitation when they wanted to enter the building.

"To the *Sissie*, I believe," he said. He glanced at Adele, but she was already getting into the vehicle. He went around to the other passenger door.

"I entered all of Sattler's files," Adele said as Hogg—who was apparently driving back—started the engine. "Though his security was surprisingly good. He's making quite a lot of money from smuggling rice out of Sunbright—and arms in, of course. But he's not an Alliance agent, and he's not involved with the rebellion itself, which is rather a pity."

The car lifted on its suspension and made a needlessly hard U-turn to head back to the harbor. Traffic was light, but Hogg still came close to broadsiding a truck as he pulled out.

"So this trip didn't help us after all?" Daniel said when he was sure that Adele had said all she intended to for the moment. Her data unit was live again.

"No, I wouldn't say that," she said toward her display. "I think the details of Master Sattler's smuggling enterprises are very useful indeed."

Chapter Four

HOLM ON KRONSTADT

Since Adele wanted Cory and Cazelet present for the discussion because they helped her with intelligence gathering, Daniel had included Vesey, his first lieutenant, and Woetjans, the bosun, as well. Adding them was mostly a political decision.

Woetjans wouldn't care one way or the other: she was by no means stupid, but she regarded planning as something her betters—better born, better educated—did. Unless the plans involved clearing top-hamper after something disastrous happened to the rig, of course, or hand-to-hand fighting. You couldn't find a better choice for clearing a path through a mob than Woetjans with a length of high-pressure tubing.

Lieutenant Vesey, a slim, blond woman, was a more complex subject. She had come to the *Princess Cecile* as a midshipman on Daniel's first voyage after the Navy Board confirmed his lieutenancy. From the beginning she had been an excellent by-the-book astrogator, and she had absorbed Daniel's training—passed on from Uncle Stacy—in the *art* of the Matrix as no one he had met before or since.

In all technical respects, Vesey was as fine an officer as one could ask for, and of course she didn't lack courage. Daniel didn't recall ever meeting an RCN officer whom he thought was a coward, though there had been no few whom he doubted could consistently put their shoes on the correct feet.

Vesey's problem was that she lacked the particular kind of ruthlessness which Daniel referred to—not in Vesey's hearing—as killer instinct, the reflex to go for your opponent's throat. She could set up a step-by-step attack, but she wouldn't reflexively see and exploit an enemy's weak point.

That lack was a serious handicap for an RCN officer, and it made Vesey—who was more self-aware than was useful—unsure of herself. That was probably why she continued as the *Sissie*'s first officer when her skills fitted her for a command of her own even after the cutbacks which resulted from the Treaty of Amiens.

Daniel was sorry that Vesey's career had stumbled in such a fashion, but the *Sissie* had gained by her misfortune. He could have left astrogation to her if he hadn't loved the process himself, and Vesey's ship-handling in normal space, now that she'd become comfortable with it, was better than his.

"I told you about our new mission when I returned from meeting the regional commander," Daniel said, passing his wry smile across the command group as he spoke.

"Yes, and we don't deserve it," said Cory angrily from the astrogation console. "I think it's a bloody shame!"

Daniel had decided to hold the briefing on the *Princess Cecile*'s bridge. A corvette had very little internal space in civilian terms, but he and his officers had been together on the *Sissie* for years. She was home to them.

He looked at his second lieutenant. Cory had been Vesey's classmate, but initially he had been so cack-handed at everything he tried that Daniel had wondered how he had graduated from the Academy. The boy had demonstrated a flair for communications, however, which had blossomed under Adele's direction.

To Daniel's amazement and probably Cory's own, the midshipman had then developed into a serviceable astrogator and a useful all-round officer. The Navy Board had confirmed the promotion to lieutenant which Daniel granted Cory after the bloody victory off Cacique.

"Mister Cory," Daniel said. He wasn't angry, but complaints about the decisions of superior officers weren't a good use of time. "If we had what we by rights deserve, we would all be dead and the *Sissie* would be a ball of gas in any one of a dozen star systems. If we may return to business?"

"Sorry, sir!" Cory muttered toward his clasped hands.

"Officer Mundy informed me that she sees a way to attack the problem," Daniel said, nodding toward Adele. "Since I certainly don't, I'll ask her to proceed now."

There were two consoles each on the port and starboard sides of the compartment, with the command console in the far bow. The gunnery console was forward of Adele at the communications console to starboard, and Vesey, whose normal station was in the Battle Direction Center in the stern, sat there now. The missile station where Midshipman Cazelet was sitting was astern of the astrogation console to port.

The gunner and the chief missileer had been ousted from the bridge for the time being, because this discussion didn't involve their skills. Chief Engineer Pasternak was in the Power Room, for the same reason and for an even better one: had he been present, hc would have remained in seemingly comatose silence, as bored as a frog listening to a sermon.

"Captain Leary interviewed Bernhard Sattler, the Alliance representative here," Adele said without preamble. "He's involved in trade with the Sunbright rebels, though this is simply a commercial matter. He appears to have no political interests."

The console seats could be rotated toward the interior of the compartment. The officers—and Woetjans, who stood with her back to the closed hatch—were facing the others present; except for Adele, whose eyes were on her display. Small images of her companions' faces were inset into the top of her screen.

She coughed to clear her throat, then added, "I found on reviewing the record of Sattler's conversation that he admits these activities."

Daniel blinked. Adele had been *present* at the conversation. What did she mean by "on reviewing the record"?

"It appears that other Kronstadt merchants are similarly involved," Adele continued, "though probably none to the extent that Master Sattler is."

Adele's body was in Sattler's office, Daniel realized with a grin that he tried to hide. But her mind had been dancing down a score of information pathways, unconcerned about the sounds coming through her ears. She knew that if anything important was being discussed, it would be available on the recording her data unit was making. As indeed it had been....

Everyone in this group respected Adele too much to doubt that she had a reason for the current lecture, but Daniel suspected he wasn't the only one to wonder where she was going with what seemed a pointless sidetrack. Sattler had told them all he knew, and that had brought them no closer to the Sunbright rebels.

Vesey said, "Isn't there still a problem with shipping goods to the rebels from Cinnabar territory? If the Funnel authorities capture some of the ships, that is, and they're bound to capture *some*."

Hogg sat quietly on the jump seat across from Daniel at the command console; Tovera faced Adele at Signals. The servants had no business at this meeting of the ship's command group, but there was no reason to exclude them, either. Nobody worried about either of them speaking out of turn.

"Sattler owns a one-third interest in Calpurnius Trading on Madison," Adele said. She didn't react sharply to the interruption, as Daniel had seen her do in the past. He had the feeling that this was what she had planned for the next point in her presentation anyway.

"All goods for the rebels are purchased and shipped by Calpurnius," she went on, flicking a wand to cascade files to the officers listening to her. None of them bothered to examine the data now; or ever would, Daniel surmised. "I doubt that Sattler's financial involvement would appear to anything less than a full investigation, and that by unusually competent investigators. He hasn't put Alliance-Cinnabar relations at risk."

Daniel didn't try to hide his smile this time. Adele had found the link in a matter of minutes. Granted that she had been in Sattler's office, but it was pretty certain that she would have done the same thing just as quickly if she had been given access to the Calpurnius Trading offices.

"But Madison is an Alliance world," Vesey said, frowning in puzzlement. She didn't doubt what Adele was saying, but she didn't understand it. "It's a sector capital, in fact?"

"This far out from Pleasaunce...," said Midshipman Cazelet. His family had owned a shipping line operating from the Alliance capital, Pleasaunce, before they had incurred the displeasure of Guarantor Porra and disappeared into his dungeons. "It's just a matter of knowing who to slip the bribe to. And the bribe won't have to be very large, I'd expect."

"There's a political aspect as well," Daniel said, speaking to end the discussion before Adele did so. She had a tendency to jerk the leash harder than necessary to bring her wandering listeners back to the path she had chosen. "Madison *is* a sector capital, but Sunbright and its problems are in a different sector."

He coughed and added, "Go on, Officer Mundy."

Adele smiled minusculely, not at him but very possibly toward his image on her display. "Master Sattler has no immediate plans to send someone inspect his investment on Madison," she said in her usual dry tone, "but based on similar situations on other planets, it wouldn't surprise the staff of Calpurnius Trading if he chose to do so. I propose that I go to Madison as a passenger on the *Princess Cecile* disguised as a private ship, and that I present my credentials as Sattler's agent to his partners there."

"By the gods, yes!" said Cory in beaming excitement. "The ship is private, after all, except we're under RCN charter right now."

Daniel didn't interject, but the circumstances were more complex than Cory implied or perhaps even knew. Daniel personally owned the *Princess Cecile*; he had bought the former Kostroman corvette out of RCN service several years earlier with some of the prize money which he had gained in the course of a short but very fortunate career.

However, the *Sissie*'s present charter was not with the RCN but rather with the External Bureau so that she could carry an official to an Alliance protectorate without Cinnabar naval involvement. There hadn't been time to change the paperwork in the rush after they had arrived on Cinnabar, then lifted at once with the dispatches to Admiral Cox.

While his officers chattered and his conscious mind focused on a legal technicality of the sort his sister Deirdre, a banker, spent her life with, Daniel's subconscious fitted the varied pieces into a decision. He said, "Fellow spacers?"

The two lieutenants and Cazelet continued arguing about whether to arrive on Madison as the *Princess Cecile*, whether to pretend to be a Trinidad-registered schooner, or whether to land on Trento and send the "inspector" to Madison on a short-hop freighter. They also disagreed about who should pretend to be Sattler's representative, though all agreed that it shouldn't be Adele.

"Pipe down and listen to Six!" Woetjans said; even Daniel jumped. The bridge was armored, but he was willing to bet that everybody in the rotunda beyond the closed hatch had heard the bosun's shout.

The three officers sat upright at their consoles, their eyes straight ahead and their lips tightly together. No one spoke.

Adele's smile was too slight for anyone but a close associate to have recognized the expression, but it was enough to make Daniel grin broadly in return.

"Thank you, fellow spacers," he said politely. "I will visit Calpurnius Trading myself. If this excellent plan works out, the representative will continue from Madison to Cremona and then on to Sunbright. Officer Mundy's virtues are too well known for me to bother listing them in this group, but I do not believe she could pass as a working spacer on a blockade runner."

Vesey's face went blank; Cory and Cazelet stared at one another in surprise. It took Woetjans a moment to put Daniel's deadpan words together with their meaning; then she laughed as loudly as her shouted command of a moment before.

"Sir?" said Cory. "You can't take a risk like that yourself—it wouldn't be proper. I can—"

Cazelet and Vesey had their mouths open to object and doubtless to offer their own proposals. Daniel stopped all three of them with a cold smile and a raised finger. He said, "I'd hate to think that my bosun had more authority aboard the *Princess Cecile* than I do. But I'm sure Woetjans would be willing to restore order, eh?"

"Sorry, Six," Vesey muttered to her hands, though she hadn't actually spoken. Cory and Cazelet just nodded.

"You're good officers," Daniel said, looking again around his command group. "You wouldn't be aboard the *Sissie* if I didn't trust you, you know that."

He paused and felt his grin harden before he went on, "But I'm Six, and you know that too. I'm going to do this because I think I'm the right choice for the job, and the *Princess Cecile* isn't going to become a democracy on *my* watch."

Adele rotated her seat so that she faced the other officers. For her to do that could only be a piece of theater, as everybody on the bridge knew. She said, "I would appreciate it if you explained your logic, Captain Leary."

Nobody else would have asked, Daniel realized, so Adele had asked. You never had to wonder if Adele Mundy would do whatever she thought was necessary.

But not in this case necessary for *her*. She understood already, which is why she had made such a circus turn out of her question.

"Of course, Adele," Daniel said. He *never* treated Adele casually when they were on duty in public. His choice of address created a deliberate balance to her overformality.

"First," he said to the group, "I personally, and the *Princess Cecile* through me, have been tasked to remove from Sunbright a presumed Cinnabar citizen going by the name of Freedom. This is our sole duty at the moment; we have no greater purpose. Not so?"

Cory was blushing in embarrassment; Vesey looked pale and miserable; and Cazelet had a withdrawn expression as though he had just been told the date of his execution. None of them spoke, but Woetjans nodded vigorously.

"I can easily play an RCN lieutenant beached on half pay by the Treaty of Amiens," Daniel continued. "That's what I'd be now if I hadn't been extremely lucky."

For an instant he thought that both Vesey and Cory were going to protest, but neither of them did. Adele's sniff had a suggestion of humor in it, though, if you knew her well.

"Any of the three of you—"

Daniel gestured to the commissioned officers. Even Cazelet had passed the tests for lieutenant, though he hadn't been—and, if the present peace continued, might not be for a decade—granted the rank.

"—can command the *Sissie* in my absence. A yacht owner would be lucky to hire a captain as skilled."

"And the mistress can be the owner, right?" Woetjans said, excited as the concept came into focus in her mind. "She can carry it off because she *is* a fine lady, even though she's, you know, the mistress too!"

That was exactly the conclusion that Daniel had come to also. As he opened his mouth to say so, however, Vesey objected, "But why would a yacht be carrying a passenger? Perhaps you—"

She turned to Daniel.

"—should be the hired captain, but when you get to Madison you quit for some reason?"

"Oh, that's no problem," Woetjans said with a toss of her big hands. "Six can play at being the lady's fancy man. And, you know, looking for an easier berth."

Vesey, Cory, and Cazelet went perfectly blank. From the stiffness of Daniel's own face, he supposed he did also. Hogg guffawed, and Tovera tittered like a crazed weasel.

"Based on my past experience," Adele said calmly, "it should be quite easy to get people to believe that."

"I dare say it would," said Daniel, pleased that he sounded relaxed. "But I think we'll explain that Bernhard Sattler and Company handled the yacht's refit on Kronstadt in return for her ladyship—"

He dipped in his seat as though bowing.

"—delivering me to Madison to make an inspection."

He cleared his throat and went on. "Now, we have to assume that a trading firm will be knowledgeable about ships, and the *Sissie* is obviously Kostroman-built. How do we explain a Cinnabar noble owning a yacht built on Kostroma?"

"I've looked into that," said Adele before anyone else spoke. Her control wands dipped and crossed; the hologram of a ship formed in the center of the compartment. "To begin with, I won't be a Cinnabar noble—"

"—because for our purposes it makes much better sense that I be a Kostroman," Adele said. "As some of you will remember, I was for a time in Kostroma City as Electoral Librarian."

She smiled. Daniel smiled back more broadly, and Woetjans—who then had been building bookshelves for the Electoral Librarian on Lieutenant Leary's orders—nodded with enthusiasm. Adele had met Hogg and Tovera on Kostroma also, but the servants held their silence; they had no part of this discussion.

The post on Kostroma had provided Adele with shelter of a sort, food of a similar sort, and even her pay occasionally. In those categories she was better off than she had frequently been since the Proscriptions which followed the Three Circles Conspiracy had left her a penniless orphan.

Otherwise the post had very little to recommend it, even before the bloody coup which made Adele—because she had survived—a member of the RCN. Depending on how you judged time, that had happened either several years or a lifetime in the past.

"I don't think I'll have difficulty in convincing those we meet on Madison," she said, "that I'm the deposed Principal Hrynko, travelling for my health. That is, the former chief of the Clan Hrynko, who retained enough power to negotiate the transfer of power to her stepson rather than to have him replace her in a less expensive manner."

"That's not the *Sissie*," said Woetjans. She had focused on the holographic ship in the middle of the compartment instead of listening to what Adele was saying. "This one's got the E and F rings staggered instead of straight."

The bosun frowned, then added, "I've seen Kostroman ships rigged that way, but never the *Sissie*. Even if she'd been changed to the standard rig before we grabbed her, her hull'd be dimpled where the mast steps used to be."

Daniel smiled with the delight of a happy infant. "I wouldn't have noticed that, Woetjans," he said. "I didn't notice it. But I will another time, thanks to you."

The bosun grinned and slammed the heel of her right fist into the palm of her left hand. Adele realized again that people had very different ways of expressing pleasure.

Adele said, "The image is the *Archduke Wilhelm*, laid down at the same time as the *Princess Cecile* but in the Isocha Yards instead of in Kostroma City. She was wrecked on landing within a standard year of her first liftoff. She was sold to Krishnamurti and Wife for scrapping, but the broker instead repaired her and passed her on to the Bijalan Navy. That was twenty-three standard years ago."

"Bijala has a navy?" Cory said in surprise.

"If they do, their officers probably have bones through their noses," Cazelet replied contemptuously. "We had some Bijalan spacers sailing for us at Phoenix Starfreight. They were pretty handy as riggers, but you had to be careful not to test them with something complicated like a screw fastener."

"Kostroman government records simply indicate that the *Wilhelm* was sold out of service," Adele said. She hadn't dealt with Bijalans personally, so she was glad that Cazelet's firsthand experience confirmed—colorfully—the impression which published sources had given her. "While I was on Kostroma, I assembled all the data I could. That included the files of Krishnamurti and Wife, which is how I learned about the Bijalan connection."

As Adele heard herself speak, she remembered that in most groups she would be asked why she had scooped up the records of private brokerage firms on a planet where she happened to be working. She didn't have to explain to her shipmates on the *Princess Cecile*: they took it for granted, as they took for granted that despite years of starfaring, Officer Mundy had to be watched carefully if she went out on the hull lest she drift off unawares.

The Sissies also took it for granted that the information Adele gathered compulsively would help them time and time again. As it was doing here.

While Adele spoke, Daniel turned to his display and began going through the data which she had transmitted. He didn't have Adele's skills at sorting information, but she had seen before that his knowledge of ships allowed him to take intuitive shortcuts to insights that no amount of study would have gained her.

The junior officers turned to their displays also. They followed Daniel's lead like a school of fish moving as a single shimmering entity.

"I don't have any record of what happened to the *Wilhelm* after she left Kostroma," Adele said, "but it appears to me a reasonable bet that we won't be unmasked if we claim to be her."

"Given Bijala's climate, the *Wilhelm*'s a pile of rust on a mudbank by now," Cazelet said flatly. "Nobody on Madison will have seen the real thing to compare with us."

"Nobody on Bijala will have seen the real *Wilhelm,* either," said Daniel in a tone of amazement. "Look at the surveyor's report—"

Adele didn't bother with her console. She used her personal data unit as a controller for the console anyway, so she simply switched to the little unit's own display. It was adequately sharp for this purpose.

"See, the *Wilhelm* broke her back when her aft thrusters failed and her stern hit the dock. That's why they scrapped her. Now, look at the repairs that the brokers made."

As Daniel spoke, he highlighted sections of the reports. His subordinates mirrored his display, while Adele kept watch on all four consoles. The pattern was a work of art if you had the right sort of mind, she supposed.

"They replaced two thrusters," said Vesey, speaking for the group as its most senior member. "Which left the *Wilhelm* two thrusters short of specifications, but that isn't critical if the officers know what they're doing. But they should have replaced twenty feet of hull, and instead there's just a six-foot band of structural plastic as a stiffener."

"And it's not even bolted on properly, just tacked!" Cory said. "Not that that would matter. Look how the skin on both sides is crumpled! You couldn't anchor bolts in that."

"I don't understand how they could get officers to lift in a ship in that condition," said Cory cautiously. He seemed to be feeling the results of being clouted twice for having spoken— or almost spoken—out of turn. "Real spacers, I mean."

"Cory got to the main point," Daniel said, cutting off the discussion without raising his voice. "The *Wilhelm*'s sailing master—"

The corvette had actually been renamed *Demon of Fanti* before liftoff, but Adele caught herself before she interrupted.

"—was from Cazador, but he'd drunk his way out of his captain's license. The remaining officers were Bijalans, and the crew were whoever the Bijalans could hire from the waterfront in Kostroma City. I don't imagine they were all spacers, and I'm certain that none of them were both sober and holding an able-bodied rating. Most were neither, I suspect."

There was general laughter. Woetjans said, "Like Six said to start out, if that lot didn't crash on liftoff, then Kostroma was the last planet they saw in their lives. So—"

She looked around.

"—when do *we* lift, sir?"

"In about eighteen hours, by my calculation," said Daniel. Grinning broadly, he added, "But perhaps we should ask former Principal Hrynko, the *Sissie*'s new owner. Eh, Adele?"

Adele gave the room as warm a smile as her personality allowed. "I'll discuss that matter with my officers," she said, "but for now I think we can expect to lift in about eighteen hours. I should point out, however—"

They are my friends. They are more than friends; they're my family.

"—that my yacht is named the *House of Hrynko*. I hope you'll all remember that, and I hope that I will remember it also."

The laughter resumed as Woetjans undogged the hatch to get to her duties.

Chapter Five

HOLM ON KRONSTADT

There were six spaces reserved for commanding officers in front of the Operations Annex, three ahead and three behind the space marked Admiral; four were empty. Hogg pulled into one, rode up the curb, and straightened out. The car was half into the admiral's spot, but Daniel was pretty sure that Cox wouldn't arrive in the next few minutes.

Hogg looked at him truculently and said, "We're bloody leaving the planet in a couple hours, aren't we?"

Daniel got out with a smile. "Quite right, Hogg," he said. He walked toward the entrance carrying the small chip case. "I don't expect to be long."

A blue pennant with the single silver star of a captain dangled from the standard on the car's right fender. Closely examined, one would see that Hogg had picked out the previous name *Cossack* and embroidered *Princess Cecile* in its place. He wasn't the most polished servant an RCN officer might have, but even in matters of display he was more useful than an outsider might have guessed from his scruffy exterior.

The four guards at the front door were spacers, not Marines. They watched those entering the building, probably checking uniforms, but they didn't bother looking at IDs. That would have been a major bottleneck given the crush of traffic caused by the deployment warning order, as well as being a pointless waste of time.

The Operations Annex was a converted warehouse whose wooden floor held the odors from the spices which had been stored here in former days. Daniel stepped out of the doorway but then paused to close his eyes and take in the mixture of scents. He understood his fellow humans well enough to know that the personnel working here must complain bitterly about the stinking conditions, but to Daniel it was trip back to his childhood and Uncle Stacy's tales of wondrous worlds among the stars.

DEPARTURES in holographic red letters hung over two consoles in front of an enclosed office in the corner. The bar which framed them was also of coherent light. A lieutenant in utilities talked heatedly to the enlisted clerk at the console on the right, but the other clerk was shifting data with no outside interference.

Until now, Daniel thought. Wearing a pleasant smile, he strode to the left-hand console, waited a polite moment, and then said, "Excuse me, technician. I'd like to file my departure request—"

The technician—thirtyish and more fit than the normal run of desk jockeys—looked up with a sour expression.

"—and because we're operating directly under Admiral Cox's orders, I decided to deliver the information in chip form rather than transmitting it with the risk it might go into the wrong bin."

Phrased that way, the statement wasn't quite a threat. Despite Daniel's smile, the clerk was certainly aware that it could become a threat in a heartbeat.

"Ah, all right, sir," said the technician, reaching through his holographic display to take the case. He opened it, removed the chip, and inserted it into an access slot on his console. "This would be...?"

"I'm Leary of the *Princess Cecile*," Daniel said. "We'll be lifting for Sunbright at 1700 hours, carrying out the regional commander's directions."

"Sunbright?" the clerk said. He stared at the data which the chip had just thrown onto his screen. It merely expanded on what Daniel had just told him, of course. "*Sunbright*? Ah..."

His index finger made quick gestures on a virtual touch-screen. He said, "Ah, Captain? If you wouldn't mind waiting for a moment, I'd like to show this to the deputy head for his input. That is, your plan's in order, but there are some—"

The door of the office behind him opened; a lieutenant commander wearing Grays stepped out. He was a short, slim man with a dark complexion and hair as black as cannel coal.

"Sir?" he said, his eyes fastening on Daniel. "Captain Leary? I'm El-Tee-See Shiniviki, the deputy operations officer. Might I see you in my office for a moment?"

Daniel walked into the office with no more than the faint, friendly smile he had been wearing since he arrived at the annex. It was a struggle not to laugh out loud, though.

Daniel had come here to convince everyone in the Macotta

Squadron—and by extension, everyone to whom they talked—that the *Princess Cecile* was heading for Sunbright; and in addition, that her captain was a ninny. He was having greater success than he had even hoped.

"Please take a seat, Captain," Shiniviki said, nodding to a chair as he sat down at his console. "I realize that you're not under the squadron's operational control, but I feel that I'd be derelict in my duty if I didn't offer some advice."

He cleared his throat, then added, "My advice is that you not go to Sunbright."

Daniel sat carefully. The chairs were extruded metal, standard RCN issue; they were no different from those in the *Sissie*'s wardroom except that these were not bolted to the deck.

"But Commander," Daniel said in apparent puzzlement, "Admiral Cox was very clear about what he expected me to do."

Shiniviki stared at him, frowning in concentration. *He's trying to imagine how somebody so stupidly literal could have gotten the reputation and quick promotions that I have,* Daniel thought. *And he's about to put that down to extremely good luck.*

"Look, Captain," the lieutenant commander said, "Admiral Cox needs to demonstrate that we, that the RCN, are making a proper effort to repatriate this rebel leader. But the admiral doesn't care—that is, *nobody* really believes that you can succeed. That's if the rebel even exists."

He leaned back and spread his arms. The walls of the office were real wood, probably a local variety. They had been varnished instead of being painted; the crossing diagonals of the grain gave the impression that the smooth surface was faceted.

"Our intelligence section doesn't believe there's a rebel using the name Freedom at all," Shiniviki said. "He's just an excuse dreamed up by the Sunbright government to explain why they can't put down the rebels after four years of fighting."

"Well, I'm sure you have reasons for your belief, Commander," Daniel said. He opened his eyelids still further to give the impression that he was a popeyed innocent. "But orders are orders, as our friends in the Alliance are fond of saying. I can but try."

"Sir...," Shiniviki said, obviously struggling to find the right words—and not to use the wrong ones to an officer who was his superior in rank despite being several years younger. "Ah. We're at peace with the Alliance, of course, but Sunbright itself is under blockade by the Funnel Squadron, and there's quite a lot of action between Alliance patrols and blockade runners of all descriptions. Accidents can happen, and—"

He grimaced, looked at Daniel and looked away. "Look, sir," he said. "There's a lot of people in this region who believe that we're behind the trouble on Sunbright. That Cinnabar is, I mean. Now, it's not true, but you know how frustrated spacers can get on blockade duty. It wouldn't do to have an incident between an Alliance patrol and an RCN warship, you see?"

That's almost a plea, Daniel realized. Shiniviki knew the kind of trouble there'd be in the Macotta Region if an Alliance destroyer put a missile into a yacht in Cinnabar service— or worse, if the firebrand in command of the Cinnabar ship managed to gut an Alliance patrol vessel. Beyond that practical consideration, though, the lieutenant commander seemed really worried that a foolish outsider was getting into trouble more complicated than he could imagine.

"Commander," Daniel said, rising to his feet. "I fully appreciate your concern. I will not act in a fashion that will complicate life for the personnel of the Macotta Region, and if somebody else isn't as careful—"

He felt his grin harden. At this instant, he probably didn't give the impression of a hapless dimwit as he'd been trying to do during the interview.

"—I'll work very hard to avoid making the situation worse. But—"

His thawed his face back to harmlessly cheerful.

"—I'm not going to spend my time drinking with Funnel officials in their sector capital and moaning about what a terrible thing this business on Sunbright is. I'm going to do my job, to the best of my ability."

Shiniviki shrugged. "Then I can only wish you the best of luck, Captain," he said.

As Daniel left the office, he thought he heard the lieutenant commander add, "And that's what I hope for the Macotta Region too."

Adele browsed information about Sunbright at the communications console, feeling the *Princess Cecile* shudder as the pumps cycled reaction mass. There would be plenty of time to strap in when it was really time to lift off; and if she forgot, as sometimes happened, it was unlikely to make any difference.

"Testing H," Pasternak warned over the command channel. The ship wallowed in a pillow of steam which roared from the slip beneath the sternmost starboard thruster. The unit was

operating at low flow, with its nozzles irised fully open so that the plasma developed minimal thrust. Even so, the exhaust boiled cubic yards of water and raised a plume sparkling with ions which hadn't yet been slaked by the atmosphere.

Some of the *Sissie*'s ports must still be open, because Adele felt the soggy warmth of steam and a moment later sneezed when ozone bit her nasal passages. Spacers tended to be blasé about conditions which would have most laymen screaming about health risks. Yes, of *course* there were health risks in shepherding a starship through the Matrix.

The roar of exhaust silenced momentarily. *"Testing A,"* Pasternak said. He was running up the thrusters one at a time. This time the bloom of steam and noise came from below the port bow.

When Adele first had lifted as signals officer of the *Princess Cecile*, she had turned her whole attention to data on her display; that way she didn't have to think about what might happen to the ship. Now—

She grinned as broadly as she ever did, though a stranger wouldn't have noticed the expression.

—she turned her whole attention to data on her display. because she didn't worry about what might happen to the ship. The more things change, the more they stay the same.

Pasternak shut down his thruster, then lit the next in sequence. The Power Room boards were echoed in miniature on Adele's display, but the numbers and gauges meant nothing to her. She put them up simply from a desire for completeness.

"Adele?" said Daniel over a two-way link. *"Do you perhaps have something that a half-pay lieutenant could do*

while the ship's officers are preparing for liftoff?"

Adele expanded the little image of Daniel set into the top of her display along with those of the *Sissie*'s other officers. He was now in profile.

She smiled again, tightly: that meant he was looking at her, kitty-corner across the compartment. Even at so short a distance, the holographic image was sharper.

"I don't have any duties at present, Daniel," she said, continuing to use the intercom. Even without the roar of the thrusters, the bridge of a starship preparing for liftoff was too noisy a place to easily call from one console to another. "I'm just studying the situation on Sunbright. Ah—you're really giving up command for the sake of your role as Lieutenant Kirby Pensett, then?"

A roar that was louder but more diffuse shook the corvette, rocking her from side to side and slapping water violently against her pontoons. A larger ship must be lifting from a berth nearby. Adele switched the top third of her display to an optical panorama to see what was going on.

"That'll be the Blanche," Daniel said. He hadn't bothered to check anything but what memory and his ears provided. *"Admiral Cox put the* Blonde *in orbit instead of the usual destroyer as soon as we sent down the orders to proceed to Tattersall. Now he's sending her sister ship up to replace her while she lands, loads consumables for the voyage, and tops off her reaction mass."*

He cleared his throat and said, *"I, ah, have a tendency to take charge, you know. If I happen to do that while I'm supposed to be a passenger on the, ah,* House of Hrynko, *the results might range from bad to very bad. I'm trying to avoid that. And besides…well, it's a bad habit. Any of my officers can handle this mission without me looking over their shoulders."*

Adele sniffed. "*My* officers in that case, I believe, Lieutenant Pensett," she said.

She checked to be sure that her automated systems were harvesting communications: between Macotta HQ and the ships of the squadron, and among the ships themselves. The systems were, of course, and she wouldn't lose anything by waiting to review the data until they were in the Matrix.

She said, "All right, since we're both superfluous to the vessel's requirements at the moment, I propose to brief you on Sunbright."

"*I'm in your hands, Lady Hrynko,*" Daniel said, then chuckled. "*During the voyage, I'll read the files you've compiled, but I'd appreciate an oral précis.*"

This is my duty, Adele thought as she hesitated a moment to organize the data in her mind. *Not to brief Daniel, but to entertain him when he's feeling uncomfortable because he's removed himself from his normal duties.*

Pasternak had completed his individual thruster checks. He and Vesey—Captain Vesey—were discussing Unit E with a minuteness that irritated Adele despite the mere shadow of attention she gave it.

The ship's officers were obviously just as uncomfortable performing in front of Daniel as he was in watching them do so. She hoped that Vesey and the others would shed that overcaution when they were on their own; even a signals officer/librarian could see that E's three-percent-below-average output was insignificant in any real sense.

"The administrative capital, Saal, is the part of Sunbright which is really under Alliance control," Adele said as strands of data settled into place. "Saal includes the starport and the logistics base—"

"The base whose construction set off the rebellion?" Daniel said.

"The causes of the revolt are more complex than that," Adele said. "But the influx of construction workers and staff was certainly a factor."

She coughed and went on. "In any case, Saal is more extensive than even its population, some twenty percent of the planet's total, implies. There's a fence and bunker line, so though rebels certainly get in and out of the city, they're unlikely to attempt a head-on attack."

She had almost said, "They wouldn't attempt a head-on attack." That was the sort of thing that people said when they didn't think, since even a little reflection would remind them that people often did equally wild things—and that sometimes the attempts succeeded, because their enemy had been caught completely off guard.

It irritated Adele to—almost—speak thoughtlessly. Irritation was almost the only constant in her life, however, so perhaps she should probably be thankful for the near blunder.

With her lips forming the shadow of a smile, Adele continued. "There are Alliance administrators for all the communities, and often they actually live in these communities."

"Often *they do?*" Daniel said.

"Yes, though of course some administrators prefer to remain

in Saal and carry out their duties electronically," she explained. "But ordinarily they won't have any problems with the rebels if they keep out of the way during the hours of darkness and more generally avoid rocking the boat. So to speak."

Daniel's image was frowning. *"So basically,"* he said, *"the government, the administration imposed from Pleasaunce, controls the Fleet base. Which is really the only thing which is really important to the Alliance."*

"Yes," said Adele, pleased again by her friend's quick understanding. "The Alliance problem is that the population outside Saal is large enough and—thanks to Freedom—hostile enough to require a very expensive garrison for that base."

Two thrusters, balanced bow and stern, lighted again. This was the start of liftoff procedure.

Adele shrugged. "I suspect that Guarantor Porra and his advisors would willingly give up all revenue from Sunbright rice—pink rice, it's known in the trade—if they could get rid of the rebellion. But at this point a significant element of the population would continue to attack Alliance facilities even if the government withdrew from everywhere but Saal itself. And anyway—"

Adele checked the list of Alliance officials on Sunbright to make sure of the name.

"—Governor Blaskett appears to be too hard-line to consider backing down. I would say that he has at least as much to do with the rebellion as Freedom does."

"Rice smuggling funds the rebels?" Daniel said.

Adele wondered if he particularly wanted to learn that information or if he were simply "showing interest." Probably the former, since the *Princess Cecile* was not proceeding directly to Sunbright as they had worked to convince everyone on Kronstadt that they were. Getting into the rebel structure through their suppliers would be a good method, if it were possible.

All eight of thrusters were running now, but their nozzles were flared to waste their energy into the water of the harbor. The roar was nonetheless visceral, and enveloping steam shook the corvette.

"I can't find any other source of funds," Adele said. Her tone was neutral, but the fact galled her. "Obviously the available records on smuggling are partial. Available to me, but I think to anyone; there's no centralized control, and even when I get the Sunbright records—"

She had no doubt that she *would* have those records eventually.

"—they'll only give a further portion of the whole."

She pressed her lips together sourly, then went on. "I think rice smuggling and raids on stockpiles on Sunbright itself probably equip the rebels' current operations. They don't explain the initial investment, the start-up funds, which must have been considerable. There were mobile anti-ship missiles around the export warehouse at Tidy when the first group of interloping traders landed to pick up the rice. A missile destroyed the gunboat *Panther* when it approached to capture the smugglers."

Daniel's face went perfectly blank. *"I see,"* he said. *"Yes, that does imply a considerable initial outlay."*

Then he said, *"Adele, is it possible that Cinnabar is behind this rebellion? Because to be perfectly honest, I don't see anywhere that the funds could have come from without government involvement."*

"Yes, that's possible," Adele said; bluntly honest, because she was bluntly honest. On a matter of such importance, there was no option anyway. "I find no evidence that rogue elements in the Macotta bureaucracy are involved, but I'll continue to look."

"Yes," said Daniel. *"And if you find that* is *the case, we'll deal with it ourselves. Since we won't be able to trust the local authorities."*

He laughed. *"You know?"* he added. *"I'm rather glad that Admiral Cox handed us this mission. It sounds as though it may be more interesting than anything that our friends in the Macotta Squadron are going to find on Tattersall."*

"Liftoff!" said Captain Vesey. The thruster petals closed; the *Princess Cecile* shuddered, starting to rise again to the stars.

Chapter Six

Daniel stood with Cazelet on the topgallant crosstrees of the Ring D dorsal antenna, watching mixed teams of riggers and techs from the ship's side shift the port and starboard Ring F antennas sternward by thirty inches. Woetjans was in charge of the operation, with Vesey on the ground taking direction and learning from the bosun's years of experience.

"Does staggering the F Ring really make the ship more maneuverable, sir?" Cazelet asked, his eyes on the scene below. He was up here because he had a view of the whole operation and could direct the teams if they needed it. Daniel liked the view from high up a mast, but he was here today because it put him with Cazelet in privacy.

A diamond saw screamed, cutting the last bolt head off the Port F mast step. Six spacers, in rigging suits without helmets, held the cables which would support the heavy step when Woetjans herself broke the grip of the rust which would continue to hold it.

"Well, I can't say, Cazelet," Daniel admitted. "I've never been aboard a ship with this rig, not till now. Nobody but some Kostromans use it, and not many of them in this generation. But there've been some great Kostroman spacers."

Rigging suits—hard suits—were stiffened with fiber. The armor could turn strands of frayed cable which would tear an airsuit and the flesh beneath. Hard suits wouldn't save a spacer who was under a falling spar, but wearing them was a reasonable safety precaution for the present sort of job.

Daniel grinned. Woetjans—predictably—didn't think hard suits were necessary; Vesey had overruled the bosun. That was good, because otherwise Six would have had to reappear aboard the *Sissie* for long enough to give the order himself. He wasn't going to have his people crippled because Woetjans thought any concession to safety was a form of cowardice.

Cazelet had been leaning over to look down. He straightened and bent backward, rubbing the small of his back with both hands.

Daniel grinned. The midshipman was balancing on steel tubing almost a hundred feet above the curve of the hull, and the hull's eighty feet more above the sheet of solid ice on which the *Sissie* stood.

ME8*9JB was a charted location, not a name. The planet had a breathable atmosphere and vast quantities of water in the form of ice, but there was no other encouragement to colonization and no indigenous life. Ships stopped here often to replenish their reaction mass, and a number never rose again; half a dozen were visible from the crosstrees, metallic glints against the glacier. Using his visor's magnification,

Daniel saw that the hulks had been stripped. Some had even lost sections of hull plating, leaving the frames bare.

"This is the sort of place you only land if you're having trouble," said Cazelet, surveying their surroundings. Basalt ridges thrust up a mile to east and west of the corvette, channeling the slow river of ice; snowfields stretched beyond, occasionally marked by another black peak. The sun was a tiny blue-white dot in the high sky. "Sometimes the problem won't be soluble."

"But eventually," Daniel said, "somebody else with a problem will land, and maybe you can make one ship out of the parts of two or three."

Cazelet's comment had been intelligent and on point. He'd entered the RCN as a midshipman by Daniel's dispensation. The boy hadn't been trained in the Academy, but experience he'd gained while working up from the bottom in his family's shipping firm, Phoenix Starfreight, made him the superior of ordinary midshipmen in many aspects. The main gap in Cazelet's learning, missile tactics, was something that—

Daniel grinned.

—Captain Leary was as well-suited to teach as anyone in the Academy.

"That's a penterio," Cazelet said, pointing his extended left arm toward the ship farthest to the south in the ice stream. "None of them have been built since Santander rebelled against the Alliance a hundred and more years ago."

Daniel raised his magnification. Penterios displaced about five hundred tonnes and carried cargo externally on a spiderweb of spars and cables. That netting spread the vessel's weight and kept her from sinking out of sight in the decades or longer in which she must have rested on the ice.

"I landed on Santander once," Cazelet continued, "while I was purser on the *Kelly Maid*. It's a thriving place now—in a small way, of course. It was re-colonized from Pleasaunce and Greenhome after the reorganization which followed the mutiny."

He turned toward Daniel; Daniel turned his head also, to meet the younger man's eyes. Cazelet said, "The old culture was completely gone, of course. Not enough of the original population survived to maintain it."

"Yes," said Daniel, looking down at the rerigging.

He had learned when he was very young that it was a bad idea to discuss matters of academic interest to you with someone to whom they have great emotional weight. He was well aware of the brutality of the Alliance of Free Stars in dealing with what its leaders considered rebellion.

Rene Cazelet, however, was an orphan because Guarantor Porra had decided his parents were a threat to the state. He had come to Adele as a suppliant, sent by his grandmother, to whom Adele owed a debt of gratitude; and Adele had asked her friend Captain Leary to find a place for the boy.

Daniel grinned slightly. The RCN, and the *Princess Cecile* in particular, had gained a very useful officer through that turn of events.

He wasn't about to discuss brutal suppression of dissent with Cazelet, however. Corder Leary, Daniel's father, had put down the Three Circles Conspiracy in a thoroughly savage manner, after all; as Adele, also an orphan, could testify.

Woetjans was shouting triumphant directions to the crew

on the cable. They shuffled sternward, bringing the step along with them. The bosun planned to set the base into its new position on the hull directly; the holes were already drilled, and a senior technician waited with a drift punch the length of her forearm to slide it the last quarter inch into place.

Cazelet cleared his throat. Looking at the distant horizon rather than Daniel, he said, "Ah, sir?"

Daniel turned toward him. "Yes, Cazelet?" he said gently.

"Ah, you may know that Lieutenant Vesey and I have been seeing one another socially," Cazelet said. The air was bitter, and gusts of wind sent snow dancing over the ice sheet, but sweat was beading his forehead and his cheeks were flushed. "When we're on the ground and off duty, that is. We've tried to be discreet about it."

"Go on, Cazelet," Daniel said. He thought, *I'd be a bloody poor commanding officer if I didn't know that, midshipman.*

"Well, I just wanted you to know that because Elspeth, that's Lieutenant Vesey, is captain of the...the *House of Hrynko* now, we decided it wouldn't be proper that we continue seeing one another," Cazelet said. He glared at the horizon as though he wanted to eviscerate it with a grappling hook. "Even on the ground. Because the captain isn't ever off duty, not really."

"I'm glad to hear that, Cazelet," said Daniel, as mildly as he'd spoken before. "Because that means I don't have to transfer you to becoming the officer in charge of sewage lagoons on, say, Aristogeiton's World."

"Sir?" Cazelet said in surprise, his face jerking around to meet Daniel's eyes.

"I believed you both had good judgment," Daniel said.

Nobody watching them, even with magnification, would imagine they were discussing anything of more emotional significance than the *Sissie*'s sail plan. "But if I were wrong about one or both of you, well, I'd correct my mistake. A commanding officer can*not* be sleeping with a subordinate on a ship as small as this one."

"No, sir," Cazelet said. He swallowed. "Anyway, you weren't wrong. I—thank you for letting us think it through ourselves, sir."

Daniel nodded mildly and returned his attention to the teams beneath. "Got it!" shouted a technician. One, then two, impact drivers began to burr home the bolts anchoring the repositioned mast step.

Daniel wondered if Cazelet fully understood the risks he'd faced if he hadn't made the correct decision. The boy was Lady Mundy's protégé. If he had let his behavior risk the safety of Adele's new family—the crew of the *Princess Cecile*—she might have treated the breach as a matter of honor.

Rene Cazelet would not have survived that decision.

"Ma'am?" said Cory, rotating his seat at the astrogation console to face Adele. "I'd like you to look at this."

He was facing her back, of course. She didn't bother to turn, and Cory knew her too well to expect that she would. If he was more comfortable looking at her back than he would be speaking to her holographic face, that was his business.

While Vesey and Cazelet—along with Daniel—were involved on the *Sissie*'s exterior with the rerigging, Cory was on watch on the bridge. Because he was a good officer—in part because Adele had trained him—he was using the time for work rather than games or pornography.

"Yes," she said aloud, adjusting her display to echo that of the astrogation console.

Adele didn't mind being called away from her analysis of rice production—according to official statistics—on Sunbright over the past ten years, broken down by district. All information was potentially valuable, as well as being worthy for its own sake, in Adele's opinion. That said, the practical benefit of these data was yet to be proven.

Cory had been looking at a pattern rendered in sepia monochrome. Lines ran roughly from top left to bottom right, crossing occasional beads of varied shape. It was unintelligible without context: Adele could imagine it being anything from a graph to a magnified view of the fabric of her trousers.

She started to follow the current image back through its history to determine what it was. Before—momentarily before—she executed that plan, she caught herself and smiled wryly. She turned to face Cory, punishing herself for so determinedly shutting out the RCN family of which she was—by the gift of fate, because she didn't believe in gods—a member.

I don't really believe in fate, either. Well, in luck, then. I certainly believe in luck.

"Please tell me what we're looking at, Cory," she said.

"Well, ma'am," Cory said. He turned to his display and highlighted a faceted lump in the flow of lines. "If you'll take a look here."

Adele thankfully returned to her display also. Signals

officer was a junior warrant rank, equivalent to bosun's mate and several steps below a commissioned lieutenant like Cory. Despite that, he and Cazelet treated Adele as though they were young boys and she was dowager matriarch of their family.

The attitude of the enlisted personnel, including Woetjans and Pasternak, was simpler yet: they were peasants, and Lady Mundy was mistress of the estate. That bore no resemblance to proper RCN protocol, and it certainly wasn't anything Adele encouraged.

She admitted to herself that she didn't mind the situation, however. She had been raised as a Mundy of Chatsworth, and the Sissies' behavior fitted *her* instinctive sense of rightness as surely as it did the crew's.

"We did an all-spectrum scan of the region as we were coming in," Cory said. "This is the valley on ground-penetrating radar, so it's without the ice, you see. Ships show up—"

Beads expanded one after another, just long enough to be identified as shapes in steel before Cory shrank them back to scale.

"—on the surface. Where the ice flow has carried them into one wall of the valley or the other, there's scrape marks in the rock."

His hands poised on his virtual keyboard, preparing to raise the magnification of striations upstream of the bead slugged HEPPLEWHITE, OUT OF KOSSUTH. Adele had already done that with her wands. She didn't need to see the markings—that was equivalent to proving the existence of gravity, so far as she was concerned—but it was useful to remind Cory that she hadn't become a completely helpless ninny.

Aloud she said, "Yes, I see."

"Well, that's all what you'd expect," Cory said earnestly. "Except for this one."

He expanded the highlighted bead until it filled the display. It was a ball formed from pentagonal plates. "Ma'am, this is on the valley *floor*, under three hundred feet of ice. It displaces about three thousand tonnes, and there's no ship in the *Sissie*'s database that looks anything like it."

"It sank through the ice, then?" Adele said, frowning. She restrained her reflex to sort for dodecahedral spaceships, because her conscious intellect assured her that Cory wouldn't have made a mistake when he told her that. He had been well trained.

"Ma'am, maybe," Cory said, but the anguish in his tone meant that he was contradicting her. "But if you look at the scrape marks behind her—"

This time he didn't try to magnify them. Adele's wands flickered, expanding and following the track up the valley; a very long way up the valley.

"If the ice has been moving at the rate it has for the last twelve years—figuring from the marks the *Manzanita Maid* left—and I know it maybe hasn't, but anyway that's *a* figure; it ought to get us into the right order of magnitude...."

"Yes, I see that, Cory," Adele said. "Get on with it."

"Well, the track computes to about thirty thousand years," Cory said apologetically. "Which the model says is about when the planet's orbit got eccentric because a dark star passed through the system."

"In other words, the ice began pushing—"

She decided not to call it a ship.

"—the object as soon as the glacier formed thirty thousand years ago. That doesn't tell us how long it had been sitting on the valley floor before it started to move."

"Yes, ma'am," Cory said in relief. "That's what I thought too. But I don't know how it could be."

Adele sniffed; another person might have laughed. "Nor do I, Cory," she said. "It should be possible to answer some of the questions by melting the glacier with our plasma thrusters, as we'll be doing to fill our tanks of reaction mass, though of course on a much greater scale. But—"

She rotated her seat to face the young lieutenant; he was staring over his shoulder at her.

"—I think that will have to wait until we have more time. At present, we have to find a rebel to repatriate to Cinnabar."

There was a clang against the hull and a cheer from outside loud enough to be heard even though the corvette was closed up against the bitter wind. It appeared that the *Princess Cecile* was now the *House of Hrynko*. They would be lifting shortly.

"Fellow Sissies!" Daniel said from one of the star of five consoles in the Battle Direction Center. He was speaking to the whole ship, his image appearing on all displays and his voice coming through commo helmets and the loudspeakers in every compartment and corridor. "You've all known something was going on. This is what is going on."

Vesey would normally have been here in the armored BDC as first lieutenant, ready to take command if a missile destroyed the bridge. Now she was at the command console in the bow, and Cory, the new first lieutenant, had moved back.

"I'm about to become Kirby Pensett," Daniel said. "Formerly a lieutenant in the RCN but now on half pay and a passenger on this vessel, the *House of Hrynko*. That's the story, and it's *bloody* important that you remember it when you're talking to outsiders. Talking even to each other, because we never know who'll be listening in when we're on the ground."

Tovera, like Hogg on a jumpseat folded out from the bulkhead, glanced at Adele with a reptilian smile. Adele, seated at the console to Daniel's right, was probably aware of her servant's amusement—nobody was going to eavesdrop on the *Princess Cecile* when Adele was aboard—but she gave no reaction herself.

It's still the right thing to say. Even sober, spacers were notoriously loose-tongued, and the chance of a spacer being sober on the first night or two of liberty wasn't very high.

"You're the crew of a yacht owned by a Kostroman noblewoman, the former Principal Hrynko," Daniel said. "She looks a lot like Lady Adele Mundy, but you *won't* call her that any more than you would the real Lady Mundy. You'll say 'ma'am' or you'll say 'sir' because she scares the crap out of you. She's got a temper and you know how these wog nobles can carry on—"

He grinned at Adele. She grinned, broadly for her, though she didn't look up from her display. She had at least his face inset in the image area, along with those of the other officers.

"—but she pays on time and the grub on the *Hrynko* is pretty bloody good. Just about RCN standard, *I'd* say."

There was general laughter at that, in the BDC and trailing down the corridor through the open hatchway. Private owners were notoriously liable to scrimp on the quantity and quality of the rations they provided their crews. An RCN captain checked the quality of all the consumables that came aboard, then signed his approval. A captain who cut corners on food or drink had problems not only with crew members—who knew the regulations—but with the Navy Board.

"Mistress Vesey is captain," Daniel said. His tone was cheery and bantering; handled clumsily, the situation could go from unfamiliar to frightening—a very small step for veteran spacers, who believed that surprises were either bad or fatal; as in space they generally were. "Principal Hrynko doesn't know any more about astrogation than some high-born librarian from Xenos would."

The laughter was even louder this time. Adele continued to smile while her control wands twitched and jabbed. Daniel didn't have the faintest idea what she was working at; it could be her family tree, for all he knew.

He didn't care. Adele said that everything was connected, and for her it was. Her mind was always working, a fact that regularly led to unexpected good results for those around her.

"Now," Daniel said, getting to the nub of it, "if you were any other crew than my Sissies, I'd tell you that this was going to be dangerous. We'll be landing on Madison, an Alliance sector capital, claiming to be a Kostroman ship. Well, you and I have done worse than that to the Alliance, haven't we, spacers?"

The response this time was a bloodthirsty roar from the body of the ship, though the sound had been reduced to tinny echoes by the time it reached Daniel. Nobody inside the BDC actually cheered, though it wouldn't have been a surprise if Fiducia and Rocker, the missileer's mate and gunner's mate, respectively, had joined in.

"But there's something else you ought to know, spacers," Daniel said, pitching his voice a little lower to suggest that he had reached the serious part of the discussion. "Admiral Cox doesn't know what we're about to do. He thinks we're going straight to Sunbright. *Everybody* in Macotta HQ thinks we're going to Sunbright."

"Who bloody cares what the farmers out here think?" somebody shouted. Daniel thought the voice was Woetjans', but if so, she spoke for everybody aboard—Captain Daniel Leary included. Certainly the cheers seemed universal.

In fact the tricky part was going to be keeping up the pretense of being Kostroman while they were on Madison. He'd slipped past that when he told the Sissies it was minor compared to what they'd done in the past.

The deception wasn't dangerous in the sense that the Alliance authorities would shoot them if the trick was detected, but it would certainly be embarrassing and might very well mean months or years of internment while diplomats discussed the matter in measured tones. Daniel didn't imagine that the Macotta bureaucracy would strain itself in helping uppity naval personnel who'd come out from Xenos with an attitude.

Very few of the *Sissie*'s crew were from Kostroma, perhaps six or eight out of over a hundred. That in itself wouldn't surprise Alliance port officials. Spacers were a nation unto themselves. That was less true of a warship's complement than it was for civilian vessels, but even so, no more than half the crew of the corvette *Princess Cecile* had been born on Cinnabar or worlds under the Republic's hegemony.

"Well, Sissies," Daniel said. "We're going to come through this fine, like we have before, if we all do our jobs. This time for you that means mostly watching what you say when we're on the ground. And for me, that means being Kirby Pensett, who used to be an RCN officer. Can we carry it off?"

There were so many variations in the reply that they merged into a growl, but they all amounted to "Yes!" generally with a word or words of emphasis.

"Then for the last time until we've succeeded, let me say it's an honor to command you, Sissies. Six out!"

Over the cheers, Vesey's amplified voice from the bridge said, *"Captain to ship! Prepare for liftoff in thirty, that is three-zero seconds."*

Unexpectedly she added, *"Next stop Madison, spacers."*

Daniel grinned. Vesey tended to seem colorless, and it wasn't often that she raised a cheer. She got one this time.

Chapter Seven

ASHETOWN ON MADISON

Daniel walked down the Harborfront wearing mottled-gray utilities without any markings. A veteran might recognize them as RCN in cut and color, but in dim light they would be indistinguishable from the fleet's gray-green or from similar garments worn by spacers all over the human universe. The clothing wasn't a statement of allegiance, though it did imply his profession.

That would have been a safe bet anyway. Most people at the waterside of a spaceport were spacers or had been spacers.

"Ah, young master," Hogg said in a falsely righteous tone as he viewed the storefronts. "What sinks of iniquity! How I long for the good clean air behind the pigsties back at Bantry."

"You're being unjust to the establishments, Hogg," Daniel said, pursing his lips judiciously. They were looking for the Miltiades Hotel, where the offices of Calpurnius Trading were located.

The Grand Hotel Pleasaunce was to their right, a three-story establishment with a ship chandler and a jewelry store on the ground floor. "They're quite upscale, it seems to me. Now, if we were to wander down an alley, *that* might be another thing altogether."

Though the air did have an unpleasant pong; indeed, Daniel would almost call it a texture. It didn't have anything to do with depravity, however. At a guess, the algae on the surface of the harbor included something that fixed sulfur, which became hydrogen sulfide at the touch of plasma exhaust.

The patches of virulent yellow which floated among the greens and browns were a good candidate for the culprit. Chances were it was an off-planet species which had travelled through the Matrix on a starship's floats and now was adapting to Madison. Viewed in the right way, it was an uplifting story of triumph over adversity.

"Well, anyway it don't half stink!" said Hogg, completing the thought which his master hadn't spoken aloud. Daniel chuckled.

Small boats lined the seafront. The naval harbor had concrete slips, but the commercial side of Ashetown Haven used floating walkways and docks—the *House of Hrynko* was tied up to one—or, for the majority of traffic, anchorages at pilings in the open roadstead with lighters and water taxis to reach dry land.

"And here we are, I believe," said Daniel, nodding to the building across the intersecting street—Fifth Street, according to the sign suspended on cables in the middle of the intersection. The wicker railing of the second-floor balcony was woven to read MILTIADES HOTEL in brown letters against cream; above the tile roof were steps to a miniature widow's walk.

The wall of the building's ground floor was pale orange stucco with CALPURNIUS TRADING in florid black letters, and

CONTRACTORS AND PURVEYORS in smaller script beneath them. There were no windows, only a heavy door which was held open by a doorstop in the form of a bronze dog.

As Daniel started across the street, a handful of ragged boys rushed toward him, crying, "Spare change, Captain, spare change!"

"Sorry, lads, I'm on the beach my—" Daniel started to say. There was a loud *whap!* and a cry behind him. He looked over his shoulder to see another boy staggering away, bent over and holding his left ear.

Hogg picked up the shears the boy had dropped; he had been reaching out to cut the straps of Daniel's belt wallet. Hogg clenched and opened his other hand, working feeling back into his fingers; he'd slapped the boy instead of using his fist. From his own youthful experience, Daniel knew that such blows felt like those of a wooden bat.

Hogg twisted the shears till the steel snapped, then dropped the pieces behind him. "Cheeky little sods," he growled. "Did they think I'm blind? Or my arm's crippled?"

The other boys had vanished like mist as the sun rose. "Not anymore, I'm sure," Daniel said, and he stepped into the premises of Calpurnius Trading.

Three young male clerks were at desks behind the counter to the left. A capable-looking middle-aged woman sat to the right of the doorway. Her console had come from a starship, probably a passenger liner of the previous century. Even as old as that, an astrogation computer was more than sufficient for any planet-bound task. The back wall was wooden with two doors; both were closed.

"Yes, gentlemen?" the woman said. Daniel hadn't seen her send a signal, but an interior door opened and two men came out.

"I'm Kirby Pensett, late of the RCN," Daniel said, withdrawing an identification chip from his belt pouch. "That name doesn't mean anything to you, but I'm here as representative of Bernhard Sattler, whom you do know. I'm to speak either to Mistress Sysco or Master Bremington."

"Why has Bernhard sent an agent?" said the older, better dressed of the two men. His companion looked like a stevedore. "Are you here to inspect us, is that what you mean?"

"Master Bremington?" Daniel said. "I'm here to inspect Master Sattler's investment. Which is significant enough to justify inspection—in my opinion, but much more importantly, in his. Do you have a problem with this?"

"He's who he says he is, Picque," said the woman, who had inserted Daniel's chip into her console. "Look, we've got nothing to hide. If Bernhard wants to look things over, I guess I don't blame him."

Bremington made a sour face. "Well, I suppose I can't complain that Sattler didn't give us warning," he said. "And of course, we don't have anything to hide. That is..."

He paused and gave Daniel a concerned look.

Daniel spread his hands. "I'm here on Master Sattler's behalf," he said. "If it may be that some port duties or the like didn't get paid, that's something for a government to worry about—not me. I would say that so long as the profits are being shared properly, then anything that benefits the company, benefits Master Sattler."

Bremington gave Daniel a slight smile, the first break in

hostility since he entered the lobby. "Come on back to my office," he said, "and after we've talked for a moment, I'll set you up with a console and full access codes."

He cleared his throat and added, "We'd have gone bust seven years ago if Bernhard hadn't raised our capitalization. I'd cheat my mother before I'd cheat him."

"Thank you, Master Bremington," Daniel said with a half bow. With a deeper bow to the woman, he added, "And thank *you*, mistress."

"I'll just wander around, if that's all right with you, sir," said Hogg. The words were more respectful than the tone in which he spoke them.

Daniel followed Bremington down a short hallway. Before the door behind him closed, he heard Hogg said, "I wonder, mistress, if there's a place nearby that a poor man might find a drink and a game of poker?"

The pale russet robe Adele wore in her guise as Principal Hrynko felt unfamiliar but not uncomfortable. She wore khaki utilities beneath it, and the rigger who had run it up for her had placed long vertical slits along the sides as directed. Through them she could reach her pistol or her data unit as easily as she could have normally.

"Hallelujah, I'm a bum!" her escort chorused. She wasn't sure how the Alliance staff would to react to the details of her escort, but she suspected no one on Madison except her had more than a passing acquaintance with Kostroman nobility. *"Hallelujah, bum again!"*

Techs had built Adele's litter from high-pressure tubing and bats of insulation. Covered with ribbons and bunting from the ship's stores, it was flashy enough to appeal to any real Kostroman. Spacers felt that the more decoration, the better; a taste shared by most cultures once you got past the sophisticates of Xenos and Pleasaunce City.

Adele's data unit was already operating in passive mode, gathering inputs according to the instructions Adele had programmed before she left the ship. She didn't suppose she'd need the pistol at Forty Stars Sector Headquarters, but there had been unpleasant surprises in the past. They had been *less* unpleasant because she had been able to shoot her way out of trouble.

They'd reached the plaza in front of the Alliance Building. Adele said, "Set me down here."

Tovera was ahead of the litter, walking with Woetjans at the side of the ragged column. She took the command through her earbud and spoke crisply though inaudibly to the bosun.

"Hallelujah, give us a handout—"

"Halt!" Woetjans shouted. Some of the locals—loungers in the portico as well as those entering or leaving the entrance on business—leaped to the side in surprise; spacers laughed at them.

Three of the four riggers carrying the litter started to put it down. The last was a moment behind the others, with the result that Adele would have pitched out onto the flagstones if she hadn't grabbed the stringers with both hands.

Riding with Hogg has sharpened my instincts, she thought. *Perhaps if I live another fifty years, I'll rise to the level of landsman in the opinion of my shipmates.*

Woetjans had suggested that riggers carry the litter because their job required them to be agile. They weren't used to working as this sort of team, however, and marching in step wasn't part of *any* spacer's training. The twenty Sissies accompanying Adele each wore a russet sash over the right shoulder to indicate that they were Hrynko retainers, but beyond that they were as disparate a group as you could find.

They didn't carry real weapons, but they had clubs of various sorts. That was normal practice on Kostroma, and it wouldn't have raised eyebrows for a member of the nobility in Xenos. Nobody expected a senator's daughter to be jostled in the street by laborers. The Alliance authorities here might object, but they wouldn't be surprised to see it.

Adele stepped out of the litter, feeling thankful. She had—reasonably—felt on the verge of disaster all during the procession from the Harborfront. It might very well have been that a member of the escort would have caught her if the litter-bearers had flung her out, since they'd learned to be alert on the *Princess Cecile* lest Mistress Mundy fall or drift into serious trouble. Nonetheless, it had been an uncomfortable sensation.

The whole escort moved toward the double doors of the entrance, several of them sliding pipes or batons from under their belts. A pair of slender, forties-ish women in blue uniforms were leaving the building. They saw the oncoming gang and turned back inside with startled chirps.

Adele opened her mouth to object, but Woetjans was already bellowing, "Dasi, Barnes, and Creighton *only*, you wankers, just like I said! Any of you who can't obey orders can spend their liberty polishing thruster nozzles! Yes, I mean you, Hatchett."

Adele stared coldly at the confusion, her natural expression under the circumstances. Spacers slunk away from the door and gathered around the litter, tucking away cudgels or, in the case of one technician, a knife that he shouldn't have been carrying.

Tovera nodded. The spacers pushed open the doors and marched into the atrium. Adele followed them, and Tovera brought up the rear with her attaché case held waist high in her left hand. Though the building didn't have a military detachment, the pair of security guards inside were fingering their shock rods as they scowled at Woetjans and her spacers.

Adele felt the humor of the situation, though she didn't let it reach her lips. With Tovera in the room, nobody else could be considered really dangerous. The mental smile hardened: except perhaps for Tovera's mistress.

The double-height atrium was semicircular, with doors opening off the curve. There were a dozen people watching Adele's arrival at ground level, and a similar number peered down over the mezzanine rail.

"I am the Principal Hrynko!" Adele said, her words filling the big room. She had grown up in a family of politicians; even her little sister, Agatha, had known how to project her voice. "I am here to meet your Admiral Jeletsky, as one leader to another!"

The male receptionist at the central island was in urgent communication with someone over the intercom, but he kept his eyes on Adele and her entourage. Nobody actually responded to Adele.

She pointed to a man in lace-trimmed trousers and jacket who stood at the open door to his office. The style had been briefly popular on Pleasance about five years earlier, marking the fellow as a local who was trying to pass as a citizen of an Alliance core world. He was probably a mid-level functionary and therefore as frightened of overstepping his authority as he was of doing the wrong thing.

"You!" Adele said, pointing with her right arm. "Take me to the squadron commander!"

"Mistress?" said the receptionist in a desperate voice. "Your Ladyship? Please, someone is coming. He'll be here very shortly, so if you—there he is! Deputy Quinley, the, ah, Principal Hrynko is here to see you."

Quinley was short, tubby, and at the moment, red-faced. Over an ordinary business suit with puffed sleeves he wore a blue sash; the pretty blond aide trotting with him through an interior doorway was trying to tug wrinkles out of its glossy fabric.

He stopped and straightened when he saw Adele. Bowing, he said with unexpected dignity, "Your Ladyship, I am Deputy Controller Quinley. How may the Alliance serve you here on Madison?"

"I am here to see Admiral Jeletsky," Adele said. "I am a leader, and I will meet with your leader."

What Adele was *really* here to do was to cause a stir that would cause all departments in the building to check on what was happening—and by so doing, to open their systems to her personal data unit. She wasn't looking for information at the moment; that would require her input, choosing the pathways and circumventing security. All she expected to get from this were the internal addresses.

"Your Ladyship," Quinley said quietly but firmly, "Admiral

Jeletsky is a Fleet official. Unless you're here to declare war, your business is with the Sector's civil government. I am the highest Alliance representative available. If you'll come back to my office, we will deal with your concerns as expeditiously as possible."

He looked at Woetjans and added, "My office isn't overly large, Your Ladyship. It would be better if you left your companions here to amuse themselves. And better still if they were to wait outside."

Adele looked stern in a calculated fashion for a moment. Then she said, "My secretary will accompany me."

To the bosun she added, "Woetjans, you may wait at the litter while I deal with this bureaucrat."

If Quinley was offended by the description, he avoided letting the fact show. "Follow me, please," he said and walked back the way he had come. Adele, Tovera, and finally the aide followed.

A security guard opened the door into a hallway. He and Quinley exchanged glances; then the guard faced front and stood with no more expression than the wall behind him while "the Kostromans" passed.

Quinley's office was on the ground floor, but the back wall was glass with a door into the small garden beyond. The deputy controller touched a belt fob as he entered, and the sidewalls became a creamy blank. Everything in the office was virtual except for the chairs and desk of a synthetic with the sheen of black onyx.

"If you'll give me a moment, please," Quinley said, sliding behind the desk and bringing up a display on which he concentrated.

Adele had to restrain her reflex to take out her data unit. As a loud semi-barbarian, she was a harmless joke. If she showed herself to be technologically capable, she would become more interesting—especially since Quinley was showing himself to be a good deal more than a pompous nonentity also.

The aide smiled brightly and said, "Won't you be seated, Your Ladyship, mistress? And can I have some refreshment brought to you?"

Adele sat down. Though the chair looked like stone, it deformed firmly but comfortably to her weight. She said, "No, I have my own food aboard the yacht."

Tovera stood against the wall, on the hinge side of the door panel. If it opened, she and her attaché case would be concealed from the person entering. Neither Quinley nor the aide paid her any attention: Tovera was as colorless as the walls.

"I see," Quinley said in a neutral voice. He shrank his holographic display—it had been merely a haze of light to any eyes but his—and looked at Adele. He said, "I've reviewed the records, Lady Hrynko. So far as I can see, there's no reason you couldn't have let the port authorities handle the clearance in the normal course of business. That might take a day or two, but since you're the owner but not the listed captain, your employees could have made the declarations without troubling you."

Adele raised her head slightly, so that she was speaking down her nose at the deputy controller. It was acting, of course, but her mother had been a very good role model for this sort of thing.

"I should let flunkies come aboard my yacht?" she said. "Even if I am on emeritus status, I am owed the honors of a Principal of Kostroma!"

"As you wish, Your Ladyship," Quinley said equably. He brought up his display again, then narrowed it to a single column so that he could meet Adele's eyes.

"Since I'm acting as clearance officer, Your Ladyship," he said, "I'm curious about the size of your crew. One hundred and fifteen effectives would be heavy even for a warship the size of your yacht. Why is that, please?"

When Adele didn't respond instantly, Quinley added, "I'm officially curious, that is. An answer is a requirement of your presence on Madison."

Not at all a pompous nonentity, Adele thought, pleased at the realization. She liked to meet competent people, even in cases where her job would have been simpler if they were like the dullards who vastly outnumbered them.

Aloud she said toward the corner of the ceiling, "Should the Principal Hrynko allow a booby from Vitebsk—"

She had recognized the deputy controller's accent.

"—to question her motives? But no matter."

Adele met Quinley's eyes again; he had flushed at the reference to his origins. "I explained," she continued, "that I was emeritus; that is, that my stepson guides Hrynko in my place. I considered becoming Elector of Kostroma but decided that the position was unworthy of me in the final analysis. Elector Cargill, who took the position when I renounced it, arranged a pension for me sufficient to support my love of travel."

Anyone with a feeling for politics would hear Adele's statement as an admission that Principal Hrynko had lost the struggle to rule her planet but that she retained enough power that the victor had preferred to buy her off instead of carrying the fight to the end. From the way Quinley relaxed, *he* certainly heard it that way.

Adele turned her hands palms-up. "I have chosen to invest part of my pension in safeguarding my person," she said. "Instead of spending larger sums to ransom myself from the pirates who infest many of the regions in which I may travel. Should anyone question my judgment?"

Quinley smiled, then touched a keyboard control. "I certainly don't question it, Your Ladyship," he said. "I've cleared your yacht. Enjoy your stay on Madison."

The aide had been standing across the doorway from Tovera. "Wycherson," he said. "Please show her Ladyship out."

Adele followed the aide down the corridor at a stately pace. There was nothing more to do here, but rushing off to check what her data unit had gathered would threaten the pose of aristocratic foolishness which she had taken pains to cultivate. Patience was always a virtue, and here it was a necessary one.

"Feel free to call on us, Your Ladyship," the aide called as she held the entrance door open for "the Kostromans." Adele swept past without deigning to look at her.

Woetjans shouted an order, but the Sissies were already sorting themselves out. There were different spacers on the litter poles; this time they were techs from the ship side rather than riggers. It appeared that even the bosun had decided that the riggers' individual initiative wasn't the best choice for teamwork on the ground after all.

Adele waited until they had lifted the litter before she took out her data unit; through sheer effort of will she waited till they had paced a block back in the direction of the yacht before she switched on the display. Tovera walked alongside instead of being ahead with Woetjans.

Adele looked at her servant. She would have spoken, but a ship lifted from the roadstead just then. Though the vessel was small and a mile offshore, its three plasma thrusters hammering at full output were loud enough that she would have had either to shout or to speak through the earbud, in which case Tovera could not have responded.

When the sound had died away, Tovera looked up and said, "Mistress?"

"Most of the departments might as well be without any security at all," Adele said. "Which I suspect means that there will be nothing to help us in their files."

Tovera shrugged. "The exercise was healthy, I suppose," she said.

The techs moved more smoothly by far than the riggers had; with a little practice they would probably become quite good at the business. Though if Adele never had to ride on a litter again, it would be too soon.

Aloud Adele said, "I said 'most of the departments,' Tovera. The exception was Fleet Intelligence, which seems to be walled off securely."

Tovera frowned, a momentary parochial irritation overcoming her usual detachment. "The Fifth Bureau didn't have a high opinion of Fleet Intelligence," she said, making her opinion impersonal in form.

"No," said Adele, "nor do I—in general. Since the Forty Stars detachment is such an exception, I think I'd better learn more about the Commander Rudolph Doerries, who runs it."

Daniel got up from the console. He braced himself in the doorway of the office and pushed hard against both jambs. His muscles had stiffened while he went over the Calpurnius Trading files.

It might have been useful to have Cazelet with him—or for that matter, to have Cazelet in his place—but Daniel was confident that he would have spotted a problem if there were one; at least he would have spotted the fact that there *was* a problem. His sister Deirdre handled the Leary family's extensive investments, but Daniel himself wasn't a babe in the woods when faced with a ledger.

Bremington must have heard the movement, because he came out of the adjacent office where he'd been working since he unlocked all files on his personal console and left Daniel alone with it. Obviously he was making a point—but it was precisely the point an innocent man would want to emphasize.

"Are you satisfied, Pensett?" he asked.

"I am," said Daniel, looking over his shoulder as he shifted and thrust against the doorway in the other direction. "Both with your good faith toward Master Sattler and with the good business judgment with which Calpurnius Trading is run."

Daniel had the impression that Bremington made sure that the shipping side went smoothly while Mistress Sysco ran the front office and was the partnership's public face. He hadn't seen Sysco since starting work on the files: an earnest-looking young man was still at the reception desk he had taken over when Sysco had offered to show Hogg some nearby establishments where he could relax.

Daniel grinned. How relaxing Hogg had found the afternoon

was another matter—and none of the young master's business.

"Well, give my regards to Bernhard when you next see him," Bremington said. "Is there anything more we can help you with?"

Will you please get out of here and let me do my job! Daniel translated mentally. He smiled. Aloud he said, "There is, sir, but I hope it won't be a burden. Master Sattler wants me to follow a shipment of his goods to Sunbright. I'm a spacer, of course, so I'm more than happy to work my passage."

"To *Sunbright*?" Bremington said with a rising inflection. "Why in the name of the infernal does he want to do that? Our sales are Free Alongside at Ashe Haven. If the buyers want to dump the goods into the sea after they pay for delivery, that's no skin off our noses—us or Bernhard either one."

"I didn't figure it was my business to ask," Daniel said, shrugging and spreading his hands. "I'm being paid and paid pretty well. Besides which—"

He grinned engagingly at Bremington.

"—it occurred to me that when I get to Sunbright, there might be a more interesting job than supercargo available for an RCN-trained astrogator. At any rate, I can ask around."

Hogg came in the front door and bowed as he held it open for Mistress Sysco. Both looked flushed but cheerful. Hogg seemed to have had more than a little to drink, but Daniel had never seen his servant too drunk to function.

Of course it might have happened when Daniel himself was passed out drunk. That had happened a few times; or maybe more than a few. But not recently.

Not *very* recently.

"*Good* afternoon, young master!" Hogg said, straightening

with pie-eyed care. "And if I may say so, it has been a very good afternoon, an afternoon of great exceptionableness!"

Bremington seemed to be taken aback to see his business partner leaning across the reception desk, bracing her weight on her arms. The boy seated there stared at her with a horrified expression.

"Ah, Madge?" Bremington said. "Lieutenant Pensett wants to travel to Sunbright on an interloping trader. I was thinking of sending him to the *Savoy*?"

"That's a bloody good idea, Picque," Sysco mumbled to the desktop. "Whatever you say is a bloody good idea. You go on and do it, why don't you?"

"Yes, of course," Bremington said. He was beginning to smile. Turning to Daniel, he said, "The *Savoy* has a load of solar-charging lasers which we provided. She'll stage from here to Cremona, then make the jump to Sunbright. I'll call the owner, Kiki Lindstrom, and tell her you're coming."

"Thank you indeed," Daniel said, dipping his head in something between a nod and a bow. "Is Lindstrom the captain as well as owner?"

"No, she's got somebody from Novy Sverdlovsk for astrogation," Bremington said. "I guess she knows a console well enough that she could probably find her way to a planet by herself if she had to."

He pursed his lips, then added, "I haven't met the captain. I've never had much use for folks from Sverdlovsk, though."

Daniel shrugged. "I've sailed with them," he said. "They can be all right. Still, any help you can provide in getting us places would be appreciated."

"It's Berth 54," Bremington said. He looked at Hogg, leaning against the doorframe. "Ah, would you like me to call you a surface car? That's about a kilometer north of here."

"The walk will do us good," Daniel said with a laugh. "Come along, Hogg. Duty calls."

"Faithful to the last, young master!" Hogg said, straightening. He immediately began to wobble, but with Daniel's touch to steady him he started out onto the Harborfront.

"But one bloody minute," he added. He turned and bowed again.

"My red-haired lovely," Hogg said. "I will never forget you. Never, never, never."

They marched northward along the Esplanade. Daniel glanced back. Mistress Sysco was still bent over the desk.

It wasn't a bad view, given that she was much older than Daniel's tastes lay.

Chapter Eight

ASHETOWN ON MADISON

Daniel would be whistling if he felt like this, Adele thought as she pattered up the *Sissie*'s companionway toward Level A and her console on the bridge. Tovera was ahead, though not even a paranoid sociopath like her servant was really worried about someone waiting ahead in the armored staircase to attack them.

Adele didn't regret her inability to whistle, but it pleased her that other people might have done so if they were as content as she was now. She wasn't going to take off her clothes and dance up the stairs, either.

Though now that she thought about it, she *had* tossed "Principal Hrynko's" gown behind her when she reached the entry hold. She probably ought to send someone back for it in case she was suddenly required to impersonate a Kostroman noblewoman. Well, one of the spacers would probably bring it up unasked; and if not, she would worry about it later.

Adele had new data to pore over—and the promise of still more shortly. She planned to visit the Assumption Library this afternoon, as soon as she had set her systems working to harvest data from the Forty Stars Headquarters. She could justify going to the library—the *Assumption* was the colony ship by which Madison had been settled before the thousand-year Hiatus in star travel—on reasons of duty, but in truth she was hoping to find ancient documents which had been lost to scholars on other worlds.

Tovera led her into the rotunda just aft of the bridge. The forward dorsal airlock opened onto it, as well as the companionways. Nobody on a starship, not even the captain, used the wrong set of stairs. That was true even—indeed, especially—in an emergency, when people tangled in the tubes, which were the only ways to get from one level to another, would make disaster certain.

Until Adele entered, Cazelet, sitting at the astrogation console, was alone on the bridge. He was checking the communications intercepts which Adele had set her equipment to make in her absence. She supposed that was as useful as anything else the watch officer could do under the current placid conditions, and it was more Cazelet's taste than reviewing crew-discipline records or the rate of water usage during the past thirty days.

"Mistress?" he said. Cazelet wasn't much better than Adele herself in following protocol when addressing his fellows aboard the corvette. Like her, he was a well-born civilian who had not gone through the Academy. "There's something interesting going on in orbit."

At the same moment, a sidebar on Adele's display pulsed with a message in purple from Cory in the Battle Direction Center: COMMUNICATIONS SWEEP INDICATES FREIGHTER BEING ATTACKED IN ORBIT, with an icon which would take her to the same input as the icon Cazelet had put on her sidebar after alerting her verbally.

Adele felt more frustration than amusement. The young men were not twins, but her training seemed to have turned them into the professional equivalent of that. She wasn't a martinet who hammered every peg into a hole of the same size!

She brought the incident—it was still evolving—up on the left half of her display while she finished arranging to download the files from every database in the Alliance HQ, save for those in the Fleet Intelligence bureau. Years before, she had developed a template for that task, so executing it on a new target was only a matter of making sure that the software was working as expected.

The *Princess Cecile* had spent less than twelve hours on Cinnabar between arriving from Zenobia and lifting again for Kronstadt with orders issued and signed by the Navy Board. That was a sufficient interval for Mistress Sand's messenger to give Adele updates for Alliance codes. Because of how far Madison was from Pleasaunce, the latest codes might not have reached the Forty Stars Squadron itself.

Only when Adele had set her console to work did she switch her attention to what had her disciples excited. It had taken her thirty seconds to complete the initial task; while that *could* be the difference between life and death, anything could be the difference between life and death. It was worth a good deal to her to avoid the irritation she felt at being interrupted, and the choice of which task to do first was random on the information she had thus far.

Cazelet's icon sent Adele to a plot-position indicator centered on Ashe Haven; two beads in orbit were highlighted, red and blue. As soon as she started to adjust the range of the image, it shrank to the minimum size needed to encompass both vessels. That was a degree of automated helpfulness which Adele neither needed nor wanted, but it wasn't important enough to discuss at this moment.

The blue dot was out-sun of the red dot; about 60,000 miles separated the two, according to the scale. The display would give Adele a figure accurate within inches if she queried it, but that wasn't necessary for her present purposes.

A thin line the same color followed each dot, showing its track for the previous seventeen minutes; dotted lines—they hadn't been visible at the original large scale—projected the vessels' future courses, which were converging. Each dot was slugged with a full name rather than the usual three-letter identifier: blue was the *Estremadura*, red was the *Sister Kate*.

"Estremadura, *this is piracy!*" said the *Sister Kate*. She was—full data on both ships had appeared twice on Adele's sidebar—a 600-tonne freighter registered on Cremona, an independent world in the Funnel. It was the closest world to Sunbright in time of passage through the Matrix. *"You have fired on a friendly vessel within a system belonging to the Alliance of Free Stars. You are pirates, and I'm reporting this to Forty Stars Headquarters! Over."*

The little freighter—from the timing, she was the ship which had lifted as "Principal Hrynko" was leaving the sector headquarters building—was using tight-beam microwave to transmit to the *Estremadura* and, through a separate antenna, to a communication satellite above Madison. That was to be expected, as the captain hoped to be rescued by the Forty Stars Squadron.

The *Estremadura* was also transmitting to Madison Control as well as to the freighter. That *was* a surprise, though Adele's patch into the military observation constellation would have brought the details of the incident to the *Princess Cecile* even without the parties being so helpful.

"Sister Kate, *this is the Fleet Auxiliary Cruiser* Estremadura," the other vessel responded. The speaker was male and had what Adele thought was a Pleasaunce accent. *"We have warned you to lie to. The manifest you filed before liftoff is false. We have a true manifest, showing that you are carrying arms and other contraband to the rebels on Sunbright. If you attempt to evade us by maneuver or by inserting into the Matrix, we will destroy you under authority of our commission as an auxiliary in the Funnel Squadron. Do not doubt me! Over."*

The sidebar—twice, of course—gave the particulars of the *Estremadura*. She had been built eighty years before as an anti-pirate cruiser on Hallowell, a Cinnabar client world in the Macotta Region. She was now registered on Sunbright and commissioned as a Fleet auxiliary.

The cruiser displaced 3,000 tonnes compared with the *Sissie* at 1,300 under full load. It didn't carry missiles because its intended prey was lightly built pirate craft of a few hundred tonnes, but it mounted eight 4-inch plasma cannon in separate mountings.

Adele scrolled back in time, running the verbal exchange between the ships as text at the bottom of her screen while she watched the business unfold. Madison was the second planet of this system. The *Estremadura* had been keeping station thirty million miles out-sun, in the orbit of the third planet. It had made a short hop through the Matrix, extracting a hundred thousand miles above Madison only minutes before the *Sister Kate* lifted from Ashe Haven.

The *Sister Kate* rose to orbit and lighted her High Drive motors to accelerate. When she reached what her captain considered sufficient velocity, she would insert into the Matrix and slip through a sequence of bubble universes in which the constants of space and time differed usefully from those of the sidereal universe. While a ship could multiply its existing velocity in the Matrix, it could not accelerate until it returned to the universe in which it properly existed.

The *Estremadura* had ordered the freighter to shut off her motors and lie to. When the freighter's captain predictably ignored the challenge, the cruiser fired two plasma cannon at the smaller vessel. The range was too great for the bolts to seriously damage the freighter, but there was risk to the sails and to anyone on the exterior of the hull, even in a rigging suit.

Perhaps more to the point, until the burst of plasma dissipated, the *Sister Kate* could not escape into the Matrix. In order to insert, a starship's surface charge had to be in perfect balance, which couldn't be achieved while loose ions were dancing on the skin and rigging.

The freighter's captain had yelped, complained, and transmitted bills of lading which indicated his cargo was ten-megawatt fusion generators being carried to Cremona. That was the point at which Adele had begun observing in real time. The cruiser continued to approach the *Sister Kate*, ignoring all protests.

"*Mistress?*" said Cory. "*Two separate guns fired at the freighter—they don't mount them in twin turrets like ours. Both bolts were centered, just perfect. That's RCN-quality shooting; better than that, even, for most ships.*"

Adele was pleased to see that though Cory was using a private intercom channel, he had opened it to Cazelet as well. The officers were young males with all that implied to anyone with a grounding in biology, but they were also courteous professionals who appeared to like one another personally.

Adele shrank the PPI to an inset and used the bulk of the display for her own search. The two officers continued to watch the capture of the freighter, but that—though dramatic—wasn't important. The important thing to learn was how it came to be captured.

The *Sister Kate* either was or was not a blockade runner carrying a load of contraband. The RCN neither enforced the blockade nor wished to circumvent it, so what was happening in orbit did not affect the *Princess Cecile* or her crew.

Adele didn't smile, but she felt a touch of pleasure at the situation. She had gone to the heart of the problem while Cory and Cazelet were both lost in trivial side paths. On the other hand, that meant that there had been a flaw in the training they had received from Officer Adele Mundy.

Adele let the smile touch her lips after all. Their education wasn't over; it wouldn't be over till they died, if they were the men she hoped and believed they were. And neither was her own education.

She found the signal at about the time she expected it to have been sent, thirty-one minutes before the *Estremadura* had left its distant station to appear in Madison orbit. It had been transmitted by laser from a civilian comsat, though Adele used the military constellation to locate it. A signal beamed thirty million miles out had to be tightly focused, so there wasn't any difficultly tracking it back to the sending head and in turn identifying the feed from the ground.

The last stage of Adele's search was to locate the terminus where the call had originated. Since she had given herself full access to the civilian communications system within hours of the *Sissie*'s landing on Madison, that wasn't very difficult either.

As she expected, Cory and Cazelet were now echoing her search instead of wasting time on a freighter of no significance. She smiled, this time with complete justification.

The call had come from a secure warehouse a few blocks from the harbor. The district was a mix of similar wholesale/storage facilities and tenements, saved from being a slum by the commercial activity bustling in it. Cory had already found real-time satellite imagery, so Adele decided to enter the site's internal communications system.

And failed. As best Adele could tell, the line by which the signal had been sent to the *Estremadura* simply did not accept incoming data. She didn't doubt that there was a way to conduct two-way traffic from within the warehouse, but it was separate from the line which delivered information—or orders—to the waiting cruiser. At a guess, it was hardwired to a location at some distance from the warehouse.

Adele touched her lips with the tip of her tongue, considering how to proceed. A flicker on her sidebar caught her attention—as Cazelet had clearly meant it to do. She called it up with her wands.

"*Mistress?*" Cazelet said, using the intercom to include Cory in his discussion. "*I followed the money trail for the rental. It led to Forty Stars HQ; the only further information is the slug* "Platt/Restricted.'"

"Very good, Cazelet!" Adele said. "Could it have come from the Fleet Intelligence Bureau?"

"*Adele, there was* no *further evidence,*" Cazelet said, with no more sign of irritation beyond the fact that he was repeating what he had already said.

Adele grimaced. Cazelet had a right to be peevish: she had treated him as though he was one of the many who used words in a sloppy fashion when reporting to her.

"*But I then did a sort through general records for other files marked that way,*" Cazelet continued, obviously working *very* hard not to sound smug. "*I found references to the* Estremadura *had the same slug, and there was a further notation to refer all reports to the Intelligence Bureau and take no further action.*"

"*Caz, that's bloody brilliant!*" Cory said.

"Yes, Cazelet," Adele said. "I agree."

She started to examine what Cazelet had found, though his oral report had probably covered everything of interest. She noticed Cory had put an icon on the sidebar also, to a very different location from Cazelet's. Adele followed it, smiling as broadly as she ever did.

The link took her to real-time security camera outputs; four of them. Two gave kitty-corner views of a walled courtyard, one was an exterior view of the street beyond the gate of that courtyard, and the last was toward the gate from the inside, from a camera mounted on the roof of the building which the courtyard served.

This was the warehouse which Adele had viewed through satellite imagery. Cory had penetrated it after all.

"The exterior guard posts aren't shielded the way whatever's going on inside is," Cory said with quiet pride. *"I thought it might be that way."*

"You've both done very well," Adele said. *And if your teacher were a third party, I would say that she has done well also.*

The sliding gate in the courtyard wall was steel and wide enough to pass a full-sized truck. To the left of it, a cylindrical tower peeked over the high wall. There were firing slots on the tower's inner side, but the armored door was open for ventilation; a guard with a carbine lounged in it.

The front of the single-story building was pierced by four roll-up vehicular doors and a pedestrian door in the middle. There were gunports in the doors, though none in the masonry itself. Whatever the building might have been originally, it wasn't a simple warehouse now.

"There's a vehicle," Cory said. *"Yes, it's turning in. It's a delivery truck."*

Adele didn't expand the image from the gate camera beyond its present quadrant of her display. That scale was sufficient, and something of even greater interest might be about to happen in the field of one of the other cameras.

The high angle didn't give any detail of the black van other than the presence of two figures in the cab. The driver stuck her head out and called something; very likely she had honked as well.

The guard who had been dozing in the tower doorway got up and disappeared inside. After a moment, the gate opened slowly, jouncing on at least one flat roller. The truck pulled in, but the gate started to close before the driver and her assistant got out of the cab. That was surprisingly good procedure, given the slovenly fashion in which the guards seemed to behave in general.

The pedestrian door into the building opened. Two guards, in khaki like the man in the tower, stood in the doorway; they held carbines, but the muzzles were lowered.

The woman and the man from the truck wore nondescript civilian clothes. They walked around to the back of their vehicle and pulled out a boy of eight or ten. His wrists and ankles were bound, and he appeared to be gagged as well; the camera's resolution wasn't good enough for Adele to be sure.

They carried the boy to the door, holding him by the elbows. He tried to kick, but he went limp when the driver clipped him over the ear with her free hand. They handed him to the guards, then walked quickly back to the truck while the door into the building closed.

"*Now, that's interesting,*" Cory said in puzzlement.

"Yes," Adele said. She paused, plotting her further course of action; plotting it all the way to the end. Because she was fairly certain how it was going to end.

"Cazelet," she said. "Learn what you can about who is

paying for this operation. Cory, follow that truck to wherever it goes and learn everything about it and its crew."

She had no authority to give orders to RCN officers. She knew that; the two men knew that; and they *would* do as she directed.

Adele got up from her console. She said, "Tovera and I are going to the Assumption Library. It's what I had intended, and..."

She paused, choosing her words. "I have spent much of my life in libraries," she said. "I think well in that setting. And I have important thinking to do."

Lady Adele Mundy strode off the bridge of the *Princess Cecile*; Tovera followed her in grinning silence. What Adele contemplated was not the business of an RCN officer.

The *Savoy* was the fifth and outermost vessel in the slip, but the fact she was tethered at a concrete quay rather than moored to a buoy made her royalty among the thirty or forty blockade runners in Ashe Haven. A suspension bridge crossed the twenty feet—more or less; the bridge dipped or tightened as the side moved—from the entry hatch to eyebolts on the quay, but Daniel paused to look at the vessel before he boarded her.

Hogg had recovered well enough on the walk that Daniel wouldn't have guessed that he'd come back from lunch staggeringly drunk. He grunted as he looked at the *Savoy*. "Not much to write home about, is she?" he muttered sourly.

"Neither are the cowsheds at Bantry, Hogg," Daniel said with quiet cheerfulness. "What's important in a blockade runner is function, not a statement of national pride. That ship has made seven landings on Sunrise since the beginning of the rebellion and has returned a very handsome profit for her captain and backers."

The *Savoy* was a 600-tonne single-decked freighter. The hull was a rusty steel cylinder floating just above the harbor surface on two pontoon outriggers; they were rusty also, at least the portion above water. The crew compartment was a capsule forward. The fusion bottle was in the hold; there was no separate Power Room.

She had four antennas spaced around the hull amidships. Astern, a short jack was mounted at 45 degrees to the ship's axis; there was probably a similar jack at 225 degrees, out of sight from the quay. The fixed jacks gave the astrogator leverage to slew the central antennas against the Casimir radiation by which ships adjusted their courses in the Matrix.

A light was on in the entrance hold, but no crewmen were in sight. Daniel could hear voices from within, though: a man and a woman. The words weren't audible, but the angry tone was beyond question.

"Hello the ship!" Daniel called, pitching his voice to carry. "Hello, Captain Kiki Lindstrom! Permission to come aboard the *Savoy*!"

There was silence for a moment. A woman of forty-odd stepped into sight in the hatchway. She wasn't precisely unattractive, but the first adjective which would occur to a man meeting her was "solid." A man, younger but only dimly glimpsed, followed her from the crew capsule.

"You're Lieutenant Pensett?" she said. "Yes, come aboard."

Hogg would have started across, but Daniel held him

back and took the lead. The treads were steel with non-skid perforations, while the suspension cables were woven from beryllium monocrystal.

Though the construct was strong enough to support an armored personnel carrier, it swayed, jiggled, and bounced like gossamer in a breeze. Even spacers with years of experience of starships' rigging might be uncomfortable with the slack support and the wind coming off the sea.

Daniel grinned. The catwalk took *him* back to his youth, when he clambered about every building and tree on Bantry, the family estate. He murmured over his shoulder, "Hogg, you never tried to keep me from doing things because they weren't safe."

"And how much would ye have listened if I *had* tried to do something so silly?" Hogg growled. His greater weight joined Daniel's on the walkway, their steps syncopating. "Besides, you needed to learn how to fall so that you'd learn to pick yourself up again. You mother told me to take care of you, didn't she?"

"I suspect she meant what I would've called coddling, Hogg," Daniel said.

"Well, that's not what *I* bloody meant," Hogg said. His tone of certainty put an end to the discussion.

The man stepped forward to stand beside Mistress Lindstrom. He was taller than Daniel and perfectly proportioned, with broad shoulders and a trim waist; his hair was short and a blond so pale that at a distance in bright sunlight he would look bald.

"We don't need you!" he said, arms akimbo.

"Petrov!" the woman said. "I told you this was my decision!"

"You certainly don't need me," Daniel said, because it was as easy to be polite. "The *Savoy*'s record of success is all the proof of that one could ask for. I need you, though, and I'll work my passage at any position on the ship. I can both rig and astrogate, and I took my Power Room training in the RCN Academy."

"We've got riggers," Petrov said, speaking to Lindstrom now. He was trying to moderate his tone, but he was obviously angry and not well-enough controlled to keep that out of his voice. "You handle the fusion bottle, we don't need that, and *I* astrogate better than any pansy from Cinnabar. He's not worth the food!"

"I can bring my own rations," Daniel said mildly. "And I've never been aboard a ship which couldn't have used another pair of skilled hands when things got hairy. As they're pretty sure to do now and again for a blockade runner."

He was beginning to suspect that Petrov's problem wasn't with Daniel as a rival spacer but rather with him as a rival *man*. There wasn't any polite way for Daniel to say that he wasn't interested in Mistress Lindstrom's favors, regardless of the wishes of the lady herself.

"You really can run a fusion bottle, Pensett?" Lindstrom said, her eyes narrowing. She glanced at Petrov and said, "Look, Peter, I'm all right with the bottle so long as everything's running normally, but I'm *not* a trained tech. We could be deep in the muck if we're over Sunbright with a cruiser bearing down on us the next time she starts running high so I have to shut down."

"We'll be all right!" Petrov said. "We've *been* all right!"

"A Power Room certificate is required for commissioning in the RCN, Mistress Lindstrom," Daniel said. "As I'm sure you know. I'm not an engineer, but I can tease a fusion bottle back into the green without shutting her down."

"Look—" Petrov began.

"No, *you* look, Peter," Lindstrom said, turning toward her astrogator with a flash of anger. "We can—I can, this is *my* ship—use another hand with the rigging. There's so many splices that we're bound to have as many cable jams as we did on the last run. Besides which—"

Petrov had opened his mouth again to speak. Lindstrom stuck a blunt, capable finger in his face and continued in a louder voice. "*Besides* which, I bloody need help with the bottle! Pensett ships with us and that's final. Do you understand?"

Presumably Petrov did, because he sneered and walked off the ship past Daniel. His soft boots—they were standard spacers' boots, intended to be worn inside rigging suits— wouldn't bang on the catwalk, but he certainly tried.

"We'll be lifting in forty-eight hours," Lindstrom said, "but get your traps aboard tomorrow. I'll introduce you to the crew then, and you can go over the setup. There's nothing unusual if you've sailed in ships this small before."

"I have," said Daniel, "and smaller. But one thing, mistress? My man Hogg—"

Hogg had done a remarkable job of keeping his mouth shut. Now he straightened and seemed to be trying to stand at attention. Even sober and as cleaned up as he was ever likely to be, he would look like a rumpled countryman. The attempt was either sad or amusing, depending on the observer.

"—is an important part of my researches for Master Sattler. I'll pay—"

"Is he a spacer?" Lindstrom said curtly.

"Sure, I am!" Hogg said.

Daniel would have backed the lie if he'd thought there was any chance of it succeeding. Starting with Hogg's heavy boots, he was as unlikely a spacer as he was a striptease dancer.

"No, mistress," Daniel said firmly, "but he's a bloody useful man to have around for any number of reasons. And Master Sattler will pay passenger-liner rates for bare food and passage."

Lindstrom shook her head. "No," she said. "Having you aboard is stretching accommodations, but it's short runs to Cremona and then to Sunbright. I won't have another body, though, and that's flat."

Daniel had seen Lindstrom angry, and he didn't intend to turn her anger on himself pointlessly. He wasn't going to change her mind—and he didn't really disagree with her. A small blockade runner wasn't a place for extra bodies.

Hogg must have reached the same conclusion, because there was desperation in his voice as he said, "Look, ma'am, you won't know I'm there! I swear, I'll be as quiet as the ship's cat, I *swear* it!"

"Got anything on for tonight, Pensett?" the woman said as though Hogg hadn't spoken. "I've got a room at the Criterion; I don't sleep on the ship while there's a choice. I thought we might have dinner and a drink, then go over your duties?"

"Thank you, sir," said Daniel with false enthusiasm, "but I have preparations to make tonight. Perhaps another time, though!"

He grinned brightly. He thought, *But no time in* this *lifetime, I hope.*

He touched his servant on the shoulder, then used firmer contact to turn him away. "Come on, Hogg," he said. "Let's get outside of a drink or ten, shall we?"

Hogg shuffled across the catwalk like a sheep in the slaughter chute. When they had reached the other side, Daniel guided the older man toward one of the smaller, darker taverns on the other side of the Harborfront.

Hogg turned to look at Daniel. "Lad," he said quietly, "I didn't try to wrap you in gauze, you know that. But I wouldn't have let you try to fly from the top of a cloudscraper pine either."

"Now, it's not as bad as that, Hogg," Daniel said, trying to sound cheerful.

"Yes, it bloody well is!" Hogg said. "You and that Petrov won't both reach Cremona alive. Since you won't stab *him* in the back, that means betting on you to survive is a sucker's bet."

"It'll look different when we've wet our throats, Hogg," Daniel said.

But in his heart, he wasn't finding much wrong with his servant's assessment.

Chapter Nine

ASHETOWN ON MADISON

Daniel raised his hand to the barman and pointed to the beer pitcher. It wasn't empty, but he took care of that problem by splitting the remaining contents between his mug and Hogg's.

"It tastes like dog piss," Hogg muttered. He lowered the level in his mug with a series of deliberate gulps.

The barman nodded to Daniel, but he was waiting with a quart of whiskey in his hand while the trio of locals at the bar agreed on which of them would pay for the round. Hogg and Daniel were at the rearmost of the four small tables; the pair of hookers at the front table had made a desultory try, but Daniel's curt "Not now!" and a glance at Hogg's face had stopped them in their tracks.

"Well, I don't know, Hogg," Daniel said. "It's not up to our Bantry Brown Ale, I'll agree, but it seems to me to have plenty of kick."

He took a swig and rolled it around his mouth. In a judicious tone, he went on. "I don't have any experience with dog piss, of course. That I remember. I'll admit that there've been mornings that I woke up and really wondered what I'd been drinking."

Hogg half lifted his mug to drain it again, then set it down. He looked fiercely across the table.

"Look!" he said. "We can joke and tie one on, even on this dishwater the wogs here sell for beer, and we can say it'll all be fine. But it *won't* be fine, young master. Unless you've figured out a way not to sleep for, what? Seven days running? Maybe ten? If you go to sleep, you're not going to reach Cremona alive and that bastard Petrov won't even pretend it was an accident. Why should he? And you *know* I'm right!"

The bartender started filling a fresh pitcher. Daniel sipped, then drank deeply and met his servant's eyes. "Hogg," he said, "there's risk, and I know there's risk. But I don't know a better way to carry out my orders. It's my duty."

"Well, it's not bloody worth your life!" Hogg said.

Daniel shrugged. "Maybe you're right," he said. "Maybe I ought to settle down on Bantry and be the squire. I could buy the estate through Deirdre, I'm sure. I don't have any better use for my prize money. Is that what you want me to do, Hogg?"

"What bloody difference does it make?" Hogg said angrily. "You're not going to do that, whatever I tell you. And you'd go off your chump in six months with just a bunch of yokels to talk to."

He snorted. "Same as I would," he added, "after all we've seen these past years."

Four spacers came in the front door. "I'll be with you in a moment, gents," the bartender said. He set down the fresh

pitcher and swept up the three local coins—pistoles with
square holes in the center—which Hogg had set out. Daniel
had realized ruefully when they sat down that he had only
Cinnabar florins in his purse.

"Look, maybe if you work on Lindstrom—" Hogg said.

The spacers in front of the bar carried lengths of tubing or
steel reinforcing rod. Another man entered from the back alley
and stood in the doorway. *Peter Petrov, and he's carrying a
solar-charging laser from the* Savoy's *cargo.*

"*No*, Hogg!" Daniel said, grabbing his servant's right wrist
and pinning it to the tabletop. His eyes were on Petrov. "No,
no trouble now."

"That's right, no trouble," Petrov said. He was holding the
laser waist-high, as though it were the nozzle of a fire hose.
"Our little Cinnabar friend here has decided he doesn't want
to go to Cremona after all, and he's coming into the alley with
us so that we can explain why."

The bartender had tensed to get back behind the bar
where he probably had a weapon. He would have had to
push through the spacers with clubs to get there; instead, he
moved into the back corner behind the tables. The whores had
retreated to the other corner.

"And if anybody gets bright ideas, I'll toast him *good* with
this!" Petrov said, his voice rising as he slapped his weapon's
eight-inch lens with the palm of his left hand. "You better
hope I don't trigger it in here, because it'll light this whole
place like a pile of straw!"

The business end of the laser was a foot-long cylindrical mirror
array which multiplied the pulse twelve hundred times before

releasing it toward the target. The charging panel unfolded from the stock. The lasers were better for hunting than for military use, but their power and the fact that they didn't need to be supplied with ammunition made them useful for sniping and the sort of hit-and-run attacks that rebels were likely to make.

"I'm sure we can discuss this like officers and gentlemen," Daniel said, keeping his fingers on his servant's wrist as he stood up. "Hogg, stay here till Captain Petrov and I sort this out, please."

He tried to sound casual, but he could hear his voice tremble. That was all right, because Petrov would take the rush of adrenaline as meaning Daniel was afraid.

"That's right, hobby!" Petrov crowed. "You stay right where you are or you'll be a *real* crispy critter!"

The four men with clubs were presumably the *Savoy*'s crew. They seemed hesitant, but Daniel didn't doubt that they'd pound him within an inch of his life—or beyond—if only because they were afraid of Petrov's laser.

He walked toward the door, smiling pleasantly. Keeping the laser aimed at Daniel's midriff, Petrov backed ahead of him into the alley. He didn't appear to be concerned by his victim's attitude. The crewmen followed, bumping over an empty table.

The alley was paved, but the surface was covered with filth which had accumulated since the most recent rainstorm washed the previous load into the harbor. None of the businesses on this section of the waterfront bothered with a latrine. There was no streetlight, but illumination scattered from the Harborfront and quays where vessels were loading made it brighter than the bar's interior.

"Now you just stand there, kiddo, and—" Petrov said.

Daniel stepped forward, grasping the laser just behind the mirror array. Petrov pulled the trigger; nothing happened.

"Hey!" Petrov said.

Daniel kicked him in the crotch. Petrov doubled up in pain, and Daniel pulled the weapon away.

Taking the stock with both hands, Daniel clubbed Petrov over the head. There was a loud *bong!* and the laser array deformed. The mirrors were polished metal, but nobody was going to be using *this* weapon again except as a club.

Daniel turned to the crewmen. They stood shocked and openmouthed.

Hogg stepped out of the bar behind them. He held a pistol in his left hand and a knife with a knuckle-duster hilt in his right.

Daniel was gasping, and his muscles trembled. "Drop those bloody clubs!" he said in a shrill voice.

Hogg called the crewmen's attention to his pistol by firing into the coping of the building across the alley. There was a *crack* from the electromotive pulse and a crunching hammerblow as the osmium pellet blew a chunk of concrete into gravel.

One spacer screamed; the rest threw themselves on the pavement. The fellow who screamed continued to hold his length of pipe, but his legs slowly gave way; he slumped to his knees.

"Pushing your luck, wouldn't you say, young master?" Hogg said in a conversational voice. He walked through the groveling spacers. The man whose hand he stepped on whimpered but didn't try to get up. Hogg seemed casual, but the pistol slanted down—not toward the ground, but rather toward the terrified men.

"He'd taken the laser from the cargo after I left the *Savoy*," Daniel said. "He couldn't have charged it this late in the day."

"You *thought* he'd just taken it from the cargo," Hogg said with gentle emphasis. "And it seems you were right. Which I'd give a prayer of thanks for, if I was the sort who prays."

He turned at Daniel's side and looked down at the spacers. "How'd you feel about me breaking them up some, young master?" he asked. "Give them something to remember the next time they think about taking pipes to a Leary of Bantry."

"That won't be necessary, Hogg," Daniel said. "They're the crew of the *Savoy*, I believe, and I need them healthy."

He coughed into his cupped palm and added, "You gentlemen are willing to serve me ably and willingly, aren't you? I'll be Mistress Lindstrom's acting captain, you see."

The answers were muffled by muck and fear, but Daniel was sure that they were all some variation of "Yes, sir!"

"Very good," he said. "Now you may stand up."

The spacers took their time about it. It appeared that they were afraid that the first head to rise was going to be clouted back down as a reminder.

Daniel grinned. He wasn't that sort of person, but Hogg had been known to deliver lessons of that type. Not now, though.

"Very good," Daniel repeated. The men wouldn't meet his eyes, but that would come. "Now, which of you knows where Mistress Lindstrom will be at this time of day?"

The tallest of the four wiped his mouth with the back of his hand. "I guess she'd be in the bar of the Criterion," he mumbled. "I mean, that's where she is most nights we're in port here."

"Then," said Daniel, "you go and ask her to come back to the

Savoy ASAP, where the rest of us will be waiting. Understood?"

"Yessir!" the man said. He looked behind him, then hesitated.

"Hop it, buddy!" Hogg said. "Or I'll show you how a length of wire can cut your throat right down to the spine!"

The spacer bolted down the alley in the other direction. No doubt he would be able to find Lindstrom's hotel in good time.

"Now—" said Daniel.

"One moment, young master," Hogg said. He wasn't asking permission. "We have one more thing to do. Now, 'hobby,' what Petey-boy called me. That's short for 'hobnailed booby.' That's right, ain't it?"

"I believe so, yes," Daniel said. He was being deliberately nonchalant. "A term for a countryman. An insulting term."

"Right," said Hogg. "Well, I'm a countryman, sure enough, but I'm not wearing hobnails because they don't go with steel floors on a ship."

He drew back his right leg as he turned to the sprawled Petrov. His boots were of the heavy-soled country style—but without the usual cleats, as he had said.

"Which is a bloody shame," Hogg said. "But we'll make do."

He kicked Petrov in the face. It sounded like a maul striking a watermelon.

The jitney that carried Adele was intended for four passengers but carried a dozen during most of its leisurely course through the city. The seats had been removed, but nonetheless the little vehicle was badly overfilled.

Initially Adele had wrapped her right arm around a window pillar and stood with one leg on the outside footrail and the other in the air. When a place to stand inside opened, she had taken it despite the determined opposition of a large woman with a day's shopping in a string bag.

When the local had grasped Adele's shoulder with the apparent intention of pulling her out, Adele had rapped the woman's front teeth with the muzzle of her pistol. The woman had toppled backward with a shriek, spilling potatoes and unfamiliar fruit on the street around her.

The jitney started off, accelerating more slowly than a child on a tricycle. Adele put the pistol back into her pocket. The other passengers didn't give her more room—they couldn't—but they were obviously straining not to crowd her any more than they had to.

The local woman had been lucky. If Tovera had been present, she would have informed the woman that her behavior was discourteous. In all likelihood, the method Tovera used would have been less delicate than what Adele chose.

The jitney was approaching the western edge of the city. Instead of tenements, houses stood on their own lots with tall trees growing between them; deeper forest hung as a curtain beyond the dwellings. Flying creatures with translucent pastel wings fluttered out of the treetops, floated for a few moments in the sunlight, and disappeared into the foliage again.

The jitney stopped. The driver turned in his saddle and said to the four remaining passengers, "This is as far out as I'm going. Get off or go back with me."

"You said you would take me to West Slough," Adele said.

"Well, I was wrong," the driver said. "Get off or go back, you hear?"

The man who had been standing beside Adele when she moved inside the vehicle now leaned forward and whispered something to the driver. The driver said, "*What?*"

He stared at Adele for a moment, then faced around and continued westward down the street. The jitney accelerated much more quickly with a reduced load.

About the distance of three blocks later—there was only one connecting street, a mud lane that made a T intersection with the main road—the jitney reached what Adele supposed was West Slough. The driver pulled around in a half circle and stopped; he studiously avoided turning to look at Adele as she and her fellow passengers got off.

Well, she hadn't wanted to have a discussion with him. She walked to the pilings on the waterside and looked at her surroundings.

From orbital imagery Adele knew that the "slough" was actually a resaca, a loop of the river cut off when the channel shifted west. The *Phoenix of Assumption*, the colony ship which made the initial settlement on Madison, had landed here rather than in the ocean a few miles south, and Port Madison had grown up nearby.

The river had changed course during the thousand-year Hiatus following the war between Earth and her principal colonies. When star travel resumed on Madison, the port had been relocated to an artificial harbor on the ocean, and Ashetown had shifted south as well. What remained was called West Ashetown, but most of the original warehouses and tenements had sunk into the muck.

The colony ship remained, however, as a museum and a library of pre-Hiatus documents on a man-made island created by a coffer dam. A causeway connected the island to this shore, and a few water taxis were tied to bollards along the waterfront for those who needed to cross the resaca; occasionally the mist cleared and Adele glimpsed buildings on the other side.

To Adele's surprise, the development along the waterside wasn't merely a slum, though there were a number of wooden hovels which would have looked abandoned were it not for ragged people sprawling in doorways or against the walls. There were several apartment blocks of plasticized earth, their ground floors given over to shops and restaurants, and a certain amount of light industry as well. A metal-roofed shed to the right was a repair garage which sheltered several partly disassembled vehicles; glimpsed in a blurred fashion through the mist to the left was a barge drawn up to a large building.

Adele had found reference to some regional offices being moved to compartments on the *Phoenix*. They were apparently funding a renaissance of sorts for the neighborhood.

She started across the causeway. It had recently been repaired by pouring a sheet of some synthetic onto the gravel surface. Adele reached for her data unit, then decided to leave it in its pocket. She continued on. She would check when she was within the ship and had a dry place to sit.

She was wearing a nondescript business suit. Her only concession to her supposed Kostroman nobility was that the fabric was russet with thin black piping on the seams of the jacket, the colors of the House of Hrynko.

She had considered going with an escort as she had to the sector headquarters, but she didn't want to attract attention and she *did* want to think. The chatter of a dozen Sissies wouldn't have disturbed her, but the feeling of responsibility for them would have been a serious problem.

Adele had too much experience now to doubt the kind of trouble which bored spacers were likely to get into. Escorting spacers were certainly going to be bored as they waited on a mudbank while the mistress indulged her love of old books.

Animals squeaked, shrilled, and boomed from the vegetation at the water's edge and covering the shallows to a distance out from the shore. The creatures ranged down in size from the length of Adele's palm and extended fingers to smaller than her thumb joint, but they were all on the same pattern: lizard-like bodies with powerful hind legs and pipe-stem arms which they folded against their torsos except when snatching food.

I'll have to tell Daniel, Adele thought. Her interest in natural history had initially been academic, but she had so often listened to Daniel's enthusiasm or looked things up for him that she was gaining an appreciation of the subject.

Some of the creatures were fully visible on mats of the weed; others clung to the causeway's pilings. One even scampered ahead of her along the railing, swaying its head and tail side to side to balance the thrust of its legs.

A pair of office workers approached from the other direction, chatting to one another. The little animal rose on tiptoe, then hurled itself off the rail with its legs windmilling furiously. Its feet had bright scarlet webs. Perhaps they slowed the creature's descent, because Adele heard only a gentle *plop!* as it hit the water.

The *Phoenix* towered overhead as Adele approached. The ship was a sphere, a volume-efficient design with a score of serious disadvantages which Adele knew from discussions with RCN officers. A ship even of this enormous size would today be cylindrical, but such globes had been common before the Hiatus.

The *Phoenix* had brought ten thousand settlers to Madison, having kept them alive during a voyage of fourteen months. Adele smiled faintly. Alive, but probably not very happy.

Well, Adele had endured conditions no better than those of the colonists during the years she lived in the slums of Blythe City on Bryce. Her teacher and mentor, Mistress Boileau, had done what she could, but not even the director of the Academic Collections could arrange more than a minimal stipend for a Cinnabar citizen in the midst of all-out war between Cinnabar and the Alliance.

The would-be colonists had hope before them; the orphan Adele Mundy had seen nothing better ahead of her except death. But things *had* become better after all, better for the person the real Adele was, than they would have been had her life gone in the track she had expected while she was growing up as the studious daughter of a powerful Cinnabar political leader.

Adele had the whole RCN as a family, and she had Daniel Leary for a friend. Her father had had power, but he had neither friends nor family in the sense that Adele had come to understand the words.

The artificial island around the *Phoenix* had been turned into a garden with walkways through its plantings. Adele thought,

Daniel would know whether the trees are native species.

She reached for her data unit, thinking, *Well, all I have to do is find the catalogue of the garden's holdings and compare it to the database of species native to Madison.*

She caught herself again. This time she came as close to laughing as she had done in weeks or longer. *I'm not in competition with Daniel. If I decide that I have to compete with him, I should focus on a skill like clambering about the rigging. That would have some practical application.*

An aircar approached from the mainland side. Adele wasn't particularly interested in vehicles, but she looked at this one, an enclosed gray six-place car, because it drove low and near the causeway. The only passenger sat behind the driver. He eyed Adele as he passed.

If Tovera were here, Adele thought, *she would step between me and the car—and she would have her hand on the submachine gun in her attaché case.*

Adele didn't reach into her left tunic pocket, but she *consciously* didn't reach into it. She wasn't as paranoid as Tovera, but she knew that she could get into that state very easily if she didn't constantly fight the tendency.

The aircar slowed and turned inward when it crossed the wall protecting the island. The causeway ended in a circular plaza from which narrow paths led into the garden while a broad one continued to the starship's entrance. The pavement was probably synthetic, but it was patterned to mimic brick.

The driver angled the car between two of the stone benches set around the perimeter of the plaza. It settled, and a guard at the entry port a hundred feet away shouted angrily.

The driver idled his fans; the passenger, a short, tubby man, got out of the back and walked toward Adele. His hair was intensely black even over a swarthy complexion.

The guard shouted again and started toward them; he wasn't armed, so that wasn't an immediate problem. Adele lifted her pistol; she didn't bring it out of her pocket *quite* yet.

"Lady Hrynko?" the little man called. He was twenty feet away and coming closer with short, quick steps. "I am Liber Osorio, the Cremonan trade attaché here on Madison. Can we go somewhere to discuss a business proposition?"

"No," said Adele. She thought for a moment. "If you'd care to sit on one of these benches, though—"

She gestured with her right hand. Pedestrians were walking around them, and the guard was coming closer. He had taken a communicator out of its belt pocket.

"—I'll give you a few minutes."

Osorio turned and shouted to his driver, "Go to the other side of the water and wait for us."

The car lifted. It hovered for a moment, then obediently drove over the water toward the mainland side at a moderate pace.

The benches were backless, slightly curved, and about six feet wide. She sat on the left end of the closest and gestured Osorio toward the midpoint when he tried to sit closer to her.

Adele said, "Before you tell me your proposition, Master Osorio, explain how you happened to meet me here."

Her hand was still in her pocket.

Chapter Ten

WEST ASHETOWN

"I didn't mean to surprise you, Lady Hrynko," Osorio said, smiling at Adele; he spread his hands to his sides to echo his mouth's curve. "I had you watched so that I could speak with you without arousing the comment which would ensue were I to visit your yacht, that is all. I must say—"

He gestured toward her, probably meaning to indicate her simple costume.

"—I wasn't expecting to find you alone."

"I am incognito," Adele snapped. "I am here to bathe my soul in the artifacts of Ancient Man!"

She couldn't imagine a real Kostroman Principal saying that, but she had been on Kostroma long enough to have seen equally—if differently—eccentric behavior among the clan leaders. She thought it would sound bizarre but believable to Osorio; which appeared to be the case.

"You are clearly a person of great refinement, Lady Hrynko," the little man said, dipping in a seated bow. "As I said, I am my planet's trade representative here, a position which requires a relatively coarse outlook. I ask your pardon for that. But—"

He gestured to the sides again. His smile made Adele want to slap him.

"—I too have a spiritual side. I dream of a free Sunbright. I am one of a group of like-minded souls on Cremona who are working to help the citizens of Sunbright throw off the yoke of Alliance domination. We hope that you will be willing to aid us—for a fair price, I emphasize. You are a stranger in this region and cannot be expected to care about the hopes of us and our neighbors."

Adele didn't speak for a moment. *I shouldn't be offended by this—he believes I'm who I claim to be, after all. But does he think I'm brain damaged or a child?*

Aloud she said, "You're talking nonsense. If you have a proposal consistent with my honor, make it. Otherwise . . ."

She sniffed and let her voice trail off.

Osorio bowed at the waist again. "Yes, of course, Your Ladyship," he said equably. "We Friends of Sunbright are Cremonese citizens who have banded together to provide supplies to the Sunbright freedom fighters. The Alliance Funnel Squadron attempts to capture our ships—our ships and those of like-minded shippers—over Sunbright, but this is a difficult task and the blockaders are rarely successful. You understand this, Your Ladyship?"

He must *think that I'm a moron,* Adele marveled silently. *Or else he has a lower opinion of foreigners than even Hogg does.*

She sniffed again. Kostroma was a far more sophisticated

place than anything she had heard about Cremona.

"Yes, I understand," Adele said. "Explain what that has to do with me?"

"Now, most of the ships and supplies running the Sunbright blockade," Osorio said, "come through Madison here even though they make the final approach from Cremona. Madison is a major trading world; we on Cremona do not have either the industry or the volume of shipping to supply the materials needed by the freedom fighters."

Or to broker the pink rice, Adele thought. Cremona didn't have a planetary government so much as it did a club in which members of a criminal gang got together to brag and to discuss further banditry.

"Why doesn't the Funnel administration discuss the matter with their colleagues here on Madison?" Adele said, helping to keep things moving along. "Surely if the Forty Stars Squadron cooperates with the Funnel Squadron, they can end their problem easily. They can end your blockade running, that is."

Osorio tried to laugh lightly, but Adele was pleased to hear an underlying note of strain. Granted that the fellow wasn't patronizing Lady Mundy, she still found his attitude irritating.

Was there *any* adult too stupid to realize that the Friends of Sunbright were profiteers who were getting rich by supplying the rebels? If the Alliance forces had needed arms, the Friends would willingly have supplied them. The bloodshed was of no concern to them.

Adele shrugged. The bloodshed didn't particularly concern her either. She had shed a fair amount of it herself over the years.

"Mistress?" Osorio said in confusion.

"I was thinking of something else," Adele said, regretting that she had allowed her expression to change, a visible warning. "I was thinking that fighting, whether for freedom or not, is likely to lead to death."

Her lips—barely—smiled. "But since everything leads to death," she said, "that doesn't matter, does it?"

"Ah," Osorio said. He cleared his throat and said, "Well. You were asking about the Forty Stars Squadron cooperating with the Funnel blockade. This will not happen. The authorities hate each other! Sector Administrator Braun here is pleased to see the trouble Kolpach of the Funnel is having. But there is a better reason!"

"Go on," Adele said. The Cremonan attaché had already given the correct reason—regional rivalry—for why the Forty Stars government winked at local support of the Sunbright rebels. It was beyond her how any reason could seem better than the true one, but she had long ago learned that most people seemed to have a different opinion on the matter.

"Cinnabar is behind the rebellion!" Osorio said with his usual heavy-handed emphasis. "No, I don't mean just that Cinnabar sent one of its top secret agents to lead the rebellion under the name Freedom. I mean that the Cinnabar Navy intelligence section on Kronstadt has planned the whole thing. They set up the supply network before the rebellion started *and* they provided enough weapons to make the initial stages practical. It was anti-ship missiles which made the first raid at Tidy possible!"

Adele's mind cascaded analyses:

I don't believe that.

It is possible that a Naval Intelligence section here on the fringes of the empire could go rogue.

If Cinnabar's Naval Intelligence is behind the Sunbright rebellion, it means the war will resume very shortly.

None of the thoughts reached her tongue. She looked at a couple walking beside a pool in the garden, not far from the causeway. The man was ... overattentive; the woman shied away, but not very far away. From their clothing, they both worked in the government offices on the *Phoenix*.

Osorio must have taken Adele's silence as meaning that she had not understood the importance of what he had just told her. He leaned forward and said urgently, "The Cinnabar Navy wants the Forty Stars Squadron concentrated around Sunbright with the Funnel Squadron. Then Cinnabar will capture Madison! But Admiral Jeletsky here knows that, and he won't be tricked away. You can see that he's ready to move at any moment, though. The squadron has been on high alert for twenty days!"

"I see," Adele said, since she realized that she was expected to say something. "I still don't understand what this has to do with me. With the Principal of Hrynko."

Osorio started back. There was nothing in her words to disturb him, so he must be reacting to her face.

Adele had been considering options for correcting the situation if she learned that Cinnabar personnel were really behind the rebellion on Sunbright. It certainly wasn't the section on Kronstadt, but some other element of the RCN might be responsible.

Mistress Sand would need to be informed, but time would

THE ROAD OF DANGER

be of the essence. It might be best to solve the problem first, then report it. Adele was confident that she and Tovera would be able to take care of the matter without help from Xenos.

"While the Alliance Navy can't catch many of our supply ships," Osorio said, meaning the blockade runners which were making him and his friends rich, "the governor of Sunbright has commissioned a private vessel, the *Estremadura*, which is another matter. It operates in the Madison system—where ships from the Funnel Squadron would not be permitted— and along the route from here to Cremona. It carries ships it captures to a prize court on Westerbeke, where they're always condemned."

He puffed up his chest with an air of angry injustice. "*And*," he concluded, "they always know the real cargo, no matter how careful the owners have been in creating believable documents!"

"I still don't see—" Adele began, though in fact she finally had a glimmer of understanding of what the Cremonan was getting at.

"You will see!" Osorio said. "You have a real warship, do you not? You can fight. The port officials here say this."

"Yes," said Adele. Her suspicion, unlikely as it had seemed, was correct.

"We will hire you!" Osorio said. "The Friends of Sunbright will hire you to protect our shipping. You will have a Cremonan commission so that you will not be pirates—you need not be afraid. We have power in our government!"

The government of Cremona is a joke, Adele thought. *And if a Cremonan naval vessel attacks an Alliance naval vessel, it's an act of war. Even if both ships are auxiliaries.*

"You are authorized to commit your government and to pay the fee I might demand for undergoing this danger?" Adele said coldly. "I would need proof, which I doubt you could provide."

She pursed her lips and added, "I would be paid in Alliance thalers. *If* I were to do this. Or Cinnabar florins. That would be all right."

"Then you will do it!" Osorio said. Which was, after all, what Adele's answer implied, despite the qualifiers she had used to couch it. "I do not have this authority, no no, but you will take me to Cremona. The Council of Friends will meet you; and when we have agreed, the government will issue your commission. On my honor as a gentleman of Cremona!"

I have heard oaths that impressed me more, Adele thought. Aloud she said, "I will give this matter thought, Master Osorio. I will inform you if I decide we have anything further to discuss."

In other words, she thought, *I will talk the matter over with Daniel, and we will form our strategy together. But I really want to look into your claim that Cinnabar provided missiles at the beginning of the rebellion.*

Reacting—again—to Adele's lack of immediate response, Osorio said, "Come!" as he rose to his feet.

He made an upward gesture with both hands as though he were tossing grain to winnow out the chaff. "We will eat together, and you will understand my position. They have good wines here on Madison, very good wines!"

I already understand your position, Adele thought. *You, however, don't appear to have heard a word that I've said.*

The Cremonan attaché shied again at her expression, which this time pleased her sourly. Aloud but calmly she said, "I now will go about my business. I do not require your presence, Master Osorio. If I wish to see you again, after I have considered your proposals, I will inform you."

"Can I carry you somewhere?" Osorio said, waving vaguely toward his car.

Not a single word, Adele thought.

"All I *want* of you," she said, "is your absence. Do you understand?"

"Yes," Osorio said with a false smile. "Yes, of course, Your Ladyship. We will speak soon!"

He sauntered toward the causeway and his vehicle. Adele watched him for a moment—Osorio was the sort who might suddenly turn around to offer some further absurd argument—before she took out her data unit. The Principal of Hrynko didn't have to be a technological illiterate, but Adele hadn't chosen to emphasize her abilities in front of the Cremonan.

Cory had just sent her a file slugged DOERRIES. She smiled faintly as she opened it: Cory and Cazelet kept one another very much on their toes when she set them similar tasks. Though either would have been a good assistant regardless.

The smile faded as she viewed the material. Cory had searched the database of the Ashetown police, looking for files which were closed with the slug which they had linked to Doerries.

In addition to mentions of the black utility van and the converted warehouse, there were nine files concerning the death and mutilation of street children. Some included images of the bodies, which had mostly been found in the harbor. To Adele's untrained eye, they were not even identifiable as to gender.

Adele sent a terse message to Tovera, then slipped the data unit into its pocket and turned. Osorio was just past the midway point of the causeway.

Adele began running, a thing she never did, and shouted, another thing she never did. "Master Osorio! I'll take a ride after all! Master Osorio!"

Tovera would need some time, but Adele wanted to be ready to leave the *Princess Cecile* as soon as her servant arrived with a suitable van. They had work to do.

"Master Osorio!"

ASHE HAVEN ON MADISON

A taxi which had driven up the quay now stopped beside the *Savoy*. Daniel was surprised when Kiki Lindstrom got out. The Criterion Hotel was only one further block from the water, on the street which paralleled the Harborfront. That distance scarcely required a—

Lindstrom staggered. The tall crewman who had gone to fetch her squeezed out of the taxi behind her and gripped her arm for support. The shipowner might not be falling-down drunk, but she was well on the way there.

The driver snarled a demand for money. The spacer flung her a bill. Her complaints continued till she looked at it; then she drove off. Daniel wondered how much the crewman had paid in his haste, but that was a problem for a later time.

Lindstrom had the necessary spacer's ability to walk a

gangplank even when she was too drunk to see straight. She marched onto the boarding ramp where Daniel waited for her. Hogg and the other three crewmen stood behind him in the cabin.

"All right, Pensett!" she said in a slurred growl. "What the bloody hell is this? Hargate wouldn't tell me a bloody thing, just that I had to come. I own this bitch! You don't give me orders!"

She squinted to take in the group facing her. "And where the bloody hell is Petrov, since everybody else is here?"

"Captain Petrov has resigned, mistress," Daniel said. He stood at Parade Rest, with his heels six inches apart and his hands clasped behind his back. He met her eyes without flinching. "I will take over his duties. I'm glad to say that the crew—"

He nodded over his shoulder. Hogg grinned like a drunken cherub; the other three men stood as closely to attention as fear and their lack of training allowed them to.

"—have announced their willingness to sail with me as their captain. Under your ultimate command, of course."

It occurred to Daniel that the crewmen had expected the laser to incinerate him. They were probably more frightened by what they took as an act of insane courage as they were by the beating he and Hogg had given the former captain.

"Resigned?" Lindstrom said, puzzlement replacing anger. She reached the compartment and stood without swaying; the situation seemed to have sobered her.

"He had health problems," Daniel said, as though he were explaining.

"He'll stop having any kind of problem if he shows himself around here again," Hogg said.

"Ah," said Daniel with a nod. "And I should mention that you'll find your cargo is short by one laser; which I'm afraid is not repairable, since Captain Petrov brought it to the discussion he forced with me."

Lindstrom stared as though the words had been in an unfamiliar language; then she began to laugh so violently that she lost her balance again. She would have fallen if Daniel had not held her by the shoulders.

"Is that so, Pensett?" she said between renewed guffaws. "Is that bloody so?"

She hugged Daniel, then stepped away to survey him and the others. "Well," she said, "maybe that isn't such a bad thing after all. You're a pretty sturdy lad to've seen off Peter if he came looking for you."

She pinched him affectionately at the base of the ribs. He grinned but said nothing. Lindstrom was buying only his professional services, and he wasn't a professional in *that* field. Still, he saw no need to disabuse the lady until they had lifted from Madison.

"Before we all leave," said Hogg, "there's another piece of business. Which is that now that there's a berth empty, I'll be coming along."

He had been looking at Mistress Lindstrom, but now he glared straight at Daniel himself. "This ain't a question, young master," he said. He didn't raise his voice, but nobody could have doubted that he meant it. "It got decided when that jumped-up wog pointed a gun at you. Understood?"

Daniel stood silent for a moment, considering choices. Suddenly he grinned. "Yes," he said. "Under the circumstances,

I think that's a reasonable decision. As you can see, I'm sure, Mistress Lindstrom."

Even half drunk, the shipowner pursed her lips at the statement; again, it wasn't a question. Then she guffawed.

"Call me Kiki and it's a deal," she said. "I'll even feed him." She chucked Daniel under the ribs again.

Chapter Eleven

ASHETOWN ON MADISON

"I look forward to hearing from you soon, Your Ladyship!" said Osorio as they settled to the quay beside the *Princess Cecile*. The aircar's running lights gleamed from the water of the slip and the wet aluminum surface of the catwalk.

"Thank you," Adele said, opening the door and getting out. Because the passenger compartment was enclosed, the Cremonan could no longer see her face. She preferred the anonymity, because her mind was far away from Osorio and his problems. "I will inform you of my decision."

She started across the floating catwalk to the corvette's boarding ramp. She sniffed. Indeed, her duties to the ship and to the Republic itself were far from her mind. Well, there would be time for them later, if there was a "later."

"Hail to Lady Principal Henkow!" shouted Gildas, a technician and one of the spacers on guard in the entrance hold. He was willing and good-hearted, but she had met spaniels whom she thought were of greater intellectual capacity.

This was a typical example of Gildas overdoing a task out of enthusiasm and stupidity. Dasi, the chief of the watch, had been talking on the internal communicator mounted beside the hatch. He turned and snarled Gildas into silence.

The business helped Adele back into what passed for normalcy with her. There was no harm done: the real Principal Hrynko would have stupid, ignorant spacers in a crew she hired also. The aircar purred away behind her.

"Ma'am?" Dasi said. "Six is on his way down here. Ah, Lieutenant Pensett is, you know?"

At least he didn't shout loudly enough to be heard three slips over, Adele thought grimly. Well, she and Daniel had known all along that most spacers weren't skilled at deceit; and besides, it was unlikely that anyone was looking for evidence that the *Sissie* and her crew were not what they pretended to be.

"Why—" she began aloud.

Her question was interrupted—and answered—by the speaker above the main hatch. In Vesey's voice, it announced, "Ship, this is the captain. In a moment our passenger, Kirby Pensett, will address us from the entry hold. Those of you who do not have access to a good display may either go to the bridge or to the BDC, or join Pensett in person in the hold. Captain out."

Daniel strode out of the companionway, talking over his shoulder to Hogg. He was wearing mottled RCN utilities without insignia, typical garb for an officer on half pay who didn't have family money to fall back on. He caught Adele from the corner of his eye and brightened beyond his normal infectious enthusiasm.

He makes even me happier. Well, less grim.

Daniel bent close to her ear and murmured, "Adele, I'll be travelling to Cremona and I hope Sunbright as captain of the *Savoy*. I worked out the details with the owner this evening."

Hogg, standing close, grunted. Though he wasn't looking at them, he was certainly listening.

"That is, *Hogg* and I are going," he said with an affectionate grin toward his servant.

Spacers were coming down the companionway with bangs and chatter; others pushed in from the axial corridor to the stern. The hold was filling up.

"Excellent," Adele said. "A Cremonan backer of the rebels wants me to carry him home to meet his consortium. They hope to hire the *House of Hrynko* to attack an Alliance privateer that is capturing blockade runners leaving Madison."

Twenty-odd spacers were within the compartment, so she and Daniel were scarcely talking in private. Boots on the steel deck and echoing conversations in a score of hoarse whispers were too loud a backdrop for any crewman to overhear them. It was equally unlikely that it would matter if one of them did.

Daniel pursed his lips. He said, "Do you expect to accept the offer?"

"I wanted to hear your opinion," Adele said austerely.

No additional crewmen were joining those already in the compartment, though the audience had spilled onto the upper edge of the boarding ramp. It must be about time for Daniel to make his address.

"Yes," he said, a placeholder as he considered the situation. "I recommend that you take this agent to Cremona and listen to the proposition. It's likely to give us—"

THE ROAD OF DANGER

He grinned broadly.

"—to give you, that is, an opportunity to get information that we couldn't get any other way. Beyond that—"

He shrugged.

"—we don't have enough data to make a decision. Decide as seems best to you at the time; with, one hopes, more information."

"I agree," Adele said. She tried to clear her throat of the lump there. "I hope we'll meet on Cremona, then."

She nodded toward the loudspeaker. There was an audio/video pickup in it, though they had to be switched on from the bridge.

"Yes," Daniel repeated, facing the speaker and letting his face settle into his usual cheerful grin. "Fellow spacers!" he said. He waited for the cheers of his immediate audience to die down.

She and Daniel had come to the same conclusion after viewing the data. That was scarcely surprising: it was the correct conclusion, and Daniel rarely made mistakes in the professional arena.

Her lips quirked slightly in the direction of a smile. Since he had met Miranda Dorst, he had been less often involved with mindless young women in his private capacity too; though Adele wasn't sure that he had yet come to view those bimbos as mistakes.

"I'll be leaving the *Sissie* this evening," Daniel said. He had obviously decided to drop the pretence of the *House of Hrynko* for the time being. Though the hatch was open, sound propagation out of a crowded compartment would be extremely poor. "I hope to rejoin her and you after we've reached our destination separately. Now—"

He had been speaking toward the pickup. He lowered his
eyes to sweep them over the audience with him in the hold.

"—I need not tell you that I expect you to do your duty by
Captain Vesey and by the RCN. You're my Sissies; of *course*
you're going to do your duty!"

There was another babble of cheers and laughter. Daniel
smiled until it cleared, then said, "Until we meet again,
fellow spacers!"

As the crew cheered, Adele leaned closer to Daniel and
lifted onto her toes to speak into his ear. "May I address
them?" she asked.

"Of course," he said with a raised eyebrow. He turned
toward the pickup again and raised his hands. "Fellow
spacers!" he cried.

The audience quieted; at first slowly, but then with a rush
to near silence.

"Her Ladyship wishes to address you," Daniel said,
sweeping his right hand toward Adele. He was grinning,
probably at his pun on her civilian rank and the persona she
had adopted for this mission.

Adele fixed her eyes on the pickup. She was used to
communicating through electronics; used to the process and
comfortable with it.

"Fellow spacers," she said. She would never be an orator.
Her father had been a brilliant speaker, a man whose verbal
skills had carried him high in the Republic . . . though ultimately
to the top of Speaker's Rock.

"Captain—Six, that is, Six—is depending on us," she
continued, picking the words carefully. She could not afford

to be mistaken. She knew that people often heard tone, not words; but they had to hear, to *believe*, her words; for Daniel's sake and for their own. "He has put Captain Vesey in command of the ship, because he has implicit confidence that she is the best suited to support him."

Adele coughed into her hand. She knew that Vesey wouldn't like what she was about to hear, but Adele was going to say it anyway.

"Now," she said aloud, "I know that everyone in a crisis would do anything Six ordered without hesitating. But some of you might think, 'That can't be right,' when Captain Vesey tells you to jump. Don't let that happen, on your lives."

Daniel was watching her, his face unusually quiet. There was no disapproval in his expression; just a sort of alert calm.

"If members of this crew endanger the life of Six—"

Adele nodded toward Daniel.

"—by hesitation or inattention to orders," Adele said, "they will answer to me. It will be a very short meeting, and their last. On my oath as a Mundy."

There was silence in the compartment for a moment; a literally breathless hush, because the spacers seemed afraid to breathe. Suddenly Dasi shouted, "Count on us, ma'am!"

To Adele's utter amazement, Sissies started cheering. *All* of them were cheering! What was there to cheer about? She had just warned them that she would kill anybody who failed Daniel—and they knew she meant it.

Daniel touched her arm, then bent close. "They had been told that Vesey speaks for me," he said. "Now they really *know* it, more clearly than they would from anything I could say."

Adele grimaced. She didn't understand human beings, probably because she wasn't one herself. Even when she got it right—as she appeared to have done this time—she did so for the wrong reasons.

"Ma'am?" said someone. She looked up. Dasi had stretched out his hand, but he'd stopped short of touching her sleeve.

Before Adele could snap harshly because of her discomfort at the situation, she saw that the rigger's other hand pointed out toward the quay where a black utility vehicle had just pulled up. Tovera was driving.

Adele glanced at her outfit. She had intended to change into something gray or blue, but this dull russet would do.

"Daniel," she said, "I have business which doesn't concern the ship."

Without waiting for a response, she walked down the boarding ramp and across the gangplank without a slip or a wobble. She was in a different mindset now.

She walked around the van and got in the passenger side. It was a ground vehicle whose small wheels were mounted on four trucks. From the singing of the motor, it was a diesel. As soon as she got in, Tovera made a hard turn and started off.

"This looks very much like the van we saw," Adele said, comparing the present vehicle with the imagery of the one which delivered the street children.

"Yes," said Tovera. "I thought that was the best choice. The former owners don't need it anymore."

Adele nodded. She looked over her seat into the rear compartment. A ten-year-old boy lay on the bare floor. Tovera had cinched him to both sides of the vehicle with elastic cords so that he wouldn't bounce around too badly, but he wasn't bound. She must have drugged him.

"I believe we have everything we need," Tovera said.

"Yes," said Adele. She didn't bother to tap her tunic pocket. She could feel the familiar weight of her pistol without checking.

Daniel heard the aircar dawdling down the Harborfront. It was fifty feet in the air, high enough that the downdraft wouldn't do damage. The throb of the fans would be unpleasant to anybody beneath it, though.

The hatches on the *Princess Cecile*'s bridge were open for ventilation. Now that Cory had been promoted to first lieutenant and gone aft to the BDC, Daniel was using the astrogation console as a passenger and supernumerary. He got up from it and looked out the port hatch.

"Suppose it's the mistress coming back?" said Hogg, voicing the unstated hope that had brought Daniel to his feet. "Do you know where she was going?"

"No idea at all, Hogg," Daniel said with an appearance of calm. Hogg had been drinking off and on all day. The alcohol had apparently affected him enough that he hadn't noticed Adele's expression when she strode off the ship.

Daniel had seen his friend's face change when she saw Tovera driving the van which had just pulled up. He didn't question Adele about her business anyway, but *nobody* who'd seen her eyes at that moment would have chosen to speak to her.

The aircar cut the corner over the adjacent slip and slanted down as it drove along the quay toward the *Princess Cecile*.

The vehicle had a windscreen but not a roof. The driver was a middle-aged woman in a business suit, a stranger to Daniel, but her passenger was Kiki Lindstrom.

"Come along, Hogg," Daniel said, scooping up the barracks bag which held the personal effects of Kirby Pensett. "It isn't Adele, but it seems to be our business somehow."

He started toward the companionway. The only others on the bridge were Sun and a rigger named Wesley who was striking for gunner's mate; they were practicing deflection shots on the gunnery console.

"You hook 'em for us, sir!" Wesley called. "And you can count on us to set the gaff!"

"The lad was raised a fisherman," Hogg explained over the echo of their boots on the companionway treads. "On the east coast, where it's nothing like the seas we get off Bantry; but he's got promise, I do believe."

Daniel reached the entry hold as Lindstrom started across the catwalk. He dropped his bag on the deck—it was little beyond toiletries and a spare set of utilities—and said over his shoulder, "Watch the gear, Hogg. And come when I call you."

The guard had changed since he'd addressed the crew; Barnes, Dasi's partner, was in charge now. He bobbed his head as Daniel went past, an acknowledgment somewhere between a salute—which spacers didn't attempt on shipboard—and a tenant's bow to the squire.

Daniel grinned as he started down the ramp, waving Lindstrom back toward the quay. Nobody was going to touch his bag, but he didn't want Hogg with him while he learned what the shipowner wanted.

The trouble with Petrov had keyed up Hogg and had also supported his jaundiced view of the operation. Nothing he added to the coming discussion would be helpful.

Lindstrom frowned for a moment, but her face cleared and she stepped back onto the concrete to wait. Daniel judged the period of the catwalk's wobble—three pontoons supported the surface; the structure was safe enough, but it certainly wasn't stable—and hopped to the quay as it rose.

"I hadn't expected you to come for us, mistress," Daniel said with an engaging smile. "Though I suppose we're ready to go, if that's what this is."

"Not 'with me,'" Lindstrom said, "and not your man—"

She nodded toward Hogg, standing in the hatchway with his hands in his pockets.

"—this time either. There's a man wants to talk to you, one of our backers. He sent the car and driver to take you to him. And bring you back."

"I see," said Daniel, who was sure only that he *didn't* see. His tone was mild. "Who is this man, precisely?"

"Look," Lindstrom said in frustration. "It doesn't matter who he is. We just do what he says. You were Cinnabar Navy, right?"

"Yes," said Daniel.

"Then he's a friend of yours, that's all you need to know," she said. "That's all *I* know. I don't know his name and it doesn't matter. His money's good and he supplies stuff we get top dollar for."

Daniel considered the situation. "All right," he said. "I'll go, but Hogg will accompany me."

He gestured. "There's enough room in the car."

"No," Lindstrom said, irritation showing in her voice and scowl. "He said you were to go alone. I *told* you that."

"Yes," said Daniel. "And I'm telling you that anonymous strangers don't get to set the terms for a meeting which they want and I see no need for. I think that's simple enough."

"Are you afraid?" Lindstrom said. "Is that it? You need that yokel to hold your hand?"

"Master Petrov used the term 'hobby' to describe Hogg," Daniel said, grinning in the direction of his servant. "That turned out to be an unfortunate choice of words."

His humor dropped away. "I'll be clear. I am your astrogator and shipmate, mistress. I am *not* your flunky, and I am certainly not a dancing monkey to entertain your unnamed friend."

The shipowner snorted, then let her expression soften. "I'll make a call," she said.

She walked back to the aircar and got in. After a few words with the driver, she unclipped the handset of the communicator and touched a preset. She spoke into it, paused, then closed the connection and returned to Daniel.

"Have it your way, Pensett," she said. She looked tired and a little disgusted. "And you might as well take your traps along. Watchly says she'll take you both to the ship when you've had your talk."

Daniel looked at the driver, presumably named Watchly, and nodded. "All right," he said.

He waved toward the *Sissie*'s hatch. "Bring our bags, Hogg," he called. "We're travelling in style."

He watched the shipowner trudging down the quay toward

the *Savoy*. He wondered why she didn't want a ride back with them. Maybe despite her protestations she wasn't really sure what kind of a meeting was planned.

And maybe she did know....

Chapter Twelve

ASHETOWN ON MADISON

The aircar had curved well out to sea, so Daniel had nothing but time and estimated speed to judge their location by. That was sufficient for him to guess that when they cut the shoreline again, they were about ten miles east of the harbor and therefore well beyond the settled fringes of Ashetown.

Hogg could probably estimate a good deal closer than that, though it didn't matter: satellite tracking from the *Sissie* would give precise course data. Adele wasn't aboard, but Cazelet and Cory were following events in real time.

Daniel bent over the seat back and said, "Are you a native of Madison, Watchly?"

The driver glanced toward him, then back to her course. "Master Pensett," she said uncomfortably, "the Chief will tell you anything he wants you to know. I have nothing to say."

Daniel leaned back on the cushions, smiling cheerfully. Adele would probably have known where Watchly had gone to grammar school, but even he could be confident that the driver's accent meant she was from one of the Alliance homeworlds.

She was no ordinary driver, either, though she did drive well. Watchly had the look and mannerisms of a senior aide; with near certainty, she was her "Chief's" personal assistant.

She brought the car around and dropped toward the yard of a disused farm. They had overflown a right-of-way which a dual-track railroad shared with a highway for self-powered vehicles; that was about a mile behind them now, providing another—unnecessary—data point.

The car landed on the high grass behind a rambling farmhouse. Watchly shut off her fans. The aircar was out of sight from the main road as well as from the driveway leading to the house; Daniel had noticed as they approached that the gate was closed and chained.

"I'm to take you in, then leave you alone with the Chief," Watchly said. She glanced meaningfully at Hogg.

Hogg raised an eyebrow toward Daniel. Daniel grinned and said, "I'll scream for help if anyone attempts my virtue, Hogg. Until then, perhaps you could interest the fellows there in the shed—"

He gestured toward the small outbuilding some twenty feet beyond where the aircar was parked. The door was ajar; there had been movement inside as the car came in to land.

"—in a game of poker, do you think? You'll be more comfortable here on the back porch, though, I think."

They both looked at Watchly; she flushed. "That's Martensen, the caretaker," she said uncomfortably. "I can call him out, if you like. We just—the Chief wants to see you privately."

"And so he shall," Daniel said cheerfully. He gestured

toward the back door. "I suspect I can find my own way, mistress," he said. "But if you prefer to introduce me...?"

"I'll take you through," she said, stepping onto the porch and opening the door. The hallway beyond was dark. She gestured Daniel inside—that was safe enough with Hogg waiting behind her with his hand on a pistol—and followed; a glowstrip lighted as soon as the door closed.

She walked past Daniel again and tapped on the interior door. "Yes," a muffled voice called.

She opened the door and gestured to Daniel. "The Chief is waiting for you, Lieutenant Pensett," she said.

Though dim, the ceiling glowstrip was adequate to show all the details of the room beyond. That was in part because there was little to show. A figure faced the door from behind a desk; a distortion screen turned him and the holographic display he was watching into a grayed-out blur. There was no other furniture.

Daniel wouldn't have been sure even that the Chief was male had it not been for the bass voice in which he said, "How long ago did you graduate from the Academy, Lieutenant Pensett?"

"Five years," Daniel said. Pensett had been his classmate, though the physical resemblance between them was limited to height and gender. That should be enough out here in the Macotta Region. "I was on active duty until the Treaty of Amiens, so I've kept my skills up."

He hesitated, then added, "I assure you that my astrogation abilities are well beyond anything to be expected in the merchant service."

"Do you have any particular memories of your Senior Cruise on the *Swiftsure*?" the concealed figure asked. He seemed to have ignored Daniel's answer to the previous question.

"I bloody well do," Daniel said. "Cinnabar orbit after we lifted off was the closest I've come to getting killed on duty, and that was *too* close. A cable snapped as we were raising the rig. One end came near as near to taking my head off my shoulders!"

The incident was true, though Cadet Pensett had been in the bow section and therefore not in danger. Cadet Leary, on the other hand—

"How did that happen?" the Chief said. He continued to sound bored.

"Ventral K Antenna had been cross-rigged," Daniel said, his mind going back to a very vivid memory. "It was the crew ahead of ours—we'd just reached orbit, so this was the first time we had the rig up. As the antenna extended, one of the lines tried to tighten instead of running out. A battleship's hydraulics have a lot of thrust, and even beryllium monocrystal has a tension limit."

He shrugged. "I saw strands popping on the cable and ducked just in time," he said. "Colley—no, Colling his name was, Colling—he was looking the other way. The cable whipped like you wouldn't believe. It cut him in two at the waist, rigging suit and all. I don't think they ever did find where the leg half went."

Daniel licked his lips; they were suddenly dry. "There was blood all over," he said. "I thought the right sideplate of my helmet was cracked because I couldn't see out of it. It was Colling's blood. That cable had slung it everywhere."

With a continued lack of emotion, the voice said, "Who was your classmate Cadet Halevy dating, then?"

Daniel shrugged. "Hell if I know," he said. "It wasn't me. I didn't know her well enough to care."

He paused and added, "She was bright, I give her that. But that's all I'll give her. She had trouble with her PT scores. I had the feeling that if she wasn't so bloody bright, she'd have left at the end of the first year."

The figure across the desk shrank his display to look directly at Daniel. Until then it had been a rectangular sheen within the otherwise featureless blur of the distortion field.

"Look," Daniel said, letting his disquiet at the situation enter his voice; he hoped his tone would read as bored irritation. "Are you going to get to the point? Because if you want to hear about my dear old schooldays, you can wait for my memoirs while I do something useful."

"I assure you that this is useful, Lieutenant," the voice said. "I had to determine that you were not an imposter before I opened the matter to you."

The portentous tone struck Daniel as false, but it might well have been no more false than that of any other man pretending to himself that the fate of the nation was in his hands. There were no few of those, which Daniel had learned as a child in the house of Speaker Leary.

Corder Leary himself spoke with the unemotional precision of an architect describing a housing block. Nothing in his voice ever suggested that there was more than casual importance to the order he was giving, though it might mean the immediate murder of some thousands of men and women . . . along with a number of children, inevitably gathered up in haste and error.

"I need a messenger to carry dispatches to Sunbright," the

hidden man said. "They must be put into the hands of Freedom himself. There are any number of adventurers here on Madison, let alone Cremona, who would contract to carry them, but they would be venal or worse. You are an RCN officer, Lieutenant; you are therefore a man of honor and a patriot."

I wouldn't say..., Daniel thought. But considering the context and the RCN officers he had met—before as well as since he entered the Academy—the statement was a pretty fair approximation of the truth.

Aloud he said, "I hope I am a man of honor, yes; and I'm certainly a patriot. I don't see how my patriotism is involved with the problems of scruffy foreigners here at the back of beyond, however."

The Chief laughed. "That is a matter for higher ranks than yours, Lieutenant," he said, "but I assure you that my statement is quite true. All you have to do is to carry out your duties with the skill and determination to be expected of an RCN officer. Are you willing to do that?"

"I was planning to look for, well, a position, after I reached Sunbright," Daniel said cautiously. "Is this business going to affect my chances of doing that?"

"It will not," the other man said. "But this duty is a paid position also. Here are—"

He slid his right hand through the distortion screen. His fingers were short, pudgy, and well manicured. He lifted and withdrew them to display ten high-denomination coins.

"—a thousand Cinnabar florins. The fee is yours upon your oath as an RCN officer that you will use your best efforts to deliver the dispatches—"

His left hand appeared, pushing a chip case, then withdrew.

"—into the hands of Freedom. I depend on your honor; but the Republic also depends on you."

"A thousand florins?" Daniel said in surprise. He leaned forward to view the case more closely, being careful not to touch it. It was a standard RCN model, which meant that unauthorized opening would destroy the contents and probably the hands of the thief.

"It will be a difficult task," the Chief said. He continued to sound like a recruiting spiel for an elite combat unit. "And an extremely dangerous one. You will earn your pay, Lieutenant."

Daniel chuckled. He dropped the coins into his breast pocket, then slid the chip case into the right cargo pocket of his utility trousers.

"I was going to Sunbright anyway," he said to the blurred figure. "For a thousand florins, I don't mind looking up somebody on the ground there."

He took a step back and said in a challenging tone, "I don't believe your story about this being my duty to the Republic. But that doesn't matter one way or the other, since I'm on half pay till notified. Are we done now?"

"We are done, Lieutenant," the Chief said. His voice had returned to the calm boredom with which he had begun the interview. "Watchly will take you and your man to the *Savoy*."

Daniel turned on his heel and walked out, trying to hide his delight. He didn't trust anything the Chief had just told him—but it really didn't matter.

He couldn't have given himself a better excuse to find Freedom if he had planned the whole meeting.

* * *

Tovera was wearing a loose gray sweater and darker gray slacks. The garments didn't fit very well, but they probably hadn't fitted the original owner, either.

Without glancing aside from her driving—Tovera was a very *earnest* driver—she said, "There's another set in the back that will do for you. There's plenty of time for you to get them on before we reach the warehouse."

Adele leaned into the back and found a sweater with broad horizontal stripes of blue and maroon—both colors originally dark but badly faded—and a pair of slacks indistinguishable from those Tovera was wearing. They were so loose that she pulled them on over the clothes she was wearing, then transferred her pistol to a trouser pocket.

She didn't ask about the boy; his condition wasn't important at this moment. Tovera was one of the most consciously observant people Adele had ever met, however; she caught her mistress' glance toward the rear of the van after she had finished dressing.

"He'll have a headache when he wakes up," Tovera said. "And a hundred pesetas in his pocket. He'll be fine so long as things go well. If they don't . . ."

She shrugged, smiling.

"He takes his chances with the rest of us," Adele said without concern. They hadn't asked the boy's opinion, because they didn't care. They needed bait of a particular type, and the boy had been drawn from the bait bucket.

Why would a Mundy of Chatsworth care what a feral

youth thought about a necessary action? In the longer term it would benefit him and his fellows, but that had very little to do with Adele's fierce determination, either.

I couldn't save my sister Agatha.

Adele reached for her data unit to check how far they were from their destination; the borrowed trousers covered the unit's pocket. She pressed her lips tightly together, more in irritation at herself than because she couldn't get the information.

She *had* the information: when she looked out the window, she saw that they were turning north off the Harborfront and onto the street where the former warehouse was located. A repair garage on the corner was unmistakable: it had walls of pinkish beige.

I have to be willing to accept information directly though my eyes and ears. I'm nervous, and I'm letting reflex rather than intellect control my behavior.

She looked at Tovera and said, "I'm not an animal! That is, I'm not only an animal."

Her servant raised an eyebrow but didn't turn her head. "No, mistress," she said.

She was smiling. She was a sociopath without true emotions anyway.

Tovera turned the car toward the gate in the brick facade and stopped in the street. The wall was a little lower than Adele had guessed from the imagery, closer to nine feet than ten; the guard tower projected another four feet above it. The guard had a window of armored glass. The three gunports below it were flared to provide full coverage of the street.

Theoretical coverage, that is. Adele doubted that anybody

could hit a target from the port while aiming through the glass panel. Certainly not with a carbine.

After waiting a moment with no response, Tovera depressed the van's attention signal, which turned out to be a high-pitched bell. No one appeared at the window; Tovera rang again.

Adele grimaced. The bell was unpleasant, and Adele of course could open the gate herself with a moment's business with her personal data unit.

She didn't need to do that; she was just impatient. She should be thankful that the guards were somnolent.

The gate slid sideways, jerking and squealing on its track. Tovera drove in, scraping the van's left fender on the post because she was concentrating on the gate itself on the right side. There were enough dents and scratches in the vehicle's finish that this wouldn't arouse the guards' suspicion.

There were four surface cars in the courtyard; there had been only three nondescript sedans when Adele had last checked satellite imagery. The new vehicle was a small three-wheeler with flowers stencilled onto a bright yellow background.

The gate banged shut and a heavy crossbar slid into place. Adele stepped out her door and walked to the back of the van, where Tovera met her. Tovera wasn't carrying her attaché case.

The door in the back of the gate tower was open, as it had been on the imagery. The guard, a paunchy man, stepped onto the landing. He hadn't bothered to bring his carbine.

"We didn't get a call about you this time." he said. There was doubt in his voice.

"Well, we're here anyway," Adele snapped without looking up at the fellow.

Tovera opened the back of the van. Adele waited a moment for her to unhook the elastic cords holding the boy in place, then leaned in to help pull him out. He was as limp as a half-full bladder of water.

"How come he's not tied?" the guard said. "Say, did you drug him? Why'd you drug him?"

"Don't worry about it," Adele said. "He'll scream just fine when the knife goes in. Now, tell them to open the bloody door so that we can get out of here, okay?"

Her back was to the tower. She brought out her data unit under cover of her body. When she heard the door into the one-story building start to rise, she switched off the security cameras.

Tovera held the boy up by the collar with her left hand. She had taken the submachine gun from her waistband where the sweater had concealed it. Two guards stood in the doorway; they didn't step into the courtyard.

Leaving her data unit on the floor of the van, Adele turned to the tower. The guard had gone back inside. The staff knew what went on here. At least the man at the gate tonight was squeamish about it.

"Hey, fatty!" Adele shouted. "Come give us a hand, lard-ass!"

The guard stepped onto the landing again. He shouted, "Who the bloody hell do you—"

Adele shot him twice in the throat. She didn't aim at his head silhouetted against the evening sky for fear that her light pellets would hit the cranial vault instead of the eye sockets and perhaps not penetrate.

The tower guard grabbed his throat with both hands, gagging in blood. His feet twisted under him so that he fell back on his side. His legs kicked for a time as his body ran down.

Tovera's weapon had snapped out two short bursts. When Adele turned, one of the two guards in the doorway was sprawled limply while the other one had stiffened like a mannequin. The submachine gun's muzzle glowed red.

Adele and Tovera stepped over the bodies; they didn't need to discuss the plan.

The drugged boy lay on the pavement at the back of the van. From any distance he would look identical to the three guards. The difference between life and death might be no more than a faint breath—or a few ounces' pressure on a trigger.

Chapter Thirteen

ASHETOWN ON MADISON

Adele held the pistol out at her side. Though she had only fired twice, the electromagnetic flux that propelled the pellets had heated the little weapon's barrel shroud hot enough to blister her thigh through the cloth if she dropped it back into the trouser pocket.

Besides, she was likely to use the pistol again very soon.

Facing the outside door was the guardroom where the pair now sprawled in the doorway had waited until the van arrived. Adele hadn't been able to view the interior of the building while she planned the operation, but the files of a Madison architect had provided as-built drawings of its original warehouse configuration.

A corridor now ran across the front of the building. Tovera turned right, toward what had been the warehouse office and was probably now the administrative control room: the security cameras and intercoms were run from a console there.

Adele went the other way.

There was a steel door to the right at the end of the corridor. Over it was a security camera on a different circuit from the external system; it would have gone blank also when Adele ordered the control console to shut down for a system check. There was no keypad on this side of the door, and the intercom would be dead also.

She rang the knuckles of her right hand on the center of the door panel. If she had had something hard she might have used that instead, but the sharp *cling-cling-cling* on the steel was adequate.

She wouldn't use her pistol as a mallet, of course. It was a specialized tool whose mechanisms were more delicate than many people seemed to realize.

Someone shouted from the other side of the door. Adele smiled slightly and knocked again. She didn't bother trying to make out the words.

Bolts withdrew from wall sockets at both the top and bottom of the door. It had been designed much like a spaceship's hatch. The panel opened toward her, slowly because of its weight.

"What happened to the camera and—" the guard inside began. There was no concern in his voice, merely the irritation of a dull man when his routine is interrupted.

He didn't notice Adele's pistol before she shot him twice through the right eye. His body spasmed backward, kicking the door panel hard enough to open it wider. Because he was wearing soft-soled boots, the sound was only a muffled thump.

The guard had been in an anteroom with a door on the other end as well. Its only furnishings were a low stool and a holograph projector loaded with—

Adele touched the unit to check. She loved information, no matter how valueless, the way an alcoholic craves the bottle.

—pornography involving women, more women, and animals. At least she assumed it was pornography. She had never pretended to understand the allure of sex, but it puzzled her that *any*one could find these images titillating.

She looked down at the dead man, wondering what had happened to the pair of soldiers who had killed her sister Agatha. No doubt they would have explained that they were just doing their jobs, but logic as well as Adele's anger argued that men who cut off the head of a little girl were not likely to die in bed themselves.

The inner door wasn't locked. Adele pushed it open.

The space beyond was a single room thirty feet deep and twenty wide. On the right-hand wall was an electronics suite that would have done credit to the bridge of a battleship.

The floor to the left was a stainless steel tray with upturned edges. On it was a floodlit operating theatre. A child, probably an undernourished ten-year-old rather than someone younger and healthier, was strapped to the table.

The man who had been bending over the child was in his sixties and fat, with lifeless hair. He was nude except for splotches and splatters of blood; he seemed to have dipped his thumbs in the blood to paint designs on his chest.

He held a scalpel. It and his hand were dripping.

Light reflecting from the door's inner face must have drawn him from his leering concentration. He rose and stared at Adele in surprise and anger. "Who the hell are you?" he said. "Get out!"

"Put down the knife," Adele said. She kept her eyes on the

fat man as she walked toward three linked consoles against the wall.

Her personal data unit was out in her right hand. It didn't have to be in contact with a console, but it was probably safer sitting on one than it would be anywhere else in the room for the next short time.

"I told you to get *out*, you stupid bitch!" the man said, raising the scalpel as he started around the table. There were drains in the floor.

Adele shot him through the wrist. He didn't drop the scalpel until three spaced rounds had puckered the skin, smashing the cartilage and delicate bones into grit and gelatine. She set the little data unit on the console's fascia.

"What did you do?" the man shouted in disbelief. "*What did you do?*"

He lunged toward Adele. She shot him twice through the right knee, then twice more through the other. He finally twisted to the left and fell, still shouting.

Sheer mechanical damage had brought him down; he didn't seem affected by pain. Either he was heavily drugged or the endorphins which his brain released from delight at torturing children protected him from what should have been agony.

Adele walked to the boy, keeping the table between her and where the naked man had fallen. Blood had stopped leaking from the network of shallow cuts, but she touched the victim's throat with the tips of her right index and middle fingers.

There was no carotid pulse. She supposed that was just as well. Having carved out the boy's eyes, the man had cut his vocal cords, too.

"Are you police?" the man said as Adele walked back around the table. "You've made a mistake, a terrible mistake! I'm Charlie Platt. Talk to your watch commander. You're not supposed to be here!"

He wheezed suddenly; perhaps the pain was getting through after all. "Oh, what have you done? You bitch, you stupid bitch!"

"I'm not the police," Adele said. She checked her little unit as it mined the consoles and transferred their data to her base system on the *Princess Cecile*. Though it purred along happily, it hadn't completed its tasks yet. There must be an amazing amount of information in Platt's system.

The man on the floor had fallen half on, half off, the tray under the operating theater. He must have begun noticing discomfort from the raised steel gutter, because he tried to squirm off it. That flexed his right knee; he screamed, and his whole body quivered.

"I thought I might need access codes from you," Adele said. "Apparently not, since my unit is mirroring yours without difficulty. Your external security was very good, though."

"I'll pay you," Platt said, breathing quickly. "I can pay any amount, *any* amount. I'm a very important man!"

Platt had fouled himself when his leg bent. He was an aging fat man who wore only his own feces and a child's blood, and he was bragging about his importance.

"You *must* be very important," Adele said in a calm, reasonable tone, "to be allowed to do this."

She gestured toward the operating table with her right hand.

"Even on a frontier world like Madison, that's amazing."

"I was the chief of systems at Fleet Prime on Pleasaunce!"

Platt said. Adele wasn't sure whether it was breathy enthusiasm or only pain that she heard in his voice. "I should have been promoted to technical director, but some officious fool started making trouble and I had to, well, I came here. I—"

He paused and panted for a moment while he retrieved the thread of his argument. At last he said, "I know powerful people here. They'll give you whatever you ask to free me. *Anything!* Just ask."

"Your protector is Commander Doerries of Fleet Intelligence here?" Adele said. She backed a few steps to glance sideways at her data unit without looking away from Platt.

"That doesn't matter!" Platt said. "I can get you more money than you dream, *that's* what matters!"

"No," said Adele, "it isn't. Even if I cared about money, it wouldn't matter now."

She shot Platt through the eye; twice, as she had been trained to do. He spasmed and went flaccid.

You don't torture a cockroach.

"Coming through!" Tovera said from the doorway. "Coming through!"

Adele slid the data unit into its proper sheath beneath the borrowed trousers. She continued to hold the pistol out. It would have cooled sufficiently to pocket by the time she stepped into the open air again.

"I'm almost done here," she said, turning. "Bring a—ah. Yes, of course you would."

Tovera gave Adele a snake-like smile. She held two of the automatic carbines which the dead guards had dropped.

"Step clear, mistress," she said, holding one of the carbines sideways at her waist. The other was slung over her shoulder.

Adele obediently walked toward the door. When Tovera was satisfied that Adele was at a safe distance, she fired into the first console. Because the impellers were smoothbores, rifling didn't twist the barrel to the side, but the fully automatic burst did lift the muzzle slightly under recoil.

The thirty osmium pellets spaced themselves across the body of the console and halfway into its nearest neighbor. Sparks, fragments, and the sizzle of short circuits followed the line of destruction.

When the weapon was empty, Tovera tossed it into a corner—the muzzle glowed a yellow which shimmered toward the white—and unlimbered the other carbine. Her second long burst was in perfect alignment with that of the first.

She dropped the carbine onto the steel floor; it sizzled and stank in blood. "I'll lead," she said, drawing her submachine gun as she stepped ahead of Adele at the door.

"No problems?" Adele said.

"The woman on the console tonight had her girlfriend in to improve the time," Tovera said. "I expended six rounds instead of three, that's all."

She held up a keychip in her left hand. "I thought we'd leave the van here and go out in the girlfriend's car," she said. "Nobody will connect that with this business if it gets noticed before we're back aboard the *Sissie*."

"All right," said Adele. It was very improbable that anyone would notice the slaughter for days if not weeks, given the care that Platt and Doerries had taken to keep the location secret.

Adele didn't care. She wasn't sure she cared about anything at the moment.

The three-wheeler's back wouldn't have held an adult, but they easily folded the drugged boy into it. Tovera got into the driver's seat and switched the vehicle on. Adele took out her personal data unit by rote.

"The boy back there?" Tovera said without looking at Adele.

"He was dead," Adele said. She opened the gate for Tovera to accelerate into the street, then started it closing again.

Adele looked at her servant. "Tovera?" she said. "Does what happened to those children disturb you?"

Tovera did not look away from the road. "It bothers me, mistress," she said, "because it should bother me. It bothers you."

"Yes, it bothers me," said Adele. She thought about Agatha. "It bothers me a great deal."

Daniel and Hogg got out from opposite sides when the aircar landed. Its fans blew grit across their ankles as it lifted and curved away from the quay where the *Savoy* was berthed. Watchly didn't look back at them.

"I chatted some with Martensen, the guard back to the farmhouse, you know?" Hogg said in a quiet voice, his hands in his pockets. He hadn't spoken about the farm or the people there during the return journey.

"Ah?" said Daniel. Kiki Lindstrom came to the *Savoy*'s entry hatch, probably summoned by the sound of the aircar. She didn't call to them or start across the catwalk. Her face was impassive in the high light standards on the quay.

"We didn't talk about much," Hogg said, still facing in the direction Watchly had driven off. "But his boots were Fleet issue. And the poncho he was wearing had G 37 stencilled on the back."

"*Ah*," Daniel repeated in a brighter tone. "There's a destroyer *G 37* in Fleet service. Probably not first-line by now; the class was laid down about twenty years ago, which is a long time for a destroyer."

"Martensen isn't a kid," Hogg said reflectively. "He's a husky fellow, though." He shrugged. "Anyway," he said, "I thought you might want to know."

"Yes," said Daniel, "thank you. It confirms my suspicions."

He didn't know what it meant. The fact that an Alliance officer was pretending to be a Cinnabar officer certainly meant *something*, but it might simply be that the Chief was a grafter who thought that patriotism would make former RCN Lieutenant Pensett more willing to lend himself to some black-market scheme.

Daniel touched the RCN document case in his pocket. Adele would be able to open it safely, he was sure, but he didn't want to take it straight back to the *Princess Cecile*. There was an obvious chance that Martensen or someone of his ilk was watching "Pensett's" activities, or that Lindstrom herself would contact her backer if she decided Daniel's behavior was suspicious.

Daniel—or perhaps Hogg—would have a chance to deliver the package tomorrow, when he was sure that Adele had returned to the *Sissie*. He wasn't going to risk this heaven-sent opportunity to meet Freedom without a better reason than he had thus far.

"Let's go aboard, Hogg," Daniel said, "and choose our bunks."

There was an old girl who lived in Cairo Port..., he whistled as he preceded Hogg across the catwalk. *How I wish that she was dead!*

Chapter Fourteen

ASHETOWN ON MADISON

Adele entered the Battle Direction Center and sat at the empty console beside Cory's. She had left the borrowed overgarments in the three-wheeler when she and Tovera abandoned it in an alley behind a row of brothels.

Someone would probably steal the vehicle before morning, but that didn't matter. There was no harm done if the car remained where it was for however many days it was before the authorities discovered the owner's body was one of many at a massacre site.

"Mistress!" Lieutenant Cory said. "I didn't expect you back here. Ah—that is, I'm glad to see you. It feels, well, I'm used to being on the bridge, so this station isn't... I mean, even though it's a promotion to first lieutenant."

Adele looked at him. The others present in the BDC were Fiducia, the missileer's mate, and Knibbs, a technician whom Cory had been instructing in astrogation simply because he was willing to learn.

And Tovera, of course. It was easy to overlook Tovera, while things were quiet.

Captain Vesey, as she had become, was at the command console on the bridge. Although she would not have questioned anything Adele did, Adele would feel constrained in Vesey's presence. Vesey felt that she *ought* to understand what Lady Mundy was doing.

Cory didn't feel anything of the sort. If Adele had begun tap dancing on the seat of her console, the most Cory might have done was ask if he could help. She'd chosen the BDC for no better reason than that.

"I suppose it's the opposite with me," Adele said. "I thought this would be a more comfortable setting for a task I have to do. Though I hadn't connected the cause and effect until you spoke, Cory."

In fact, she realized, she wasn't making many connections at all since the shootings. She had subconsciously divorced herself from everything that was going on around her.

She felt a touch of wry humor, though nobody looking at her face would have recognized it. The disconnected way she had felt since leaving Platt's sanctum wasn't very different from her normal state of existence.

Cory's enthusiasm cooled as Adele looked at him without emotion. "Ah," he said. "I'm watch officer, but since it's quiet I thought I'd go over procedures with Knibbs here. If you'd like us to leave...?"

"Not at all, Cory," Adele said as she synched her personal data unit with the console. She preferred to use her little unit as an interface. She found the wands with which she controlled it to be her fastest and most efficient input method. "Strictly speaking, this isn't really RCN business."

"I better get back to the Power Room," muttered Knibbs. He got up without looking at Cory or Adele. Fiducia had already slipped out of the BDC.

I didn't care, Adele thought wearily. *But I couldn't have cleared the compartment more quickly if I'd waved my pistol.*

"I could—" Cory said.

"Sit down," Adele said, much more sharply than she had intended. She grimaced. She was on edge, but that was no excuse for snarling at a—well, at a *friend*—who was simply trying to be polite in a confusing situation.

She met Cory's eyes and tried to smile. "I uncovered a sexual predator here in Ashetown," she said. She was explaining as a more tangible form of apology to him. "I'm transmitting the information to the authorities. As I say, it isn't strictly RCN business, though it seems to involve Fleet officials in some fashion or other."

"Sexual predator," Cory repeated. Something had changed in his face, though Adele couldn't have said exactly what the difference was. He cleared his throat and said, "Mistress, if you thought it might be better for a couple of us to talk to the fellow informally...?"

And what is there in your background that causes you to react that way, Lieutenant? Adele thought; her face remained expressionless. Aloud she said, "Thank you, Master Cory, but I'm sure no further action will be necessary."

"Yes, mistress," Cory said. He relaxed and his smile spread. Perhaps he understood more than had been in Adele's words.

He'd been in close contact with her for long enough to know what she was besides a scholar and a signals officer.

She checked her display; the file transfer was complete. She hadn't dumped the whole assemblage which she had netted from Platt's consoles, just enough from a quick sort to give the proper authorities a handle on the rest.

"Ah," Cory said. "If Fleet officers are involved, could I help? Even if they weren't, you know, it would be an honor to help. And Rene too, of course, though I think he's in town now looking for clothes."

Cazelet looking for clothes? But of course: lingerie or the like for Elspeth Vesey; to be given her after she stepped down as captain of the *House of Hrynko*.

Adele thought of the mass of data. Her two unofficial aides *could* be useful, during the initial sort and probably later on as well.

"Yes," she said, transferring a file to Cory's console. "This man claimed to have been chief of systems at Fleet Prime and in line for the post of technical director. I don't know what period this would have been going on, but today he appeared to be in his sixties."

"Yes, mistress," Cory said; he was already at work. "Is there anything in particular I should be looking for?"

Adele pursed her lips. "Platt implied he was working for Commander Doerries, head of the Fleet Intelligence office for the Forty Stars Sector," she said. "Platt's skills were of a high enough order that his claims about his rank on Pleasaunce may well be true. If so, how did he come to be transferred to this backwater?"

"Guarantor Porra," Tovera said, "is something of a prude."

Adele didn't twitch in surprise, but Cory did. It was as though one of the jumpseats folded against the bulkhead had joined the discussion.

"*Porra* is?" Cory said in amazement. "Why, he's...he's done..."

He let his voice trail off. Perhaps he was remembering that Tovera had been a member of the Fifth Bureau, the intelligence agency which reported directly to the Guarantor—that is, dictator—of the Alliance, and which was the tool he used for his most brutal acts of repression.

"Guarantor Porra has done many reprehensible things," Tovera agreed with a terrible smile, "but personally he is prudish. He might well order children to be tortured as a matter of policy, but it would disgust him to learn that one of his officials was torturing children for sexual gratification. I suspect you'll find that Platt wasn't transferred—he was running ahead of Fifth Bureau executioners."

She giggled. "He didn't go far enough, as it turns out," she said.

If Platt was a fugitive, Adele thought, *then whatever Commander Doerries is doing isn't a sanctioned operation.* With luck the data grab from Platt's consoles would eventually give them full particulars on that operation, though it still might not have any bearing on RCN business or even on Mistress Sand's broader objectives.

Adele's smile was barely a quiver at the corners of her lips. There was no useless information; there was only information for which she hadn't yet found a use.

"Master Cazelet?" Tovera said. She spoke loudly enough for Cazelet to hear as he entered the compartment, but the real purpose was probably to call Adele's attention to the new arrival.

"I, ah...," Cazelet said. "The captain told me that you were...*both* of you were in the BDC. I thought I'd...well, I'd see if there was something I could do?"

Adele smiled faintly. She shouldn't be surprised to be surrounded by people who looked for work rather than for ways to avoid work. That was her own attitude, after all; and more important, that was Daniel's attitude.

"Find a console," she said without looking over her shoulder toward Cazelet. "I'll send tasks to you when that's appropriate."

The console Adele was using threw a pulsing amber attention signal onto the upper right corner of its display. It took her a moment to cycle back to the present and determine which of her various automated operations had borne fruit.

She expanded the icon. As soon as Daniel informed her of his plans, Adele had cued her intercepts of squadron internal message traffic to alert her if the word *Savoy*—among many others—appeared. It just had.

She scanned it, then copied the link to Cory, Cazelet, and— after a heartbeat's hesitation—to Vesey on the bridge. This might well become a task for the corvette *Princess Cecile*, not just a matter of intelligence gathering and dissemination.

A man named Petrov—the name wasn't familiar; she would track him down later—had reported to squadron headquarters that the yawl *Savoy* was carrying weapons stolen from Fleet stores and intended for the rebels on Sunbright. Though the squadron was on four-hour alert, the Operations staff had authorized Captain von Trona of the cruiser *Marie* to sequester the yawl pending survey and possible condemnation of her cargo.

The *Marie* carried a company of fifty-six naval infantry. They had no duties during liftoff preparations. There wouldn't be a problem if they were absent and the squadron received emergency orders to lift for Sunbright—or for Tattersall, as the case might be. Von Trona had told the company commander, a naval major, to take a platoon to the *Savoy* that night.

"I thought the blockade runners bribed the Fleet authorities here to look the other way?" Cazelet said. "We *know* the authorities have been bribed. I've tabulated the payments over the past three and a half years. What caused the change?"

Adele didn't consider the question, because for the moment it wasn't important. The only important task was to reach Daniel before the Alliance troops arrived. Since the *Savoy* was tied up at a quay, it was possible that the ship had landline communication through the Ashetown network.

"It isn't a change," said Cory. "Lindstrom and her backers are bribing the squadron *base* establishment. This Petrov obviously knew that, so he sent his information to the squadron itself. If the Fleet is anything like the RCN, the real spacers hate the base wankers worse than they do...well—"

His small image on Adele's display grinned.

"—worse than they hate us. The RCN may kick their asses in battle, but we're not going to rob them blind on the ground. I suspect somebody on Jeletsky's staff—and von Trona for sure—is doing this to stick it in the base establishment's eye."

The *Savoy*'s berth did have a landline connection. Adele

called it while she prepared to send a microwave signal to
the blockade runner also. The *Sissie*'s stern sending head had
a direct line to the yawl, but success presupposed that the
Savoy's receiver was switched on.

It would be bad if an RCN officer were arrested aboard
a blockade runner carrying arms to the Sunbright rebels. If
by some chance the RCN officer were identified as Captain
Daniel Leary—that would be very bad indeed.

Answer me, Daniel!

"Mistress Lindstrom?" Daniel said, nodding to the shipowner
as she backed out of the hatchway to allow him and Hogg
aboard. "I thought I'd familiarize myself with the electronics
tonight. Tomorrow morning I'll go over the rigging, but that's
a job for daylight, right?"

"The rigging's all right," Lindstrom said. "It got us here,
didn't it? Why wouldn't it get us back to Cremona?"

Daniel waited till she met his eyes. If she hadn't been his
superior officer—at least until they lifted off—he might have
taken her chin between thumb and forefinger to turn her face
toward him.

"Since you're not a moron, mistress," he said, "you don't
really mean that. Please tell me what the problem is, so that I
can at least try to fix it."

Lindstrom glared at him. Daniel tried to keep his face
quietly neutral, but he was tense inside as he waited for one
from a familiar catalogue of shouted or snarled responses:

Nothing's wrong!

You're the one with the problem, so you tell me!

Why should I bother? It's no use talking to you!

The fact that Daniel didn't have the faintest notion what he'd done wrong wouldn't help. At least it had never helped in the past.

Lindstrom's face softened from anger into the nervous misery she had been trying to conceal. "Oh, bloody Hell," she said, not shouting. "I don't know what the trouble is. I'm just feeling jumpy. I felt the same way when we extracted over Sunbright on our second run and we were bloody near on top of a patrol ship."

"And you got out of that fine," Daniel said. "Let's go over the console together. And I packed light, but not so light that I didn't find room for a bottle."

He was feeling such relief that his knees trembled. What with one thing and another, he'd had a lot of women screaming abuse at him over the years. While he wouldn't say that he'd come to long for a quiet life, he *did* increasingly appreciate Miranda Dorst's calm intelligence.

"I've got one open," Lindstrom said, turning with him toward the crew capsule. "Maybe we'll move on to yours later."

After a step she added, "And call me Kiki, will you?"

The hatch was only wide enough for one at a time. "Ma'am?" said Hogg as the owner led the way through.

Daniel backed out of the way; Lindstrom paused and turned her head. Without warmth she said, "Right?"

"D'ye have any guns aboard?" Hogg said. "I mean, for using. I don't care what's in the cargo."

"There's a pair of carbines in the locker here," she said,

tapping the vertical chest starboard of the hatchway. "For when we're on the ground on Sunbright, just in case. But I'm the only one with the key."

"Well, ma'am," Hogg said, his eyes turned toward the deck. He was so perfectly the bashful rustic that Daniel wanted to burst out laughing. "I don't know squat about consoles and electronics, but guns is different. I figure I could sit out here in the hold and go over the carbines so that I'm sure they work if we need them. Though you could do worse for a club, I suppose."

Lindstrom was silent for a moment. Then she said, "Right," and fished out a key fob attached by a length of monocrystal line to a loop on her equipment belt. She touched it to the lock plate, then stepped into the crew capsule. Daniel followed her.

The owner's bunk had a railing so that it could be curtained off from the remainder of the tiny cabin, but the curtain itself was missing. A stack of four more bunks folded against the opposite bulkhead, battered outward because of the hull's curve. The vertical space between bunks would be tight, but no worse than would have been the case in the midshipmen's berth of a battleship.

With Hogg aboard, there couldn't be assigned bunks. That didn't matter. The large crews of warships always shared bunks, and that was normally the case on smaller merchant vessels as well.

Lindstrom sat on the edge of her bunk and reached under it, coming out with a bottle. She looked at Daniel and patted the bedding beside her.

With careful nonchalance, Daniel walked past her and sat at the console as though he hadn't noticed the invitation.

Only after he had touched a few keys to bring up the system diagnostics did he turn beaming and say, "Kiki, this is a first-class piece of hardware! It's not new, but I trained on older systems at the Academy. This is much better than I expected!"

Daniel's enthusiasm—perhaps a little exaggerated for effect, but the astrogation computer really was a solid unit—smoothed Lindstrom's brief scowl away. She unstoppered the bottle, took a slug of its faintly violet contents, and offered it to Daniel. Because the compartment was so small, he didn't have to rise from the console to take it.

"We gutted the *Savoy* and replaced all the controls," Lindstrom said, warming. "The hull was fine and the rigging was too, except for the cordage—we replaced that. The only problem's been the bloody fusion bottle."

Daniel sipped the liquor and sluiced it around the inside of his mouth to get the flavor. It was smooth, though from the tingle, he suspected that it was roughly the same proof as industrial alcohol from the Power Room. It had the floral taste which its color suggested.

He swallowed. The aftertaste reminded him of a wreath left over from a funeral held some weeks past. He took two proper swallows and handed the bottle back.

"I don't think we'll have serious problems," Daniel said honestly. "Your spacers are experienced, and I'll have a chance to get to know them on the leg to Cremona. Getting through the patrols above Sunbright will be a little trickier, sure, but I know how difficult it is to intercept a little yawl like this in anything but a dedicated pirate-cruiser with a crew which knows its business. I won't promise, exactly, but, well—"

204

He grinned, but what he was about to say was the truth if ever he'd spoken it.

"—I'd be pretty disappointed if somebody trained on Novy Sverdlovsk could do a better job of ship handling than a Cinnabar Academy graduate."

An amber light pulsed from behind, flooding the compartment and startling Daniel. He jumped to his feet and turned; his left arm was out with the fingers spread, prepared to block whatever had started to happen.

The console display had been pearly and neutral; now it sequenced from bright amber to black. Daniel lowered his arm sheepishly and said, "What *is* that, mistress?"

"That's an incoming call," said Lindstrom, rising to her feet also. "But it's the landline, so it must be a wrong number. I haven't given the number to anybody; I just use it to call out."

There's one person who could find an address that everybody else thinks is secret, Daniel thought. He sat at the console, his back to the owner, and brought up a menu.

"What are you doing?" Lindstrom asked.

The incoming call was an icon to the right. Daniel opened it. Without hesitation, Adele's voice said, "I need to speak to Lieutenant Pensett immediately. This is Principal Hrynko, and I need him *at once*."

"Speaking, Lady Hrynko," Daniel said, as smoothly as if they had rehearsed the routine. "Go ahead."

"On the basis of information given by a man named Petrov," Adele said, "a platoon of marines is coming to search the *Savoy* and arrest you. If they find contraband, that is, and I gather that they will. They're not treating this as an emergency, though, so you have at least an hour to return here. Ah, where you'll be welcome, of course."

Daniel felt his lips purse as he considered. Changing from his initial wording—of *course* Adele was sure he would have at least an hour, because she wouldn't have said so otherwise—he said, "Warn me if there's a change in the troops' schedule, if you please. I'll be here, and I've—"

He brought the whole communication's suite live.

"—switched on the microwave in case something happens to the landline. I believe we can lift off comfortably ahead of their arrival. S—"

He caught himself.

"Pensett, that is, out."

"If you say so, Master Pensett," Adele said. Her voice was as cold and dry as a desert night. She broke the connection.

"What's going on?" Lindstrom said. She had heard the whole conversation, but she obviously hadn't been able to take it in. "They won't arrest us. Do you know how much money I've put in the hands of the port commissioner?"

"Hogg!" Daniel called, but his servant already stood in the interior hatchway. He held one carbine muzzle-upward by the grip like a large pistol, and the other by the fore-end, butt toward Daniel.

"We won't need those, Hogg," Daniel said tartly. "I don't propose that you and I fight the Fleet by ourselves. Or even one cruiser squadron."

He turned to the owner, who was now gaping at Hogg instead of at Hogg's master. He said, "Kiki, do you know where your men will be now?"

"Pretty much," she said. "I've been doling out their pay from the last run at a bit each night so they don't wind up broke or dead right away. There's maybe a half-dozen bars along the water that they might be at, starting with El Greco's."

"Find them," Daniel said. "Get them aboard *fast*. Hogg, escort her in case somebody needs convincing or is just too drunk to walk."

"As the master says," Hogg murmured. He disappeared into the entry hold. The arms locker banged closed a moment later.

"What are you doing, Pensett?" Lindstrom said. "They can't be coming to arrest us, I tell you!"

If Adele says that's what's happening, Daniel thought, *it's happening. I'd believe her over a choir of angels singing otherwise.*

Aloud he said, "I'll be running through liftoff checks and making sure the tanks are topped off. Now, move it! You have forty-five minutes. I don't care if the men come aboard drunk, but I'll lift short-handed if I have to."

Lindstrom opened her mouth, perhaps to object that she owned the *Savoy*. She deflated and turned silently toward the hatch. Hogg said, "Shake a leg, sister! You heard the young master!" But the prodding was unnecessary.

Daniel started the pumps that circulated reaction mass to the plasma thrusters and studied the flow. There was corrosion or a pinch in the line to the number one thruster, but it wasn't serious enough to change his plans. He began to whistle.

Father and I went down to camp, along with Captain Bony...

He felt very much alive.

Chapter Fifteen

ASHETOWN ON MADISON

Adele, seated at the Battle Direction Center console she had appropriated, watched imagery of the *Savoy* lifting off. Exhaust curling upward from the plasma thrusters curtained the blockade runner, though the ship was generally visible as something between a shadow and a lumpy cylindrical shape. It was thirty-seven minutes after Principal Hrynko had warned Kirby Pensett that his ship might be seized.

I wondered whether—I doubted whether—Daniel was correct in believing that he could get away in an hour. I'll apologize when we're next together.

The BDC was an armored box of irregular shape, designed to protect the equipment and personnel within to the greatest degree possible. As with the Power Room, there were no piercings to weaken its structure save for the hatch onto the corridor.

Cory and Cazelet had gone to the wardroom, just forward of the Battle Direction Center on the starboard side. That compartment had an external hatch from which the two

208

officers were watching Daniel lift off. They wore RCN goggles whose lenses would filter the dangerous actinics and could magnify the image if they chose to.

Adele considered the situation with part of her mind. Cory and Cazelet were spacers. They used holographic displays constantly and with great skill, but they were even more at home on the hull of a ship in the Matrix—directly viewing not just stars but the very cosmos in its majesty.

Adele was a librarian. Given the option, she preferred to observe her surroundings through an electronic interface. The male officers were *doing* the same thing—their goggles were as surely electronic as the console at which Adele sat—but they were subconsciously counterfeiting direct observation.

A smile almost reached her lips. Cory and Cazelet were her students, but she had not turned them into her clones. For that, the RCN—and their RCN careers—could be thankful.

Nor was either of them a particularly good shot. *They* should be thankful for that.

Another alert throbbed on her sidebar. She opened it as text, though she kept Daniel's liftoff as background to the message.

The signal was from Forty Stars HQ to the *Estremadura* in distant orbit, but it was routed through Platt's station as a cut-out to protect the identity of the initial sender. Though Platt and Commander Doerries were careful about communications security, Adele had retrieved their internal codes as part of her haul from Platt's sanctum. She now could read the contents instead of just knowing that there had been a message.

Doerries—whom she had identified with certainty from reviewing Platt's records—was ordering the *Estremadura* not to disturb the *Savoy*. Adele had not yet determined what game—or games—Doerries was playing with the blockade runners, but he apparently had his reasons for wanting the *Savoy* to get through.

That was all very well, since Adele very much wished Daniel to have a safe trip also. Unfortunately, because Adele had destroyed the retransmission station and killed its operator, the message was not going to reach the *Estremadura*.

Dropping the clutter of the *Savoy*'s liftoff from her display, Adele instructed one head of the *Sissie*'s stern microwave cluster to lock on to the lurking cruiser—and froze. Doerries had placed this message at his highest security level. Instead of sending it through the planetary satellite network, it had to go by direct microwave link. The handshake between the systems was achieved through a pair of randomizing chips which were identical at the molecular level.

I can't duplicate the signature. The necessary chip in Platt's station was irretrievable, even if it hadn't cracked from heat stress during the short circuits.

She would punish herself at leisure for her mistake—for her choice; it hadn't been a mistake, because she had made the correct judgment under the circumstances. If the choice cost Daniel his life, she would punish herself till she died, and that day couldn't come soon enough. For now, though, she had to mitigate the damage.

Adele switched to the laser transmitter. It wasn't ideal— there wasn't a good way to communicate with a ship lifting off—but it was more practical to punch coherent light through the optical haze of the exhaust than it was to drive microwaves through the RF hash caused by the volume of ions changing state.

"*Savoy*, this is Hrynko," Adele said, her voice as dry as salt fish. "Respond at once. I repeat, respond at once, over!"

"—*at once, over!*" Daniel's commo helmet said in what he believed was Adele's voice. The helmet eliminated static from the signal, but it could only fill in the holes with flat approximations of what the algorithm decided were the missing particles.

"This is *Savoy*," he said. The helmet wasn't his personal unit from the *Sissie*—that had Six stencilled above the visor—but it was RCN standard. It wouldn't strike anyone as unusual that a lieutenant dumped out on half pay would manage to liberate a commo helmet before he strode down the gangplank for the last time. "Go ahead, Hrynko, over."

Starships didn't—couldn't—accelerate very quickly. Not only were they underpowered for the purpose, accelerations more than three gees would torque the hull even of a warship and leave a trail of rigging in the wake as tubes sheared and clamps vibrated off.

Civilian vessels were even less sprightly than warships. The *Savoy* was straining upward at less than two gees, as much as her three thrusters could manage. Daniel could have walked about the cabin if that were necessary; holding a normal conversation wasn't a strain.

"*Savoy, the* Estremadura *was alerted twelve hours ago to make a particular effort to capture you,*" Adele said, her voice sounding even more emotionless than usual. *"The information provided to the* Estremadura *includes the four alternative course plans in your computer for the route from here to Cremona. The cruiser entered the Matrix as soon as imagery of your liftoff reached its location three light-seconds out. Ah, over."*

"Roger, Hrynko," Daniel said, smiling in fond amusement. "Thank you for the warning. I think we should be able to put matters right shortly. *Savoy* out."

He realized that though Adele might worry in part because the patrolling cruiser was targeting the *Savoy*, most of her concern was because she herself wasn't aboard the blockade runner to work some sort of magic. Perhaps she would have come up with some amazing trick—she certainly had before—but Daniel didn't imagine it would be necessary. A yawl commanded by Captain Daniel Leary, RCN, ought to be able to run circles around the yokels here in the Macotta Region.

The *Savoy*'s only acceleration couch was his on the command console. The four crewmen—West and Hargate wore the ship's two rigging suits—were seated on the folded-down bottom bunk, and Hogg was on Kiki's couch with her. He sat at the foot and wasn't being overcompanionable, but Daniel knew that his servant hadn't asked her before he chose his location.

He thought of warning the others, but the *Savoy* didn't have a PA system. Nor was there room for the whole console to rotate as it was designed to do, and Daniel wasn't willing to turn the seat alone at this juncture: he needed to keep his eyes on the display more than he needed to keep the others abreast of what he was doing.

The *Savoy* was thirty miles above Madison's surface. If Daniel had been commanding an RCN ship, he would have switched to the High Drive by now to conserve reaction mass. On a commercial vessel there were other factors to consider. The throats of *Savoy*'s High Drive motors were already badly eroded. It made sense to minimize the further damage inevitable when antimatter atoms which hadn't combined in the reaction chamber flared into an atmosphere.

Daniel finally shut down the thrusters. Instead of switching directly to the High Drive, he adjusted controls to bring the electrical balance of the yawl's surface as close to zero as possible.

"Preparing to insert!" he shouted. He wasn't sure if anybody but Hogg—who had covered his ears—could hear him. Though the ship was simply coasting on inertia, the thrusters' roar had been numbing to unprotected hearing. Like most civilian spacers, the *Savoy*'s crew didn't bother with pansy frills like sound-cancelling earphones or even earplugs.

"Pensett, what are you doing?" demanded Lindstrom, who must have heard something after all.

"Inserting!" Daniel said as he pressed the red Execute button. The console was so old that the keyboard was real instead of virtual, and the tactile *thunk* through his thumb was immensely satisfying.

The yawl slipped from normal space into the Matrix. The physical sensations accompanying the change of state were entirely imaginary and in Daniel's case had differed on each of the by-now thousands of times that they had occurred. This time he felt as though he had dropped fifty feet, been brought up short by a rope anchored in his solar plexus, and then dropped twice more in similar fashion.

He leaned back on the acceleration couch, gasping and hoping that his insides would settle down before long. Knowing that the experience was purely psychological didn't make it any less real—or exhausting.

"What in hell have you done, Pensett?" said Lindstrom, bending over Daniel's couch to shout. Hogg had gotten up also. Obviously neither of them had been as badly affected by the recent insertion as Daniel was. "We don't have any way on yet!"

Daniel set the rigging to deploy, extending the antennas and unfurling the initial sail set, before he looked up at the owner. He didn't care to have anybody bellowing at him, but he formed his lips into an engaging smile.

The expression was as much for her sake as his own. He didn't want Hogg to change the situation with the enthusiasm he'd been known to show when he decided that somebody was threatening the young master.

"We had an Alliance cruiser coming down on us, Kiki," Daniel said. "We won't need to go far, I hope, to confuse them for long enough that we can set off in proper fashion."

West—the oldest of the crewmen; he was sixty if he was a day—and Hargate had risen and were settling their helmets in place. It was nearly certain that the rigging wouldn't work properly the first time it was deployed after liftoff, so the crewmen were preparing to go out to clear kinks and jams.

Daniel straightened. He thought for an instant, then said, "No, stay inside for now. As the boss says—"

He grinned as he nodded to Lindstrom, who had returned

to her couch. Hogg remained standing in the center of the compartment.

"—we don't have much way on, so we're not going anywhere in particular. We'll extract and accelerate for a while; *then* you can get your exercise."

"Suits me, Chief," Hargate said, giving Daniel the first smile he had seen on the man's face. "This suit—"

He clacked his gauntleted fingers against the stiffened chest plate.

"—lacks about two inches of what it ought to have for height, and with the helmet locked down I feel like somebody's trying to pound me through the deck."

"I see," said Daniel. "When we hit ground on Cremona, I'll see if we can't promote a hard suit that fits you a little better."

Hogg could probably arrange something. Quite apart from common decency—hard suits of the wrong size were miserably uncomfortable—he didn't want the ship's safety to depend on a rigger whose suit hobbled him when he needed to move fast.

Daniel returned to his display. The equipment on the hull was hydromechanical; electric current would have generated magnetic fields. They could randomly and sometimes enormously affect the sails' resistance to the Casimir radiation which shifted a vessel through the Matrix. In a well-found modern vessel the hydraulic input was converted to electricity within the hull and appeared as readouts on the console.

The *Savoy* had instead four pointers above the airlock. Three were vertical; the fourth—the starboard antenna—was at ninety degrees, indicating that the antenna had only partially extended.

Daniel grinned. A jam at this point didn't matter, as he had told the riggers. More to the point, he had no reason to believe that the gauges were working properly, either.

"Preparing to extract," he said. One real benefit of a small vessel was that insertion and extraction were relatively simple procedures. An 80,000-tonne battleship might be five minutes completing either operation, even with a crack crew.

Daniel pulled the sliding control toward him, saying, "Extracting!"

Ice water trickled inward from each finger and toe, meeting in the center of Daniel's chest for one freezing moment; then the extraction was over. The yawl had reemerged in the sidereal universe, and all her external sensors were live again.

Daniel had set his display to a naval-style Plot Position Indicator simply out of habit. The *Savoy*'s console was old, but it had originally come from a warship—certainly Pantellarian, and probably a destroyer.

He lighted the High Drive as soon as a quick glance showed that the *Savoy* was still headed outward. His quick in-and-out of the Matrix could have reversed the ship's attitude in normal space, and they were close enough above Madison that diving toward the surface could have serious consequences.

The second order of business was to locate the *Estremadura*. With luck, the cruiser had extracted half a million miles away or even farther. That would give the *Savoy* plenty of time to build up speed before Daniel had to take her into the Matrix again.

The *Estremadura* wasn't visible on the PPI, which meant she was still in the Matrix. Since the *Savoy*'s console was a naval unit, it would have shown the cruiser on a predicted course even if she were momentarily behind the planet from the yawl's vantage point. Daniel had deliberately allowed plenty of time for his opponent to extract from her initial jump toward Madison.

Are they completely incompetent? That could certainly happen, but it wasn't a safe assumption to make about an untested opponent.

Speaking of untested, the yawl's two High Drive motors were buzzing in nearly perfect synchrony, making the vibration in so small a ship not only unpleasant but potentially dangerous. When there was time—which there certainly wasn't now— Daniel would adjust the units to syncopate one another with their pulses. Their present output created harmonics which could fracture electronics and might very well crystallize metal if it went on for long enough.

Daniel wondered if Petrov had deliberately aligned the motors' phases in some mad quest of a perfection that actually degraded performance. The gods alone knew what naval officers were taught on Novy Sverdlovsk!

The PPI highlighted the precursor effects of a ship extracting from the Matrix about 19,000 miles from the *Savoy*'s present location, some three light-seconds outsystem from Madison. That could be chance, but even if it *were* chance—

"Prepare to insert!" Daniel said as he slammed the paired High Drive feeds shut. The yawl wouldn't be able to insert until they'd coasted beyond the haze of antimatter atoms finding atoms of terrene matter with which to immolate themselves, but she was far enough out now that her surroundings were hard vacuum.

"Sir?" said one of the crewmen on a rising note. "Sir? What's going on?"

Lindstrom wasn't speaking this time, but she'd gotten up from her bunk and was hovering—literally; they were in free fall—beside the console, maneuvering expertly by taps on the bulkheads. Daniel couldn't blame the others for wondering what was going on, but it certainly wasn't helpful.

"Inserting!" Daniel said.

He didn't notice the transition this time because his mind was wholly focused on his display. He got a momentary glimpse of the ship which had returned to the sidereal universe just as the *Savoy* was leaving it. As he had feared, it was the *Estremadura*.

And when his console enhanced and enlarged the image, Daniel could see that the cruiser's guns had been aligned to bear on the yawl.

Chapter Sixteen

ASHE HAVEN ON MADISON

The *Savoy* and the pursuing cruiser had vanished into the Matrix. Neither Cory nor Cazelet could predict the result of chase, and they knew Adele too well to offer hopeful platitudes. Yes, Daniel was very skilled, but so was Captain Regin of the *Estremadura*, and the cruiser's large crew made it handier than the yawl.

Adele had nodded at the analysis and turned to what she could control. She lost herself in the broad expanse of the data she had harvested from Platt's station until a purple crawl at the bottom of her display announced OSORIO ARRIVING WITH VEHICLES ON QUAY. The slug at the close of the message indicated it was from the command console, where Vesey was acting as watch officer—despite being captain now and no longer required to stand watches.

"I'll go down and meet him," Adele said, letting the console reform her words into a prose response. She transferred her work to the signals console then, stripped the work off the BDC console instead of locking the files.

Only then did she get up. "Our passenger has arrived," she said to Cory and Cazelet. She preceded Tovera out of the BDC.

Daniel generally had stood watches also, even when the *Princess Cecile* had enough officers that it wouldn't have been necessary. Captains were permitted to be eccentric.

Adele glanced down at her clothing. She was still wearing the outfit she had put on to visit the Assumption Library... which she hadn't entered after all. The clothes were rumpled from hard use, despite being covered by borrowed garments while she and Tovera cleared Platt's station.

In particular, there was a blotch on the arch of her right boot. It was almost certainly blood, though she couldn't say without chemical analysis whether it was Platt's blood or that of his victim.

Kostroman nobles were permitted to be eccentric also. It was unlikely that Osorio would observe any more than Principal Hrynko looking disheveled when at leisure on her own yacht.

Tovera stepped in front of her, the attaché case waist-high and slightly open. Before Adele entered the corridor, she looked back and said to the young men watching her, "Continue with what you're doing."

Then—because they would understand—she added, "I would much rather remain here doing something useful instead of this playacting."

As they strode together toward the forward companionways, Tovera said quietly, "You wouldn't do it if you didn't believe it was useful, mistress."

Adele sighed and said, "What I should have said is that I

don't care to do this sort of thing, despite the frequency with which I'm called on to do it. I suppose I would be wiser to adjust my attitude rather than to expect the universe to change reality."

They went down by the bow companionway instead of the one immediately outside the BDC hatch in the stern. The central corridor on D Level ran past bulk storage compartments to the boarding hold, but A Level was familiar territory to Adele and required less of her conscious mind. She nodded by rote to crewmen going sternward or calling their respects through open hatchways, but her brain kept poring over the question of whether they would meet the *Savoy* on Cremona—and what Adele would do if they didn't.

Platt's files indicated that the *Estremadura* sent its prizes to Westerbeke to be condemned. Adele had not yet constructed an excuse for Principal Hrynko to take her yacht to that out-of-the-way port in the Funnel. Of course they could ignore duty and simply focus on saving Daniel; but Daniel wouldn't approve of that decision, and neither would she.

Adele and Tovera stepped into the boarding hold just as Osorio reached the guards. Heberle, a Tech 8 and the senior spacer on duty, had just started talking on her commo helmet when a rigger with a submachine gun patted her wrist and pointed toward the principal and her aide. Heberle braced to attention and shouted, "Her Ladyship!"

Tovera giggled. There were as many guesses about how to treat Principal Hrynko as there were Sissies. Adele had decided that lack of uniformity in address was less of a danger than trying to drill the crew into a particular form and have a confused spacer blurt something about Lady Mundy. Even sober that could happen; and sufficiently flustered spacers could probably find a drink to relax them.

"Master Osorio," Adele said. Looking beyond the Cremonan to the train of vehicles which had brought him—a ground car and a pair of small tractors pulling carts filled with luggage—she added, "And what is all this? Do you mistake my yacht for a merchant vessel?"

"I have lived on Madison for three years, Your Ladyship," Osorio said with a deep bow, "but I am going home to stay now with those of my possessions which I haven't disposed of here."

He gestured toward the car. "I sold my aircar, for example. Surely it will be possible to stow my household goods on so large a vessel?"

He probably sold the aircar at a very tidy profit, Adele realized. They weren't manufactured on Madison, and Osorio—as a government representative—wouldn't have had to pay the heavy import duty levied on luxuries.

Rather than answering directly, Adele turned to the detail commander and said, "Heberle, can that quantity of cargo be stored aboard without harming our combat efficiency?"

Heberle had a muttered conversation with the other ship-side spacer in the guard detail. She looked back at Adele and said, "Yeah, we can stuff it in, likely. We're low on some of the fungibles, and there's room in the forward magazine besides. What doesn't fit there we can cram into the cabin you assigned his nibs, I guess."

"All right," said Adele. "Inform Captain Vesey that I want this cargo loaded. Also tell her that I want to lift off as quickly as possible when that task is complete."

She looked at Osorio, who seemed startled. "Come with me to the bridge, then, my man," she said. "I usually watch liftoffs from a console there. You can sit at the training seat on my console."

Adele turned and started back the Up companionway. Tovera was immediately behind her. Spacers banged into the entry hold as Adele left it, on their way to striking down the passenger's luggage.

Osorio followed—she glanced out of the corner of her eye as she entered the armored tube—after a moment of puzzled hesitation. He hadn't expected to be treated as a foreigner of no importance.

Adele smiled faintly. It was as well that the Cremonan attaché wasn't travelling with servants, though they could be stowed also—with as little ceremony as the luggage, and probably with what a landsman would consider as little comfort.

Her smile slipped. She did very much want to lift off. If the *Princess Cecile* had been ready to lift when the cruiser made for Daniel, Adele would have done so immediately, regardless of her cover as Principal Hrynko. As it was, all she could do at the moment was to determine what had happened. Later she would right it, if possible.

Adele entered the bow rotunda and strode across it to the bridge. Tovera was a silent shadow a step behind, and Osorio panted audibly at the unpracticed effort of the steep helical staircase.

The Cremonans wanted to hire to *House of Hrynko* to destroy the *Estremadura*. Adele would force them to make a reasonable offer for the services of her yacht, but that was

223

only because the businessmen backing the project would be suspicious if she didn't demand that.

But the money really didn't matter: Adele had already determined that. The *Sissie* and her crew would eliminate the cruiser. She only hoped that she would be punishing the *Estremadura*'s crew for worrying her, rather than taking revenge for Daniel's death.

THE MATRIX

Daniel finished a series of computations before he rotated his couch and grinned at his companions. Hogg appeared nonchalant. The expression might be feigned, but probably not. Hogg had complete faith in the young master's infallibility regarding anything to do with a starship, so he saw nothing to worry about.

"*What* the bloody hell are you playing at?" Kiki Lindstrom demanded. She looked furious. To a degree the anger could be hiding her fear, though Daniel's cavalier behavior toward her ship and herself gave plenty of reason for her to be pissed.

The faces of three of the crewmen ranged from worried to frightened. The fourth, Blemberg, had no expression at all—as always before in Daniel's experience. Daniel couldn't tell at this early point in their acquaintance whether Blemberg was unflappably stolid or if he was simply too stupid to understand that they were in danger.

"There's a cruiser here in the system, targeting blockade runners," Daniel said. "The *Estremadura*."

Lindstrom nodded, suddenly looking thoughtful. "I've heard of her," she said. "She's a privateer, really. The governor of Sunbright hired her because the Funnel Squadron couldn't catch its ass with both hands. But she operates above Cremona, mostly, and sends her prizes to Westerbeke."

"Well, for now, she's in Madison orbit," Daniel said. "She's coming for us, and her captain is bloody good. That's why I've been bouncing around like a training exercise."

He was glad to see that the crewmen, too, were relaxing. When he started discussing a real danger, they realized that their captain and the only astrogator aboard hadn't suddenly gone crazy—which was the best explanation they'd previously had for his behavior.

Lindstrom backed to her bunk and seated herself again. "The *Estremadura*'s been in this system before but didn't bother us when we lifted off?" she said. Her tone made the words a question.

"Well, that's changed," Daniel said flatly. "If we'd been fifteen seconds later in inserting, she'd have hit us with her guns. They couldn't have done a lot of damage at this range, but we wouldn't have been able to insert if she kept hitting the hull. So we have a problem."

"Sir?" said Hargate. "Can you get us out? If they carry the ship to Westerbeke and condemn it, they just dump us spacers out on the beach there with the clothes we stand in."

"I think we'll be able to handle it, yes," said Daniel. He smiled again, but this time with the hard triumph of a chess player about to make a move which he is sure will take his opponent by surprise. "The *Estremadura* expects us to sail

225

to Cremona—they have our course projections. I don't know how, but they do, and whoever is captaining that cruiser will know what to do with the data. So—"

He paused to let the delay add drama.

"—we'll go directly to Sunbright instead. I've plotted the course, and I'll be out on the hull most hours to refine it en route."

"But we can't do that!" Lindstrom said, her voice cutting through the spacers' disconcerted babble. "We don't have food for a straight run, and I don't know that the reaction mass will last out, either."

"We have enough food," said Daniel flatly, "and the reaction mass will be fine too. I checked them both as soon as I recalculated the course. We'll drop into normal space when we're ten light-minutes out from Madison on the present course. That'll give us time enough to build up speed before the *Estremadura* catches up with us again, if she even tries. Then—"

He repeated his artificially bright grin.

"—we don't enter the sidereal universe again until we're in the Sunbright system."

"Can you do that?" Lindstrom said, rather as though Daniel had said he planned to dance on the hull without a suit.

"Can't be done," said West much more forcefully. "*Can't* be done! Never *heard* of nobody doing that!"

"Nonsense," Daniel said in a brusquely cheerful tone. "We did it in the RCN every day. Well, every voyage, pretty much."

That was a flat lie, but it was closer to the truth than West's denial. Any RCN Academy graduate should be able to bring her ship close enough to an intended point after seven straight days in the Matrix that she could at least find her goal after extraction.

The problem was the human cost. People saw things after long immersion in the Matrix. Seven days was long enough for spacers to see a corridor where they knew there was a solid bulkhead; and sometimes to see someone or something approaching down that corridor.

Daniel had once seen his mother. She had stared at him in horror, then walked on very quickly and disappeared.

"You done that?" West said, but the words sounded like a prayer for absolution.

"Many times," Daniel said, truthfully this time. "Now, I've got the new course loaded. Hargate, I'll need your suit for the initial watch. West, you and I will go clear the stuck antenna or whatever the problem really is. Hogg—"

He smiled at his servant. *So far, so good.*

"—I'll bang three times on the hull with a wrench when we're ready. When I do that, you push the red button."

He pointed to the Execute button on the console. At one time it would have been protected with a hinged cage, but that had been lost in the distant past.

"Got it?"

Hogg grunted. "Guess I can handle that, young master," he said. "In between trying to learn how to pour piss outa a boot, y'know."

Hargate was stripping off the ill-fitting hard suit with enthusiasm. He might have doubts about seven straight days in the Matrix, but he was certain he didn't want to wear the suit.

Lindstrom, though, frowned and said, "Look, Pensett, we're not RCN, you know, even if you are. I'm not sure—"

"What *I'm* not sure about, mistress," Daniel said, "is what

227

these yobbos on the *Estremadura* are going to do if they find an ex-RCN officer on a blockade runner. I don't worry about a trip to Westerbeke, but instead it just might be a dive out an airlock without a suit. And if they space me, well—"

He shrugged.

"—they're not going to leave witnesses, are they?"

There was silence in the cabin for a moment. Then Lindstrom sighed and said, "Sunbright it is, I suppose. But I tell you, Pensett, we didn't have any of this trouble before you came aboard."

"Don't fret, mistress," Daniel said as he started getting into the hard suit with Hargate's help. "It'll be a smooth run from here on out, and at the other end—"

He grinned at the glum-faced crew members.

"—we'll all be able to get just as drunk on Sunbright as we could've done on Cremona."

ASHE HAVEN ON MADISON

As Adele entered the bridge she felt the circulating pumps start, a necessary preliminary before testing the plasma thrusters. The big pumps in the stern throbbed a moment later, drawing water from the harbor. For the moment the draft would be wasted back into the slip, but when thrusters were lighted those pumps would replenish the reaction-mass tanks.

Vesey had rotated the command console inward. When she saw Adele, she shrank her display so that their eyes could meet without a holographic veil between them.

Adele felt a flash of irritation: she much preferred to be anonymous, a shadow ignored by the others present. She swallowed the reaction since it was manifestly unjust. Everyone aboard was faced by an uncertain situation, and they had to take their cues from Officer Mundy.

"Carry on, Captain Vesey," she said aloud as she settled onto her console. Her voice was no colder nor more clipped than it would be if she had just been given wonderful news. "I have some matters to discuss with our passenger, and I've chosen to do so here on the bridge."

The only wonderful news Adele could imagine at the moment was a report that Daniel was safe. A believable report, because she didn't indulge in wishful thinking.

"Yes, sir," said Vesey and expanded her display again. Adele brought hers live.

Sun had gotten up from the gunnery station beside Adele's and was showing Master Osorio how to use the training seat which folded out from the back of the signals console; Chazanoff at the missile station had half turned to be able to look sidelong at Adele across the compartment, while Tovera watched the whole business with cold amusement from a jumpseat against the aft bulkhead.

Adele supposed it *was* amusing if viewed in the correct fashion: everyone was staring at the woman who preferred to be invisible. Perhaps at some later point she would actually be able to feel the humor instead of merely accepting it intellectually; for now, she was satisfied that nobody looking at her would understand what she was thinking.

Pasternak announced over the PA system and the general

intercom channel—the general push, as Adele had learned to call it in the RCN—*"Testing thrusters one and eight!"*

A moment later thrusters roared. Shortly after that, steam and the sting of ozone drifted into the bridge through open hatches.

She echoed Vesey's display on her own. Cory was in charge of the liftoff, with Vesey overseeing the maneuver; Cazelet was ghosting it from the astrogation console.

Adele allowed herself to compare the *Sissie*'s array of talent with what she knew of the officers on ordinary commercial vessels in the Macotta Region, or anywhere on the fringes of human settlement, for that matter. Most astrogators would be trained or half trained by apprenticing with people who were themselves without formal training. The exceptions were generally drunks or officers who for similar reasons had been driven from the core worlds. Only one or at most two people to a ship had even that training, with perhaps a spacer who knew how to program the computer to give a lowest-common-denominator solution.

Adele's present life was as close to perfect as she could imagine it being. She was a member of the most efficient ship of the finest navy in the human universe. Her friends and colleagues cherished and respected her, and they constantly displayed themselves worthy of her respect—and of her love, as she understood the meaning of the word.

But to achieve this perfect—in Adele's terms—life, it was necessary that the Mundys of Chatsworth have been massacred and that Adele have gone on to kill more people than she could count; people who often visited her dreams in the hours before dawn. Everything had a cost, she supposed.

The image of Osorio at the top of her display seemed to be speaking, though Adele couldn't have heard unaided speech over the thruster roar even if she hadn't already raised the sound-cancelling field around her station. She felt a moment's regret at her behavior: she didn't like the Cremonan attaché, but it had been discourteous to bring him up here and then ignore him.

She adjusted the cancellation field to encompass the console's back as well as its front station, then said, "The crew is testing the thrusters, Master Osorio. There'll be nothing to see until we lift, but—"

Adele used the override controls on her side of the console to provide Osorio with a panorama of the harbor as viewed from a sensor on the knuckle of the Dorsal A antenna, at present the highest point on the *Sissie*. As an afterthought, she added her own image to the top of his display so that he could look at her. He seemed to be completely at a loss with the console controls.

"—that shouldn't be long. In the interim, you can explain how you sell the prizes captured by Cremonan privateers."

Adele had that information already from Forty Stars files, but she was interested in how Osorio would react. His willingness to be frank—let alone honest—would give her a gauge of his character.

"Well, technically they're not Cremonan privateers, they're Sunbright Republic privateers," he said, "but most of them are fitted out and crewed on Cremona, of course. The lesser Names"—members of the Cremonan noble class—"own most of them, because that doesn't require much capital. And they sell their prizes on Bailey's Horn, an independent world but in the Forty Stars, you see?"

"You personally own privateers, then?" Adele said—a question that she *didn't* have the answer to. Osorio was surprising her positively. It was very probable, given her mindset, that surprises would be positive ones.

"I have shares in two or three," Osorio said casually, "but the real profit comes from blockade running if you have enough capital to buy merchandise. And to accept the occasional run of bad luck."

His image shrugged. "Four ships in a row that I had half interests in were captured. Even so, with profits of five hundred percent on each successful cargo, it has been a very good investment."

Adele kept her brow smooth, but she was frowning mentally as she reviewed the data already in her files. "Are you and your fellows, your Friends of Sunbright, outfitting all the blockade runners, then?" she said.

The Forty Stars records indicated there were about a hundred ships occupied in the trade at any one time. Though most individually were quite small, they and their cargoes added up to a very considerable outlay.

The yacht's hatches were ringing closed. The rumbling which Adele felt through the fabric of the ship was a gear train raising the boarding ramp to become the main hatch. Osorio couldn't identify the chorus of sounds and vibrations as normal and harmless, though. Instead of answering, he looked around in concern—because he was at the back of a console that would show him only the starboard hull—and said, "Is everything all right?"

"Yes," Adele said. "The crew is readying the ship for

liftoff. I asked if the Friends of Sunbright owned most of the blockade runners."

The words were a verbal slap rather than a question this time around. Surely the man had travelled on a starship before, to bring him from Cremona to here if nothing else. And not so very long ago!

"Ah," Osorio said, nodding as he tried to raise his mind from a slough of fear. "No, no; that would be wonderful, but even together we could not support more than a quarter of the ships trading with the rebels. The trading houses outfit most of them, but even they take money from off-planet investors. From Cinnabar, yes, but from Pleasaunce too, I'm sure."

He shrugged, relaxing in the contemplation of profits—and apparent irritation at the fact that others were making most of those profits. "The biggest houses on Cremona are from Alliance planets," he said, "and they all have correspondent firms on their homeworlds. They own as many blockade runners as everyone else together, or very nearly so!"

Adele looked at his image, though that was merely a place to rest her eyes as her mind considered the avenues which the situation offered to their mission, the *Sissie*'s mission. *If* Osorio was being truthful and accurate, of course; but he was in a position to know the true situation, and he didn't seem to her to be lying.

"It isn't fair that the foreigners make so much more of the money than we Cremonans do!" he added bitterly, as if to underscore her belief that he was honest.

Adele continued to look at him. Alliance and Cinnabar estimates agreed that the Cremonan Names controlled ninety percent of the planet's wealth. They also agreed that the Names paid no taxes whatever to the central government, which explained why Cremona's government was even weaker than the norm of similarly benighted fringe worlds.

"The universe has never appeared to me to be particularly fair," Adele said at last. "I think some people should be thankful for that reality."

After a moment, she said, "Many more people should be thankful than appear to be, in fact."

Before Osorio could respond—if he even intended to—Cory's voice boomed through the speakers in unconscious attempt to mimic Daniel, *"Ship, this is Five! Prepare for liftoff!"*

The roar of the eight thrusters began to build. At full output they filled the world of all those aboard the *House of Hrynko*.

THE MATRIX, EN ROUTE TO SUNBRIGHT

Daniel waited in the *Savoy*'s airlock with his gauntlet on the pump housing. The panel was fitted with red and green lights to indicate whether the atmosphere within the lock was balanced with that on the other side of the hatch, but they didn't work. Waiting until he could feel the pump shut off gave the same result.

The vibration stilled. Daniel opened the inner hatch with one hand and lifted off his helmet—he had already unlatched it—with the other. Hogg helped his master step over the coaming. Daniel started to object, but a sudden, unutterable weariness stilled his tongue.

Hogg walked him toward the owner's bunk. Lindstrom got out of the way without objection.

"I've seen you look this bad before, young master," Hogg said, "but you'd been having more fun than you seem to be now."

Daniel sat heavily with his legs splayed out before him. He would have collapsed had it not been for Hogg's support. West, who had the next shift on the hull, and Lindstrom herself began stripping off his hard suit.

"I was going to set some course adjustments at the console," Daniel said. He thought he sounded hoarse. His voice was so soft that he wasn't sure the others present could make out his words. "I think I'd better get a little sleep first, though. Don't let me sleep more than an hour."

Hogg snorted. "You'll sleep longer than that," he said, "and I'll try to fix up some of the raw patches where these bloody suits've been rubbing you. They're eating you alive, bugger me if they ain't!"

Hogg glared at Lindstrom, who didn't look up. Working in concert with West, she wriggled the lower half of the hard suit down and off Daniel's legs. He felt sudden relief, followed as suddenly by jabs of pain as the compartment's cooler air touched the sores which the ill-fitting hard suits rubbed in him. He could wear either suit, but they merely punished different portions of his skin.

Lindstrom and West—Hargate and Blemberg were asleep, and Edmonson was still on the hull—unlatched the upper portion of the suit.

Hogg began daubing Daniel's left ankle with salve from the medical kit. "Wish I had proper lanolin salve like I would back at Bantry," he growled in a savage tone.

"It's not just what the suits cost," Lindstrom muttered defensively. She was careful not to meet the eyes of either Hogg or his master. "It's volume. You see how tight it is with two hard suits. This isn't a luxury liner here."

The remainder of the suit came off. This particular one scraped Daniel's collarbones instead of his elbows like the other. Hogg lifted away the folded rags which at least absorbed the matter leaking from the sores and got to work with the salve again.

"Oh, well, it's a cheap price to pay for Sunbright's liberty," Daniel said cheerfully.

Lindstrom snorted. "Liberty?" she said. "Is that what you call it?"

"More like rats in a pit," said West, sitting on the deck to slide his legs into the suit Daniel had relinquished. "With no food."

He looked up at the shipowner. "Nothing against you, mum," he said, "but I might not've made the run this time without Petrov promised us a bonus if we'd..."

He must have been very tired to have said that, Daniel thought as West stopped speaking with his mouth open. He seemed frozen, afraid to turn his head for fear of seeing either Daniel or Hogg.

If West had been in any doubt regarding what kind of reaction was possible, Hogg dispelled it by saying, "*I'll* give you a bonus, boyo. I won't cut your balls off just now—if you're lucky."

"That's all water under the bridge, Hogg," Daniel said. Necessity allowed him to chuckle pleasantly, which he found helped considerably with the discomfort of his long hours on the hull. "West, you've shown yourself an able spacer, and I'd be glad of your presence in any crew I commanded."

That was stretching the truth somewhat, but the old fellow did know his way about the rigging. The propulsion system was a closed book to him, even for so simple an operation as polishing the throats of the High Drive motors with emery cloth. On a ship of any size, however, there would be riggers and techs, neither of whom would be expected to know the others' job.

Daniel bent and straightened the fingers of his left hand while Hogg worked on his right shoulder. Neither set of gauntlets was comfortable, either, but at least they were overlarge rather than pinching.

"What do you mean about rats?" he said aloud, smiling as he looked at West. He didn't want him being so frightened of Hogg that he missed his hold out on the hull and went drifting into oblivion with half the *Savoy*'s inadequate stock of rigging suits. "From what I've seen—"

In Adele's typically excellent briefing materials.

"—the Alliance governor is brutal and grasping even for, well, out here. It's not my fight, but I can certainly understand the locals deciding they've had enough and trying to do something about it."

He'd almost said, "...even for this far out in the sticks." Which was true but was impolitic, since everyone aboard the yawl apart from himself and Hogg was from the Macotta Region.

"I don't know about the governor," Lindstrom said. "I didn't get involved on Sunbright till I started these runs, and I wouldn't be the sort to get invited to the governor's palace anyhow."

She stepped away from West, who now had the suit on. He got up with the slow care of a spacer whose suit fits badly.

"But what it is now . . . ," she said, sitting down on the other side of Daniel from Hogg. She reached across and took the liter-sized tube of salve. "is a bloody shambles."

Lindstrom began salving Daniel's right shoulder. She was used to the work; her hands were no firmer than they needed to be when they covered the sores themselves.

"It's easier work taking rice from the gang in the next vestry," she said, "than it is going up against the Naval Infantry and the Alliance Guards that're sitting in any place big enough to rate a garrison. And it's easier still to loot civilians who don't have a garrison or a local gang claiming to own them already."

West stepped into the airlock and dogged it behind him. He was still holding his helmet, though he'd have to latch it down soon.

"There's a lot of money in running these cargos," Lindstrom continued, her voice growing softer. "More than I could make any other way, a lot more. And the risk, well. We've been doing all right, Pensett, and I guess we'll do better with you than we did with Pete. But . . ."

She shrugged. The whine of the pump evacuating the airlock made the bunk quiver. The vibration was more noticeable through the cabin fittings than within the heavily framed lock itself.

"People are paying off old scores, now that they've got guns and there's no police to worry about," Lindstrom said. She had begun massaging Daniel's shoulder muscles instead of spreading salve. "And I guess that's all right, it's no skin off my butt, but they're pretty much treating anybody who *doesn't* have a gun as the real crop, not the rice those folks were growing. And I'm kinda tired of that. It gets old fast."

"What about the fellow running things, Kiki?" Daniel asked. Hogg had edged away slightly, giving him and Lindstrom as much privacy as the cramped compartment allowed. "The one who calls himself Freedom."

He didn't want to show too much knowledge, but it was reasonable that somebody being sent to Sunbright would have gotten a little information about the place. Besides, Lindstrom seemed to be looking for somebody to talk to.

Lindstrom frowned as though she was really puzzling over the answer. She said, "He lit the fuse, but I guess he couldn't control it once it all started going. He's there on Sunbright, he shows up here and there, but nobody knows where his base is."

She shrugged. "He can't control it—there's no 'thing' to control. Each gang does what it wants, *takes* what it wants. That's the truth of it. Nobody can stop it now, not even Freedom if he wanted to. It's going to go on until every plantation on Sunbright's been burned, and every adult outside the garrisoned cities is in a gang or's been killed by somebody who is. There won't *be* any children. And I—"

Lindstrom's fingers were no longer kneading Daniel's shoulders; instead they were clamping hard. It cost him effort and the certainty of bruises not to break the spell by saying something.

"—am making great pots of money by selling them the guns to kill themselves with. Bloody wonderful business, isn't it?"

Daniel thought in silence for...he wasn't sure how long. His mind was swimming through colored lights which sometimes formed images either from memory or of his present surroundings. He wasn't always sure which of those were which, however.

Aloud he said, "I'm very tired, Kiki. I'm sorry but I'm—"

Daniel lurched to his feet; Hogg steadied him as he walked across the compartment. The bottom bunk of the four-high tier was empty, which was a blessing. Though he would probably be able to grip the frame of a higher one while Hogg swung his legs up onto the mattress.

My brain still works, he thought with a faint smile. *Though complex problems may require a little longer than usual.*

He sat down, bending forward so that his shoulders didn't thump Hargate, who slept on the next one up.

"Kiki?" he said. "There's a way to fix it, I know there is. But you're going to have to give me a little time."

He collapsed sideways onto the mattress. Lindstrom was staring at him as if he had gone mad.

Chapter Seventeen

ABOVE SUNBRIGHT

"Extracting in five seconds," Daniel shouted. Everybody was in the cabin, but he wanted to be sure that Edmonson and Blemberg could hear him even though they were wearing the hard suits.

He mashed the button with both thumbs, a habit dating back to his first real insertion on the training vessel *Ganges*. He had been worried that the execute button would stick—as every cable and antenna in the ancient battleship's rigging seemed to—and was determined not to allow *that* to go wrong. "Extracting!"

The *Savoy* dropped into normal space with a suddenness that took Daniel by surprise, even though he had experienced it before. There were advantages to a yawl even over a relatively small warship like the *Princess Cecile*...though *how* he wished he were back in the *Sissie*!

The *Savoy*'s sensors were rudimentary, but her warship-class console processed the data instantly. Daniel had set the sensitivity to equal that of *Princess Cecile*, though of course that meant there was a great deal of electronic speculation at the higher ranges. For his present purposes, that was acceptable.

They were 350,000 miles out from Sunbright. Kiki Lindstrom, leaning over his shoulder, crowed, "That *is* Sunbright below! Brilliant, Pensett! Bloody brilliant!"

Daniel grunted. The only thing that pleased him at the moment was that the owner had remembered not to clap his raw, bruised back, as he had tensed himself to receive. But in truth—

It really was respectable astrogation to bring the *Savoy* this close to the intended location after five—almost five— days of dead reckoning from their most recent observations in normal space. He would expect to do better—very much better—in any proper warship, let alone in the *Sissie* with the crew he had picked and trained; but he was in a yawl with a minimal sail plan and a maximum of two riggers available at any one time. He should cut himself some slack.

Daniel grinned. *Not likely*. Not even a suggestion that anything short of perfect was really acceptable.

A yawl much like the *Savoy* was 100,000 miles out from the planet, accelerating on her High Drive. The slug on Daniel's Plot Position Indicator abbreviated her name to Ell which, when highlighted, expanded to Ella 919.

"That's Captain Tommines' ship," Lindstrom said, pushing uncomfortably closer to the display. "But I think he's on shares with a trading house on Cremona. *I* own the *Savoy* free and clear."

She peered further at the display and added, "Bloody hell. They don't have a prayer, do they?"

Daniel had been weighing the same question. The blockade runner was being pursued by a pair of Alliance gunboats, the *Flink* and the *Tapfer*. They had her boxed and were closing in. If the *Ella* shut down her motors for long enough to balance charges and insert, one or both of the gunboats would close and bathe her in ions before she could enter the Matrix. If the *Ella* didn't shut down, they would catch her before long anyway.

Unless Captain Tommines was a complete fool and had lifted directly into the path of the Alliance patrols, he had probably been a little careless and a little unlucky. In combat, either alone could be enough for a disaster.

To confirm his suspicion, Daniel said, "Tommines is a regular on this run, then?"

"I should say so!" Lindstrom said. "Why, he must have made it a dozen times! He'd have retired long since, I guess, but he gambles on dog races and he's got no bloody luck."

"Tommy gambles on anything," Hargate said; he shook his head. "I've seen him bet on which raindrop was going to run down the window of the bar first—and give odds if nobody'd take him on at evens. But a good skipper."

"Not a prayer," Lindstrom repeated sadly as the gunboats continued to near. Flecks of static across the RF spectrum indicated that they were beginning to fire with plasma cannon. If they were equipped with the 5-centimeter popguns which were all their frames and scantlings could bear, they still weren't within range—even to prevent their target from inserting.

The commander of the Alliance patrol must have recognized the *Ella* and made his plans based on information from her previous runs. Most captains let their computers handle liftoffs and landings; the machine didn't make mistakes, and it corrected faster than most humans could if something went wrong—a thruster failed or an antenna broke its lashings under acceleration and swung violently.

But computers always provided the same solution to the same question. The gunboats could hang well out from the planet and, when the *Ella* lifted, insert on a course they had refined for a week or more, and then extract close enough to their target to trap her.

Unless the Alliance captains were extremely good, they had still been lucky to pinch the *Ella* so closely, but some captains *were* very good. All spacers knew how much luck their trade involved.

Daniel checked both his calculations. There were risks involved, but he took a risk every time he rolled out of his bunk.

He grinned. Actually, he'd clouted himself a good one on the temple with the stanchion when he slid *into* his bunk the other day. It had stopped bleeding, but the lump was still there.

"Inserting in five seconds," Daniel said.

What?/Why?/Roger... He ignored the last and similar acceptances as surely as he did the protests from Lindstrom and from Edmonson, who fancied himself as an astrogator. Edmonson could just about push Execute after the console had calculated a course....

"Inserting!" Daniel said. His guts flip-flopped, but because he hadn't lighted the High Drive after extracting, the process was as painless as it could be.

Safely back in the Matrix, he turned to face his companions.

He smiled and said, "I thought we'd give Tommines and his crew a helping hand. And maybe—"

His smile spread.

"—we'll remind whoever's commanding those gunboats that it's not just the Fleet that teaches its officers to maneuver."

Hogg grinned with pride. He knew even less than the spacers did of Daniel's plans, but he knew the young master was about to stick it to the other fellow.

Lindstrom and the crewmen looked blank—or blankly horrified, in the case of West. Still smiling, Daniel rotated his seat to face the display again. Three process clocks were counting down, but the PPI was blank: the *Savoy* was her own separate universe here in the Matrix.

There were solid reasons why Daniel should not do what he was about to. The best were that he might fail—unlikely—or that some critical piece of the *Savoy* might break and leave them at the gunboats' mercy. Beyond those material dangers was the fact that even if successful, he would be marking the *Savoy* and himself for special attention from the Alliance forces.

Some—Adele, for one—might even have added that such boastful behavior was beneath a noble of Cinnabar.

Others were entitled to their opinions. He was Captain Daniel Leary, RCN, and he saw nothing wrong with grinding an opponent's face in the dirt when he saw the chance.

"Extracting!" he called to his companions, and he pressed Execute.

* * *

HALTA CITY ON CREMONA

"Your Ladyship?" Vesey called over the crackles, hisses, and pings which filled the boarding hold. Adele turned to see the slim blond woman emerging from the companionway, looking concerned.

An instant later, the main hatch undogged in a clanging chorus which overwhelmed any attempt at speech. The hold was the corvette's largest empty volume; echoes from its steel surfaces multiplied sounds a thousandfold.

The ramp began to squeal down on the thrust of hydraulic rams, allowing steam and ions to curl into the hold. The bite made Osorio close his eyes and sneeze, though the spacers—Adele included—took the familiar unpleasantness without reaction.

"Captain?" Adele said. She didn't really expect Vesey to be able to hear her, but she cocked an eyebrow toward the younger woman to show that she had heard. *What in heaven's name is Vesey coming to me here for?*

Adele glanced at Master Osorio out of the corner of her eye, but he was too lost in the misery of the moment to be interested in what the principal was doing. She nodded toward Vesey and moved to the back of the compartment, through the spacers who would be her escort.

Adele didn't care for commo helmets, but under ordinary circumstances she would have been wearing one now. They were short-range, but when their signal was piggybacked onto the local communications net—as Adele regularly arranged every time the *Sissie* made landfall—they could cover as much of the planet as the system itself did.

It was acceptable—necessary, in fact—for Principal Hrynko to be eccentric. It would send the wrong signal if she were technically proficient, however; that might cause the Cremonans, or at least the more sophisticated elements of Cremonan society, to take precautions which wouldn't occur to them while dealing with a blustering, arrogant noblewoman from a third-class planet.

Mind, "third class" was more complimentary than any term Adele would use for Cremona, but the locals probably didn't see it that way. Proving how benighted they were.

"Your Ladyship!" Vesey said. Her lips were almost touching Adele's right ear, but she had to shout regardless. "Since the *Savoy* wasn't in harbor, I asked Lieutenant Cory to check local records of her. It doesn't, that is, it doesn't necessarily mean there's a problem, but I'm afraid there's no evidence that she or a vessel that could be her has landed in the past five days."

Adele turned to Vesey and forced a smile. "Thank you, Captain," she said, enunciating clearly but not trying to bellow over the ambient noise. "I'm sure that the appropriate parties are dealing with the situation in their usual able fashion."

Vesey was covering a tragic expression with professional calm. If Osorio hadn't been present, Adele would have patted her hand—as a bit of theater for the younger woman rather than anything Adele herself found natural.

As soon as the *House of Hrynko* reached orbit above Cremona, Adele had entered port records and the records of all the major trading houses in Halta City. Cazelet—and a moment later, Cory—had informed her that the *Savoy* wasn't among the hundred-plus ships in Halta Harbor nor in any of the outlying anchorages scattered across Cremona.

The yacht's sensors were set to automatically search for starships on the surface of any planet they orbited. The information was not infrequently useful; and besides, it was always Adele's goal to have more data rather than less.

Vesey didn't know that. She had always been an excellent astrogator and had improved her shiphandling to a high degree of skill under Daniel's tutelage, but she had no more concept of what an information specialist really *did* than Daniel himself.

Daniel, however, assumed that Adele knew or could quickly learn everything. That wasn't precisely true, but it was actually a better default option than Vesey's subconscious belief that the only data Adele had were those things which Adele had explicitly stated she knew.

It didn't matter that Vesey had gone out of her way to provide Adele with unnecessary information. It did matter that she'd tried to help Adele and that she had come down to the entry hold in person to take the sting out of what she knew was bad news.

Adele compromised between a coldly professional response and the pat—or even hug, though she never could have brought herself to hug another person in public—by adding, "I understand your concern, Captain Vesey, but I have trained myself to examine probabilities. In this case, the probabilities—based on the considerable information about the personnel that we've both amassed over the years—are overwhelmingly in favor of a good result."

The boarding ramp clanged against its cradle on the yacht's starboard outrigger. Woetjans shouted "Hup!" and led a team of riggers to roll out the pontoon-supported gangway which would reach the rest of the way across the slip.

The dock had a floating extender, but now at high tide it had risen level with the concrete spine, where a small aircar waited. Idling fans spun swirls from the steam which the *Hrynko*'s thrusters had boiled up from the harbor.

Adele joined Osorio as he recovered himself enough to turn and wonder what had happened to his hostess. She said, "Where is the transportation you promised?"

"There on the quay," the Cremonan said. He started down the ramp at a quickstep; arriving back on his home planet seemed to have revived his mincing arrogance. "Come, don't you see the car?"

"That little toy?" said Adele. "I have an escort of twenty, my man. My position demands it."

"Not here in Halta City," Osorio said, too brusquely to have picked up on Adele's tone. "This is merely a business transaction, you agreeing terms with me and my friends. It is better that you be alone. We don't want to call attention to your presence, you see. We have rivals."

They reached the car, which was tiny. Instead of cushions, the backseat was cast out of the same thermoplastic as the body; the vehicle hadn't been luxurious when new, and it was by now at least twenty years old. Adele restrained her reflex of bringing out her data unit to identify the car precisely.

It doesn't matter. It really doesn't matter. But then, nothing really matters against the certainty of the heat death of the universe.

Adele smiled faintly. Most people would not find that

thought as reassuring as she did, so it was probably a good thing that she didn't volunteer it often.

"This is not acceptable," she said dismissively to Osorio. "Bring proper vehicles for my escort and myself or—"

She turned her palms upright as though scattering trash on the wind.

"—I will take myself off. To Sunbright, perhaps, to consult with the governor there. Blaskett is his name, is it not?"

Osorio opened his mouth to shout what would probably have been an order couched in insulting terms. His glare melted as the full import of what Adele had said struck him. Enlightenment came just in time to prevent the Cremonan from making an uncomfortable mistake.

Barnes and Dasi were in charge of Principal Hrynko's escort. The very least Osorio could have expected was a punch in the belly with the tip of a truncheon. There was a better chance that the riggers—either could have managed it alone, but they were used to working in concert—would have tossed him into the slip.

"Blaskett is a beast and a criminal, Your Ladyship," Osorio said, looking downward rather than meeting Adele's eyes. "You would not be treated well by him and his, whatever they might say at first."

In context the statement was self-serving, but Adele knew it was basically true. "You will arrange for proper transportation to my meeting, then?" she said coldly.

"Please, Your Ladyship," Osorio said. "Too public an appearance will really cause the wrong kind of attention. We Cremonans are civilized, but it is true that there are gangs here in Halta City who could be hired by unscrupulous opponents. For your own sake, please—you come with me alone to meet my fellows. The car will truly not hold more than you and me."

And the driver, Adele thought. She turned her head slightly and said, "Tovera, can you drive this car?"

"Certainly," Tovera said. "But if it stays in ground effect, it'll carry four. Master Osorio is a cute little butterball, so I don't mind sharing the back with him."

Grinning, she pinched the Cremonan's waistline. He yelped and jumped back, but that may have been outrage rather than pain.

Osorio looked toward the aircar, then back at Adele. The driver was watching the proceedings with obvious amusement. Now he volunteered in a Pleasaunce accent, "Room's maybe a problem, but the weight of all you three isn't. I can hug the ground if you like, but it's quicker if we fly."

Grinning, he added, "Besides, it's nigh three weeks since the last good rain, so the streets are filling up with garbage. *I* don't need to be down in it."

Osorio started to speak but paused; started again but looked at first Adele, then Tovera. He had probably been wondering if he could ask Adele to get in the cramped backseat with her servant because she would fit better than his rotund form.

At last he sighed and said, "All right, all right, let's get going. We'll fly, and I'll squeeze into the back with your secretary, if she must come."

"She must," Tovera said. "Cheer up, cutie. It might be more fun than you think."

She giggled.

"Ma'am?" said Woetjans as Adele stepped into the passenger compartment of the vehicle. The bosun wasn't a member of the intended escort, but she'd reached the quay to lash down the boarding bridge ahead of Adele and her companions.

"Yes?" said Adele.

"Look," said the bosun, "if you figure it's all right for you to go off with just Tovera, then I guess it is. But you know all you gotta do is holler and we'll come for you. Right through the heart of this city, and burn it down behind us if that's what it takes."

"Thank you, Mistress Woetjans," Adele said calmly. "I'm sure that won't be necessary, but if it were—"

She gave Osorio a smile, of sorts.

"—there's no one I would rather trust with the business than you and your shipmates."

She seated herself in the bucket seat beside the driver. Osorio was wheezing behind her. Perhaps that was just because he fit so tightly into the available space.

ABOVE SUNBRIGHT

"You've killed us!" Edmonson shouted to Daniel in amazement. "What were you *thinking*, Pensett?"

He reached for the controls, apparently believing that Daniel—that Kirby Pensett—had blundered and was frozen in horror. The yawl had extracted between the two Alliance gunboats.

Normally the first thing captains did on extracting was to engage the High Drive to gain velocity in normal space before they reentered the Matrix. Daniel hadn't done that for a bloody good reason.

He slapped Edmonson's hand away. He didn't bother to bellow "Keep away from the bloody board when I'm on it!" because Hogg had already caught the spacer's wrist and twisted it up behind his back to move him away from the young master.

"Wait for it, all of you," Daniel said pleasantly.

The gunboats were on courses that would eventually converge with the *Ella 919*. The *Savoy* had extracted dead astern of the other blockade runner, but on a reciprocal; she was headed directly toward the Alliance ships. Daniel grinned tightly. That had been a *very* neat piece of maneuvering, if he did say so himself.

The *Flink* and—no more than a heartbeat later—the *Tapfer* rotated to bring their ventral surfaces—with the High Drives and plasma thrusters—in line with their present course. Both gunboat captains were reacting identically to the information, though they hadn't had enough time to coordinate their maneuvers. The *Ella* was a probable capture; the just-appeared *Savoy* was a certainty if they could brake to come aboard her.

"Inserting," Daniel said, "*now!*"

He pressed Execute. The *Flink*'s captain must have understood what was happening, because the gunboat began firing. The range was too great for anything less than a heavy cruiser's 15-centimeter cannons to be effective.

The last thing Daniel noticed on his display was that the *Ella 919* had shut down her High Drives as she prepared to insert. "Good luck, Tommines," he said under his breath. "But you're on your own now."

Transition from the sidereal universe froze Daniel's spine into a column of ice. The sensation spread outward along his nerve endings, then passed. The *Savoy* was safe within the Matrix.

"What did you do there, Pensett?" Lindstrom said in the calm which immediately followed their insertion. She didn't sound angry or frightened, just...intrigued would be the best word, Daniel decided. "I don't pretend to be an astrogator, but I know you did *something*."

"I thought he'd killed us," muttered Edmonson. Hogg continued to glower in warning at the fellow, though he had released him after walking him back to the bunk tier.

The spacer looked at Daniel and said, "I did, sir. I thought you'd screwed up and they'd catch us sure, then put us out the lock without suits. I'm sorry, but I'm still not sure how you did it."

"It was a matter of timing," Daniel said. Speaking of which, he needed to keep an eye on the process clock still running. There was plenty of time available for a full explanation, though. "We didn't—"

Meaning "I didn't," but there was no advantage in rubbing the others' noses in the fact that they were completely under his control.

"—dare chance anything that involved a rigging change, because that could stick. But we knew what the present conditions in the Matrix were because we'd just extracted, right? A timed in-and-out—and in again, of course—would put us anywhere we wanted to be in the Sunbright system with just using our current sail plan. As we did, to the benefit of *Ella 919*."

He grinned at Lindstrom, then at the gaping spacers. She simply accepted what Daniel said at face value, but the crewmen had learned enough misinformation in the past to think what they had just heard was impossible.

"You can ask Captain Tommines to buy you all drinks the next time you see him," Daniel added. "Actually, I suspect he'll volunteer to do that without you asking."

It really had been as simple as he'd described it being, but an astrogation computer by itself couldn't have planned the maneuver: what the *Savoy* had done wasn't within the parameters loaded into the unit. Someone who knew his way around the software, however, could exceed the preset options by orders of magnitude.

Spacers crewing small craft here in the Macotta Region— or even in the heart of Cinnabar territory, like as not— would never have met an officer who really knew how to wring out the best of his computer. That led to the common human mistake of believing that because you'd never seen something done, it therefore couldn't be done.

"They're going to be laying for us when we extract," said Edmonson darkly. "It's not just the *Ella* got away, it's you made monkeys out of 'em with all this school-trained nonsense. I shouldn't wonder they brought up the whole gunboat squadron and we'll play hell trying to get down!"

Daniel smiled at the spacer. That was the ill-tempered bitchiness of a poseur who now couldn't even convince himself that he was good as Daniel. That Edmonson had ever imagined otherwise was proof in itself that he lived in a fantasy world.

But bitchy or not, the point was valid.

"I don't think there'll be a problem," said Daniel mildly. "We'll extract quite close in above the planet in a little under a minute."

In forty-three seconds from the word "minute," to be precise.

"The Alliance forces won't have time to react, and I very much doubt that either of those gunboats would be willing to transit to within seventy-five miles of the surface anyway."

Edmonson opened his mouth as though to speak, then closed it. West, in a tone of puzzlement rather than objection, said, "Sir, can you do that? I mean, I'd always heard—"

"If we didn't have an excellent console here," Daniel said, patting the unit as he spoke, "and if I hadn't had plenty of time to judge the Matrix, it'd be risky operating so close to a gravity well, yes."

And also if he hadn't put the *Savoy* in a situation where the risk of *not* cutting a few corners was greater than that of a close approach through the Matrix.

"As it is, we'll be fine," he concluded, beaming at his companions.

He returned to the display. Raising his voice, he said, "Hargate and Blemberg, you'd best get onto the hull as soon as we extract. We'll need to get the rig in for a very fast landing at Kotzebue. Anything that sticks and you can't manhandle into place is going to come off in the stratosphere."

The third clock reached zero. "Extracting!" Daniel called.

Chapter Eighteen

KOTZEBUE ON SUNBRIGHT

"All right, open the hatch!" Daniel called toward the entry hold. The *Savoy* had no method of internal communication beyond the unaided human voice, so he had to shout if he didn't want to walk into the hold himself. That would have meant leaving the console, which was the only way he could view their surroundings until the hatch was down.

Instead of the carillon of hydraulic pumps withdrawing the dogs securing the *Sissie*'s main hatch, the yawl provided a squeal, a metal-to-metal screech, and finally a clunk. A moment later steam, ozone, and the stench of burned organic matter puffed from the hold into the crew capsule.

They'd landed in a former rice paddy. It was obvious that manure had been used to fertilize the crop.

"Well, that's bloody pathetic," Hogg said. He stood to the left of the console, holding a carbine for himself and another for Daniel if the occasion warranted. He could have been referring to any one of several things and been correct.

The yawl's exterior sensor was a low-resolution optical lens. It was supposed to rotate fully but instead stuck within ten degrees of ninety. Daniel hoped that was the most important wedge to see, since it showed anybody approaching the hatch. He couldn't help wondering, though, if there was a bloody great plasma cannon aimed at their port side.

A small flatbed with seven floatation tires and a much smaller road tire was angling toward the yawl's hatch. Two men rode in the open cab and two more—holding carbines—in the back. The paddy's thin mud formed an undulating wake, but the tires weren't sinking to the wheel disks.

"That's Riely," said Lindstrom, who had been leaning over Daniel's right shoulder to view the display. She straightened. "It's all right, then."

Hogg snorted, but that was probably true. Lindstrom was already walking toward the hatch. Daniel rose and said, "If you're leaving the cabin, we'll need somebody on the console."

"There's no need," said Lindstrom. "We'll still be aboard."

Daniel had landed close enough to a dike that one could enter or leave the *Savoy* without necessarily sinking to the knees in muck, but it was a quarter mile to a cross-dike which led to the town straggling along the unflooded slope. The four crewmen were watching out the main hatch, waiting for a ride in the truck.

Each man clutched a purse of Alliance thalers, payment for the outward run. Spacers preferred coins to credit chips in the dives that serviced them. They could still be cheated when they were given change, but it wasn't quite as easy. There was a Sunbright currency, but apparently nobody used it.

"Hargate, watch the display for now," Daniel said as though the owner hadn't spoken. "The lens is higher than we're going to be, so if somebody comes toward us and you're not sure they're friendly, give a shout so we're ready to discuss it with them, all right?"

"Hey, I'm looking forward to a proper drink, you know," the spacer complained, but he went into the crew capsule as directed anyway. He glanced at Lindstrom, but she pretended not to see him.

"If there's a *proper* drink to be had up there," Hogg said to Daniel, nodding to the lights of the town, "then I'm a choirboy. But there's some sort of popskull, and I figure he's no fussier than I am."

"Are you expecting trouble, Pensett?" Lindstrom said as the truck slowed to turn parallel to the dike across which the ship waited. The paddies were scarred by perhaps a hundred previous landings. They were no longer in production, as best Daniel had been able to tell from orbit with the yawl's sensors, but continued irrigation made them a safe if messy place for blockade runners to land.

Three craft similar to the *Savoy* were already on the ground. A hopper car of pink rice waited beside a cutter two fields out, where half a dozen stevedores manhandled the inbound cargo onto trailers. The tractor pulling them mounted an automatic impeller on a ring on the roof.

Daniel let his wrist brush the document case in his cargo pocket to reassure himself. "No," he said truthfully.

He was pretty sure the *Savoy* had outrun anybody who might have sent a message to Sunbright about what he was carrying. "Still," he said, "the situation here is fluid—and if that turns out to mean there's a gullywasher on the way, I'd rather know it sooner than later."

Riely's truck pulled up with a final slosh of mud. A slender, bent-looking man wearing knee boots stepped from the driver's seat onto the dike. He was probably in his early thirties, but his slouch made him look decades older in the poor illumination from the yawl's hold.

"Master?" Hogg said quietly, pressing the butt of the extra carbine into Daniel's thigh to remind him of it. Instead of speaking, Daniel waved off his servant with his open left palm.

Riely hopped onto the yawl's ramp; his companion, a dull-looking, heavyset man, followed with a thump. The guards remained on the vehicle.

"I got the manifest you radioed down from orbit, Lindstrom," Riely said without enthusiasm. "If it checks out, I'll be able to fill your hold with the rice and there'll still be some on account. *If*, mind you."

"The lasers are there," Kiki said. "When can you start loading? Because I don't want to spend any longer here than I need to."

"Neither do I," the agent said, shaking his head in dismay. "I don't know how much longer I can stand this. It's worse—"

Gunfire crackled from the town: a short burst, probably a submachine gun. Daniel's head turned, but there was nothing to see in the darkness; Hogg started to present the carbine in his right hand, but he lowered it again before he'd gotten the stock to his shoulder.

"It was too far away for a pellet to even reach us," Daniel

said mildly. "Even if it'd been aimed this way."

"Bloody buggering hell," Riely whispered toward his boots. He looked up, suddenly sharper, and said to Daniel, "You're the courier to Freedom?"

"Yes," said Daniel. "You transmitted my message to him?"

He had sent the message, as directed, in a standard Alliance administrative code—the sort of thing that would be used for personnel records, but with a few changes which would prevent an unmodified receiver from translating it. That said, an experienced signals officer could decode it quickly, and an expert—let alone Adele—could do it in his sleep. It kept complete outsiders from reading the contents, but little more.

"I sent it on through the missile battery," Riely said, gesturing vaguely toward the town. "They've got a link to the system. I don't. Look, come back to my office with me. I want to talk with you."

"Not before you've checked the cargo," Lindstrom snapped.

"Mayer can do that," said the agent. "Mayer, you and Mistress Lindstrom go over the manifest. I'll send the car back for you as soon as I've gotten to the office."

"I'm coming," said West.

"And me!" said Hargate, joining the others in the compartment.

"Hey!" said Lindstrom. "You're not leaving me here alone. And Hogg, hand over those guns. They stay with the ship."

Daniel thought briefly. "Hogg," he said, "give Mistress Lindstrom one of the carbines. Mistress, we'll return the other as soon as we're able to find something of our own, which I don't think will be hard in this environment."

As if to underscore his remark, there was a single gunshot and the *crack! whee-e-e* of a ricochet from the south end of town. Daniel grinned.

"And Edmonson, you stay with her till she releases you," he added.

"Who do you think you are to give orders to me!" said the outraged spacer.

Hogg straightened his left arm and tossed Lindstrom the carbine Daniel had refused. Facing Edmonson he growled, "Who he is, boyo, is the fellow who's going to kick your balls up between your ears. Just like he did your buddy Petrov. Remember?"

"Oh, screw you both," the spacer muttered, but he said it as he turned and hopped into the crew capsule quickly enough to dodge a boot if Hogg had decided to aim one at him. Instead Hogg smiled, though Edmonson's quick retreat had probably saved him a kick—or a jab with a buttstock.

"I never checked in a cargo by myself," whined Mayer.

"Well, then it's bloody well time that you learned how!" the agent said. He stepped to the dike, then into the vehicle's cab and slid behind the steering yoke. "All right, get aboard, those of you who're coming. Pensett, you sit in the front with me."

Daniel obeyed with a faint smile. The agent—his contact with Freedom as well as the consignee on this cargo of contraband—should be more polite, even though he didn't know he was dealing with a Leary of Bantry.

On the other hand, teaching Riely to keep a civil tongue in his head wouldn't benefit the needs of the Republic. The poor fellow was obviously feeling the strain.

They pulled away from the dike. The vehicle wasn't

articulated, but all eight wheels were steerable. Daniel had always found that kind of system to be more trouble than it was worth, but Riely used it expertly. They crossed the paddy at a rumbling trot, keeping just below the speed at which the big tires would rain mud on everyone aboard.

"Have you met Freedom in the past, Pensett?" the agent said. He kept his eyes on the terrain and his hands on the yoke.

"No," said Daniel. "And I've never been on Sunbright before. Is there much fighting in this region?"

"It depends what you mean," Riely said. "If you mean with the government, no. Alliance troops only leave their enclaves in heavily armed convoys, except sometimes a squad of Special Troops lifts by spaceship from Saal and inserts into waste country to raid on foot. Kotzebue is five hundred kilometers from Saal, and there's too many people with guns around here to make a commando raid better than suicide. There's at least a dozen gangs, and most of them have mortars and automatic impellers by this time."

He twitched the steering yoke, angling to intersect the steep bank at a precise ninety degrees. That puzzled Daniel for a moment: his own reflex would have been to approach at a grazing angle to reduce the effective slope. Then he realized that this truck had a high center of gravity and was likely to overturn on a sideslope.

I suppose I can accept a certain lack of courtesy from a driver as good as he is, Daniel thought, letting the smile show.

"But if you mean fighting as in people killing each other every bloody night," said Riely, "*that* we've got in plenty. If the gangs don't have the Alliance to fight—and they don't—they'll fight each other or just shoot anybody who happens to be around!"

He slowed slightly as the front wheels touched the bank, then fed in more power to climb at a steady rate. At the top he paused momentarily so that when they toppled onto level ground the front axles took the shock without slamming them all forward.

The truck turned right on the broad, unpaved street. The permanent buildings—or semipermanent; some were solid-framed but fabric-roofed—were all on the left, but there were hovels of various sorts on top of the dike.

Some were commercial, in the sense of three-sided cribs for cheap whores or a thimble-riggers table; most just provided a bum with a modicum of protection from the weather. Since there was no street lighting, and vehicle headlights were likely to be mud-covered, the shanties must be driven over fairly often. Presumably nobody cared very much, including the victims.

The establishment just ahead to the left must have a fusion generator; the frontage was as brightly lighted as that of a spaceport terminal. Its walls of earth stabilized with a plasticizer were only waist high, and the louvered shutters which would keep out rain had been swung up against the corrugated roof. The lights threw a broad fan of illumination across the road and the wooden pole—a tree trunk—on the edge of the dike.

For a moment the pole was a blur at the edge of his vision, less interesting than the act on the stage of the dive across the street. Then Daniel jerked his head around and reached for the helmet in his bag. He wasn't wearing it because the distinctive outline would call attention to him, but he very much wanted the magnification and light-intensification that its visor would have provided.

"What *is* that, Riely?" he demanded. "That pole? It seems to be covered with human hands!"

"They're hands," Hogg confirmed from the truck bed. "Some've been there long enough to dry, but from the pong there's plenty of fresher ones too."

"They were traitors," Riely said, driving on at a sedate twenty miles per hour. There were plenty of pedestrians, alone or in pairs and gaggles, but thus far at least the truck had avoided them, or vice versa. "Or somebody said they were traitors."

He glanced at Daniel, the first time he had taken his eyes off his driving. "And I don't know what they did to make them traitors," he said. "You'd have to ask the people who killed them about that. Though I recommend you don't, because anyone who could give you a truthful answer would be likely to consider the question traitorous."

Riely stopped in front of a building with the look of a blockhouse or a prison. A man with a slung carbine swung open the gate into the walled yard; the automatic impeller in the roof cupola was pointing north down the street toward the bulk of the town.

The agent got down from his side as Daniel and Hogg swung from theirs. To Daniel's surprise, that left only the guards in the back; the *Savoy*'s crew must have jumped off during the truck's saunter down the Strip.

"Garmin," Riely said, "you and Kelly drive back for Mayer. Tell him to radio from the ship when the manifest is cleared."

They entered through the gate with Hogg walking backward behind them to watch the street. Daniel said, "Is Kotzebue the only place like this? That's in this condition, I mean."

"No, it bloody isn't," Riely said bitterly. "It's the whole planet, or it will be before long. And when it's over, there won't be anybody outside the enclaves. The rice won't be planted because the farmers are dead, and the gangsters will have left because there's nobody around to rob. And I guess I'll have gone. Or maybe I won't—I'll be dead too."

He took a deep breath. For a moment he looked ancient, a skull covered with parchment skin. He said, "You can wait here, Pensett. I don't know how long it'll be before somebody contacts you. I just pass on messages. After that, it's out of my hands."

Riely opened the steel door into his warehouse, then looked over his shoulder to meet Daniel's eyes. "It's none of my business," he said. "You do what you please. But what I *advise* you to do is get off this hellhole as quickly as you can. Because it's only going to get worse."

Two pistol shots sounded, in the street but very close. Somebody screamed until a third shot silenced her.

Riely shut the door behind them.

HALTA CITY ON CREMONA

Adele gripped the side panel as Osorio's driver pulled the aircar into a tight spiral to keep up speed as they landed in the tight space. Tovera would probably have tried to drop vertically on lift alone. The driver seemed skillful, so he was probably correct in doubting that this car's fans could safely hold it in a hover.

The bow lifted slightly as they touched down, killing their forward velocity in less than a foot after contact. They were between a pair of ground cars decorated in an ornately tacky fashion; one seemed to ape an animal-drawn carriage. The several additional vehicles included another aircar.

Tovera looked at the parked cars as she got out. "Hogg would be very impressed," she said, so dryly that a stranger would not have heard the implied sneer.

Osorio's presence had prevented Adele from gathering information about the building they'd arrived at. It was built around a courtyard with a three-story front and two stories on the remaining sides. It seemed to be a hotel, though Adele's glimpse of the legend painted on the porte cochere had been too brief to be certain.

Less than a minute with my data unit would tell me so much!

Unfortunately, it might also tell the locals too much about Principal Hrynko. She had chosen not even to wear an earbud, though Cazelet would send a warning by way of Tovera if his data search turned up a problem.

Adele almost smiled. While Cazelet pored through records, Cory was using satellites to keep a real-time watch on the building and its surroundings. She supposed that with assistants of their quality, she could afford to take an hour off for other duties.

Master Osorio waited until Tovera was out before until he climbed out of the car. He had squeezed himself as tightly as possible into the left side, facing Tovera with his knees drawn up to his chest.

She had merely smirked during the short flight. Adele was

grateful for her restraint, but she probably wouldn't have intervened if Tovera had chosen to needle Osorio further. The little man and his presumptions had been offensive from the first.

Adele had no idea of what her servant's sexual proclivities were. The subject didn't interest her to begin with, and she was fairly certain that nothing she learned about Tovera's personal life would help her sleep better at night.

There were a number of men, probably chauffeurs, chatting with inn servants around a large outside sink. The aircar's driver went to join them without asking permission.

Osorio fluffed his garments, then beamed professionally toward Adele. "Very well," he said. "I see that my colleagues are already present. We will go in and introduce you!"

"Indeed," Adele said without inflection. "Get on with it then, sir."

Doors in each two-story block opened into the courtyard. Osorio wove around the back of the carriage and minced to the larger arched doorway directly opposite the passage through to the street in the front.

Adele expected to see guards, but though the open barroom to the left was boisterously full of beer-drinking attendants, none of them appeared to her to be armed. Tovera's expert opinion might differ, but at any rate she wasn't walking into the armed camp she had expected of a conclave of clan leaders on a backward world.

Perhaps she had done Cremona an injustice. But perhaps not.

A watchful attendant opened the door on the right side of the hallway. Osorio nodded and said, "Lady Hrynko will enter with me."

"As will my aide," Adele said, before the attendant—or potentially much worse, Tovera herself—could speak.

Osorio grimaced without looking at Adele and said, "Yes, yes, both of them since it must be!"

People—almost all of them men—had turned to the door when it opened. An oval table with six matching wooden chairs—two were empty—stood on a patterned carpet in the center. Its longer axis was in line with the door on one side and the fireplace—a convection heating unit sat in the alcove, but soot indicated that it had at one point been used for real fires—opposite. On either side twelve chairs of molded plastic, most of them occupied, were in double lines facing the table.

"My fellows!" said Osorio, flourishing his hand like a conjurer. "I present to you Lady Hrynko, owner of the warship which I promised to bring you. Lady Hrynko has agreed to help the cause of Sunbright liberty when we have answered her questions."

Adele walked to the empty chair directly in front of the fireplace, ignoring the one on a long side. She didn't expect anyone to shoot her in the back, and with Tovera standing behind her, anyone who tried would have had his work cut out for him. Still, she didn't care to have people at her back when she was forced to interact with the world directly. So long as she had her console display to escape into, she didn't care who might be behind her on the *Sissie*'s bridge.

"So, Lady Hrynko," said the man facing Adele across the length of the table. "How can we help you understand how important it is that you take a moral stand on the question of liberty or servitude?"

Osorio was svelte compared to his fellows on the long sides of the table, and this fifth man was grotesquely obese. The chair in which he sat was twice the size of the others, but he filled it like a cork in a bottle.

Adele changed her mind and placed the personal data unit on the table before her. The wood was lustrously dark, and its grain was a spiral of fine black lines.

Daniel would love this. Oh, if I could have his day cabin paneled with it as a surprise!

If she ever saw Daniel again.

"The morals of a principal of Kostroma are none of your concern, my good man," she replied. The feed from Cory identified the fat man as Master Mangravite; he had arrived by the faux carriage. "The running costs of my yacht are approximately seven thousand thalers daily, however, and there will be a further charge to amortize the cost of the ship herself. Shall we say—"

Adele had been looking at her holographic display. She minimized it to meet Mangravite's eyes across the table.

"—an even ten thousand? With the first ten days in advance, and thereafter five days' payment every fifth day."

"Do you chaffer like a street vendor?" Mangravite thundered. "I understood you were a person of quality, like the rest of us at this table!"

"In my eyes, my man," said Adele in the cold, haughty voice she had learned from her mother, "you and the others of your ilk are indistinguishable from the roaches scuttering around your kitchens. I do not chaffer with you. I *direct* you!"

There was a risk that her new approach would cause these

assembled Friends of Sunbright to attempt physical violence, but Adele had decided, as soon as she saw the people she was dealing with, that the original plan would fail. Since she had to take a risk to succeed, she took the risk.

If the Friends did attack her, Adele was confident—she smiled mentally—that she and Tovera could kill everyone in the hall by themselves. They were going to run out of ammunition shortly thereafter, however, unless Tovera was even more paranoid than she had demonstrated in the past.

"Who do you think you are, woman?" Mangravite said. He slapped his hands down on the tabletop and put enough weight on them to make his flesh wobble, though not enough to really lever him out of his chair.

"I am Principal Hrynko," Adele said, raising her voice more than she cared to do. The uproar made it necessary, and even so only those seated nearest to her would be able to hear. "I own an armed yacht which my officers assure me is capable of removing the costly thorn from your flesh. As you have no other choice of dealing with the *Estremadura*, I am telling you my terms."

A real Kostroman principal might have been just as arrogant, but she would not have displayed the same perfect control; *that* also Adele had from her mother. Esme Rolfe Mundy had been committed to the principles of the Popular Party, which her husband led. She had cared deeply about the plight of the common people and told those around so at every opportunity.

That said, her mother had been acutely aware that common people *were* common, and she, a Rolfe by blood and a Mundy by marriage—two of the most noble houses on Cinnabar—

was nothing of the sort. It would have been no kindness to allow simple folk to get above themselves.

Her daughter had a different and much clearer view of the lower orders, having been a member of them for the fifteen years following her parents' execution. When necessary, however, she could still ape her mother; and it was necessary now.

Adele had visualized Cremona as being as sophisticated socially as it was technologically: a crude copy of Cinnabar or Pleasaunce. In fact, the planet was organized like a small town run by shopkeepers.

The five men at the table were wealthy by Cremonan standards, but Osorio had admitted that the bulk of the blockade running was done by off-planet factors because most of the locals couldn't afford the outlay. Privateering—or crude piracy—was as much as they were capable of.

The lesser gentry filled the chairs set to either side. A few of them appeared to have risen well into the middle class. The rest were farmers or mechanics; in a good line of business, perhaps, but obviously more comfortable wearing work clothes than in the frilled dress clothing they had squeezed into for this meeting.

An advantage to dealing with people face-to-face, Adele thought in conscious self-mockery. Given an hour and their names—which she could have gathered herself within another hour's searching—she would have known just as much about the Friends. It had only taken her a few seconds to scan the room, but she would rather have spent a few hours on the bridge of the *Princess Cecile*.

"Lady Hrynko?" said Master Osorio.

By a conscious effort of will, Adele turned her face toward Osorio instead of twitching the image into view on her display. Of the fifteen people in her direct vision at the moment, he was the only one who seemed at his ease.

"You have stated your terms, Your Ladyship," he said. "As businessmen ourselves we can appreciate both your restraint and the limited ranges of options open to us—as you noted. How quickly are you prepared to undertake the mission should we Friends agree to your terms?"

In describing the situation while they were still on Madison, Osorio had said that five of the major nobles were the real power of the Friends and that the score of other members were merely makeweights. Now that Adele had seen the Friends in conclave, she would have amended that to say that Master Mangravite, a landowner who also owned a significant trading house, was himself the Friends of Sunbright, and that four of his noble colleagues had significant shares in the risks and profits—but not in the direction.

Osorio obviously had ideas about changing the last point. He was—in a very conscious way, it appeared—using Lady Hrynko's presence and power to erode Mangravite's autocratic rule. The pudgy little man was a good deal more clever than Adele had believed.

I wonder if he has consciously been irritating me in the expectation of how I would react when I met Mangravite? He can't possibly be that clever, can he?

"I won't go into the tactics which my officers have outlined to me," Adele said, "but we will need two additional vessels of no great force in order to eliminate the *Estremadura*. Under the circumstances, the rental costs will be tantamount to purchase. Because of the risk, that is."

What Adele had taken for a window on the wall beyond Osorio was actually a bull's-eye mirror that provided a panorama of the entire room. There was a similar mirror in the opposite wall. They accomplished through simple optical methods what her personal data unit did by very sophisticated imaging software.

I shouldn't hold the Cremonans in contempt for their lack of sophistication. At any rate, I shouldn't hold Master Osorio in contempt.

"The additional ships will need crews, of course," she said. "I'll provide commanders and perhaps some key personnel, but the common spacers will be hired locally."

Mangravite had subsided briefly in the face of Adele's frozen haughtiness. The business discussion had allowed him to recover, however. He said, "What do you consider the proper conversion rate between Alliance thalers and our credits, Your Ladyship? Since of course we will be paying in Cremonan currency."

"The exchange rate doesn't enter into the matter," said Adele. Cazelet had briefed her on this point before she left the corvette. "I can't pay my crew in credits—which are scarcely useful to buy rotgut in your dockside taverns! And even if I were willing, I have to buy—procure, at any rate—ships and crews. Unless you gentlemen—"

She surveyed the room with the air of a hawk scanning a meadow for prey.

"—and both you ladies care to provide the ships and crews out of your private resources, I'm sure that the owners will require hard currency. As will the spacers, since the blockade runners they would otherwise sign with pay in thalers. Or florins, of course."

The room broke into general discussion, occasionally heated. The men to Mangravite's right and left both leaned toward him and began to speak with worried earnestness. Mangravite snarled at the beginning but then subsided. He clenched his huge fists and hunched like a lion being pelted by hail.

Osorio smiled toward Adele in a commiserating fashion. After waiting with his hands before him for long enough to let the first edge of the arguments pass, he rose to his feet and raised his right arm.

"My fellow patriots!" he said, turning to sweep the room with his attention. "A moment, if you please!"

When the level of noise reduced abruptly, Osorio said, "My friends, we are being discourteous to our guest. Please, for the honor of Cremona and of our assembly, let me discuss what I see as a possible solution. Do I have your approval?"

Adele happened to glance at Mangravite at the other end of the table. *If looks could kill...,* she thought.

The fat man's face had swelled in purple fury. All the renewed babble was agreement with Osorio in some fashion or other. *It won't matter how rich you are if you burst a blood vessel in your brain.*

Osorio bowed to one side of the room, then the other. Still standing, he said to Adele, "Lady Hrynko, we Friends cannot quickly raise such sums in hard currency, but we can provide you with notes to be redeemed in hard currency which you can negotiate."

"That isn't acceptable," Adele said. "I would have to discount them by ninety percent to get anyone to take them."

She would never be a financier, but years of learning to manage her increasing wealth—and the training which Daniel's elder sister, Deirdre, had provided in handling that wealth—had taught her a great deal. Deirdre Leary approached finance in the same spirit and with the same genius as her brother showed for astrogation.

"Not by so much, I hope," Osorio said, nodding, "but with a significant discount of course. We would adjust the notes to reflect a portion of that discount. And—"

Adele raised an eyebrow as she waited. She wondered how much of this performance was for Osorio's fellows rather than really aimed at her.

"—after your victory over the *Estremadura*, the value of our notes will increase to near par, providing Your Ladyship with a very handy profit, is it not so?"

There was a gasp of delight among the Friends who understood the proposal, and a wash of whispering among those who did not. Finance at this level was unfamiliar territory for many of those present.

Adele considered the matter. Osorio was putting a very positive face on the proposition, but it wasn't completely unreasonable. Adele needed a plausible reason to do what she intended to do anyway: punish the *Estremadura*. This offer provided that color, though she would ask Cazelet to knock down the details.

There was one other point to pursue, not so much for its own sake as because it would further Adele's plans to learn as much as possible about the affairs of the Sunbright rebels and thus their leader, Freedom. She let her eyes rest on the fixtures which flanked the door, cascades of dangling crystals that diffused the light efficiently while sparkling like the sun on wavetops off the coast of the Leary estate.

"Insofar as the hire of the *House of Hrynko* is concerned," Adele said, "I accept Master Osorio's offer as a matter for detailed discussion with my business manager. That does not cover the hire or more likely purchase of two subordinate vessels and payment for their crews, however. *That* will require hard currency, as you put it, and I will *not* defray those expenses myself."

Again there was a babble. Osorio, still standing, settled his face warily. He had been grinning broadly about the room, though he was careful not to let his gaze settle on Mangravite. From the fat man's expression, it was not beyond imagination that he could be goaded into lurching from his chair and crushing his rival like an avalanche.

"I can suggest an alternative to you Friends finding the thalers yourself," Adele continued, raising her voice. Silence spread in waves. Those who had understood what she had said whispered to those nearby until everyone in the room had been informed.

Adele looked left, then right, before focusing on Osorio. The Friends *could* provide hard currency in the necessary quantities: the five major members each controlled shares in blockade runners to the equivalent of two full ships apiece. It would require many days and the publication of their private financial records—which Adele could do, but which would make an enemy of each member affected—in order to get that money, however.

"I believe your group has influence with the government of Cremona?" she said blandly. Mangravite sneered, and both men to Adele's right at the table chuckled at the idea. They knew, as she did, that the government of Cremona was whatever a wealthy and powerful individual wanted it to be.

"Very good," Adele said. "If the government is willing to give me authorization, I will raise the necessary sum in the form of loans from the foreign factors here in Halta City. Can you procure me that authorization?"

This time the chatter was delighted. Mangravite sat silently, his fists clenched like hams on the table before him.

"I believe that should be possible, since the proposal doesn't affect any member of this group," Osorio said, cutting through the enthusiasm.

He turned and for the first time looked directly at his rival. "That is true, is it not, Master Mangravite? Do you agree that we Friends of Sunbright should use our influence to permit Lady Hrynko to solicit loans for this purpose?"

"The factors will never agree!" Mangravite said. His words were almost lost in their growling overtones.

"I believe you're wrong, my good man," Adele said, the syllables sounding like whipcracks. "But in any case, I do not require anything of you save the legal authorization to try. Do I have that agreement?"

No one spoke for a moment.

Adele put down her control wands, though she kept her hands on the tabletop for now. "Do you grant me that authority, Master Mangravite?" she repeated.

"Yes, damn you!" the fat man said. "And much good may it do you!"

Shouts of delight filled the room. Several Friends clustered about the beaming Osorio.

It will, Master Mangravite, Adele thought as she leaned back into her chair for the first time since she sat down. *It will serve my purposes very well.*

Chapter Nineteen

HALTA CITY ON CREMONA

Osorio's driver set the aircar down on the apron in front of the three-story brick warehouse. Adele had asked to borrow him with the vehicle. Not only was the fellow very skillful, he could stay with the car while she and Tovera were inside. There were bollards to keep trucks away from the building except at the loading docks, but he had simply skimmed over them.

"I'll do my best, mistress," Tovera said as she eyed the Wartburg Company headquarters. "But there'll be a lot of places to snipe from inside, and if we have to fight our way down from the penthouse..."

The walls on the ground floor were solid, though orbital imagery had showed that there were windows on the courtyard side. The warehouse wasn't air-conditioned, so the multi-pane casements on center pivots the length of the second and third floors were necessary for ventilation as well as for light during daytime. The glass was clear, in a manner of speaking, but its coating of grime would block vision as thoroughly as muslin curtains.

"We'll hope it doesn't come to that, Tovera," Adele said austerely as she started for the pedestrian door, which had been propped open by what seemed to be the stator of an electric motor. "Master Brock agreed politely to meet me in his office, after all, so I can scarcely object to where that office is, can I?"

Adele wore a russet pantsuit rather than formal robes. She was no longer the technological illiterate she had portrayed on Madison and had intended to remain on Cremona. Her current role—for this too was acting; she was acting in all her appearances outside the hull of the *Princess Cecile*, which had become her real family home—was that of a wellborn woman from a world more sophisticated than Cremona.

She smiled mentally. That would be true for a real principal of Kostroma, and Mundy of Chatsworth on Cinnabar was all those things in spades.

The racket inside the warehouse was punishingly louder than it had been in the street, even with the door open. Fans thrummed in the ceiling, diesel-powered forklifts blatted under heavy load, and paired elevators—when her eyes adapted, Adele saw a set at each corner of this wing—squealed and groaned. Presumably all the same things were happening on the upper floors, adding their counterpoints.

The light banks high above were probably adequate, but for the first moments after Adele entered, she had the impression of having fallen into a deep cavern. The massive wooden beams of the ceiling were covered with soot which absorbed any illumination that fell on them. Workmen were wraiths, dwarfed by the machinery and the piles of goods among which they moved.

Adele led the way along the aisle, between the front wall and stacks of large crates which often encroached on the passage painted in yellow on the floor. The section foreman was in a miniature office whose walls were glass from above waist height. The three loading docks were beyond him, and a passenger elevator was just in back.

That elevator, like its larger brethren at the ends of the building, was a platform riding between two pillars without a cage. Again like the freight elevators, it was one of a pair on the same cables; one rose as a counterweight when the other half dropped.

The foreman was alone in the office, glaring at a flat-plate display and growling into a handset cradled between his ear and shoulder. Adele tapped on the glass politely. The foreman angrily waved them away.

Does he think I was asking his permission? Adele entered and sat down.

She didn't hear the door close behind Tovera so much as she felt the level of ambient noise reduce. The office must have an active cancellation system.

"Get your bloody asses out!" the man said with a brusque wave of the hand holding a memorandum book. "I'll tell you when I'm ready to see you!"

Adele brought out her data unit. She shrank the foreman's display and froze the console. That shut off his phone also, since outside communications were through it.

"I am Principal Hrynko," she said, her tone coldly polite. "I have an appointment with Master Brock."

"What in blazes happened to my console?" the foreman said, flipping the external power switch back and forth with no result except faint mechanical clicks from the toggle. "It just cut out!"

It would be nice if I lived in a world in which people were either smarter or more polite, Adele thought, not for the first time. *But I've learned to make do with what I have.*

Aloud she said, "Your equipment will not work until you have taken me to Master Brock. I suggest you do that so that you can go back to your business."

The foreman stared at her, his lower lip trembling. He was a brawny man in his fifties. A thin scar curved across his scalp, turning the hair white along its track, and he was missing the lobe of his right ear.

"Are you a witch?" he said in hoarse surmise.

Adele blinked. *I thought Cremona was unsophisticated. Apparently it's simply backward.*

"More like a demon if you irritate her," said Tovera. "I suggest you do what she says and avoid that danger. Of course—"

Tovera smiled. The expression was inhuman, which was an accurate description of the pale woman herself.

"—I wouldn't need to be irritated to open your belly and start winding your guts out on a stick. Why don't you take us to your master and avoid that too?"

"The elevator," said the foreman, twisting his head enough to suggest the one beside his office. He didn't turn too far to keep his eyes on Adele, however. "Just pull the cord when you get on and pull it again when you're at the penthouse."

"Thank you," said Adele. The platform would be tight enough for two, so she didn't object to the plan. She turned on his console and got to her feet.

The noise buffeted her when she stepped out, but she had a direction now and didn't notice distractions. The foreman was still gaping as she and Tovera walked around the office. He seemed to have forgotten the phone in his left hand.

Tovera stepped onto the platform. It was four feet square and supported by a cast-iron double yoke; a chain hung from each arm to a corner. The cord that the foreman mentioned ran up through the hole in the ceiling and presumably to a switch at the roof level; it didn't move with the platform.

Adele got on also. Tovera held her attaché case half-open, with her right hand inside on the concealed submachine gun, so Adele tugged at the cord. For a moment nothing happened; then the elevator began to rise with a series of individual jerks as though it was being hauled up on cogs instead of a cable drum.

Tovera was trying to look in all directions, not forgetting straight up through the hole in the ceiling. Adele was determined not to let her servant's paranoia make her equally nervous, but it was only by effort of will that she kept herself from gripping the pistol in her pocket.

Adele looked outward as the elevator rose, viewing the warehouse. The second floor looked the same to her as what she had seen at the ground level, and the third as well when the platform rose into it. The warm, nutty odor of pink rice permeated the big building, though Adele didn't identify any storage hoppers.

Men—and perhaps a few women, as genderless as spacers

in dim light and their loose outfits—worked among the vast array. They reminded her of ants, absorbed in their business, and seemed as oblivious of her scrutiny as those insects would have been.

The platform rose into the arched cover—it had no front or back, so it couldn't be called an enclosure—on the roof. It seemed silent after the cacophony within the warehouse proper.

Adele pulled the control rope firmly. In all probability the elevator would have shut off automatically at the top, but she saw no reason to trust the quality or even the good sense of the engineer—or mechanic—who had designed the system.

Turning to Tovera as they stepped off, Adele said, "I'm sure we could have jumped clear if it hadn't stopped."

"Yes," said Tovera. "But if the elevator destroyed itself, we would have been faced with starvation since we couldn't have gotten down again. Life is filled with dangers."

She cocked her head toward the penthouse—actually a shed of structural plastic, large enough for two rooms. "Of course, we could hold out for a little longer," Tovera said, "by eating Brock and any office staff he has here."

Adele smiled as she followed her servant to the door. Tovera had no more sense of humor than she had a conscience, but she had learned to imitate the sort of jokes that ordinary humans made. The problem was that a sociopath finds cannibalism just as funny as she does anything else.

So, fortunately, did her mistress.

Adele stepped in front of the door. "You can avenge me if I'm shot down on the threshold," she said.

Does Tovera realize that is a joke? she wondered. Not that it mattered, as her servant would find that response as natural as breathing.

The secretary at the console in the outer office was male, though young and attractive enough, Adele supposed. Instead of asking the newcomers' business, he turned his head toward the open door behind him and called, "Hey, boss? That Sunbright lot's here to see you. They're women."

"Well, send 'em in!" said the man within, also shouting through the door. "And tell Herrigord that I'll get back with him in ten minutes."

"You heard the man," said the grinning secretary, jerking his thumb in the direction of the door. "I'd say he doesn't bite, but I'd be lying."

Tovera grinned at him as they went past.

Adolph Brock was as squat as a fireplug. If he had been standing, his breadth would have made him look shorter than he was, but even so he probably wasn't as tall as Adele. He still had his hair, but it was white and cropped so closely that he would have looked bald at any distance.

Tovera closed the door behind them. Brock barked a laugh and said, "You needn't have done that, because you're going straight out again. I'm seeing you to tell you to your faces that I'm not giving you a loan. I don't consider lining the pockets of a monkey from Kostroma to be a good business decision. Now, out!"

Adele sat on one of the straight chairs facing the outfitter's desk and took out her data unit. The room's furniture was wooden and attractive, though of a heavier style than the appointments of her own townhouse in Xenos. She had expected functional, mismatched pieces of metal and plastic.

"Since I'm here, Master Brock," she said, "I'll explain the aspects of my proposition that I didn't choose to state on the phone or put in electronic form."

"You've nothing to say!" Brock said. For the moment, he appeared to be more nonplussed than angry. "Look, I know people in the shipping business and ex-Fleet folk too. I put your proposition to them and they say—every bloody soul of them, I mean! They say you wouldn't stand a prayer against the *Estremadura*. She's bigger, better armed, and she's got top Fleet officers and a crew they picked themselves from pirate-chasers when the Peace of Amiens was signed and two thirds of the ships went into ordinary."

He snorted. "I figure you're a con man," he said. "But if you're not, you're bloody crazy."

"I'm sorry I can't convince you that investing in my proposal will rid you and your fellow…entrepreneurs, I will say, of a serious overhead expense in the form of the cruiser," Adele said. "Still, I accept that the only way to change your opinion will be to demonstrate the fighting ability of my yacht. Before you give your final opinion—"

"Listen, bitch!" Brock said; he *was* angry now. "I've *given* my final opinion. You couldn't change it if you offered to suck me off right here in my office! Now, get out or I'll throw you out. And you'll be lucky if I don't throw you right off the roof!"

He isn't speaking to Mundy of Chatsworth. He's speaking to a principal of Kostroma, a group of people for whom I have no more regard than he does.

But she trembled slightly. Brock had started to get up from

his chair but chanced to meet Adele's eyes. He subsided with a suddenly wary expression.

"I regret that I have to do this, Master Brock," Adele said, as calm as ice again, "but have you considered the legal situation in which you might find yourself if your activities came to the attention of the authorities?"

Brock blinked, trying to make sense out of what he had just heard. "What are you talking about, woman?" he said. "I'm not violating any laws, and I don't suppose it's a secret that the government here—the people in the government; I don't know how much money trickles through to the treasury—are making a bloody good thing out of the operations of the Wartburg Company."

Adele completed the operation her wands had just directed. She met the outfitter's eyes again and smiled, in a manner of speaking.

"I've just transferred some information to your console, sir," she said. "Will you please take a look at it? It will be there when you bring your display up."

"What the hell?" Brock said, again puzzled. He punched his virtual keyboard, however. His keystrokes were as forceful as Daniel's own.

"What is this?" he said, shrinking the hologram again to look at Adele.

"That's the report which will go to the Fifth Bureau if you refuse to provide the loan I request, sir," Adele said primly. "And this—"

Her wands fluttered like ballet dancers executing a complex routine.

"—is the list of your relatives and associates living within Alliance territory. That's mostly Pleasaunce, of course, but also Conbay, Mortain, and half a dozen other worlds. That list will accompany my report, though—"

She coughed delicately.

"—in my experience, the Fifth Bureau would be able to compile it very nearly as quickly as they can read my copy. I find the Alliance of Free Stars to be a marvel of bureaucratic organization."

Brock's lips moved silently for a moment as he read. He slid the display to the side and looked at Adele.

"How did…," he began in a growl that was barely human. He stopped himself. "It doesn't matter how you learned this stuff, docs it?" he said, more normally. "It wouldn't matter even if it wasn't straight, not with the Fifth Bureau doing the checking."

He slammed his right fist down on the desk, the only external sign of his fury.

"Which it is, as much as I say off the top of my head," he said, almost conversational again.

He paused, his face hardening. "You're not a monkey from Kostroma, though, are you?" he said. "Who are you? You're bloody Fifth Bureau yourself, aren't you? It doesn't matter whether I play ball or not. It's over—"

Brock's hand jerked violently toward his holographic display.

"—for all these anyway!"

"It doesn't matter who I am," Adele said calmly. "But it matters a great deal to your off-planet associates that you accept my business proposition. Of that you can be assured."

Brock said nothing for a moment. He gestured to the display

again and said, mildly this time, "Are you going to strong-arm all the trading houses like this? Or is it just me?"

"I have appointments with the other two large houses which have links within the Alliance," Adele said. "Coincidentally, you three are the largest firms on Cremona. That spreads the risk enough that none of the houses involved needs feel that it's being backed into a corner. I don't want anyone to—"

She grinned slightly.

"—be driven to desperate measures."

"How quick do you need an answer?" Brock said.

"I'll be back in two days," Adele said, rising. "After I've discussed the proposition with Santina Trading and Loesser Brothers."

"All right," said Brock. "I'll have an answer then."

Adele started for the door to the outer office. Tovera, who had been standing beside the doorway throughout the interview, said, "Master Brock?"

"Eh?" Brock said, frowning as though his stylus had just spoken to him.

"It doesn't matter who she is," Tovera said, nodding toward Adele. "But *I* used to be Fifth Bureau. You might keep that in mind in case you decide your best plan is that we have an accident here in the building."

Unexpectedly, Brock laughed. "I didn't build this company without learning how to handle your type, mistress," he said. "Sure, it'd cost, but there's always costs. Your boss, though—"

He dipped his head in a seated bow.

"—I *can't* handle, not even if I kill her. So don't worry about tripping down the elevator shaft."

Adele led the way into the outer office. The secretary eyed them warily.

Behind her, she heard Tovera say to the secretary, "You're lucky, little fellow. Your boss is a lot smarter than most."

KOTZEBUE ON SUNBRIGHT

Daniel was watching the ditch behind Riely's storehouse when the apparent fish bobbed to the surface, just as it had done on the two previous evenings. It was the length of his finger, white and swollen as though it had already begun to decay.

Hogg stood six feet away, far enough that he wouldn't disturb his master's observations. Under his breath, he sang, *"Grieve, oh grieve, oh tell me why..."*

A pair of winged insectoids came from opposite directions, drawn by the shining white belly. Both were females, looking for carrion in which to insert their eggs. They dodged back and forth, neither willing to settle until she was certain that the other wasn't a predator preparing to attack when her ovipositor was sunk too deeply to be quickly withdrawn.

Hogg didn't move very much. He turned his head, and occasionally his torso twisted in order to allow him to scan the terrain in all directions. His left hand was in his pocket, but his right was loose and never very far from the stocked impeller leaning unobtrusively against the drainpipe from the roof of the building.

"Because he had more gold than I...," Hogg sang.

One of the insectoids eased toward the fish by tenths of

an inch, two forward and one back. At last she touched, then
settled on her eight jointed legs. A hair-fine ovipositor uncoiled
from her tail, probed the fish, and finally straightened to stab
downward. Nearly its whole half-inch length sank in.

"But gold will melt and silver fly—"

The wing-like sides of the fish's flattened body folded
upward to envelope the insectoid. The skin covering them was
dark, in contrast to the white streak along the midback. Even
knowing by now that the wings were there, Daniel had seen
only hints of the real outline of the fish below the surface of
the ditch water.

"—and he will be as poor as I," Hogg sang.

He picked up the impeller by the grip and fore-end. With the
same lilt in his voice, he added, "I think this truck's stopping
here, young master, and I shouldn't wonder if it's come for us.
Not before time, *I* say."

Daniel stood and turned. The fish flushed the white stripe to
merge with the rest of its skin coloration and wriggled to vanish
on the bottom of the ditch. The spiked edges of its wings were
already shredding its prey against the gristly back; shortly it
would extend its toothless mouth upward and suck in the bits.

The truck was a four-axle military vehicle. Originally it had
had rubber tires, but they had worn off and it was running on
the spun-wire wheels themselves. Off-road it probably made
little difference, but here on pavement the undamped *thrum* of
the wheels would be maddening.

"I suspect you're right, Hogg," Daniel said. "It's time to see
if we're the fish or the unfortunate mother."

He turned a friendly smile toward the six soldiers climbing

from the vehicle. Automatic impellers in a twin mount took up most of the most of the truck bed, so the troops in gray uniforms had been squeezed to the margins.

Hogg grunted. "I'm nobody's bloody mother," he said.

The passenger in the cab of the truck wore a tailored uniform with only the fabric color in common with the loose fatigues of his underlings. Besides that, his tunic and trousers had silver piping along the seams and there was silver braid on the saucer hat he donned as he watched Daniel approaching.

"You're the courier with the dispatches I'll take to Freedom?" the officer said. He was small and looked remarkably *neat*, even for having ridden in the cab rather than the truck's open bed.

"I'm Kirby Pensett," Daniel said pleasantly. "And I have material for Freedom, yes. May I ask who you are, sir?"

"My name is none of your affair, sir," the little man snapped. "Now, get the dispatches for me and you can go about your business."

The building's door opened and Riely stepped out. He wasn't armed, but the assistant with him carried an electromotive shotgun. From its gray enamel finish, it was a military weapon rather than a sporting gun like the ones Daniel had hunted with on Bantry.

"Hello, Kidlinger," Riely said. "Do you have an outgoing load already? I hadn't expected you for twenty days at least."

"I'm here for the dispatches," the officer said stiffly, irritated that the agent's greeting had made him look a prat even to himself; Daniel hadn't been in any doubt about the matter to begin with. "I'm to take them to Freedom."

"I haven't received orders about that," Riely said, his

expression becoming wary. "My understanding...but look, let's all come inside where we can sit down and have a drink."

"I don't have time or need for a drink," Kidlinger said, "and I don't give a fart for your understanding. Get me the dispatches and do it *now*. In the field, we don't have time to bugger around with your civilian red tape!"

He patted the flap of his full-coverage pistol holster significantly.

My goodness, he is *a little man,* Daniel thought. In a conciliatory tone he said, "I'm afraid, Colonel Kidlinger—is it colonel? I'm afraid that my directions were to hand the case over to Freedom personally."

He was careful not to touch the cargo pocket where the case had remained ever since he boarded the *Savoy*. Kidlinger appeared to think the documents were inside Riely's fortified dwelling, and at this point any indirection was a good thing.

Though Daniel continued to smile, he was thinking tactically now. Neither he nor Riely were armed. Riely's man was, but the fellow obviously didn't expect trouble, and the three assistants still inside the building couldn't get out in time to affect the business.

On the other side—six soldiers with carbines, and the driver, who might have a weapon also, still in the vehicle. Plus Kidlinger's pistol, but the officer was very far down on Daniel's list of priorities. The troops had left their truck's twin-mount unmanned, but the automatic impeller in the guard tower couldn't depress enough to bear on anything useful, either.

"I didn't bloody ask your opinion, did I, yokel?" Kidlinger shouted at Daniel. He fumbled with his holster flap. "You're on Sunbright now, and the representative of Free Sunbright gives the orders. That's me!"

If I act now, we can take them, Daniel thought. Hogg's long-barreled impeller wasn't the best choice for such close quarters, but he would make do. *If we don't have surprise, though—*

"Sir," Daniel said, raising his hands to shoulder level, palms out. "I assure you that—"

A light aircar swung around the other side of Riely's store. It must have approached at low level—*ground* level—over the hilly wasteland to the north of the town. Hogg snarled a curse and presented his impeller with a speed that would have terrified Kidlinger if he understood what it implied for his own survival had the present discussion turned into a firefight.

Two soldiers clambered back onto the truck and sat at the twin mount. The others lifted their carbines hesitantly, looking from their officer toward Hogg, then back to the aircar, which had settled to a halt.

"Put your gun up, Hogg," Daniel said crisply. "It isn't needed here."

The driver—the car's sole occupant—stood up. He wore a filter scarf which covered his lower face.

"Sir?" said Riely.

The driver pulled the scarf down. He was scarcely older than Daniel; certainly he was under thirty.

"Hello, Riely," he said, and he jumped out of his vehicle and walked toward the group. "And you too, Kidlinger, though I didn't expect to see you this far out of your area of responsibility."

"Sir, I thought...," the officer said. He stammered to a halt.

Daniel stepped forward, extending his hand. "I'm Kirby

Pensett," he said. "The Chief on Madison gave me dispatches for Freedom."

"Well met, then, Pensett," said the newcomer, shaking his hand. "I'm known as Freedom. You and I have matters to discuss."

Chapter Twenty

HALTA CITY ON CREMONA

"I don't see that a wicker cage would add significant weight," Adele said as she pulled the cord firmly. The elevator groaned to a halt. The cable was wound on a drum, as she had expected, but the teeth of the gears driving the drum were each the size of her thumbs.

"Brock will ride it more than anyone else," Tovera said as they stepped off the platform. "If he wants to kill himself, why should anyone care?"

She paused and added, "Or kill the boy. Who isn't my type."

Tovera's face was deadpan. Of course her only two expressions were that deadpan—and a grin that would etch glass.

Brock's secretary had been waiting in a folding chair leaned against the shaded west end of the so-called penthouse. As the elevator trembled to a halt, he got to his feet and executed a very respectable bow.

"The boss told me to send you through and then stay out of the way," the young man said. "We also serve who only stand

and wait, I like to say. Or sit and wait, in this case."

He opened the door; Adele bobbed her head to acknowledge the courtesy, making a mental note to learn more about the secretary. He was certainly more than he had seemed initially.

The partition between the inner and outer offices had been removed, turning the penthouse into a single long room. Brock was at his desk. The three partners who owned Santina Warehousing, and the Cortons—husband and wife—who owned Loesser Brothers, sat behind the two folding tables which had been set up facing the doorway.

"Mistress Hrynko or whatever your name is," Brock said, "you know my colleagues, since you've talked to them too. We decided to handle this together, instead of you dicking around from one of us to the next."

"I'm glad to see you all," Adele said, taking the straight chair which had been left for her beside the door. Sitting, she placed her data unit on her lap and brought up its display. "Will you tell me your decision, please?"

This whole business was mummery. She knew that the outfitters had agreed to the loan on her terms and knew also that they would be together in Brock's office when she arrived this morning.

Her tendency as a librarian was to lay all her information out immediately. The intelligence mindset to which she had been exposed if not trained in demanded that she conceal her sources and methods so that she could continue to use them.

In the end Adele had pretended to be ignorant, not because she was thinking like a spy but because she was Mundy of Chatsworth. Esme Rolfe Mundy would have been distressed to learn that her daughter was boasting of her skills—and to a gathering of tradesmen besides!

Adele felt her mouth twitch into a hint of a smile. Her mother had lived in a very simple black-and-white world. To a considerable degree, that two-value logic carried Adele through life as well. It wasn't so very different from Daniel's "Cinnabar, right or wrong!" attitude after all.

"We'll subscribe the loan," Brock said, looking across the line of his fellows. "On your terms."

"We should get at least another point of interest for the risk, though!" said Addersheim. He glared at Adele, then at Brock. He had started thirty years before as Santina's accountant and still looked the part, though he was now the senior partner.

"As I said, Lady Hrynko," Brock said wearily. "On your terms."

Addersheim muttered something, only half-audible and not a word anyway. Adele knew from her electronic eavesdropping that he hadn't been able to convince even his two partners that they should press the point: they and the other outfitters understood that this was not a normal business transaction.

He's the sort who would refuse to open the ammunition locker during a surprise attack unless he were given the correct authorization, Adele thought as she looked at the accountant.

She was more amused than not by the situation, but when Addersheim met her eyes again he started back. Well, she couldn't help it if people misread her expressions. They tended to misunderstand her words also, despite the fact—or perhaps because of it—that she was extremely precise in picking the words she used.

Aloud she said, "Since you're all in agreement, I propose that each firm now transfer its portion of the loan to an account under my control at the Venture Bank of Cremona. I chose the Venture Bank because you all have accounts there already."

That was true, but it was one of two reasons. Unusually for this region, the Venture Bank had links with Cinnabar rather than with one of the Alliance core worlds. Adele doubted that it mattered, but she had made this choice in case it did.

It was very possible that Speaker Leary, the man who had ordered the massacre of the Mundy family, was the bank's ultimate backer. Well, Adele herself kept her now-considerable prize-money account in a Leary bank also. It paid a good rate of interest to RCN officers.

Brock looked at his fellows, shrugged, and said, "*I* have no objection."

Mistress Corton was three years older than her husband and had provided the money for the purchase of Loesser Brothers. According to Cazelet, Master Corton made all the business decisions though his wife was the public face of the company.

Now she leaned forward and stared piercingly at Adele. Instead of answering Brock's implied question, she said, "You've already bought ships and hired the crews, even though you think we don't know that. What were you going to do if we refused to give in to your extortion?"

What a remarkably stupid person you are, mistress, Adele thought. Aloud she said, "Members of my staff have negotiated to purchase and crew a pair of small freighters, but the discussions weren't secret. All the drafts we've written are contingent on there being money in the account, of course."

She coughed to get a moment to think. *How would Daniel handle this?* Very possibly by sweeping the woman into his arms and kissing her. Adele couldn't see the utility in adopting that course herself.

"As experienced businesspeople," she said, trying to smile, "I think the increase in your profits from the elimination of the *Estremadura* should be obvious."

That was literally true. The statement didn't imply that Adele thought Mistress Corton would see it, or even that she would be able to put on a tunic right-side to in the morning without help.

"Look, let's move on," Brock said. His fists were clenched, and he deliberately stared toward the outside door so that he didn't let his eyes fall on Mistress Corton. "Yes, we'll transfer the funds now and be done with it."

He turned to his console. Addersheim and Master Corton brought out personal data units not very different from Adele's own.

Adele glanced at her own display. A pulsing red alert signal suffused it, then coalesced into the words—in block letters and still red—EMERGENCY! GUNMEN HAVE CAPTURED YOUR CAR!

"Stop!" Adele said to the startled outfitters. That probably confused them more than it warned them, but a part of Adele's upbringing demanded that she not take money under false pretences. Whatever was going on outside, it certainly changed the circumstances under which she had negotiated the loan.

She had several options, but she chose to activate the active sound cancellation field and communicate by voice. The little data unit's capability didn't compare to that of her console on the *Sissie*, but it would do for now.

"Go ahead," Adele said. She was focused on the display, but she was vaguely conscious that Tovera had stepped in front of her in case one of the outfitters was able to read lips.

"Mistress," said Cory, *"you need to get out now. There wasn't any trouble at first because they didn't think you'd get the loans, but now that it looks like you did, there's a dozen or more interests that've gotten together to stop you."*

Adele was looking at the data which the *Princess Cecile* streamed to her. Cazelet was probably responsible for that, since Cory was talking.

"There's naval and military officers and politicians, afraid of the power Lady Hrynko is getting," Cory continued. *"There's some investors in the* Estremadura, *and the leader's one of the Friends, a big man here, a fellow named Mangravite. There's a gang, half a dozen gangs, on the way to the Wartburg warehouse now, but the first bunch already grabbed your aircar. Over!"*

Adele expanded the map to fill her display; Cazelet had also included nodules with background data on each of the parties involved in this alliance against her. The tiny bead representing her location at the Wartburg Company was a mile and a half from the corvette's berth in the harbor.

If the aircar had been available, the only risk if they left now would have been an accident caused by Tovera's overly precise driving. As it was—

The disorganized nature of the attack worked in her enemies' favor: red beads scaled to the degree of threat were approaching along all the routes leading to the warehouse.

The force leaving the *Sissie*—a very large blue bead—would be able to shoot its way through any of them, but not *quickly* on the streets of an unfamiliar city.

"Yes, all right," Adele said. "We'll meet you on the way."

She shut down the cancellation field and rose. Tovera stepped aside; she was holding her small submachine gun openly. The expressions of the Santina and Loesser representatives ranged from uncertain to terrified, but Brock was merely guarded. His right hand was below the surface of his desk.

"Master Brock," Adele said. "Can you drive one of the trucks at your loading dock now?"

"Yeah, if it's any of your business," Brock said. The growl in his voice wasn't anger. "I can. Going to tell me what this is all about?"

"People are coming here to kill me," Adele said. "The leader is a man named Mangravite. You will drive me and my aide to the harbor, if you please, which will also lead most of the attackers away from your warehouse. From my reading of Master Mangravite, he's hoping to eliminate one—"

She glanced at the other outfitters, ignoring their gabble.

"—or several of his rivals in the process."

"*That* bastard," Brock said, rising to his feet. He dropped the shoulder holster and thrust the long pistol he had taken from his desk under his belt. "I'll give him process."

He strode through the door; Tovera was last in the short line. Outside stood the secretary, holding a shotgun that had been out of sight when Adele arrived.

"Grampa?" he said, alarmed but not frightened. *Brock didn't exclude him from the meeting. He was on guard outside.*

303

"Organize the crews," Brock said. "It seems we're going to have visitors. There's guns in the locker for the ones who can use them, but have Busoni decide who to trust."

"I'm coming along!" the youth said.

"You bloody well aren't," said Brock as he reached for the elevator control. He took up as much room as Adele and Tovera together. "And try not to get killed! Somebody's got to run this company if I buy the farm, and it's not your bloody father!"

The elevator squealed downward. Adele put her data unit away and took the pistol from her pocket.

All things considered, the situation was rather better than it had seemed to be a minute ago.

KOTZEBUE ON SUNBRIGHT

"I hope you don't mind staying outside," said Freedom as he hopped over the ditch in which Daniel had been watching the deceptively predatory fish. "Riely's office reminds me of a prison cell. I don't need an early experience of that."

Daniel had been surprised to find that he and the rebel leader were pretty much of an age. The latter was slim and an inch taller than Daniel's five foot nine; he looked fit but not athletic.

"You're in charge, sir," Daniel said. "But regardless, I prefer to be outdoors myself."

Kidlinger and four of his troops were following closely; the driver and the other pair were with the vehicle in front. Rather too closely, it seemed to Daniel, and apparently not only to him.

Freedom turned and snapped, "Keep your distance if

you please, Captain. You are not cleared for some of the information which Lieutenant Pensett has brought for me."

Freedom sat on a dry irrigation conduit mounted on knee-high posts; he started to pull off his loose coveralls. Underneath he wore a plain shirt with trousers and a matching jacket. It was the outfit of an office worker anywhere in the Alliance or the Cinnabar empire.

Daniel, working the coveralls over Freedom's ankle boots, looked at him and said, "I'm surprised to meet you, sir. That is, surprised by the person I'm meeting."

The other man laughed humorlessly. "Do you doubt I'm who I said I am?" he asked. "Perhaps I should have business cards printed? Freedom, Revolutions a Specialty. Address: the Wilderness, Sunbright."

Daniel laughed also, but without the bitterness. He sat beside Freedom and reached into his cargo pocket.

"Riely and Kidlinger both vouch for you," he said, bringing out the document case and giving it to the rebel leader. "Given that they don't seem to care for one another very much, I'll accept their joint identification."

He paused and added with a grin to take the edge off the truth, "I wouldn't mind seeing the back of Captain Kidlinger myself."

Freedom opened the document case, proving that his DNA matched the lock settings. That implied that the case could be used to identify the rebel leader. Daniel knew how to engage the self-destruct mode already—the case was RCN standard, after all—but the Chief should have emphasized the necessity of doing so if there were danger of it falling into Alliance hands.

Of course, it might be that the Chief didn't care about the

safety of *any* of the pawns in the game he was playing. Daniel was starting to figure out what that game was.

Instead of putting the chips into a reader—or using the one built into the case—Freedom looked at Daniel and said, "You're from Cinnabar itself, aren't you, Pensett?"

"Yessir," Daniel said. "From the west coast."

The real Kirby Pensett had been born in the Eastern Highlands. From things he had said when they were drinking in the same group of an evening, he had joined the RCN in the hope that it would send him only to planets where there were no words for "sheep" or "wool."

Daniel thought he was better off lying about his character's background than he would be trying to affect a Highlands accent. Besides, it was unlikely that a rebel on Sunbright had access to the amount of background information on RCN officers that the puppet master on Madison did.

Freedom absently tapped the single chip nested in the open case. He looked at Daniel and said, "This will be a list of weapons purchased, where they'll be landed, and the amount of rice which must be exchanged for them. So that we can move the anti-ship batteries into place as needed."

He gestured toward the center of Kotzebue, where the mobile battery sat adjacent to the makeshift landing field. The triple launcher wasn't visible from where they sat, but Daniel had examined it through the *Savoy*'s optics while they waited for the plasma-heated ground to cool enough to open the hatch.

Nothing less rugged than a starship could stay airborne in the hail of automatic impeller slugs which Kotzebue could throw up. In theory, ships of the Funnel Squadron could sweep in low from several directions and overwhelm the missile defenses too.

In practice, the entirety of Kotzebue wasn't worth a single starship. Taking a risk of losing three ships in a matter of seconds if the battery crew knew what it was doing would be insane.

"It doesn't matter who provides the rice, which battalion or company or gang, you see," Freedom said. "I'm the face of the revolution, but there isn't really a leader. Or perhaps money is the leader. Money's become the god of the revolution!"

Daniel didn't speak. Freedom's train of thought seemed to be going in a very useful direction already.

"I asked if you were from Cinnabar, Pensett," Freedom said, suddenly sharp again. It was like watching a gleaming fish leap up from the Slough of Despair. "Does Cinnabar support the revolution on Sunbright? Be honest! Don't worry about what I want to hear."

Unlike Adele, Daniel wasn't above shading the truth—or even of throwing a heavy drape over the truth and beating it with a stick, if the girl was pretty enough. He didn't see any cause to have done that here, however. And besides—

I don't have the faintest idea of what you want to hear, Master Freedom, he thought.

Aloud he said, "No, sir. To the best of my knowledge, Cinnabar does not support your revolution. By 'Cinnabar' I mean the Senate, of course. If you mean 'public opinion on Cinnabar,' you'll have to ask someone who knows or cares more about public opinion than I do. Than most RCN officers do, I should say."

"It's because of the massacres, isn't it?" Freedom said, leaning toward Daniel and speaking with the intensity of a prophet. "You think we rebels are nothing but brutal butchers, and it horrifies you!"

Daniel tilted slightly away from the rebel leader. That was an unconscious reaction to the sort of ideological enthusiasm that had always made him uncomfortable; an attitude he had absorbed from his father without being aware of it.

"Sir," Daniel said, "you're asking if the Senate disapproves of your rebellion on moral grounds. No, sir, it does not."

He took a deep breath and went on. "I cannot think of a case in which I believe the Senate made a moral judgment. Personally, I wouldn't encourage it to do such a thing, not that my political lords and masters would be interested in my opinion. The true reasoning behind the Senate's position as I understand it—"

He shrugged and turned his palms upward, making clear his admission of his limited knowledge.

"—is that Cinnabar wants peace with the Alliance. Not out of altruism or philosophical conviction, but because the costs of decades of war have come very near to ruining the Republic."

"The Senators aren't horrified by all this?" Freedom said with a toss of his hand. He could have been gesturing in the direction of the pole to which hands were nailed, but Daniel suspected his intention was to indicate the whole planet. "*You* aren't horrified?"

The reference to the Senate was presumably rhetorical, but the personal question was not. Daniel pressed his palms together, as though he were clapping in slow motion. Then he looked up and said, "Sir, that's like asking me if I like the taste of purple. I'm an RCN officer, trained to consider my present environment tactically. *Any* present environment. If I were studying this—"

He made a gesture which was deliberately similar to Freedom's.

"—in Xenos, in a history course, I'd look at causes and results, but I still wouldn't be ... Sir, I'm a military officer."

"Well, *I'm* horrified, Pensett," Freedom said. He got to his feet and thrust his hands into his tunic pockets.

Two of Kidlinger's soldiers stood ten yards away, between the irrigation pipe and the hills over which the aircar had arrived. When they stiffened in surprise, one started to topple from the planting mound he'd been standing on. He had to hop to get his balance.

"Get back!" Freedom said. "Damn you, didn't—"

He spun suddenly and pointed his right arm at Kidlinger, who waited near the building with his remaining troops. "You, Kidlinger!" he said. "Get your buffoons out of here, back onto your truck or the street or somewhere that I don't see them!"

"Sir, I can't risk—" the dapper officer began.

"Get them out of my sight or I'll declare you an outlaw!" Freedom said. "Do you understand? I'll double the price for the outgoing payload to the unit that takes your head. Do you doubt me?"

"Reyes, Ignacio!" Kidlinger called. His voice was controlled, but there was just enough fear in it to show that he did understand. "Get back to the truck now!"

He bowed and said, "I'll be waiting against the wall of the house when you need me, sir."

Freedom watched him for a moment, then sat again on the pipe and patted the place beside him where Daniel had been sitting a moment before. Daniel grinned and took the seat. Their backs were to Kidlinger and the town; before them, the hills softened with the approach of sunset.

"Alliance rule was an evil thing," the rebel said softly. "At best it would have been burdensome to people who had generally kept themselves to themselves, but Governor Blaskett is a brute: a thief and worse. When he can't coerce a respectable woman into his bed by threat or lead her there by bribes, he sends troops to drag her from her house."

"I'm very sorry to hear that, sir," Daniel said.

That was true, but the practical reality was that backwaters tended to get administrators who couldn't be trusted anywhere more significant. He had seen that the quality of some of the fellows sent out from Xenos wasn't a great deal higher.

Freedom didn't respond immediately, leaving Daniel to wonder if he should have held his tongue. It was hard to tell how one was supposed to react to a statement like that about people you—and probably the person speaking—have never met.

"I don't care about what happens to Cinnabar or the Alliance, either one," Freedom blurted. "If two gangs of exploiters want to bludgeon each other to death, let them. I care about the simple, decent farmers of Sunbright who were being crushed by injustice!"

"Go on," Daniel said. He nodded, his face expressionless.

The peasants of Bantry weren't simple. They had different tastes in art from those of rich city folk, and they didn't talk much about philosophy, but the years Daniel had spent in the closest contact with Hogg didn't allow him to say that he *understood* his servant; just that he could often predict what Hogg would say or do. As for decent—

He grinned broadly. For a moment he didn't care what the rebel leader thought about his expression.

—that was a matter of definition. But they'd back each other against outsiders and back the squire no matter how hard things got, and that was good enough for a Bantryman like Daniel Leary.

Freedom was so lost in his own problems that Daniel might not have gotten a reaction if he'd stuck his thumbs in his ears and waggled his fingers. "But it all went wrong," the rebel said miserably. "We didn't take Saal immediately as I'd hoped, but the rest went to plan. We took most of the planet like water soaking into a cloth. Blaskett couldn't stop us, and Pleasaunce couldn't send him more troops in the middle of a war with Cinnabar."

He raised his hands, apparently gesturing to an unseen audience. "I thought it was just a matter of time before the Alliance evacuated Saal and the people of Sunbright could work out their own destiny!"

"Instead Saal held out," Daniel said. That was a foregone conclusion when disorganized militia faced regular troops in prepared positions. The first rush might have succeeded, but when it didn't, the chances of a rebel military victory evaporated. "And the armed bands that you'd created found that it was easier to take the rice themselves rather than to fight Alliance soldiers in pillboxes. Before long, most of your forces were mercenaries or opportunists, I suspect."

"It was worse than that," Freedom said. He was a healthy,

well-fed young man, but Daniel had seen prisoners in labor camps who looked less wretched. "And I didn't set up all the bands, but I made them possible, yes. Don't think I don't know *that*."

He met Daniel's eyes. He said, "Brutes have become warlords, and the farmers are slaves. I wanted to get rid of Blaskett, but I've created a hundred Blasketts, and each one is worse than the one before. And there's nothing I can do!"

Daniel considered the situation. Freedom's political naivety startled him, though not in itself: he had learned about practical politics in his cradle as the son of Speaker Leary, but he understood that most people didn't have such a background.

The surprise was that this young *innocent*, Daniel would have said, had done such a brilliant job of setting off the rebellion. The fact that Freedom hadn't understood what he was doing didn't detract from the skill with which he had done it. And even now, without Freedom's coordination, government forces should be able to recover Sunbright with the modest increase in forces which the Treaty of Amiens made possible.

"Sir?" Daniel said. "You're confirming what I was told aboard the blockade runner that brought me here. But I think Sunbright will settle down if you leave; and anyway, you won't have to watch it get worse. It certainly will get worse, I'm afraid, if you continue to direct the rebellion. You're really very good at it, if you don't mind me saying so."

"I can't leave," Freedom said. He sounded as though he had just announced that his infant son was terminally ill. "Don't think I wouldn't have done that, but—"

He jerked his head backward without actually turning to face or point toward Captain Kidlinger.

"—I'm never alone when I'm around ships. Except in Saal, I mean. The blockade runners only land where they'll be protected by the missile batteries, so the gangs are always around. Even if I could convince a ship captain to take me aboard, the gangs trading with them wouldn't permit it. I'm pretty sure that they'd kill me and hide my body rather than let the government use me for propaganda against them."

He grimaced. "Kidlinger would kill me," he said. "He'd like to kill me now, I think, but he still imagines that he can rule Sunbright some day."

Daniel smiled wryly. He had expected the rebel leader to produce some altruistic reason why he couldn't abandon "his suffering people" here on Sunbright. Daniel wasn't an expert on accents like Adele, but he'd give odds that Freedom's voice still carried a hint of an upper-class Xenos drawl.

Aloud he said, "You mentioned Saal, sir. Can you get into the city?"

Freedom looked at him. He said, "Can *you* get me off planet, Lieutenant Pensett?"

"If you can get into Saal, sir," Daniel said, "I think I should be able to arrange something. I gather you can?"

"Yes," said Freedom. With sudden decision, he said, "Pensett, I'm going to tell you something that nobody else on this planet knows. My name is Tomas Grant, and I'm the field supervisor of the Saal Water Department."

A deputy department head would have access to the main governmental database . . . and if that deputy was a little more

313

computer savvy than most of his municipal peers, it explained how the Sunbright rebels had gathered such extremely good intelligence from the start of the rebellion.

Daniel smiled slowly. Freedom—Grant—looked as stiff as if he were tied to a post to wait for the firing party.

"Fair is fair, Master Grant," Daniel said. "My real name is Daniel Leary. I'm an RCN captain on active duty, and I'm here to get you safely off Sunbright. I have a reputation for carrying out my assignments."

That was a case of Daniel shading the truth. His orders said nothing about keeping Freedom safe. But he was Captain Daniel Leary, and by now his superiors should be expecting him to exceed his orders.

Chapter Twenty-one

HALTA CITY ON CREMONA

By the time the elevator thumped to rest on the ground floor of the warehouse, red strobes in the ceiling were pulsing while a musical but penetrating gong tolled. The light blurred through the dust of the building's interior, turning the drab space into an angry dawn.

Adele felt silly walking around with the pistol in her hand, so she returned it to her pocket. She knew from experience that she would be able to get it out quickly enough if the situation required her to do so.

The workmen Adele passed as she followed Brock's quick strides hadn't paid any attention to the pistol, however, nor to the more obtrusive weapons which her companions carried. Equipment was shutting down in response to the alarm, so the building was somewhat quieter than it had been when she and Tovera entered.

An amplified voice called, "All employees report to your section manager at once! Report to your section manager at once!"

Adele thought it was Brock's grandson speaking, but distortion from multiple speakers and the building's bad acoustics kept her from being certain. The delay before the general announcement was enough to have allowed him to give instructions to the foremen before he sent the common laborers to them.

Three trucks were backed into the loading dock: a flatbed which had arrived with a pair of sealed shipping cubes, a hopper truck into which pink rice was pouring from an overhead spout, and a three-axle vehicle with four-foot sides of corrugated steel around the bed. Brock went to the last.

The truck driver stood on the dock, looking concerned as the cargo handler who'd been with him disappeared inside at the loudspeaker's summons. A double pallet of eight-inch piping hung from an overhead track, ready to be swung onto the bed.

"Tony, I'm going to borrow your truck," Brock said to the driver. "I'll square it with Norgay, or else Klaus will if I don't get around to it. Okay?"

"Okay, Brock," the driver said; his eyes were on the big pistol whose grip protruded above the outfitter's waistband. "Hey, is everything okay? What's going on?"

Brock stepped onto the truck bed, then gripped the side with both hands and swung over to stand on a back tire. He stepped from the tire to the running board and from there opened the driver's side door.

"We've got a bloody ratfuck for the moment, Tony," he called to the driver, "but me and my friends here're going to straighten Mangravite out. Then it'll be fine."

"Whatever you say, Brock," the driver said with nervous brightness. "Hey, I'm sure not going to bet against you!"

Adele had detoured to the flight of steps at the other end of the high dock; her boot soles pattered on the concrete. Tovera remained on the platform, trying to watch in all directions. She held her submachine gun close to her chest, where its outline wouldn't be immediately obvious.

"Shake a leg, both of you!" Brock said. Adele opened the cab door and slid in. There was plenty of room for concealment under the dash if she curled her legs under her.

Tovera stepped into the truck bed. She reached for the gate with her left hand.

"Here, you can't lift that alone," the driver said, bending to help her. Before he touched it, Tovera straightened, pivoting the gate upward to clang shut; the catches snicked home.

Brock chuckled. He twisted the handle of the hand brake, then let its tensioning spring pull it open.

"Next stop, Halta Harbor," he said as he lifted the transmission lock from its detent. His foot settled onto the throttle. Motors whined; the truck accelerated slowly but as smoothly as a falling rock.

"I took this one because she's got electric motors in each wheel hub," Brock said, pitching his voice so that Adele could hear him over the chorus of whines. "Don't get me wrong—I could handle any of them. I started out in this business driving a diesel with a crunch box. But I figured not having to worry about missing a shift right now was maybe a good thing."

Adele, under the dashboard, twisted so that she could look at Brock. She was pleased to see that he was watching the road and keeping his hands on the big, nearly horizontal wheel as he spoke.

"I see," she said. "You're the expert, so of course I accept your decision."

She didn't really see. Why would the outfitter, who was driving into a gunfight with apparent willingness, be concerned that a stranger thought him unmanly for choosing a vehicle with a transmission that was less difficult to manipulate than those of the other options?

Adele would say that she didn't understand men, which was true; but that might imply that she *did* understand women, which certainly was not true. She had often thought that humans were an interesting species, but that she wasn't a member of it.

Brock swore softly, switching the weight of his foot to the back of the single, center-pivoted control pedal. The whining changed note and grew louder; each separate motor was turning the truck's inertia into electricity which it pumped back into the capacitors. Daniel had explained the system to her not long after they met, for no better reason than his enthusiasm for hardware, and she had remembered because her enthusiasm for information was just as great.

"We've got cops ahead," Brock warned. "Just keep your head down, and I think I can talk us through."

"All right," said Adele. The data unit in her pocket relayed the conversation to Tovera's earbud, but that was probably redundant. She had never known Tovera to shoot unless she thought it was necessary—or to refrain from shooting because someone else didn't see that necessity.

The truck slowed to a halt, but Brock didn't lock the transmission. He stuck his head and burly shoulders out the side window and called, "Hey, buddy? Can you give me a break? I got something hot on back at the office—*if* I get there before her husband comes to pick her up."

"Sorry, we gotta search all vehicles," said a muffled voice from outside. "I feel your pain, believe me, I do."

"Look, I just dropped off a load of pipe shipped from Norsk on the *Asphodel*," Brock whined. He reached into his breast pocket. "There's nothing to search, all right? And here's ten thalers to see it my way. Hell, here's ten for each of you. Believe me, she's special."

"Well, I dunno. Jerry . . . ?" the outside voice said. There was no reply, but his partner must have shrugged. A hand reached up to take the Alliance coins which Brock offered.

Brock's foot shifted on the pedal. "Give'r my best," the voice called, more faintly.

"Stop where you are!" a new voice shouted—more distant but making up for that with volume.

Brock came off the throttle, but he didn't rock the pedal back to brake. A submachine gun ripped out a short burst. It must have been aimed in the air, because Adele didn't hear the nasty spatter of pellets hitting something hard.

"You bloody well *stop* or the next one's through the windscreen!" the new voice shouted.

"Hey!" said Brock, heeling the brake hard. Even so, the truck slowed gently. "These patrolmen have already searched me. And what's the Navy doing stopping honest truckers anyway?"

"They didn't search you, you bought 'em off, which you

won't do with us," said the voice, now on the driver's side of the cab. "And as for the Navy—"

The passenger door jerked open. The moon-faced man in blue utilities was holding his carbine upright by the balance in the hand not on the door handle. He didn't have time to look surprised before Adele shot him through the right eye and, as his head jerked back, through the open mouth.

"Drive!" she said, but the truck was already accelerating at its slow best. She straightened to look out. Forward motion hadn't swung the door hard enough to latch, so she pulled it closed.

Tovera's submachine gun crackled a three-shot burst, then another, then a third. It sounded like water dripping into hot grease.

Adele couldn't see the first two targets from her angle, but Tovera's third burst threw forward a man wearing nondescript trousers but a crossbelt over his dirty white tunic. He had been trying to duck behind the stone steps to the entryway of an office building. The back of his tunic speckled, and he sprawled across them instead. The pistol flew out of his hand.

The policeman had probably been too frightened to shoot at the truck as it disappeared down the street, but Tovera wasn't one to take chances. Neither was Adele, not in this unpredictable chaos.

The police must have been on foot, but turned crossways to block the street ahead was a small blue van with a Navy of Cremona shield on the side in gold. The truck rolled into the van with a crunch and skidded it sideways. Brock continued to accelerate.

A tire rubbed off the smaller vehicle; the wheel rim sparked across the cobblestones until it found purchase in a crack. The van flipped onto its side, then roof, and was pulled under the truck's axles one by one, shedding parts with the scream of metal on metal.

The truck continued on; the wreckage of the van didn't catch fire. Brock seemed to be whistling between his teeth, but his mouth was set in a rictus.

The street ahead kinked slightly to the right. Two blocks past the angle and coming toward them was a flatbed truck. People standing in the back looked forward over the cab. Adele thought, *Are they—*

The windshield starred in three milky patches between her and the driver; the truck body rang like a quickly hit anvil as the slugs passed through. Brock hauled the wheel to the right, hand over hand. Their truck turned onto a cross street, lumbering over the curb. They scraped the corner of a tavern; glass and bricks shattered, spraying the sidewalk.

The gunman in the flatbed hit the back with another round from his automatic carbine, but the rest of the burst flew wide. The range was too great for Tovera's weapon to be lethal, but a light pellet in the face would throw off the aim of the most focused marksman.

The bullet-pocked windshield was as hard to see through as a heavy fog. Adele pounded at it with her right hand, but she only succeeded in stretching the sticky middle sheet of the glass sandwich even nearer to opacity.

Brock lifted his pistol and punched the barrel through the windshield in front of him. He swung his arm sideways, grinding the butt through the glass like a ship's bow crushing pack ice.

He drew back his arm, then repeated the stroke to clear the top of the windshield. When he dropped the pistol onto his lap, his wrists were bleeding. Hauling hard on the steering wheel, he turned the truck left onto a street parallel to the one on which they had left the warehouse.

Two ground cars and a light truck were stopped in the street ahead. Men with pistols, clubs, and lengths of chain were climbing out of the vehicles, warned either by radio or the sound of shots coming toward them. They all wore scarves striped red/yellow/black.

When I have a moment, I'll learn which gang uses those colors.

Adele leaned out the open side window, where she didn't have to worry about jagged edges. Two shots spun the man on the right. His right arm stretched upward like that of a hammer thrower, but his grip must have frozen on his spiked mace, because it didn't come out of his hand.

Two shots more, holding for the center of the chest because the jouncing truck didn't allow for delicacy; the driver sprawled out of sight behind the hood of the car he had started to get out of. Two more and a gunman crumpled backward into the man behind him—who dropped next, coughing up bright pulmonary blood.

Brock guided—aimed—the truck between the back fender of the car in the middle of the line and the hood of the truck behind it. There wasn't room to clear either vehicle, but the big truck bounced them in opposite directions. If Brock had smashed into one straight on and ground it down, he would have chanced ripping out his truck's wiring harness or a hydraulic line.

There were bodies on the left side of the makeshift roadblock also. Like her mistress, Tovera had started at the edge and worked toward the center.

The street ahead to the next bend was almost empty of people, though there might be some hiding on the floors of cars. Vehicles had been driven over the curb to either side and seemingly abandoned.

The visible exception was a heavyset woman in a loose, floral-print dress. She must have just stepped out of a shop when the shooting started. She had dropped her string bag, spilling brightly colored fruit, but she seemed unable even to throw herself to the ground. She gaped red-faced as the truck rumbled past.

Adele gave her only a glance. She wasn't a threat.

The shroud around the barrel of her pistol was glowing yellow because of waste heat from her shots. She had expended at least half her twenty-round magazine. She would replace it with a fresh magazine as soon as she could, but she had learned to wait until the weapon cooled. Without protective gloves, the hot barrel would raise blisters.

If, as seemed likely, Adele emptied the pistol in the next few minutes, she would have blisters tomorrow morning—if she survived. She smiled wryly: that was a cheaper price than others were paying this afternoon.

Heavy firing burst out some miles to the north; at least one automatic impeller was involved, below which a buzz of lesser weapons sounded like a swarm of wasps. So far as Adele knew, no "Blue" forces were in that direction. She wondered whether two or more gangs had collided and were slugging it out with one another due to the lack of planning for the sudden attack.

A slug dimpled the fender in front of Adele and punched downward. That tire was already flat, but to hit it from that high angle—

"Aircar!" Tovera said. "Aircar!"

Another slug hit the pavement twenty feet ahead, shattering a cobblestone as osmium sprayed in a score of vivid pastels. Adele leaned through her side window and looked upward at the aircar curling slowly into sight ahead.

The shooter leaned out from the backseat, aiming a stocked impeller. It would be an awkward weapon to use from a platform circling above the rooftops while keeping a hundred yards out from its target, but a hit with it would rip through the truck's capacitor bank as easily as it would any of those riding.

Tovera shot, but the light pellets of her submachine gun weren't accurate at half that range and the gunman was wearing a helmet with a face shield. The impeller lifted from recoil; from the muzzle puffed metal which the coils' electromagnetic flux had vaporized. The slug ticked the roof of the cab and rang through the truck bed. If Tovera had been in the way, then Adele had lost a frequently valuable servant.

Adele ducked back inside, dropped her pistol on the seat, and took the larger weapon from Brock's lap. He said, "What—"

"Drive!" Adele said. She leaned on the window frame again, presenting the heavy pistol.

The car was traversing clockwise. The impeller recoiled, but the slug hit nothing useful this time. Adele shot and shot again. Brock's pistol jolted back harder than she was used to, so it took longer than the usual heartbeat for her to bring the sights in line.

The impeller dropped, spinning like a tossed baton; the shooter had slipped into the car's interior. The car reversed its curve to dive away to the left.

Adele shot, aimed, and shot again. The aircar turned on its back. Two bodies spun away before the vehicle dropped out of sight behind the buildings. There was probably a crash, but the sound of the shredded front tire slapping the truck's wheel well was too loud to hear much over.

"Bloody hell, woman!" Brock said, but even now he didn't turn to look at Adele instead of watching the road. "What did you do? *How* did you do that?"

Adele picked up her own pistol in her right hand. It had charred a streak in the upholstery fabric, and the foam padding beneath had started to melt; there was a smear of it on the titanium shroud.

"Do what?" she said. "I shot the gunman and his driver, if that's what you mean."

If she understood the question, it was absurd. It was like being asked what the bright thing lifting over the eastern horizon at dawn was.

"From a moving truck, you shot down an aircar with a *pistol*?" Brock said.

The road kinked again, this time a fairly sharp left. Ahead was a convoy of cars two abreast—civilian and probably commandeered at gunpoint. Spacers sat on window sills and on the roofs of the vehicles, armed to the teeth.

"Friends!" called Tovera, who wasn't dead after all. *I should have checked, I suppose.* "It's the Sissies come to get us!"

"It's a very good pistol," Adele said, setting the weapon down between them. The barrel was too warm to be laid on an ally's lap. "If you hadn't brought it, we would have been in difficulties."

She leaned out the side window and waved her little pistol in the air. It would be embarrassing to be shot dead by her rescuers. She knew that the *Sissie*'s crew, though faultlessly brave, was more likely to demonstrate enthusiasm than fire discipline.

"I suppose you can drop us here, Master Brock," Adele said. "I appreciate your help. As soon as possible, I will pay for the damages you've incurred in this business. Assuming I survive, of course."

Cars were turning around or parking on the sidewalks so that Sissies could pile aboard the big truck. Cory, holding a submachine gun, jumped onto the running board and cried, "Mistress, you're all right?"

"Yes, Lieutenant," Adele said. "Thanks to your timely warning, I am."

There was room ahead to get through safely; Brock started the battered truck rolling forward again. "If it's all the same, lady," he said, "I'll take you to the dock. This has been the first real excitement I've had in twenty years."

He barked a laugh. "And I'm *bloody* glad," he added, "that I picked the right side!" throat.

SUNBRIGHT

The horizontal line below the horizon ahead was too even not to be manmade, but that was all Daniel could tell with his unaided eyes. He thought again of putting on his commo helmet. The visor's magnification would be useful, and he could switch to the infrared spectrum to search the landscape for camouflaged watchers.

"Careful!" Freedom—Tomas Grant—warned. The level of the surface didn't change, but boggy soil became a shallow pool. The car lurched; brown water sprayed to all sides.

A commo helmet looked military and more than that would be the only one Daniel had seen thus far on Sunbright. Presumably they were in general use among the Alliance garrison in Saal, but that was an even better reason not to wear one here in the backcountry. A helmet's round outline was unique for as far as it could be seen, and a stocked impeller was deadly at equal range with the right marksman behind it.

The car's underside ticked the lip of the other side of the pool as they came up; the vehicle lofted a hand's breadth into the air and flopped down again uncomfortably. Daniel grunted, though he had braced himself on his arms when he saw what was coming. Hogg cursed in a tone of familiar misery.

Daniel was in the passenger seat, though he and Hogg had traded several times. The luggage was tied onto the frame of the vehicle so that the extra man could squat in the luggage space behind. It was too narrow for Hogg's hips, but at least he wouldn't slip off if the aircar slammed hard on a bump.

The car didn't have enough power to fly safely with three grown men aboard, so they were travelling the entire three hundred miles in ground effect. That was better than wobbling to a sudden crash from fifty feet up, but the ride hadn't been a lot of fun so far, and Daniel expected it to get worse.

"That's the Grain Web," Grant said, glancing to the side and gesturing toward the line Daniel had been watching. "Part of what was completed, anyway. That's really what convinced people to support the revolt, you know."

Daniel thought back to the briefing materials he had studied during the voyage from Madison. Adele had loaded them into his helmet and had included a very good natural history database.

"How is a rail system a cause for revolt?" he said. "From—well, to an outsider like me, it looks more efficient to get the rice to market by hauling it cheaply to Saal, where bigger ships could land. Everybody gains."

"It would be a very efficient way for the person at the center of the Web to control everything," Grant said. "Which would have concerned the farmers even if they hadn't had experience of Blaskett already. And it would have cut out the small shippers, since they couldn't compete with long-haul vessels. Big ships would have ten times the capacity and could carry the rice straight to Cinnabar or Pleasaunce without transshipping."

Grant canted the steering yoke to the right, angling to mount a waist-high dike. He must use the car in ground effect frequently, because he maneuvered with the skill of practice. Control inputs were quite different from what would be necessary if the vehicle had been airborne and could bank.

"So a lot of the little shipowners would have been willing to haul arms to us even if there hadn't been so much money in it," Grant said. Then, bitterly, "But there is money, lots of money. Until everybody's dead!"

The car fishtailed as it rose onto the dike, but the rebel leader kept it under control. They could travel faster on compacted earth than they had in the paddies, where Grant kept their speed down to avoid spraying themselves with the liquid muck. The surface was narrow, even for so small a car, but they sped along it without difficulty even where a spiky native tree grew from the side and required a twitch of the yoke to avoid.

Hogg leaned sideways so that his head was between those of the others. "I could spell you on the driving, y'know," he said.

Not for the first time, of course; and perhaps not for the twenty-first thus far on the ride. Hogg's enthusiasm for driving wouldn't have been as much of a problem if he hadn't also been a really terrible driver.

Daniel didn't reply. Grant said, "We'll be coming to a farm shortly. I think we should overnight there. We have another hundred kilometers ahead of us, but it's nearly dusk now and it's unwise to try to enter Saal after dark."

They bumped up onto the right-of-way for the Grain Web. It was a magnetic-levitation system; the current-carrying rails had been buried in a smooth pavement of stabilized earth. Even after four years of disuse and damage, it seemed a real thoroughfare.

"There's a curfew?" Daniel said, glad for a change of subject.

He deliberately hadn't questioned Grant about how he was going to enter the fortified capital. The fellow was an excellent driver, but he had a tendency to look toward the person he was speaking to and wave his hand. That had already led to some near misses as a result of this broken terrain and the fact that the overloaded vehicle didn't handle the way he expected it to.

"There's no regulation," Grant said. "My identification would be checked, the same as any other time. My concern is that it would be checked in the morning, when they sent out a patrol to investigate the wreckage. The troops in the bunkers at night don't like to see vehicles driving toward them."

He slowed. "We should see a track leading to the left soon," he said, scanning the brush on that side. Interspersed with spiky bushes were hollows which were covered with flat circles of leaves. Vivid yellow spikes shot up to knee height from the middle of each green splotch.

"How is it you gallivant all over this bloody mudhole however you please?" Hogg said, sounding accusatory. Not only was he wedged into the back of the car, he really had wanted to drive—almost as much as Daniel didn't want him to drive.

"I'm responsible for Saal's water supply," Grant said, twisting to look back at Hogg. "I make inspections every—"

"Is that the road?" Daniel said, stretching his arm past the driver to indicate the wallow of mud angling into the hills to the left.

"The devil!" Grant said, turning sharply and lifting the outer edge—Daniel's side—of the car as though they were on a banked track. Even so, they skidded through brush that slapped the car's body and occasionally twanged from the fans before the vehicle looped back to the mud path.

"They've been using heavy trucks," Grant added in a doubtful voice. He was looking over the side of the car at the crushed vegetation.

"I think that tracked vehicles have come this way," Daniel

said, looking out his own side. "See the way the heavier stems are chewed, not just broken?"

He hadn't brought a weapon himself, a decision for which he now felt a vagrant regret. Still, if this was what he thought it was, a pistol—or even a stocked impeller—wouldn't make a great deal of difference.

"Tractors, I suppose," Grant said. He spoke more loudly than he needed to. "They must have gotten heavy tractors instead of using the ground-effect transport."

"There's smoke, young master," said Hogg, his lips close to Daniel's ear but his hoarse voice loud enough that Grant must have heard him. The smell was obvious regardless; not just the sharp, sneezing tickle of wood smoke but also the rasp of electrical insulation and the sludgy black stench of paint and rubber.

"Grant, perhaps you should wait here while Hogg and I—" Daniel said, but the driver had thumbed forward the verniers on the yoke. One switch controlled the fan speed, the other the blade angle.

Grant was holding the car low, but they quickly accelerated to a speed faster than even Hogg would have been willing to drive on a track punctuated with stumps and branches standing upright from toppled boles. Daniel gripped the side of the open car with one hand and the edge of his seat with the other, smiling pleasantly.

"There's a watchtower," Grant shouted. He had to compete with the throaty howl of the fans, of course. "Herrero's Farm is very well defended!"

Then, "Where's the watchtower? We should be—"

They came over the ridge at speed. Grant tilted his yoke to raise the bow, using the car's underside to brake their rush. They mushed down onto the track instead of slamming. The maneuver must have been instinctive, because his eyes and surely his mind were on the ruin ahead.

The watchtower of coarse red limestone was still there, the base at least, but the upper portion had been shot away. Daniel couldn't be sure how much was missing, but he guessed about ten feet, judging from the gravel which slugs from automatic impellers had sprayed around and beyond the remnant.

There had probably been a watchman, given the enthusiasm with which Sunbright's skin-winged "birds" fluttered over and dug into the gravel. They were tracking the scent. The stone had been crushed too thoroughly to make a good cairn.

"You really need sensors that give you warning at a greater distance," Daniel said as the car slowed to a walk. "If they knew where the tower was, and I suppose they did, then they were shooting as soon as they came in sight of it. No matter how good the watchman's reflexes were, he didn't have a chance."

"I'd have had a chance," said Hogg in a voice like rocks in a tumbler. He was looking at the farmstead itself and imagining Bantry in the place of these smoldering buildings. "*I'd* have had a bloody chance!"

"Easy, friend," Daniel said, reaching back to put a hand on his servant's shoulder. "We'll take care of what we can."

The older buildings were stone; the rest were of structural plastic. The latter seemed to have been placed on tracts between the stone ones or around the farmstead's original perimeter. The square, peak-roofed house in the center and the barn attached to it must have been ancient.

A dozen plump black-and-tan dogs had been penned behind orange plastic fencing to the west of the main house. About a dozen; Daniel couldn't be sure, since the burst from an automatic impeller had shredded them thoroughly.

"There was no call for that," Hogg said, swinging out of the car with a lithe grace that belied his cramped seating for the past two hours. He held his pistol along his right leg, where from a distance it was hidden by the baggy fabric of his trousers. "Maybe some day I'll meet this dog-shooter and discuss it with him."

"Dogs fatten on rice, and the wet doesn't rot their paws," Grant said, sounding as though he were talking in his sleep. He shut off the fans in the courtyard formed by a U of ruined buildings. "All over Sunbright, they're eaten as often as chicken or pork. It took me years to get used to that."

At least two automatic impellers had raked the farm. One shooter had simply sprayed slugs across the buildings, rarely holding below shoulder level on an adult man. The other, though, had kept his bursts at knee-height. He had brought down the front and sides of every stone building and probably killed most of those who had thrown themselves to the floor when the shooting started.

The plastic buildings fared better: small punctures at six-inch intervals dimpled the sheeting, but the plastic didn't absorb all the energy of the hypersonic slugs and shatter to dust and gravel as stone did. It wouldn't have made much difference to the people inside, of course.

"Get out of here!" a cracked voice screamed. "Get out! There's nothing left to steal!"

Hogg had vanished; Daniel hadn't seen him go. Grant whispered, "May the gods forgive me."

A man tottered out of a shed covering three carts—their drawbars canted up so that they nested—and a winnowing machine. The equipment had been riddled, but the rubber tires on the carts were the only things which could have burned, and the slugs hadn't ignited them.

"Get out!" the man screamed. He walked with two sticks, one of them a recent makeshift cut from a wooden pole. Age might have been enough to explain his feebleness, but blood stained the bandage around his head.

He tried to wave a cane, but it slipped from his grip. He slumped sideways. Daniel strode toward him, but a woman ran more quickly from the plastic barn nearby and caught the old man before he fell to the mud.

"Here," Daniel said, reaching out. "I'll—"

"Don't touch me!" the man wheezed, though he dropped his remaining cane when he waggled it toward Daniel.

The woman was younger than he'd first thought—younger than him, in fact—and would be attractive when her swollen face recovered from bruises and crying. She said, "I have—"

She gasped and doubled up, clasping her belly. *One thing at a time,* thought Daniel as he lifted the old man. He carried him at a trot to the barn the woman had come from.

As he had expected, there were shakedowns of bedding in the emptied rice-storage bins. Eyes stared at him around posts but vanished when he turned toward them; nearby a child began crying.

Daniel laid down the now-quiet man and turned to get the woman. She had followed him into the barn. She walked haltingly while pressing a hand to her abdomen, but she waved away his unspoken offer to help.

She seated herself on an upturned basket. "I suppose I'm bleeding again," she said bitterly. "Well, it could be worse, couldn't it?"

Daniel stood erect with his feet slightly apart and his hands crossed behind his back as though he were facing a superior officer. He said, "My servant and I are both countrymen. We can help with first aid."

Then he added, "I'm Captain Daniel Leary, RCN. That is, I'm from Cinnabar."

"If you'd come two days ago," the woman said, "you could have helped dig graves. In the evening, I mean. If you'd showed up any sooner, you'd just have been three more to bury. I decided we had to bury them, you know. But it didn't help with the smell. I don't think the smell will ever go away."

"Coming through!" Hogg called from outside. "Coming through!"

"Clear!" said Daniel. He wasn't the sort to blaze away at sudden movements. For that matter, he didn't have a gun at present, though he supposed he might have found one. Anyway, Hogg was being careful in a difficult situation, which wasn't something to complain about.

"There's thirty-odd more in another barn," said Hogg as he entered. He'd concealed his pistol, but he carried a shotgun in the crook of his elbow. "Kids and women, mostly."

He nodded toward the seated woman. "No others as young as her, though. And some men, but they're shot up pretty bad."

"They thought I was dead, I suppose," the woman said. "Maybe they were right."

Turning to Daniel and sitting straighter, she said, "My name is Floria Post. Emmanuel Herrero, whom you carried in, is my grandfather. Thank you."

She gestured to the barn's interior; several small children had appeared out of the bins. She said, "I brought the younger orphans here."

Grant entered the barn, looking stunned. "It was Colonel Kinsmill's force," he said. Daniel wasn't sure whom he was talking to, or if he was really talking to anyone outside his own mind. "Two of the women in the seed barn said they heard men call their leader 'King.' That's Kinsmill's nickname."

"A blond man with moustaches?" Floria said, using both hands to mime a moustache that curved into sideburns. Her voice lilted as though she were about to break into peals of laughter. "Men offered him a turn with me, but he said he didn't want sloppy thirds. More like sixth, I think, though I lost track eventually. King took my niece instead. She was ten."

The lilt turned to sobbing. The woman bent over, her face in her hands. Daniel was afraid that she was going to sag onto the floor, but he thought better of putting an arm around her for support.

A pair of middle-aged women must have been standing near the doorway but out of Daniel's sight. They entered silently. One held Floria's shoulders; the other touched her companion's elbow in frightened support.

"Kinsmill's a cultured man!" Grant said. "He's from Bryce. He was educated in the Academic Collections there!"

I wonder if he was Adele's classmate? Daniel thought. *I'm sure she would have something to discuss with him now. Briefly.*

Floria had stopped crying. She raised her eyes to Daniel and said, "Captain? What do we do now? What can we *do*?"

Daniel nodded twice, giving himself time to consider the question. The elements were simple enough, and if he didn't particularly like the answer, that didn't change reality. A ship's captain frequently arrived at answers he didn't like, and the captain of a warship did so more often yet.

"Go to Saal," he said. "You'll have to walk, but you have carts to carry invalids and enough food for the journey. I'm sorry that we won't be able to accompany you, but we have our own duties."

One of the older women said, "We supported the revolt. We always sold our rice through the Provisional Government. Always!"

Until Captain Kinsmill decided there would be more profit if he cut out the middleman, Daniel thought. Which was true, in the short term.

"I'm sorry," Daniel said. "We have to be going now."

They would sleep rough tonight rather than shelter in the remains of Herrero's Farm. They would get far enough away that no vagrant breeze would bring a reminder of the smoke and death of this tomb.

The old man's eyes opened. They were blank for a moment; then he focused on Tomas Grant and sat bolt upright.

"You!" he said, pointing a frail hand. "You did this! It's all your doing!"

The rebel leader turned and stumbled out of the barn. He didn't speak.

Daniel cleared his throat and said, "Yes, well. We need to be going also. Come along, Hogg."

"In a moment," Hogg said; he held out the shotgun to Floria. He had removed the lockplate while Daniel and the others were talking, but the weapon was back together now.

"The contacts were corroded," he said. "That's why it didn't go off. I cleaned them."

The older women shrank back. Floria took the weapon, giving Hogg a questioning look. He took three electromotive shells out of his pocket and handed them over also.

"They're just bird shot, but they're better than nothing," he said. Then with a broad, terrible grin, he added, "If you don't trust yourself with it, you could do worse than give it to the lad I took it away from. He's young, but he's got spirit, he does."

Hogg looked at Daniel and said, "Much like another tyke I knowed once back t' Bantry."

"Come along, Hogg," Daniel repeated. He strode out of the barn.

He had a lump in his throat.

HALTA CITY ON CREMONA

The truck slewed left as it pulled up in the pall of steam hanging over the *Princess Cecile*. Adele grabbed the frame of the side window again. The angle of the massive front bumper had stopped within a finger's width of the back of the car on which Dasi and a squad of spacers had been riding.

"Sorry, lady," Brock said in genuine apology. "I didn't realize I'd lost my hydraulics on the right side until those yahoos dropped anchor right in front of me."

Pasternak had shut down the corvette's thrusters as the truck and its escorting cars turned up the quay. Adele smiled in self-mockery. If it had just been spacers returning, Pasternak—and whoever warned him of the convoy's approach—might have continued running the thrusters at low output.

Mistress Mundy—she was always that or "ma'am" to the *Sissie*'s crew—was known to be as awkward as a blind bear. Nobody was going to increase the risk of her falling off the gangplank into the plasma-heated slip. And every Sissie in sight would dive in to save her if it happened, even those who couldn't swim....

"No harm done," Adele said as she stepped out into the dissipating steam. "Master Brock, I'll do my best to see that you don't regret this."

"I don't regret it now, lady," the outfitter called after them; he was out of sight in the high cab. "But Mangravite's going to."

"Mangravite certainly *will* regret this," said Cory as he waved Tovera across the floating walkway ahead of her mistress. "So will all the other gangs who contributed troops to the affair."

So that he's behind to grab me if I stumble, Adele realized. She smiled even more coldly.

He grinned and added, "We had most of them careted before I went off on my tour of the city. I'm sure Master Cazelet will have plotted the rest since then. The lairs, if you will."

Adele crossed the gangplank and strode up the boarding ramp briskly with no difficulties—as she had expected. She felt a little miffed at this particular concern, though she would never let her shipmates know that.

Yes, she was clumsy; she would never deny that. But she had a great deal of experience in negotiating slotted-steel stairs and scaffolds which had been polished by the feet of generations of librarians. She didn't slip on slick metal flooring.

But the Sissies were well-meaning in their concern. If they were also less observant than Adele might wish, well, that was true of most people. And as a general rule, she preferred to be a blur to whom no one paid attention. Still, she deliberately mounted the companionway at a pace that pressed Cory to match.

A Power Room tech was leaning over the railing to look down from the head of the stairs on A level. He vanished when he saw Adele. His voice echoed faintly down to her, however: "Five? The mistress is on her way!"

Vesey was now captain of the *Princess Cecile*, but she didn't allow the crew to refer to her as "Captain," let alone "Six." She remained in her mind—and in truth, in the minds of all the Sissies—Five, the corvette's first lieutenant.

Adele walked onto the bridge while the main hatch was squealing upward and a score of lesser hatches were clanging shut. By pairs—two/four/six/and all eight—the thrusters resumed their burning; steam roared up from the harbor in response to their rainbow breath.

The signals console was already live. Cazelet must have overridden her lock. Adele didn't think that he could have entered the Personal Access Only sectors, but—she smiled— she couldn't be sure. She had taught Cazelet well.

"Ship!" said Vesey over the PA system and the general intercom frequency. She was handling the liftoff herself, because the junior watch-standing officers were otherwise occupied. *"Prepare to lift!"*

The main hatch banged against its coaming. When the dogs shot ringingly home to seal it, they sounded like a volley of slugs hammering the outer hull. The thrusters' bellow became a bone-deep shudder, and steam buffeted the ship like an enormous pillow.

The dorsal turret would normally be lowered and locked during liftoff or landing. Now Adele heard its metal-to-metal gaskets squeal as it rotated.

She hadn't given orders, but she wasn't completely sure that her orders would be obeyed if she tried to stop what was about to happen. Officer Adele Mundy was, by the ship's table of organization, a very junior officer indeed.

However, the mistress, who had been attacked and insulted, was a person of veneration to the *Sissie*'s crew. They weren't going to ignore that.

Not that Adele had any problem with her shipmates' response. The main reason she hadn't given orders about what to do next was that she knew she didn't need to.

Instead of asking a question, Adele went straight to a preset she had prepared before the *Princess Cecile* had begun to break out of Cremona orbit. The harbor was protected by a pair of anti-ship missile batteries, and a third battery had been placed on what ten years before had been the edge of the city. That one had been swallowed by the northern suburbs which grew with the expansion of trade to the Sunbright rebels.

Adele didn't want to use the plasma cannon on the emplacements, particularly the one surrounded by civilian tenements, but they had to be taken out of action if the *Princess Cecile* was to escape safely. Using the batteries' own electronics to freeze the launchers in their safe position, locked horizontal to the ground, was just as good for that purpose as blowing them up would have been.

Someone had already locked the launchers. The missiles couldn't be fired until the software had been wiped and reloaded, a day's work for an expert—after somebody diagnosed the problem.

"Mistress?" said Cazelet over a two-way link. *"I'd been ready to override the controls since you left the ship this morning, but I didn't engage it until Captain Vesey ordered liftoff. I didn't want to chance somebody noticing the problem and maybe coming up with a fix."*

"Very good, Rene," Adele said. He just *might* be able to enter the personal sectors of her console. He had been very well trained indeed.

The ventral turret, offset to the stern as the dorsal installation was to the bow, cranked downward for use; it had been underwater while the ship was in the slip.

Ordinarily vessels rose through the atmosphere as quickly as their thrusters could lift them. A starship couldn't be streamlined. Furling the sails and clamping the telescoped antennas to the hull prevented them from being ripped off, but they still created enormous turbulence in the airstream.

The faster a ship moved near the ground, the more its crew bounced like dried beans in a rattle.

With Vesey at the controls, the *Princess Cecile* rose slowly, mushed out to sea, and began to curve back in a slight bank. A stylus would have rolled across the deck, but not quickly.

Adele's communications intercepts showed the expected amount of chatter on Halta City's emergency bands, but it was all concerned with the firefights which had rolled through the heart of town. Groups that hadn't been involved were nervous and confused. Survivors of groups that had met either the truck or Cory's relief force were in a shrieking panic. No one seemed to have noticed that the corvette had lifted off.

As a matter of reflex, Adele checked the displays on the *Sissie*'s other active consoles. Cazelet was splitting the commo board with the atmosphere controls. If Vesey had a sudden stroke, he was ready to act without hesitation.

Cory was in the Battle Direction Center. He preferred his familiar bridge station, but the *Princess Cecile* was in combat. As first lieutenant, his primary duty was to take over in the event that the corvette's whole bow was destroyed.

Cory had the atmosphere controls on half his display also. Vesey would have set a sequence in which the junior officers would take over should she be incapacitated, but which of them would be first on the rota didn't concern Adele. The remaining half of Cory's display echoed the gunnery boards of Sun, controlling the dorsal turret, and his mate, Rocker, in independent command of the ventral guns.

"Gunners, you may fire as you bear," said Vesey calmly. The

last syllable wasn't out of her mouth before a bolt slammed from each turret.

Two warehouses on the seafront erupted into mushrooms of flame. The plasma was literally as hot as the sun. Everything it touched which could burn, did: plastics, metals, even stone. A human who happened to be in the way simply vanished like chaff in a furnace.

Cory had created a targeting grid to which Cazelet had made additions. Carets in blue- or red-marked buildings, equipment lots, and three modern gunboats. The Navy of Cremona owned a destroyer, but it was a hulk; the gunboats were capable of at least intrasystem voyages.

Sun was firing single shots. One bolt from a four-inch gun was sufficient for any ordinary frame or brick building at this short range, but Adele knew that the gunner was really showing off.

The paired guns in the turrets were designed to syncopate one another to put out a nearly continuous stream of plasma which nudged incoming projectiles off course. It took a delicate hand and a great deal of practice to fire a single round, but that considerably extended the life of the cannon's bore.

Structure after structure disintegrated in balls of orange fire with flecks of iridescent plasma at their hearts. The corvette ambled in a slow arc around Halta City, uncovering additional targets as the angle changed.

The central police station was an old building—old enough that Adele felt a faint twinge of regret at the thought of Pre-Hiatus records which might have been stored there. But probably not, and anyway it was too late to worry. Rocker hit its ground floor twice. The stone walls survived to channel a roaring inferno three stories upward, lifting the roof and licking toward the clouds.

Each shot was a miniature thermonuclear explosion, shaking the corvette like a hammer blow. The shells were laser arrays aimed inward toward the pellet of tritium at the heart of each. When tripped, the lasers compressed the tritium to fusion and directed its energy toward the one missing tile in the thermonuclear furnace which was aligned with the bore.

The laser array directed the charge. The guns' iridium barrels were necessary to reduce side-scatter caused by the inevitable atoms in the jet's path in even hard vacuum. That problem and the resulting bore erosion were much worse in an atmosphere.

The gunboats were allotted to Sun, who put a bolt into the outside pontoon of each. The hull plating of even a small starship was several inches thick, but the outriggers were of much lighter material, and exploded in steam and white fire.

The gunboats tilted as they lost buoyancy, bringing open hatches in the hull proper underwater and listing further. Within a minute or two, each of the three vessels had turned turtle in its slip.

Rocker spaced four rounds the length of the naval barracks. The result couldn't be called surgical, but it was thorough beyond question. Adele thought of the naval officer who had precipitated the firefight in Halta City; she felt her lips smile.

Start a fight with the RCN and you're likely to find that we're the ones who end it, Adele thought. Her mother would have said that was an attitude unworthy of a Rolfe or Mundy; but her mother's head had decorated the Pentacrest in the center of Xenos.

Smudgy fires were burning in scores of locations, covering the city in haze that blurred or even concealed the buildings underneath it. The carets continued to give the gunners aiming points until there was no surviving target to shoot at.

The *Princess Cecile* was some distance from the sea now, having described an arc beginning at Halta Harbor. Vesey had been holding them at two hundred feet in the air. Despite asymmetrical pounding from the guns and the pulsing irregularity of the thrusters, the ship's altitude didn't vary by as much as six feet up or down.

The corvette's bank reversed, and they curved sunwise as they moved deeper inland. The turrets squealed again as they rotated to bear on the corvette's starboard broadside instead of to port.

A forest of carets sprang up, pointing to every building in a large complex surrounded by a fence and watchtowers. Adele smiled coldly; she knew what the compound was without checking—but she checked anyway.

Master Mangravite had started a fight with the RCN.

The *Sissie*'s guns slammed, destroying a pair of guard towers. *Why those?* Adele wondered, but when she magnified a surviving tower—there had been eight originally—she saw the towers mounted automatic impellers. Their osmium slugs wouldn't penetrate the corvette's hull, but they could damage the thrusters and High Drive and might even put holes in the outriggers.

Not these weapons, though: tower guards, colorfully dressed in green uniforms, were abandoning their posts so quickly that one cartwheeled to the ground after missing a rung of the ladder. A fifteen-foot fall might mean a broken neck, but at least— Adele smiled—your family would have something to bury.

Rocker's three rounds destroyed the gatehouse and the ground car racing toward it. *Somebody trying to escape.* Fragments of the car's metal body sailed off like scraps of paper in a storm.

The main house was a rambling structure of glass on stone foundations. Sun hit not the house but a shed adjacent to it. The plastic roof exploded, making the aircar underneath flip like a tiddlywink and shattering glass on that side of the house. The vehicle was still in the air when the second round hit it. Cory and Sun had planned this affair very ably.

The Sissies were cheering their lungs out. Some of the uninvolved crew could watch events on flat-plate displays in their compartments, but the rest were caught up in the moment and imagining what the cannon's regular pounding meant to the folks downrange.

Even before the *Sissie* shifted to Mangravite's estate, it had carried out the most lengthy and thorough attack on ground targets of Adele's memory. Sun and Rocker didn't aim at individuals running in terror, but they ignited every vehicle and outlying building before they destroyed the main house with half a dozen bolts.

Sun was seated beside Adele, but she expanded his face on her display instead of turning her head. The gunner moved his pipper and thumbed the trigger with a look of concentration and glee.

All the targets were gone, ablaze, or glass-edged scars raked into the soil.

The turrets fired simultaneously, devouring a small outcrop just beyond the fence line with four bolts. The rock shattered and fused simultaneously.

Sun shifted from a targeting grid to a terrain display. He leaned back against his cushions, his face glowing with perspiration and exhausted delight. He closed his eyes.

"Sun," said Adele on a two-way link. The gunner, at least, thought his job was over for the time being. "What was that last target, if you please?"

Sun turned and gave Adele's profile a beatific smile. *"Mistress,"* he said, using the intercom perforce to be heard over the rumble of the ship under way, *"it was Cap'n Vesey's idea. You see, she figured as soon as the shooting started, Mangravite would hie himself off to the bunker Master Cazelet found. So we gave him plenty of time to do that."*

"I see," said Adele, nodding. She waited for the rest.

"Last thing we did was seal the other way out," said Sun, *"which Cazelet found too, using the commo routing. Since the bunker was a big secret, there may not be anybody even trying to find the fat bastard, right?"*

"I see," Adele said, marveling at the watchwork complexity of the revenge which her RCN family had planned and executed on her behalf. She smiled. *Mother wouldn't have understood. But I understand.* "Thank you, Sun."

"Ship, this is Five," said Vesey over the general push. *"Master Cazelet, you have the conn. Carry on according to plan. Over."*

"Acknowledged," said Cazelet. Adele, watching over his electronic shoulder, saw the midshipman fill his display with the ship-status readouts. *"Ship, prepare for acceleration to orbit, out."*

The corvette steadied. Vesey had been using three-quarter

flow, with the thruster petals in their middle position. Cazelet now sphinctered the throats to maximum compression. As the *Princess Cecile* started to rise, he steadily increased the flow of reaction mass to the thrusters; acceleration built with the gradual majesty whi ch the inertia of thirteen hundred tonnes demanded.

"Officer Mundy," Vesey said over a two-way link. *"I regret there wasn't time to discuss plans with you, so I hope you'll approve. Ah, the blockade runner* Ella 919 *just returned from Sunbright, and I made the acquaintance of her commander, Captain Tommines."*

"Go ahead, Vesey," Adele said, since the acting captain seemed to have lost her tongue. Vesey viewed Daniel with religious awe. Though her professional qualifications were of the highest order, she struck Adele as emotionally younger than midshipmen several years her junior.

Vesey's relationship with Adele was more complex and not a little disquieting. Their RCN status was clear—and perfectly acceptable to Adele, who in her heart felt that the only really useful power would be the power to force people to leave her alone.

Vesey, though, appeared to regard Adele as a mixture of mother and of high priestess of the Cult of Daniel Leary. The first role disgusted Adele; the second was so ludicrous that Adele would have broken out laughing if she had been the sort of person who did that.

Daniel was a brilliant officer and a friend better than Adele had thought existed outside of Pre-Hiatus romances. He wasn't a god, however.

Her lips twitched in a hard grin. Well, perhaps one of the lustier gods of ancient myth. Adele was fairly certain that Vesey saw Daniel in a more reverent—and very false—light.

"Ah, yes, mistress," Vesey said. The dorsal turret rang against its barbette just astern of the bridge bulkhead; dogs clamped it in place. Lesser shudders were probably the ventral turret doing the same. *"Tommines was singing the praises of Kiki Lindstrom, owner of the* Savoy, *because she had drawn Alliance cruisers away from his ship and saved him from certain capture. She'd then escaped by an amazing transit into the upper reaches of Sunbright's atmosphere."*

She coughed. *"Tommines thought the* Savoy's *captain was a Novy Sverdlovsk officer named Petrov. I'm fairly confident Tommines was wrong on that point, so I set a course for Sunbright. With your permission."*

"I agree with your conclusions and with your plan, Captain," Adele said in an expressionless voice. She thought for a moment and said, "I watched the way you dealt with Master Mangravite, Vesey. Do you recall my suggesting once in the past that you might lack the ruthlessness which an RCN officer requires?"

"Ah," said Vesey. Adele didn't turn to look at her, but she could easily imagine how stiffly the younger woman sat at the command console. *"I remember a discussion, mistress, but I believe that suggestion was made by your servant."*

"If you believe Tovera made an unchallenged statement of that sort without my acquiescence," Adele said, her enunciation as sharp as a microtome, "you are mistaken. In fact I did have that concern. I was wrong to do so."

She made a chirp which was as close as she generally came to laughter. "I don't think even Tovera could have bettered the way you dealt with Mangravite, Captain."

"Ship, we have reached Cremona orbit," Cazelet announced as the High Drive kicked in. *"Next stop, Sunbright!"*

Chapter Twenty-two

SUNBRIGHT

"The ladder's on an orange support right up ahead," said Tomas Grant, taking his hand off the yoke to wave. "We'll see it in a minute or two."

Daniel was in the aircar's luggage compartment on this leg of the ride. He was younger than Hogg and a trifle slimmer, but he looked forward to getting out of the car. He leaned sideways to peer past the heads of his more comfortable companions.

The ninety-centimeter waterline roughly paralleled the Grain Web for nearly a hundred kilometers, but at this point in its course concrete and steel trusses held the pipe thirty feet off the ground. Freight trains could contend with gentle grades; water flow, barring the complexities of pumps and siphons, was a matter of gravity alone.

"I don't see why somebody don't just blow the sucker up," said Hogg, also eyeing the pipeline. The ride's discomfort had left him in a sour mood, though it was a natural question. "Hell knows you lot seem ready enough to smash anything else."

"Not infrequently someone shoots at the line," Grant said. Only the twitch of a muscle at the base of his jaw indicated that Hogg's gibe had gotten home. "People with guns, many of them drunk. The pipe's pretty durable and it's a tube, so usually there's just a dent or a even a splash of osmium on the iron. There are penetrations, of course, and that's why I make these regular trips out of Saal."

Daniel saw the marked truss at last. He wouldn't have known the paint was orange if Grant hadn't said so; years of sun and rain had faded it to a pale streak on bleached concrete. Rust from the pipe and cradle was more visible.

"But as a matter of policy, nobody, no rebel group, is going to deliberately destroy the pipeline," Grant continued. "On the one hand, that would mean discomfort or worse for rebels' friends and relatives who are living in Saal. That includes some who aren't native to Sunbright, by the way. A number of the rebels have deserted from the Saal garrison. The profit in illicit trading can be considerable, and of course the relaxed discipline is an inducement to many as well."

He turned his head and spat over the side of the car. He was obviously uncomfortable.

"Colonel Kinsmill was a lieutenant in the Army of the Free Stars and a member of the Saal garrison, for example," Grant said. "Until he deserted to the forces of liberation. My lot, as your servant put it."

He threaded the car through a band of coarse marsh vegetation and among a series of shallow ponds to pull up at the base of the truss. When he shut off the car's fans, he reached under his seat for something stored there.

Daniel levered himself out of the luggage compartment with his arms—he didn't trust his legs not to cramp—and half-stepped, half-slid onto the ground. He sank in over his boot tops, but he barely noticed the cold seepage past his ankles in his pleasure at being out of the vehicle.

"There's a platform on top," said Grant, holding the thirty-inch steel rod he had been fishing for, "but it'll be tight for three of us. If you'd like to wait here till I've turned the valve...?"

"I'll go up first and stand on the pipe," said Daniel, starting up the ladder. He didn't bother to note that the conduit was greater in diameter than a battleship's yards, let alone the lesser tubes of a corvette. "I can use the exercise."

"And I'll go up too," said Hogg, following immediately. "I've crossed my share of creeks on the trunks of fallen trees, *and* pissing down rain, often enough."

He chuckled as he climbed after Daniel. "You know, young master," he said. "We're going to look like right patsies if somebody's waiting in the bushes down there to use us for target practice."

Daniel laughed. "Are you complaining, Hogg?" he said. "You've told me often enough that everybody on Bantry expected you to be hanged before you were twenty-one. You're on borrowed time, my man."

The section of pipe here at the truss included a horizontal T; a full-diameter valve faced outward toward the semicircular platform at the top of the ladder. Daniel jumped onto the pipe with the help of his right hand. It occurred to him that the yards of a corvette in the Matrix weren't subject to breezes, and also that the long buzzing ride in the aircar hadn't been the best conditioning for his leg muscles.

Hogg climbed up to face him with his usual clumsy grace. Hogg always looked awkward, but he always turned out to have completed his physical tasks with the least possible effort as well.

We'd both rather die than lose our nerve in front of this city fellow, Daniel thought. He grinned broadly and crossed his arms over his chest.

Grant thrust the bar through the crossways hole in the end of a rod projecting upstream of the valve. He began to crank it widdershins, using both hands and his whole upper body.

"My mother was a patriot who really cared for the common people," he said as he closed the conduit stroke by stroke. "She learned that most members of the Popular Party mouthed slogans, but they were really only concerned with power. Father was that way, she said, though in the end it didn't matter: he was caught in the Proscriptions and executed. Mother had already left Cinnabar with me because she was disgusted by the hypocrisy of her fellow Populars."

The *clink* Daniel felt through his boot soles was the butterfly valve closing inside the pipe. Grant paused, breathing hard, and looked up.

"Mother told me that she expected no better of Speaker Leary and his thugs," he said, "but she couldn't stomach the so-called progressive politicians behaving the same way. She would have nothing more to do with the corrupt system, so she left."

Daniel gave a noncommittal nod. His father would have regarded Mistress Grant with contempt, if he was even aware of her. It wasn't that they had different principles; rather, their principles were of such different sorts that neither one could recognize that the other even *had* principles.

It was unfortunate for Cinnabar and for humanity more generally that Daniel's father couldn't respect Mistress Grant's viewpoint. On the other hand, it wouldn't take Speaker Leary long to handle the outlaws and murderers now overrunning Sunbright.

Grant gripped the circular wheel on the access port and leaned his weight into it; it didn't move. Daniel opened his mouth to offer to help, then thought better of it. Grant was being usefully confiding; it would break the mood to imply that he wasn't physically up to doing his job.

And of course he was capable. Grant removed the bar from the butterfly control and threaded it between the rim and spokes of the wheel. With that as a come-along, he broke the seal and began opening the valve with smooth, confident strokes. In the pauses he said, "Mother moved to Madison to save her soul, she thought. Instead she saved her life and mine."

He cranked the wheel to its stop, then paused. He looked up at Daniel again with a wistful smile on his face.

"I thought I could put Mother's principles in place here on Sunbright," Grant said. "The population was small enough and homogenous enough that true democracy was possible, I thought."

He tugged the wheel. It swung outward, releasing a continuing trickle of water. Given the size of the pipe, the leak past the butterfly valve wasn't significant.

"Maybe I was right, Captain Leary," he said. He didn't seem to have made a connection between the young RCN captain and the ruthless Speaker Leary of his childhood. "Maybe democracy was possible. But it's not what I brought to Sunbright."

"One step at a time, Master Grant," Daniel said mildly as he dropped onto the platform. It was constructed of strap iron standing on edge and welded into a series of narrow rectangles; he had supported enough of his weight with his hand on the conduit that his boots thumped but didn't cause a ringing clang.

He squatted and leaned forward to look down the pipe. Leaning back, he said, "So. We're to crawl into Saal through this?"

Grant snorted. "Saal is five kilometers west of this inspection port," he said, obviously pleased to show his superiority to the man whom he had to trust as a savior. Nobody *likes* to be a suppliant. "All you have to do is crawl one klick to the next port and get out; that's on the inside of the defense lines. I'll give you half an hour, then open the butterfly."

He patted the valve stem and started to fit the handle into it.

"Then I'll drive through the gate as normal, swing north to pick you up, and carry you into the city."

Daniel examined the smaller wheel on the interior of the port. It would be a job to open the one down-flow, but the plan was reasonable and more practical than anything he had come up with. Of course Grant knew the ground and he did not.

"All right," said Daniel, squirming into the conduit. "Hogg, I'll lead."

"I'm sorry I don't have a light to give you," Grant said, his voice attenuated. Daniel didn't bother to answer. Sound would

357

change as they neared another T-section, and his shoulder or knee would feel the difference as well.

"We'll manage," said Hogg. "Just hope we don't have to back bloody out, but I guess we'll manage that too if we got to."

He was allowing Daniel to get well ahead; Daniel nodded in approval. This was a sufficiently claustrophobic situation without the two of them crowding one another.

Behind him, the words weakened by distance and blocked by his body, Hogg said, "Just like we'd manage if the next stop was three miles away or thirty. We're the ones who're going to pull your bacon out of the fire, sonny."

The haze of light faded; Hogg must finally have entered the pipe. Daniel was grinning as he crawled along on palms, knees, and sometimes the toes of his boots.

He had left his RCN utilities in Riely's post and changed into what a farm laborer on Sunbright wore: a loose shirt with three-quarter-length sleeves, and trousers with tabs on the cuffs that allowed the legs to be rolled up and tied to the crotch for working in muck. They had looked as comfortable as a tent, but they turned out to be made from a local variety of sisal; steel wool could scarcely have been harsher on the skin.

My knees will be rubbed raw by the time I've crawled a klick, Daniel thought. *But at least I won't wear holes in the trousers.*

He grinned at himself. He knew that he was focusing on a trivial, controllable concern to avoid thinking about vaster questions that were out of his hands. The technique worked well, even though he was consciously aware of it. Human beings were remarkably good at fooling themselves—thank goodness.

Daniel found himself counting to twenty as he shuffled along—and then starting over at one. He wasn't measuring the distance, just giving his conscious mind something to concentrate on other than—for example—wondering what would happen if Grant opened the butterfly valve before he and Hogg opened the next access port.

They probably wouldn't be crushed against an obstruction in the course of the three miles of pipe; the water should have unimpeded flow on the way, after all. When the pipe reached the settling tank, however, there might well be a coarse screen to catch branches and other floating debris.

Well, that wouldn't matter: they would surely have been drowned before water pressure forced their pureed bodies through the filter.

"It ought to be about now-w-w . . . ," Hogg called, his muffled voice made fuzzy by reverberation. Blood was pounding in Daniel's ears, and that made it harder for him to hear also.

What is he talking— Daniel thought, but instinctively he reached out with his left hand and touched the locking wheel of the access port. Hogg had come within feet of judging the distance they'd travelled, despite having to crawl and being in total darkness.

"Right!" Daniel replied. "I'm at the port, and I'll get it open."

The wheel in the inner face was small, as Daniel had known, and slimy—which was a surprise, because he hadn't touched the wheel of the port they'd entered by. It was probably a gel of manganese deposited from the water, though he supposed it could have been algae.

He tried it without result. Not only was the wheel small, the pipe's narrow interior cramped his shoulders when he shifted his grip.

Maybe I should have borrowed the rod from Grant, Daniel thought. Which was silly; Grant needed it to open the butterfly valve. And besides—*bugger that! I'm Daniel Leary of the RCN, and I won't have some office worker on a backwater like Sunbright thinking that I can't manage a task that maintenance yokels are expected to do!*

Daniel used the loose end of his shirt to wipe the bronze wheel. That also gave him a chance to get his breathing under control and calm down generally. He wasn't claustrophobic, but crawling half a mile in a lightless steel tube had proven more stressful than he'd been aware of until he slowed down.

He took the wheel in his hands, tugging with his left and pushing upward with his right palm against a crossbar. Nothing moved. He continued willing more strength into his arms. This wasn't going to beat him, even if he cut his hand to the bone on the smooth rod.

There was a tiny *snap*. The wheel began to move with a grinding shudder. He changed his grip and continued to push; when blood rushed back into his right hand, it felt as though he had plunged it into boiling water.

The gear reached its stop. Daniel slammed the wheel with the point of his left shoulder, breaking the seal and swinging the port outward.

Light flooded in and made Daniel sneeze. The relief he felt as he scrambled onto the platform shocked him in its intensity. *I was a lot closer to the edge than I thought I was.*

Hogg joined him, puffing a little and with more red in his face than Daniel remembered seeing before. "I don't mind being outa that thing," he muttered as he sat heavily on the platform, his legs hanging over the edge. He leaned back against the pipe and closed his eyes.

He grinned, looking at Daniel, and added, "And whatever I told that smart-ass city kid, I'm just as glad it wasn't three miles. Though I'd've done it, I guess."

Next to the support pillar grew a tree that looked as though it had been made by sticking lengths of drinking straws together with lumps of clay. The bark was metallically smooth; sprays of purple-red leaves sprang out randomly from trunk and branches alike.

Daniel leaned closer. What had seemed to be a scar on the nearest branch was a troop of tiny insects in a circular formation.

If I were like Adele, I'd have a natural history database with me. I don't, because I depend on her to supply me at need. For so many things.

Daniel stood and swung the port closed, then locked it down by using his left hand alone on the wheel. His right was swollen, and there was still a white streak across the palm. He waggled the hand slowly to get the circulation back.

"I'd as soon wait to go down the ladder till Grant comes for us," he said.

"You don't see me moving, do you?" said Hogg. He had closed his eyes again. "Young master? What do we do when we get into Saal?"

Water began to flow through the pipe again. The rush of its passage became higher pitched as the upstream valve opened fully, squeezing the resonating air into a smaller and smaller volume.

"We stay low," Daniel said, nodding. "If the leader of the rebellion can hide in the city for years, he shouldn't have much trouble putting us up for a few weeks. I'll send a message to Adele on Cremona. There'll be ships going there, couriers if nothing else."

He grinned wryly. "Though there's not so much official trade as through the blockade runners, I'll admit," he said. "But I don't and didn't want to risk a message from an RCN captain to an RCN warship being sent by a blockade runner, just in case the Funnel Squadron captures it."

Daniel paused, staring at the disk of tiny insects as he ordered his thoughts. The bark in the wake of their slow passage had a polished look.

"We're not enemy citizens, after all: our nations are at peace. But if I'm seen to be dealing with the Sunbright rebels, the Treaty of Amiens might not...Well, let's say that there's been more war than peace between Cinnabar and the Alliance during my lifetime. I don't want to be the cause of resumed hostilities."

"So Mistress Mundy brings the *Sissie* here," said Hogg. "We sneak our young hero aboard, then we head for home?"

He straightened though he remained seated; he was looking down the brushy slope below them. He was hearing something that Daniel missed, though Daniel sat up also.

"That's the general idea," Daniel said, "but I'm not sure we could slip him aboard an RCN warship unnoticed. The *Sissie* will be watched and probably guarded."

He heard something and leaned forward. "That's the car," he said. "Well, it's *a* car."

"It's our boy," said Hogg, rising and starting down the ladder with the jolting suddenness of a dog attacking. "He'd been flying, but I guess he put her down on the ground again when he turned off to get us."

"The other problem," Daniel said, standing but waiting for Hogg to get clear before he swung onto the ladder, "is that we, Cinnabar, that is, have to be *seen* to have solved the problem. I think it's necessary to get Governor Blaskett's agreement before we act. Otherwise we risk having it appear that the whole rebellion was an RCN plot run from off-planet."

Hogg reached the bottom of the ladder; Daniel followed, gripping the rungs with his right thumb rather than his joined fingers in the normal fashion. His hand was going to be fine, but he didn't think he would strain it any more than he had to for the next day or two.

"Mind," he said as the thrum of the aircar's fans reached them; the vehicle was still out of sight through the brush, "I'm going to talk to Adele about this when she gets here. If she sees a better option, I'll delighted to hear it."

Grant's aircar nosed through a band of shrubs with thread-thin stems and foliage that could have been brushes of glass fiber. He swung around to point back downhill before he shut off his motors. Gossamer tendrils trailed from the car's seams and threatened to clog the fan ducts.

"Get the front, Hogg," Daniel said as he pulled a handful of leaves out of the back intake. The car would probably pick up as much vegetation in the other direction, but at least they could start clean, or cleanish. "And then take the passenger seat."

"At the gate, the guards were all talking about a Cinnabar warship that just arrived in orbit," Grant said. "The garrison has been put on alert. Do you know what this is about, Leary? Is it good?"

Daniel lifted himself into the luggage compartment. He no longer noticed the ache in his right hand.

"I don't know," he said. "Did you learn what the ship is?"

"Not a big ship," Grant said. "It's a destroyer named the *Princess*, the lieutenant thought."

"Ah," said Daniel. It would require about four hours to go through procedures, then leave orbit and finally to cool down the hull enough to open the ship. That should be plenty of time to get the proper garments. "I suspect that's the corvette *Princess Cecile*. And if that's correct, it's very good indeed!"

Signals Officer Adele Mundy, wearing utilities and as inconspicuous as the console at which she sat, sorted information from Saal's civil-service databases with practiced skill. Now that the yacht had become the RCS *Princess Cecile* again, command had reverted to the ranking commissioned officer, Lieutenant Vesey. Principal Hrynko had dissolved back into the fog of fantasy from which she had briefly coalesced.

That was as Adele preferred it. Her family had through the generations given the Republic many leading political figures and more than its share of Speakers of the Senate. She had found politics repugnant from age six when her father, Lucas Mundy, had paraded her before local organizers of the Popular

Party at a dinner he gave for "influential supporters"—that is, the rank and file of the political process.

Adele had found them uncouth, ill-educated, and frequently little better than brutes. She could not imagine why her father was willing to associate with such people.

If he had answered her honestly, he would have said, "For the sake of power," and she would still have been confused. What was the use of power if it didn't permit you to avoid boors who ate with their mouths open, drank too much, and couldn't have constructed a grammatical sentence for the greatest prize they could imagine?

Which for most would have been a barrel of whiskey, judging from their behavior.

Lucas had not been honest, of course. In all likelihood, he hadn't believed that his little daughter could understand if he had been willing to answer frankly.

Even a decade later, when Adele left Cinnabar to continue her schooling on Bryce and he planned the coup whose failure led to his death, he hadn't really understood how intelligent she was. Lucas couldn't *allow* himself to understand, because his daughter came to such different results from his when they both analyzed the same data.

Adele's lips twitched; in another person, the expression would have broadened into a smile. She couldn't even say that her analyses were correct and her father's death proved that his were not. Lucas Mundy had been fifty-one when he was killed and beheaded; Adele was thirty-six. Given the events of her life since she joined Daniel, it seemed unlikely that she would survive another fifteen years.

"Mistress, Flink, Tapfer, *and* Schuetze *have been alerted and are recalling their crews from liberty,"* reported Cory from the BDC. *"The* Scharf's *reaction tanks were emptied for recoating, and Commodore Pyne decided that it would take too long to fill her enough to lift safely. And the* Sicher *and* Vorwarts *are in orbit, of course. Over."*

Vesey had agreed that Cory and Cazelet were of more use mining the sudden flurry of message traffic for signs of Daniel than they were echoing the captain as she handled ordinary landing chores. She would have bowed to Adele's unofficial authority even if she had not agreed.

"All right," said Adele. That seemed to her to be an absurd overreaction to the arrival of a corvette of a friendly power, but she found on reviewing Cory's précis a copy of Governor Blaskett's screamed order to Pyne, the squadron commander.

The planetary governor had no direct authority over a Fleet officer; but if Pyne had ignored the demand and something had gone wrong, the aftermath for him would have been grim and probably unsurvivable. There was nothing unusual about an autocrat choosing to rule by fear, but Guarantor Porra was better at it—and more single-minded—than most.

Adele had set Cazelet at the astrogation console to scanning the security-force files for references to Daniel or someone who might have been Daniel. He would report when he had something to report. Beyond taking a quick overview of his progress, she left him alone.

Adele found what she was looking for. She respected the skills of Cory and Cazelet or she would not have trusted them with the important tasks she had delegated. Indeed, Daniel's location and safety were the most personally important questions on Sunbright to Adele Mundy.

She was here as Officer Mundy of the RCN, however. Her duty came first, an attitude which Daniel would not only understand but approve; but she doubted that anybody else aboard the *Princess Cecile* would understand her ability to put human feelings behind duty.

Well, Tovera would understand. She, of course, was a sociopath to whom feelings and duty were both abstract concepts and who operated on a strict basis of self-preservation.

Tovera had decided that doing whatever Adele directed was her safest route through the thickets of human emotions. Adele understood the way normal people thought well enough to function among them, and Tovera understood very well how Adele thought.

An icon winked in the upper left corner of Adele's display. "Mistress," said Tovera on a two-way link. "You'll want to look at this."

Adele opened the icon without comment or expression. Tovera was seated in her usual location on the bridge: the training station at the back of the signals console. It was intended for a striker who could observe what the trainer was doing; if the trainer chose, the striker could carry out exercises under the trainer's direction.

Adele had simply turned the station into an independent unit. She could echo—or control—what was going on, of course, but she could do that with every station on the *Princess Cecile*, including the command console. That knowledge would have shocked and infuriated the Navy

House bureaucracy and most senior RCN officers, but it simply amused Daniel.

It was not common for Tovera—or anyone else—to break Adele's concentration. She assumed her servant would have had a good reason.

Tovera had been observing their surroundings, splitting her flat-plate display between a satellite view of the spaceport and a visual panorama through the corvette's own sensors. Saal Harbor was a huge installation. Channels connected forty-eight separate pools, each big enough to hold a battleship or several lesser vessels. Less than half the pools were filled at present, and all but a skeleton staff had been withdrawn from the base after the signing of the Treaty of Amiens. Even so, from above it was more impressive than Harbor Three on Cinnabar.

Tovera shrank the satellite image to expand the real-time view from the *Sissie* alone in her pool. Because of the size of the base, a network of trams were laid on top of the dikes so as to serve each pool. A company of Alliance troops in battledress had arrived in four armored personnel carriers and had set up checkpoints on the routes leading to the corvette.

The steam of the *Princess Cecile*'s landing had dissipated. The surface of the pool still bubbled around the hull; the thick steel took some time to cool below boiling, even when immersed in a bath of water.

A tram—a long flatbed with a cabin for six in front and space for cargo and supplies of virtually any dimensions in back—had arrived. Besides the driver it carried only a pair of port officials in brown uniforms. As Adele already knew from the message traffic, Governor Blaskett had decided not to extend diplomatic courtesies to the Cinnabar vessel, so she was being met by the same customs and medical team as any tramp freighter which happened to set down.

There was also a dusty, dark-blue panel van with the legend WATER DEPARTMENT stencilled on the side. The troops had passed it through the cordon, so it must have the correct papers, but what in heaven's name was it doing here?

The driver and the two men with him on the bench seat wore coveralls, stained and faded but roughly the same blue as that of the van. The passengers got out carrying toolboxes and trudged toward the platform at the edge of the pool, where the port officials already waited for the *Sissie* to open up.

Tovera increased the magnification on the passengers' faces by ten, then by a hundred times. She must have done that earlier for herself as the van proceeded through the checkpoint.

"Right," said Adele, rising and shutting down her console. She had been using her data unit to control the console in her usual fashion; as she strode for the companionway, she slipped it into her pocket.

The personnel on duty on the bridge didn't appear to notice that Adele was leaving. Tovera swung in behind her mistress, holding her attaché case and smiling like a satisfied viper.

"Opening ship!" the PA system announced before Adele reached the companionway's Level D hatch. Vesey's words were blurred by echoes.

Pasternak, the chief engineer, waited in the entry hold with the four spacers who would be the guard detachment. Pasternak was chief of ship by virtue of his position, as the bosun was chief of rig. Vesey had delegated the duties of meeting the local officials to him, while she as captain remained on the bridge.

Adele hoped that Vesey would have made a different choice—put Woetjans on the bridge and gone to the hold herself—if the governor or other senior official had arrived to greet the *Princess Cecile*. Vesey hadn't asked if she could take Cory or Cazelet off the duties Adele had set them to, which showed clearly what her priorities were.

"Ma'am?" said Pasternak in surprise when he saw Adele. "Are you taking over here?"

The chief engineer was sixty standard years old, greatly overqualified to serve on a mere corvette and, as Adele knew, extremely wealthy. Unlike most noncommissioned spacers—and no few officers—he didn't drink and whore away his earnings; and, as senior warrant officer under the most successful captain since Anston, his shares of prize money had been enormous.

"Carry on, Chief," Adele said. The guards had riot sticks, not submachine guns as they would have on a friendly *or* a hostile planet. That was another sign of Vesey's good judgment. "I'm just here to meet the men from the water department."

"Very good, ma'am," Pasternak said, making a half bow and straightening just as the main hatch clanged into its cradle on the starboard outrigger. Technicians back in the harbor offices had already extended the gangplank from its housing on the quay to mate with the outrigger from the other side.

Adele had never asked why Pasternak continued to sail with Daniel; he certainly wasn't a man who craved excitement. The *Princess Cecile* and all those aboard her were fortunate to have so skilled and solid an officer, though.

The guards trotted down the ramp four abreast and onto the

gangplank in pairs, determined to be as threatening a barrier as they could to the minions of Guarantor Porra. Adele didn't smile as she, Pasternak, and Tovera followed at a more sedate pace. These guards and the whole RCN had been just that for decades: a barrier between Cinnabar and her great enemy.

Adele wasn't naive enough to believe that planets controlled by the Republic of Cinnabar existed in a Golden Age. She had seen enough of life in the so-called Alliance of Free Stars, however, to know that for ordinary people it was much better to be ruled from Xenos.

The pair of Alliance officials waited with increasing concern as the Sissies trotted toward them, clubs swinging in their belt sheaths. Adele suspected the locals were more concerned by the cordon of their own troops than they were by the spacers. If shooting started, they were clearly in the middle of it, and neither—from their badges, an elderly doctor and a very young customs inspector—appeared to be the hero type.

"Chief," said Adele. "Lead that pair to the side until I get the men from the water department on board."

"Ma'am?" Pasternak said, blinking as he tried to make sense of the order. Then his face cleared—it wasn't his job to understand—and he said, "Yes, mistress." He strode toward the waiting officials, gesturing them imperiously to the side.

Adele indicated the guards with the splayed fingers of her left hand. She said, "No one react as I come through with those workmen. *No* reaction."

The detachment was under Barnes, one of the few spacers who was actually a good shot with a stocked impeller. He had proven himself quite useful with a cudgel or a length of pipe also, and he was just as mindlessly loyal to Daniel—and by extension, to Adele—as any other member of the corvette's crew.

"Roger," said Barnes. He looked at his three fellows and said conversationally, "If any of you don't understand the mistress, I'll knock what she said right through your thick skulls. Okay?"

The guards laughed. "Hey," said Rossi, a short technician with the shoulders of an ox and a face which must have been ugly even before the bottle scarred it, "at least you won't shoot us, will you, Barnes?"

Adele and Tovera walked toward the workmen. Tovera was smiling.

The Water Department van drove off. Adele fitted the final piece of the puzzle into place in her mind.

"Hello, Adele," Daniel said. "Can you get me aboard the *Sissie* without a lot of fuss? I need to change into my Whites so that we can call on Governor Blaskett."

"Hello, Daniel," she replied quietly. "Yes, come this way. I've warned the guards."

Walking nonchalantly toward the gangplank, she added, "I was going to tell you that the head of the rebellion here is one Tomas Grant, the field supervisor of the Saal Water Department, but I see from your transportation that you must have learned that on your own."

Kelsey, a gangling rigger, gaped to see that Daniel and Hogg were following Adele. He didn't speak, so there wasn't a problem. Blank amazement was a normal expression for Kelsey anyway; he wasn't one of the crew's intellectual lights.

"Yes, I did learn that," Daniel said. "But how in heaven's name did *you* learn?"

The gangplank flexed with both of them on it, and a moment later Hogg as well. Tovera waited at the edge of the pool, facing away from the corvette. She was probably smiling. Adele wondered if she tried to lure people into pushing past her.

"Since Freedom was reported as having a Cinnabar accent, I checked Cinnabar emigrants to Madison," Adele said. She didn't mind the gangplank, but the steel solidity of the boarding ramp was preferable. "I found that Mistress Serafina Grant, whom I remembered as an associate of my father, had arrived with her son three months before your father broke the Three Circles Conspiracy. She was one of the Intransigents, you see; the Populars who wouldn't compromise their principles."

"Bloody hell!" shouted a tech who was inspecting the hatch hydraulics. "It's Six! Six is back!"

"Carry on, Evans," Daniel said as he followed Adele to the companionway.

Adele grimaced, but the excitement didn't matter now. The port officials were too far away to understand what was happening.

"I found that Serafina had died of cancer, but that her son, Tomas Grant, had worked in the Ashetown water department," Adele said, speaking over the companionway's echoing bustle. "He was drafted to Sunbright when the base at Saal was built. When we landed here, I found that Tomas was in a perfect location to lead the revolt. I couldn't be sure till you arrived in the water department van, but the rest was simple enough."

They stepped into the A Level corridor. Sissies stood cheering at the hatches of every compartment, including Vesey and Cazelet from the bridge.

Daniel raised his hands in acknowledgment. "I'm glad to be home, fellow Sissies!" he said. "But right now I've got to put on a monkey suit to arrange the successful completion of our mission with the local authorities!"

In a lower voice as he turned toward his cabin, he added, "Adele, I'm very glad that your deductions aren't made on behalf of the Fifth Bureau!"

Chapter Twenty-three

SAAL ON SUNBRIGHT

Adele wore her second-class uniform, her Grays, in her guise as Captain Leary's aide. Whites, like Daniel's own, would have been better, but she didn't own a pair. In most circumstances in which an RCN officer would wear a first-class uniform, Adele appeared in tailored civilian garments as Lady Mundy of Chatsworth.

This wasn't such a circumstance, so her Grays had to do. It wouldn't be surprising that the aide to the captain of a mere corvette couldn't afford Whites, but Adele would have been more proper, and therefore less conspicuous, in the more formal uniform.

The descending elevator slowed with gluey smoothness and a groan from somewhere in the shaft above. Adele didn't have any idea how far they had dropped from the ground-level entrance of Base Saal, though she suspected Daniel did.

Hogg and Tovera remained in the bare concrete foyer above. That didn't concern Adele or, she was sure, Daniel.

Both servants, bodyguards in their own minds if not the minds of their principals, were frustrated and upset.

How in heaven's name did my parents manage to function as the personal focus for thousands and tens of thousands of supporters?

Adele smiled faintly. The literal answer was that her parents had been killed and beheaded while they were still, in biological terms, in the prime of life.

"This cage is armored," Daniel said, wearing his usual friendly smile. "That's why it accelerates and slows in such a leisurely fashion. I wonder what use an armored elevator is?"

The door of the cylindrical cage rotated sideways at the measured, massive rate with which all the equipment in Base Saal operated. The glass projectiles of Tovera's miniature submachine gun would barely scratch the finish of the doors here.

Of course Tovera's case also contained blocks of plastic explosive. A very modest pinch of that would crack a hinge or shatter a lock mechanism....

The corridor beyond the elevator was concrete cast in the form of a pointed arch. There were no embellishments or furnishings, unless the two soldiers at the end in parade uniforms fell into one category or the other: they wore polished knee boots with silver helmets and breastplates.

Their submachine guns looked perfectly functional, however, and they glowered at the visitors as though they would like to open fire. Well, being confined in a bare concrete pit would sour the temper of the best-humored man.

"I've seen prisons that appeared to be more pleasant environments," Daniel said in a normal, conversational tone as he started down the corridor. Echoes blurred his words into their footsteps, but he obviously wasn't trying to conceal what he said from the guards.

Adele walked along with her friend, but she didn't try to keep in step. She hadn't been trained for it; and for that matter, Daniel had proven in the past that he wasn't very good at drill and ceremony, either.

"Captain Leary and aide to see Governor Blaskett by appointment!" Daniel said to the guard at the left of the door. They looked as similar as statues cast from the same mold; it was beyond her to see how Daniel had decided which soldier was senior.

There was a miniature camera mounted above the transom. A diode in its workings blinked; the door opened outward with a grinding noise. Neither of the guards had touched the latch or, for that matter, moved in any fashion.

Maybe they are *statues.*

Daniel walked in; Adele followed, three feet behind and offset to the left. Behind them, the door closed with another groan.

Governor Blaskett's office looked more like the bridge of a starship than the sybarite's boudoir which Adele had imagined before she first entered the lowering fortress. Of course it would have had to be the bridge of an unusually orderly starship.

Base Saal had been built as the command center of a regional replenishing base, so the building's forbidding exterior was a given. Inside, though—and especially for a man like Blaskett, who obviously felt no need to stint his appetites—one would have expected at least touches of luxury: rare woods, art glass, velvet paintings of naked women. The walls of Blaskett's sanctum were covered with real-time displays showing—to Adele's quick glance—every portion of the base, even those which were shut down under the present peacetime regimen.

Two more guards in parade armor stood in the back corners of the room. Again, their submachine guns were serious even if the men holding them looked like characters from a historical romance.

Blaskett sat in the hollow of a U-shaped desk with three holographic displays; the central one was damped for the moment to allow him to glare at his visitors. He was of average height, at least if his legs were of normal length; and though he was on the plump side, he didn't give Adele the impression of being an inflated balloon. His clothes were tailored like a military uniform, but they were bright green and had the sheen of natural silk.

Daniel braced to attention and saluted. "Sir!" he said. "Captain Leary reporting, with the compliments of the Republic of Cinnabar!"

Instead of returning the salute, the governor said, "You can stop spouting nonsense, Leary. I was warned you were coming, and I know why you're here: you plan to extract your agent now that I'm about to crush this Cinnabar provocation which masquerades as a revolt."

"Sir?" said Daniel, obviously taken aback. "Sir, I can assure you that the Republic had nothing to do with the...that is, with anything happening here on Sunbright. I've been sent to offer the Republic's help in ending the situation, that's all."

Adele considered the circumstances, then seated herself on one of the chairs against the wall. They were steel extrusions, much like those of a starship's wardroom. She took out her personal data unit, which had been operating in passive mode since before she entered the fortress. It didn't appear that anything she did was going to change the interview's tone for the worse.

"I told you to stop the nonsense!" Blaskett said, half rising and leaning forward with his hands on the desktop. Adele was interested to see that light caught droplets of spittle spraying from the governor's anger. "Well, I'm not going to give you the cheap salvation you're looking for. I'm going to capture your Freedom and I'm going to hang him and I'm going to show the whole universe that the Cinnabar Senate is a gang of treacherous liars!"

Adele avoided a smile by effort of will. She and Daniel were the children of Cinnabar senators. They had known from infancy that the Senate was a gang of treacherous liars.

Adele browsed selectively, ignored in her corner. There was plenty to occupy her. Blaskett's electronic security was no more effective than his glittering bodyguards.

The governor had told the truth when he said he had been warned to expect Captain Leary's arrival to withdraw Freedom: a courier ship had brought the information from Madison three days earlier. The sender was the chief of the Fleet Intelligence Detachment for the Forty Stars Sector, Commander Doerries.

"Sir," said Daniel. He had broken his formal posture, but he still stood very straight. "All I ask is that we be allowed to search for this rebel leader, and to take him off planet if we find him.

The Republic will sequester him where he won't do any more harm. The whole business can be taken care of very quietly."

"Now I'm going to tell you, Leary," said Blaskett, relaxing back into his chair again, "*exactly* what's going to happen. Your ship is going to lift from here within seventy-two hours. I am not required to extend hospitality to foreign warships for any longer than that, and I do not choose to go beyond my obligation."

"As you wish, sir," Daniel said in a tone of quiet restraint. "With luck that should be long enough—"

"I'll tell you when to speak, Captain," Blaskett said. "Furthermore, before you lift, you will either hand over the Cinnabar agent calling himself Freedom or my customs inspectors will search your ship until they find him. And if that means unscrewing every panel and dumping the bulk storage out on the dock, that's what they'll do."

"The *Princess Cecile* is an RCN warship—" said Daniel.

"Be silent! Your bloody warship *will* submit to a search or there'll be a tragic accident when a missile guts it on liftoff, do you understand?" the governor shouted. He was on his feet and knuckles again; Adele thought of a great ape bellowing as it nerved itself to charge. "Because I think you've already sneaked this bastard aboard, Leary! You thought you'd fooled me, didn't you, but we saw the two men pretending to be from the Water Department go onto your ship as soon as you landed!"

"Sir," said Daniel calmly, "as a courtesy to the representatives of a friendly nation, your inspectors are welcome to search the RCS *Princess Cecile* if they care to. As for the water business..."

He spread his hands, palms upward.

"...Chief Engineer Pasternak had been having leakage

problems in the forward reaction-mass tank. As we were landing, my signals officer contacted the Saal Water Department and requested caulking compound, which your officials very kindly delivered. But nobody came aboard at that time."

Daniel coughed into his hand and added, "I'm sure you can check our signals log in case your own people didn't record the call. And as I said, you may go aboard right now and search as thoroughly as you like. You won't find anyone who isn't a member of the crew."

"I suppose you think I won't!" the governor said, but by now he seemed a little doubtful. "Well, you're wrong. The inspectors are already standing by—and the missile batteries are on high alert too."

"I see," said Daniel. "Sir, I'm sorry that you have misinterpreted my motives and those of the Republic. If there's no possibility that you'll relent so that our nations can work together—"

"Listen!" said Blaskett. "Your agent has killed thousands, tens of thousands! There's no compromise with a mad dog. Just turn him over now and save yourself a lot of trouble."

"I'm afraid that's impossible, sir," Daniel said. "Ah—I trust that I'll be permitted to give my crew liberty?"

"They'll be DNA-typed as they leave," said Blaskett. "And checked back in individually. Anybody who doesn't have a match in the outgoing file will be detained. And hanged, I shouldn't wonder!"

Daniel shrugged. "Liberty is always granted subject to local regulations," he said. "This is an unusual regulation, but it won't interfere with drinking, so there'll be no complaints beyond the usual grousing. Thank you, sir."

He suddenly smiled. "My normal problem is to get the whole crew back from the bars and knocking shops, you know," he said. "There's often a few who don't make liftoff. But if you want to make sure that I don't sign on extra personnel here, that's your right."

He turned; Adele pocketed her data unit and rose as the door opened to an unseen command. They started down the corridor toward the elevator, ignoring the motionless guards.

"We won't speak until we're outside," Daniel said.

"Yes," said Adele, though she was sure that there were no listening devices in the corridor or the elevator cage.

Adele was pleased despite her lack of expression. There wasn't much information to exchange, after all. She believed she had already solved the problem.

Daniel waited at the tram stop, averting his eyes from the fierce glare as a gunboat landed with the usual thunder and lightning from her plasma thrusters. Commodore Pyne had sent the *Flink* into orbit while a tram was shuttling Daniel to his meeting with Governor Blaskett; now the *Sicher* was landing to replenish her air and reaction mass, and to give her crew liberty.

Daniel could have watched the *Sicher* land through the pair of UV-filtering RCN goggles he'd given Hogg to carry; his Whites didn't have pockets. It had been a long time since Daniel had needed more than sound to understand what a starship was doing, however, and he had more important matters to attend to.

He turned his head. "Adele," he said, "I believe it's safe to speak here. I want you to locate a ship, ideally a small one, that can be made ready for liftoff within forty-eight hours, and preferably within twenty-four."

"It is safe, yes," said Adele. "And I believe the best ship for the purpose would be the *Commune*, a former blockade runner. It has been used to insert commandos three times already."

Her eyes had been on the tram trundling in their general direction; it was still half a mile away. It might not be responding to their call for transportation.

Daniel didn't think Adele was particularly concerned with when she would get back to the *Princess Cecile*; rather, she just preferred not to have face-to-face conversations. Circumstances forced her into propinquity with him, but that didn't mean she actually had to look at her friend as they spoke.

"You knew what I was planning before I said anything about it, didn't you?" Daniel said. "Saints and angels, Adele, I *still* haven't said anything about it."

"I'm sorry, Daniel," she said—and she *did* turn to face him with a troubled, contrite expression. "I was showing off, I suppose. But I was present when the governor spoke to you, so it shouldn't surprise you that we came to the same conclusions."

She grimaced. "My mother would be ashamed of me," she said. "And rightly so in this instance, I'm afraid."

The tram was continuing around the circuit instead of pulling into the stop in the center where Daniel and his companions waited. The flatbed portion was equipped with hydraulic lifting apparatus and carried a fusion bottle. There was only one person visible in the cab.

"Wonder if he'd stop if I put one through his windshield?" Hogg said thoughtfully. "Well, I probably couldn't hit it at this range. With a pistol, I mean."

"They won't lift ship without us, Hogg," Daniel said. Secretly, though, he wondered if Blaskett, at the heart of his electronic spider's web, had disconnected the call plate at this stop as a provocation.

Though the truth was that the base was operating at less than ten percent of its designed capacity, so large portions of its infrastructure had been shut down. Indeed, there was another tram approaching the circuit now, this one apparently empty.

Daniel considered again the practicality of carrying ground transport on the *Sissie* the way the *Milton* had done under his command. The *Milton* had been a heavy cruiser, however. Even taken down to its components for stowing, a four-place vehicle was simply too bulky for the interior of a corvette.

"Daniel," said Adele. "Did you know that Governor Blaskett would search the *Sissie* before he allowed us to lift off? I had wondered why you didn't bring Grant along with you when you and Hogg boarded, though I see now that it would have been a disaster if you had."

Daniel laughed. "You give me far too much credit," he said. "I didn't expect anything of the sort. Searching us is an act of war, you realize. Though I'm sure that everyone in the External Bureau on Xenos—and most of the Senate—would be at pains to hush things up, even if Blaskett really did put a missile into us."

He sobered, trying to put in order the series of choices which he had made without slowing for conscious consideration. He had done what he thought was right; pretty much as he always did.

"I hadn't heard a great deal to the governor's credit, even before we met him," Daniel said, choosing his words. "Nevertheless, our nations are friendly now, even if not allies. I decided to assume that the governor would see our common interest in resolving the matter efficiently. I felt that was the right way to behave, as a gentleman and an officer of the RCN."

The tram *was* turning into the short loop that served the fortress. There wasn't as much traffic as Daniel would have expected to a headquarters, but he supposed the personnel were billeted on lower levels of the structure, so the process of going on and off duty didn't require leaving the building.

He shrugged. "I was wrong in my assumption, unfortunately," he said.

"You were correct in the course of action you took," said Adele. "I don't know that you would have gained points if you had done so out of a Machiavellian distrust of humanity instead of what would appear to an outsider to have been the bluff honesty and good nature of a country squire."

Her lips pursed. "It might appear in that light to someone who knew you rather well, in fact," she said. "Which is to the credit of your upbringing and of your service."

Hogg watched the tram slowing toward the stop, his hand in his pocket. He was ready to react in case someone concealed in the cab leaped up with a leveled gun.

Tovera faced back toward the steel gates of the fortress, equally prepared for an attack from that direction. Without turning, she said, "Though I wouldn't recommend a career in politics, Captain."

Her delivery was so dry that it took Daniel a moment to process what she had said. Then he boomed a laugh which wonderfully released his tension.

"Thank you, Tovera," he said. "I'll take your opinion under advisement. For now, though—"

He swung onto the flatbed portion of the tram. Hogg was already in the cab, setting the touchplate controls for Pool 28, where the *Princess Cecile* floated in lonely splendor.

"—I'll be busy committing piracy and subverting the laws of a friendly power. But doing so with as much bluff honesty and good nature as possible, I hope."

Chapter Twenty-four

SAAL ON SUNBRIGHT

The van's front seat was a bench, but it would have been more comfortable for two than with Hogg wedged between Daniel and Tomas Grant, who was driving. He took them at a good pace—not so fast that they aroused suspicion—down the straight North Meridian between Pools 8 and 16, then exited onto the frontage road encircling Pool 18, where six modest vessels were docked.

Steam with the occasional fairydust sprinkle of ions half hid the *Commune*. Her thrusters were being warmed up in response to the alert sent from Base Command. Ordinarily the noise would have drawn at least casual interest, but the recent flurry of the *Princess Cecile*'s liftoff, followed ten minutes later by the *Flink*'s landing, made the former blockade runner's four thrusters insignificant.

The other patrolling gunboat, the *Tapfer*, had already started her descent, but it would be at least fifteen minutes before she could be heard at Base Saal. The gunboat's thrusters might be visible a little sooner than that, but it was broad daylight and only someone who happened to be looking toward the west would notice.

Even then no one would wonder; or at any rate, no one would wonder except the movement control officer in the tower. That official would be puzzled at why Funnel Squadron Command had brought all its ships to the ground, leaving no one on patrol for blockade runners.

If movement control passed the question upstairs instead of merely logging the situation, then the questions were likely to be repeated in loud, angry voices. The answer was simple: Funnel Squadron Command had sent recall signals, in the proper code and with all the right indicators attached, to the ships in orbit.

Possibly some day, if the intelligence services involved in the investigation brought in sufficiently skilled computer experts, they would learn that the base communications system had been penetrated from the inside. By that time the *Sissie* would be long gone from the region.

Daniel grinned at a thought. He and Signals Officer Adele Mundy, the person who could have done the most to help them with their inquiries, might well have died of old age before the authorities reached that solution.

The sections of roadway had been laid separately, and the circular portion had settled less. The van jounced onto it at an angle, rocking badly. The empty racks rattled like an ill-tuned bell chorus.

Grant muttered a curse—he took his driving very seriously—and called, "You in the back? Are you all right?"

There was general laughter. "Hell yes, sonny," said Dasi. "Even a good landing on dry land rattles your back teeth worse than that did, and they aren't all good."

"Amen to that!" said Hofnagel, the tech who would run the *Commune*'s fusion bottle while Barnes, Dasi, and Larkins handled rigging duties, if any. All four were better than useful in a scrap, though Daniel hadn't permitted them to carry weapons on this occasion. "I'm not complaining, you understand, Six."

"Understood, Hofnagel," Daniel said. "I'm sure if the Great Gods became ships' captains, they too would have better landings and worse ones."

Grant slowed the van to a stop at the gangplank to the *Commune*. She was a 700-tonne vessel, basically of a type with the *Savoy*—and, for that matter, with the other ships in Pool 18, all of which had been captured empty or nearly empty. Blockade runners with valuable cargoes were condemned on Bailey's Horn, where there was a thriving market. Only ships which would bring no more than the value of their hulls were brought before the prize court here in Saal and bought by the Fleet itself for the Funnel Squadron's knockabout work: couriers, stores runs, and the dangerous job of inserting Special Service commandos into Sunbright's hinterlands.

There was no guard at the gangplank. Daniel hadn't expected one, since the *Commune*'s crew was too small for pointless niceties.

According to Adele, Captain Kropatchek was a Fleet petty officer, but the four crewmen were foreign spacers captured while running the blockade. They had enlisted, probably to avoid the threat of being put out into vacuum. Depending on the captain of the gunboat which captured them, that might have been more than an empty threat.

While such spacers would obey orders and do their jobs as ably for an Alliance captain as they would for anyone else, Daniel didn't expect patriotic heroism from them unless they were pushed to it. He was as confident that the Sissies he'd brought with him would obey his orders not to start a brawl as he was of their ability to finish any trouble that somebody else started.

Daniel got out as Barnes opened the back of the van. The four Sissies were standing in the aisle between racks intended for the pipes, fittings, and tools which Grant had removed from the van before he drove off in it. If others in the Water Department had wondered about his actions, their doubts hadn't risen to an official level.

The back of the van was neither roomy nor comfortable, but the vertical stanchions supporting the racks were as solid as the vehicle's frame. With them to hang on to, veteran spacers—as Dasi had said—weren't going to mind a rough ride.

Hogg slid past Daniel on the way to the gangplank. "Hogg!" Daniel said, not shouting but in a tone of command which even his old servant knew to obey. "I'll be leading, if you will. Barnes, bring up the rear."

Daniel stepped onto the gangplank. He would rather have put Hogg at the back of the column, since the *Commune*'s present crew was expecting a squad of troops. It was hard to imagine anyone looking less military than Hogg did, even if he had been carrying a stocked impeller. Now he had a pistol, a knife, and goodness knew what other weapons, but they were concealed in his baggy poaching garments.

Whoever was at the controls blipped the *Commune*'s thrusters again; not enough to be dangerous to the people crossing the gangplank, but enough to splash them with water boiling up from the pool. Daniel sneezed violently, and the ozone with traces of other ions stung his eyes.

Grant shouted in surprise. The gangplank flexed hard, but Daniel wasn't worried about the civilian falling off. Dasi was directly behind him. The big bosun's mate would carry Grant aboard by belt and collar if he thought that was necessary.

Daniel strode the rest of the way up the gangplank and into the hold. Three spacers were huddled together in a corner, glancing sidelong at Daniel and muttering greetings. They had probably known what the man at the controls was going to do, but they hadn't had any say in the matter.

Daniel ducked through the hatch and entered the crew capsule. Ordinarily six to ten heavily armed infantry would ride in the hold. The *Commune* would lift, then drop after a single orbit—a bit more or a bit less—into a blocking position against which a powerful armored column from Saal would try to trap a rebel band. Without an anvil, patrols from Saal would meet nothing but mud, mines, and the occasional sniper.

Petty Officer Kropatchek stood and stepped away from the console when Daniel appeared. Another common spacer sat against the port bulkhead at the fusion-bottle controls, but she carefully didn't raise her head or otherwise show she wanted to become involved.

Kropatchek was six and a half feet tall. He was bald, but his flowing moustaches were silky black.

"Sorry about that little mistake with the thrusters," he

rumbled. His expression would have been a smirk if his features hadn't been so brutal. "Hope none of you pissed your trousers."

"Just a little good clean fun, Captain Kropatchek," Daniel said, smiling pleasantly as he stepped close. "Giving the pongoes a bit of a shaking up, were you?"

He should have said "the grunts," since "pongo" was the RCN term for soldiers. Well, Daniel was wearing water department coveralls anyway, so Kropatchek was going to figure out shortly that it wasn't an insertion squad which had come aboard.

"Hey!" said Kropatchek. "What are you—"

Daniel gripped the petty officer's right wrist and elbow and started bending them back. Kropatchek lurched forward. Daniel shifted his balance and used the big man's rush to slam his face into the starboard bulkhead.

The technician shouted and leaped from her seat. Kropatchek turned toward Daniel, spraying blood from his broken nose. Daniel kicked him in the crotch and, as he doubled over, banged him into the bulkhead again.

This time Kropatchek hit on the point of his skull. There was a loud clang; then he slumped to the deck. There were two smears of blood on the bulkhead above him.

Daniel was breathing hard; he felt dizzy enough that he gripped the seat of the console for a moment. In a regretful voice, Hogg said, "I don't guess you'll let me finish him."

Not for a stupid joke on members of a rival service, Daniel thought. He didn't have the breath right now to get the words out. *I'm sweating like a pig.*

Hogg grabbed a handful of Kropatchek's coveralls with his left hand, perfectly judging the point of balance, and dragged him into the hold. The big man's lower legs and face dragged on the deck, which disturbed Daniel slightly but Hogg not at all.

Hogg held his folding knife in his right hand. It was a clumsy-looking weapon with a knuckle-duster hilt. Daniel had been amazed when, in his childhood, he first saw Hogg throw the weapon accurately. That no longer surprised him.

With his breathing back to normal, Daniel straightened and looked at the technician. She was flattened against the bulkhead, her eyes and mouth both wide open.

Daniel gave her a smile and said, "Go on into the hold. We'll tie up you and the rest—"

Actually, secure them with cargo tape.

"—and free you as soon as we're in orbit."

The technician didn't speak. Daniel suddenly realized that she was staring at the blood on the bulkhead. He laughed and took her by the elbow, turning her toward the hatchway and giving her a gentle push.

"I suspect your captain will have come around by then," he said. "If not, well, the console will land you without difficulties. Or you can hand control over to Base Saal, if you like."

Dasi and Hofnagel entered the crew capsule, followed by Grant and, finally, Hogg. They all carried suits.

"No trouble with the crew," Dasi said. "Matter of fact, Kepsie's an ex-RCN rigger. I'd like to sign him on if that's all right with you, Six."

"Yes, all right," said Daniel. Hogg handed him the bottom portion of a rigging suit, which he started to put on without argument. He would need it before long. "What's the suit situation?"

"Two rigging suits and four air suits," Dasi said. "Kepsie says it's really only three airsuits, the other one leaks out a bottle of air in fifteen minutes, but—"

He grinned at Grant, who looked away. Hofnagel was fitting him into an airsuit.

"—I guess that'll do for the little guy here. We'll need to make two trips, regardless."

"I'll have Woetjans bring extras when she comes over with the line," Daniel said, settling into the console and checking its readings. He set the main hatch to close; it began to whine and shudder.

Hofnagel was at the fusion controls; Hogg and Grant—the latter looking rather green—sat on the bottom bunk of the tier on the starboard bulkhead. Daniel grinned and checked flow, then lit the thrusters again.

"So far, so good," he said. "And if things go to plan in orbit, the *Princess Cecile* will have accomplished another mission!"

Neither Signals Officer Mundy nor Lady Mundy had any proper involvement with the process of bringing the freighter *Commune* and the corvette *Princess Cecile* into close enough alignment that personnel could cross between them by cable. The vessels were commanded by Captain Leary and Lieutenant Vesey, two of the best ship handlers in the RCN. Even a veteran officer would have nothing useful to add, and a mere layman like Adele couldn't even understand what she was seeing.

Nonetheless, she devoted the upper left quadrant of her

display to real-time imagery of the two ships. She supposed that showed lack of discipline on her part.

The *Sissie* was in free fall, an uncomfortable business when Adele thought about it, which she almost never did. There were always plenty of things for her to do: when there was nothing more pressing, she would sift and organize the data she had mined from Macotta Squadron computers.

She had plenty to do now. She was listening to—or trying to listen to—all the message traffic emanating from Base Saal, from the Funnel Squadron, and from individual missile batteries.

Published information assured her that ground-based anti-ship missiles were not a threat to the ships at their current height above Sunbright. Skilled people could make equipment do things that experts said were impossible. Adele wasn't willing to bet the lives of her shipmates that there was no Alliance battery commander here who was as skilled at his job as, for example, Tovera was with a pistol.

Tovera, or Tovera's mistress.

There was a jolt as a thruster fired a minuscule pulse. The *Sissie* had been rotating almost imperceptibly around its long axis; the motion stopped. The *Commune*, visible in the same true-scale image as the larger corvette, pulsed also.

"They've got it!" Sun cried from the gunnery console beside Adele's. "I thought they were going to slip the cable or have it snap, but Six—and Five too, she's doing great—brought us back together. Did you ever see anything so sweet?"

Unaided voice wouldn't ordinarily be audible on a starship's bridge, but in free fall, with all unnecessary equipment shut down to keep from affecting the linkup, Adele heard her neighbor quite clearly. She had no business bothering with extraneous conversation: Cazelet was shadowing Vesey from the BDC, and Cory was in the entry hold, prepared to act as required if something went wrong with the *Sissie*'s end of the cable. No one but Officer Mundy was surveying Alliance communications for threats.

Four figures had already reached the corvette, moving hand over hand on the line; another was starting across now, with others behind him. Adele grimaced.

"Explain what happened, if you would, Sun," she said. She continued to scan the columns of oral information converted to text.

"They'd spliced five hundred-foot lines, mistress," the gunner said, obviously glad for an audience. He was chattering to control his nervousness as Adele—she smiled grimly—was listening to control her own. "But it was paying out because the ships were both moving a bit and there wasn't time to splice in another. It wasn't hawsers that could maybe take the strain, it was just shrouds, so it'd snap if they didn't cast off in time. Well, that—"

Sun moved at the corner of Adele's eyes. She didn't look away from her duty, but she could imagine the shrug.

"—you remember what happened to Trent Johns when a line snapped, right?"

"Yes," said Adele. She had seen people killed in various colorful fashions since she joined the RCN. Johns, a rigger who had been cut in half the long way by a beryllium monocrystal cable which whipped back after breaking, was probably the most memorable, though. She hadn't realized how far the blood would splash under those conditions.

"Well, now they can all get aboard without casting off and linking again," Sun said. "It'll save time, maybe half an hour. And the only reason it's that quick is because of how good Six is, and Five too."

"Thank you," said Adele. Four more suited figures, then a fifth, were coming over the line. The first pair and last pair were swinging hand over hand, but the one in the middle must be Tomas Grant: he was linked by short safety lines to the figures immediately in front of and behind him.

Much as I would be, Adele thought.

Woetjans had carried air suits from the corvette's stores when she hauled over the line; she must be the large figure immediately preceding the rebel leader. That left an extra person coming toward the *Sissie*, but Daniel would have matters under control. He always had matters under control, even when it didn't seem that was the case.

At the top of Adele's display, along with the row of faces of the corvette's officers, she had inset an icon for the Plot Position Indicator. It pulsed orange to call attention to itself.

She brought the PPI up to full-screen to see what change had triggered the alert. The *Sissie*'s sensors were reacting to the precursor effects of a ship transitioning from the Matrix to normal space. It was a hundred thousand miles out from Sunbright but significantly closer to the *Princess Cecile* herself.

"*Officer Mundy, this is Five,*" said Vesey on the command channel, which included all the commissioned and warrant officers who were linked at the moment. "*Handle any necessary communications chores, if you will, over.*"

"Yes," said Adele. She shrank the real-time images to an icon—she should have closed it down, but she was superstitiously afraid to—and brought the location of the incoming vessel to half-screen.

The highest likelihood was that the newcomer was a blockade runner which had chosen to make a close approach to Sunbright instead of initially extracting several light-minutes out to judge the position of the blockading ships. That could have been simply an accident, of course. Most astrogators were abysmally bad by the standards Adele had learned to expect in the RCN.

Her smile was real, though it didn't reach her lips. *Let alone the standards set by the* Princess Cecile's *officers.*

The ripples in sidereal space-time gave no indication of the size or course of the extracting vessel. That became clear in a shivering rush, the way a bag expands when tugged through the air with its mouth open.

The newcomer was the anti-pirate cruiser *Estremadura.*

Adele considered the options as quickly and coldly as a computer would have done. Having decided, she locked the gun turrets, said, "Vesey, this is an enemy if it recognizes us, but I hope it won't. Break..."

She drew a deep breath. Then—using laser, because it was hardest to intercept and she *really* hoped to keep Base Saal in ignorance of what was going on—she said, "Unknown vessel, this is RCS *Princess Cecile*, Captain Leary commanding, over."

When the *Estremadura* was patrolling above Madison, it might have noticed the *Sissie* in harbor. At the time, though, the corvette was masquerading as the *House of Hrynko*, so past observation shouldn't be a danger.

The problem was that although Commander Doerries was Adele's enemy and was obviously playing some game at variance with the official policy of the Alliance, he was also thoroughly competent. Doerries might have connected the destruction of Platt's outstation in Madison with the sudden departure of Principal Hrynko and her yacht from Madison. Adele would have noticed that, and she would then have tried to match the yacht to other known vessels.

Adele was quite certain that the *Princess Cecile* was in every Fleet database, even those of outlying regions like the Forty Stars Sector. The Kostroman rig was only camouflage until someone looked at it closely, and it seemed probable that Officer Adele Mundy was as well known to Fleet Intelligence as Captain Daniel Leary was.

The *Estremadura* did not reply to the hail. That could have various meanings, but the cruiser's rig was coming down and it had lit its High Drive. Adele's display indicated that the ships were 23,000 miles apart, but the cruiser was unquestionably accelerating toward the *Sissie*.

"Bloody hell!" Sun said. He wasn't using the intercom, probably because he had forgotten about it. "Bloody hell, mistress, you've got to free my guns! She wants us so bad she's had a topmast carry away from the thrust! Mistress, she'll be launching missiles any moment, and if I don't deflect them, we've screwed the pooch for sure! We can't maneuver—we got Six out on a line!"

"*Ship,*" ordered Vesey on the general push, "*action stations. Missiles, prepare to attack the Estremadura but do not unshutter your tubes. Break.*"

There was very little chance that the missileers, Chazanoff and his mate Fiducia in the BDC, weren't already plotting attacks on the *Estremadura*. They would have done the same if an RCN battleship had appeared instead of an Alliance auxiliary cruiser.

Good missileers, just like good gunners, liked to train with real-world targets instead of simulations thrown up by the attack console. Vesey was just making explicit what they already must have assumed: the *Estremadura* was a real enemy.

Vesey was playing it safe by ordering them to leave the missile tubes shuttered also. It would require a careful observer with good optics to notice whether the *Sissie*'s tubes were closed—as they were to reduce turbulence during liftoffs and landings in an atmosphere—or opened for use; but the cruiser had been built on Pantellaria, where optics were a specialty, and the efficiency it had demonstrated in the Madison system gave no one reason to trust that its watch officers would be blind or inept.

"*Sun,*" Vesey continued. Adele would have eavesdropped on the message even if Vesey had used a two-way link, but in fact the captain was manually copying to her signals officer. "*If you argue against Officer Mundy's decision again, I will not only derate you but also transfer you out of the* Sissie's *crew. Do you understand, over?*"

"*Sir!*" the gunner said. "*Understood, sir!*"

That was a little stiff, Adele thought. But Vesey was letting Adele get on with her job, so it was only common courtesy to leave questions of crew discipline to the first lieutenant, whose duty it was.

Vesey almost certainly knew that the *Estremadura* didn't carry missiles: they would be a useless bulk and expense for a ship intended to engage pirates and blockade runners. Sun probably knew that also, though it was possible that he had forgotten in his desire to go into action.

Adele was certain that Vesey would have given the same order if a salvo of missiles had been driving straight at them, however. Six had told her to defer to Adele's judgment, so Vesey would defer.

"Unknown vessel," Adele repeated, "this is RCS *Princess Cecile*. Please identify yourself, over."

She continued to speak calmly, but she carefully injected the least note of irritation into her tone. Any emotion in Adele's voice was probably artificial, though very occasionally real anger came through.

Not when she was in a killing rage, however. Then she became icy cold.

The *Estremadura* still did not reply. Adele sighed and unlocked the gun turrets.

"Vesey," she said, "I'm going to try once more, but I think we have to assume that the *Estremadura* intends to attack us. Break. Unknown vessel, identify yourself or we will treat you as hostile. RCS *Princess Cecile*, over."

The corvette shuddered as the main hatch started to close. The vibration was worse than usual because the ship was in free fall instead of having water or even solid earth to absorb the trembling.

"Ship, they're aboard!" Cory shouted, using the general channel instead of the command push. The common spacers

were just as concerned about Six as the ship's officers were. *"I've jettisoned the line instead of reeling it in, out!"*

The plasma thrusters as well as the High Drive motors kicked in. Vesey was a careful officer who normally brought the High Drive on line gradually. That way she didn't risk an explosion in the event a feed anomaly led to a buildup of either matter or antimatter in the mixing chamber before its opposite was injected; this time she must have slammed the valves wide open.

Even accelerating at the maximum rate—a little over 2 gs—by using both propulsion systems, the loaded *Sissie's* 1300 tonnes were slow to get moving. It was unusual to use plasma thrusters in hard vacuum, because they were much less efficient than the High Drive's annihilation of matter and antimatter. Vesey was doing so to get the corvette under way as quickly as possible.

Which wasn't going to make any significant difference in the rate with which the Alliance cruiser closed with them. The *Estremadura* had extracted at .004 c. It would have had difficulty braking to land on Sunbright, but its captain appeared to have come with the intention of fighting.

"Ship, prepare to insert," Vesey said. The drives shut off as abruptly as they had been switched on. Adele's styluses no longer weighed in her fingers, and her body rose against the console's restraints.

Hatches squealed deep in the lower hull. The *Princess Cecile* shook herself in a fashion that Adele had never before experienced; she wondered if maximum thrust had damaged the ship.

The *Estremadura* had not begun firing, though it was sure to do so momentarily. At this range the bolts wouldn't damage even the *Sissie*'s rigging, but the bath of ions would prevent her from escaping into the Matrix.

The real hammering would begin shortly thereafter, as the cruiser's proper motion brought the two ships within knife range. Sun and Rocker were as good as any gunners in the RCN, but the *Estremadura*'s gunners had proven they were first-rate in Sun's estimation also. The Alliance cruiser had twice the armament and nearly three times the hull size over which to spread the damage.

A single thruster burped. The clang—it felt as if someone had kicked the hull with a steel-toed boot—was as unexpected as it was infuriating. Somebody—it was probably Woetjans—roared on the command channel, *"What the bloody hell are you playing at!"*

Even Adele knew enough to be horrified. The jolt of plasma would delay insertion by ten or more seconds, during which—

The image of the *Estremadura* blurred on Adele's display, then tightened to a false sharpness as software enhanced the signal into what it believed was the correct form. *What's happened to the sensors?*

The cruiser opened fire, six guns rippling with minimal separation between the bolts. The charges did not reach the *Princess Cecile*, but the void between the ships flared.

"Inserting!" Vesey said.

For an instant, reality for Adele flattened. She felt infinitely thin, infinitely extended—

And the *Sissie* was fully in the Matrix. Adele's display

became a pearly blur inset with the miniature faces of her fellow officers. The console was displaying the input of the external sensors, but there was no longer reality in human terms beyond the corvette herself.

Daniel, groping for the catches of his rigging suit, clashed up the final steps of the companionway and entered the bridge. He had taken his helmet and gauntlets off already. Hogg, wearing an airsuit, followed at his heels.

Vesey started to get up. Daniel said, "Sit right where you are, Captain Vesey! Start plotting us a course for Hester 27514CH."

Daniel sat at the astrogation console—empty because Cory had been in the entry hold; not that Cory would have objected if Six ordered him out. He paused for a moment and took a deep breath. Then he grinned, fully himself again.

"Ship," Daniel said, orally keying the general push. His voice echoed from the PA speakers and through the intercom. "We're safe in the Matrix instead of getting our butts toasted in normal space because Acting Captain Vesey dumped reaction mass back along our course and then kicked us out of it by kissing the thrusters. What I think—"

His face split in a smile of boyish delight.

"—is that we owe Captain Vesey a hearty cheer. Hurrah for Captain Vesey!"

The ship rang with "Hurrah!" and "Hurrah for Five."

"Up Cinnabar, fellow spacers!" Daniel shouted, and the crew echoed him again.

Chapter Twenty-five

THE MATRIX

Adele continued to review internal ship discussions as text blocks, but in the Matrix she had no communications duties proper. Instead of going back to processing data from Madison, she decided instead to learn about Hester 27514CH, the planned watering stop.

The Sailing Directions for the Macotta Region, published by Navy House, gave only a brief notation: "Uninhabitable/ Can provide reaction mass." She grimaced, then searched for information with more body.

That was readily available, because Adele always updated the *Princess Cecile*'s database with all the material she could find on the region to which the corvette would be travelling. They had paused only briefly on Cinnabar on their way from Zenobia to Kronstadt, but Adele had not stinted her information-gathering. She could sleep during the voyage, after all.

The log of a trader from Novy Sverdlovsk two centuries earlier provided the fullest account. The ship, the *Twelve*

Apostles, had landed after a reaction-mass tank had carried loose and ruptured. The crew had made repairs, then diverted to Hester 27514CH to refill the tank.

The Sverdlovians had found no land except for active volcanoes. Storm-lashed waves wore the cones down quickly if they ceased to erupt. The atmosphere was low on oxygen and poisonously full of sulfur—as was the sea, causing it to be extremely acid. Two crewmen had died when their suits failed, and a third had drowned. The ship itself had nearly sunk in the open sea when a squall swept in, and damage from the water and atmosphere had required extensive repairs when they got to their destination.

Surely there has to be a better choice for replenishment than this hellworld?

Sun and Rocker were rotating an image of the *Estremadura* on their gunnery screens, discussing aiming points and arguing whether concentrating or spreading plasma bolts across the target was the better idea. More accurately, Rocker was arguing in favor of separating the turret controls so that they could disable more of the cruiser's individual gun mountings in a given interval; Sun was adamant that a single point of aim opened the possibility of punching a hole in the *Estremadura*'s hull and ending the fight quickly.

Adele followed the discussion as text. It interested her as an observer of human behavior. Sun and his assistant were capable specialists who knew their lives were at risk unless the *Princess Cecile* performed at top efficiency. Each argued to maximize his individual authority, but they couched their arguments in terms of the general good.

Rocker wanted to control a gun turret; Sun wanted to control both turrets. Sun was senior, so the argument in favor of concentrated fire would carry the day.

Adele wasn't concerned about the question itself: the conflict would determine whether she lived or died, but she didn't particularly care which so long as she had met the standards which she set for herself. Listening to that sort of discussion, however, convinced her that she herself was a member of a species which merely shared physical similarities with human beings.

By reflex, Adele checked the file's history; she found that Cory had accessed the log of the *Twelve Apostles* shortly before she did herself. After checking Cory's console to make sure he wasn't in the midst of calculations which shouldn't be interrupted—he was merely studying the log in question and had lined up several other references to Hester 27514CH, none of them more informative than the *Sailing Directions*—she said, "Cory?"

"Ma'am?" he said on a two-way link, turning to look at her.

"Is there no better place for us to water than Hester 27514CH?" she said. "It appears to me that at best we'll be seriously damaged by landing there. Ah, over."

"What?" said Cory. He laughed. *"Because a Sverdlovsk tramp had problems? You've seen how sloppy civilian freighters get, mistress, even when they're Cinnabar flagged. And let me tell you, Sverdlovsk warships, they're no better. You put them together and you've got a ship that leaks from all the seams and a crew in suits where just the big holes are taped closed. I've seen tramps sink in Harbor Two on Cinnabar—it's the*

wogs, not the planet, where the trouble is, over."

Adele considered the matter. She discounted the notion a stranger might have had: that Cory was trying to cheer her up by putting a positive face on what he expected to be a disaster. In a crisis, RCN officers had a tendency to react with professional dispassion, which left civilians petrified with horror.

Furthermore, Adele had the impression that the Sissies were no more likely to lie to her than to the ship's steel hull. They didn't regard Officer Mundy as human, either, though they took a more positive of what she was than she did herself.

"I see," she said. Daniel, Vesey, and now Cory all believed that Hester 27514CH was a suitable planet on which to replenish reaction mass. She knew of no one whose professional opinion she would support against those three officers. "Thank you, Cory."

Tomas Grant stood in the rotunda adjacent to the bridge, surrounded by off-duty riggers. Adele could probably have seen him if she turned to look out through the hatchway, but she preferred to use imagery from the ceiling cameras.

The rebel leader wasn't involved in the discussion except as a trophy for Barnes, Dasi, and Larkins to point to as they regaled their fellows with their description of stealing a ship from the center of an Alliance base and spiriting away the most wanted man on the planet. Hofnagel was probably telling similar stories in the Power Room, but the riggers had made off with the prize.

No one seemed to be formally looking after Grant. Daniel had gone to the Battle Direction Center, leaving Vesey in the command console.

Vesey really had earned the honor. Just as Tovera studied normal human beings so that she could appear to have a conscience, so Vesey seemed to have studied Daniel so that she could appear to make split-second decisions. That meant that by force of will she picked *a* possible course of action and executed it, instead of determining which of many possibilities was the optimal course.

Because Vesey was intelligent and extremely skilled, the first choice off the top of her head was likely to be the correct one. Whether or not it was the best possible choice, remaining frozen by indecision—her natural response—was certainly the worst choice in a crisis.

It had to be very hard for her, though. Adele had once allowed a brute to strip-search her so that she could carry out her mission. It had been necessary, so she had accepted it. She was, after all, an RCN officer.

As was Lieutenant Vesey. A very *good* officer, now seated at the command console of the most efficient ship in the RCN.

"Ship, extracting in thirty, that is three-zero, seconds," Vesey announced. The riggers stepped to the edges of the rotunda, ready either to let the hull watch enter without congestion or to rush out to join them if the situation required.

"We're extracting three light-minutes out from Sunbright," Cory said, continuing his conversation with Adele. *"This is just to get us away from the cruiser so that we can build up velocity in normal space. No matter how good Six is—or Vesey, of course—it'd take us a month to reach Hester with no more way on than we had when we inserted."*

"Extracting," Vesey said.

Because Adele wasn't lost in the data on her display, the transition struck her with unexpected savagery: her left eye flared with rings of rosy light, and the right side of her body felt as though it were being shredded with garden cultivators. She gasped and dropped her right stylus.

The High Drive slammed on again, though this time without the thrusters added. Adele called up the system schematic to see how much reaction mass remained.

She became furious at her mistake. As soon as she had the answer—seven percent—she realized that she could not, and had *known* she could not, interpret the data.

"Master Cory," Adele said, speaking formally because of her embarrassment. "How serious is our lack of reaction mass, if you please?"

"Well, bad and not bad, mistress," Cory said. *"We've got plenty to get to Hester. Other than go back to Sunbright, though, that's about the choice. Once we get to Hester we'll be fine from there to Madison, if that's where we're going. Or even Kronstadt, though we'll only be filling the aft tank instead of both."*

Adele frowned, but the only really foolish thing she could do at this point would be to fail to ask for clarification when she lacked the knowledge to answer her own question. "Why won't we fill both tanks, please?"

"Oh, well, because we'd contaminate what's left in the bow tank," Cory said. He didn't sound surprised, let alone exasperated, by the question, so perhaps it wasn't as foolish as Adele had thought. *"The antimatter converters work on any fluid, but if we run sulfuric acid through the water*

purification system, it'll eat the guts out, and then we'd have nothing to drink."

"Ah," said Adele. "Thank you, Cory."

She noticed the precursor effects of a ship extracting before the watch officers did; perhaps she had her console set to higher sensitivity, perhaps it was just that she was expecting this to happen.

"Daniel, there's a ship coming," she said sharply. With a heartbeat more to remember that Daniel wasn't in the command console, she added, "Ship, another ship's—"

The High Drive switched off.

"—appearing close by, over."

In a moment she could read the scale and calculate the distance from the newcomer to the *Sissie*. It wasn't second nature to her, though, as it would have been to one of the ship's officers.

"Inserting!" Daniel said. The *Princess Cecile* shuddered out of normal space with what seemed to Adele to be a nasty corkscrew motion that only affected her lower legs. She wondered if that had something to do with the fact that Daniel hadn't allowed as much time as usual between shutting down the High Drive and insertion.

"Daniel," Adele said. Visual identification of the newcomer would not be certain at the point when the *Sissie* left sidereal space, but the electronic signature was. "The other ship is the *Estremadura*. She tracked us through the Matrix."

"Roger," said Daniel. *"Break. Ship, this is Six. I have the conn, out."*

Lieutenant Vesey had done exceptionally well. Nevertheless, Adele was sure that Vesey breathed a sigh of relief at those words like everyone else on the corvette.

It was time for the first team to take over.

Daniel had the calculated courses of the *Estremadura* and the *Princess Cecile* on his display, but he shrank the hologram because he wasn't watching it anyway. Within fifteen seconds of when the corvette had dropped into the Matrix, her enemy would have been close enough to anchor her in sidereal space if her gunners were good enough.

The *Estremadura*'s gunners were good enough.

The consoles in the Battle Direction Center faced inward in a five-pointed star. To Daniel's left was Fiducia, then Rocker, and Blumelein, a technician third class who would be in charge of the fusion bottle if something happened to the Power Room crew. The chance of there *being* a fusion bottle if the whole Power Room crew was incapacitated seemed to Daniel to be vanishingly unlikely, but he didn't argue against what Chief Pasternak considered a reasonable precaution.

Midshipman Cazelet, backing up the astrogation officer, sat to Daniel's right. He faced his display, but his hands didn't move and he was watching Daniel out of the corners of his eyes.

Grinning, Daniel turned to him and said, "If you're hoping I'll turn into a beautiful woman and pledge you my undying devotion, Cazelet, I'm afraid you're going to be disappointed."

The midshipman cringed. He still didn't look directly at Daniel. "Sir," he said, "I'm—"

He composed himself and faced Daniel with a shy smile. "I didn't want to disturb you, sir," he said. "I don't see any alternative except proceeding to Hester 27514CH at our present rate, and I'm afraid that the *Estremadura* would be able to pursue us even there."

Daniel chuckled. To put the midshipman at his ease, he said, "How long would the voyage take, Cazelet?"

"Seventeen days," Cazelet answered without hesitation. "That is, I estimate seventeen days. But you can probably cut time from that, sir."

"Though not enough to matter, I think," Daniel said. It cheered him to learn—he'd expected it, but the confirmation was nice—that Cazelet had not only plotted the course to Hester but had already calculated the time it would take the *Princess Cecile* to arrive if she were not able to accelerate beyond her current modest sidereal velocity. Vesey, Cory, and Cazelet were all first-rate astrogators, and Daniel Leary could justly claim a portion of their skill for his own efforts.

Fiducia was listening to the conversation as best he could, Rocker might be, and Blumelein was wholly lost in her display. Daniel didn't mind others listening to this conversation if they wanted to, but he was treating it as a discussion with a fellow officer whose opinion he could pretend to value. He *did* value Cazelet, of course, but at present all he wanted from his subordinate was a way to rigorously check his own speculations.

"Sir?" Cazelet said. "How are they able to track us in the Matrix? I mean, the Palmyrenes did, but they were conning their cutters from out on the hull."

"Well, partly," Daniel said, "they've got somebody good piloting them from the hull, yes. Somebody better than me, certainly. I don't know whether they've got anything as sophisticated as the mechanical hull controls that the Palmyrenes used, but there's something. And it looks like her owners hired the pick of the specialists they wanted when the Fleet put ships in ordinary when the Treaty of Amiens was signed."

As Daniel spoke, he brought up his course calculations. The *Sissie* was proceeding on Vesey's track, not his own, but he doubted there was a whit of difference between them.

Which was the problem. The route from Sunbright to Hester 27514CH was straightforward and short—only about three days if the *Princess Cecile* had been able to accelerate in normal fashion. Woetjans would have arrived at virtually the same solution by pushing buttons on the astrogation computer.

"They know where we're going," Daniel mused aloud. "I was able to shake them when the *Savoy* lifted from Madison because they didn't expect me to strike straight for Sunbright. Once they'd realized that I hadn't set a course for Cremona, it was too late for them to pick up our track."

He gestured to the display. Cazelet couldn't see the data, but Daniel wasn't really speaking to the midshipman.

"Now we have nowhere to go except to the water point or back to Sunbright. If we return to Sunbright, the *Estremadura* won't catch us but the Funnel Squadron certainly will. I don't know precisely how Governor Blaskett will respond, but I don't expect it will be a pleasant meeting after we've committed piracy. And there's Grant on board, of course."

"If we can't run, sir," said Cazelet, frowning, "what other choice do we have?"

Daniel shouted a laugh and slapped the fascia plate of the

console with both open hands. "Yes!" he said. "Of *course*, Cazelet, thank you!"

Daniel switched his display to an attack screen. He began entering calculations.

"Sir?" Cazelet said diffidently. "I don't follow you."

"We're RCN," said Daniel in a tone of pleased wonder. "We can attack. We can *always* attack."

"Well, Sissies," Daniel said, *"I believe we've run long enough. It's time to change the game."*

To Adele, his voice sounded calm but forceful. That was a fairly accurate description of Daniel under most circumstances.

"The Alliance cruiser which is pursuing us," he continued, *"is being conned very ably from her hull. Whenever we extract from the Matrix, she follows. What I propose to do at our next extraction is to launch two or, I hope, three pairs of missiles toward the point where our past experience predicts the cruiser will extract. We will insert again and very shortly extract a second time to repeat the process, if necessary."*

The plan sounded reasonable on its face. She lacked the expertise to determine whether it really could work, but Daniel was as good a judge of that question as anyone she could think of. For the first time since the *Estremadura* reappeared, Adele could imagine a future which did not involve either capture by Alliance forces or execution out of hand by the crew of the cruiser whose paymasters had been bankrupted when the *Princess Cecile* took her leave from Cremona.

"We'll be making quick insertions and extractions, Sissies,"

Daniel said. *"We've done that before. Because we've done it, we remember how bloody awful it is, and how much we all prayed that we'd never have to do it again. Well, we have to, it's that simple, so that's what we'll do. I have nothing more to say except this: RCN forever!"*

The cheers that followed were real and expected, which made Adele smile wryly. Being on a ship in the Matrix was uncomfortable for human beings. The environment led to hallucinations or perhaps to visions of things which were real—somewhere or somewhen—and were therefore even more uncomfortable to consider.

But the transition between normal space and the Matrix was infinitely worse than time spent beyond the barrier between universes. Sequencing back and forth quickly from one state to the other could leave even veteran spacers vomiting or unconscious on the deck.

As Daniel said, it was necessary. A spacer who pretended that "necessary" allowed him to choose was very quickly dead.

Adele kept the faces of fellow officers as small insets at the top of her screen. To her surprise, Sun looked doubtful instead of enthusiastic as she expected from him when they were about to see action. She echoed his display and found that though he had a gunnery board up, he wasn't participating in the computerized training scenario.

"Master Sun?" she said on a two-way link. The gunner wasn't actively involved in the immediate problem, and he certainly looked as though he would appreciate having his thoughts diverted from their present course. "Why do you doubt the success of Captain Leary's plan?"

"I never said—" the gunner blurted, spinning to stare at her. He saw only Adele's profile, of course. Though they were at adjacent consoles, she preferred to communicate through a filter. Her holographic display provided the illusion of distance even when the reality was less comfortable.

Sun's horror relaxed into a rueful smile. *"No point in trying to kid you, is there, ma'am?"* he said. *"Look, Six is playing some game, I know he is; but what he says he's doing, that won't work. The gunners on that Alliance bitch are just too good, though I hate to say it, over."*

"Explain what you mean, please," Adele said. Experts often assumed that when they had given an answer, the steps by which they had arrived at the answer were obvious to their listeners. That was even true—

She smiled very faintly.

—of experts in data collection and sorting.

"Well, ma'am, it's like this," Sun said, turning his attention toward his display but replacing the training scenario with a blank screen. He either realized that Adele would be echoing it or had forgotten about her in his focus on the question. *"We come out—"*

A blue bead appeared, though at the front in the lower right corner rather than in the usual center of the display.

"—here. And they come out here—"

The red bead appeared kitty-corner from the blue one on the three-dimensional display, on top at the upper back.

"—always at the same vector, which they do because that gives them the best angle for their guns. So Six knows where they'll be, right enough, and if nothing else happened I'd lay

odds on him fixing their wagon just like he plans. But we're too close, and their gunners, they won't let it happen!"

Adele frowned. *I need to show more charity toward people who are puzzled by what I say,* she thought.

She regretted displaying her ignorance so abjectly, but it was better to seem foolish than to take the foolish option of remaining needlessly ignorant. She said, "How is being close a problem, Sun? That leaves less time for the enemy gunners to nudge our missiles out of the way, does it not?"

Missiles weighed five tons apiece and achieved their effects by kinetic energy. They separated into three pieces after they had run all their reaction mass through the High Drive motor which accelerated them to a noticeable fraction of light speed.

There was no way to stop an incoming missile; a target could either dodge it or redirect it with plasma bolts. The metal which a bolt sublimed from one side of a missile shoved the remainder of the projectile in the opposite direction. Skillfully used, plasma cannon could save a ship, which was, after all, a point target at the ranges of a normal space battle.

"If they've reached burnout, sure," said Sun, but he wasn't agreeing. He pointed to his display. *"But ours won't, you see? They'll still have half their reaction mass aboard, and that means—"*

Pairs of azure tracks as fine as spiderwebs spread from the blue dot toward the projected course of the red dot. One by one, the tracks broke into wobbling spirals. None of them intersected the red dot or even its course.

"—they'll blow up when the gunners catch them. Which they will, as sure as we're sitting on the Sissie's *bridge, ma'am.*

The reaction mass will boil and burst the tank, and the gods alone know where the missile goes off to. It can't work."

"I see," said Adele. Her mind considered the options. Then, with what for her was a broad smile, she said, "That means there's a factor we aren't considering, Sun. I have no idea what it might be, but I'm certain there must be one. If this were a desperation play that Daniel didn't believe could work, he would have said so."

"Extracting," Vesey said.

The *Princess Cecile* dropped into sidereal space like light striking a prism. Adele felt ice in her bone marrow, but it was a sensation rather than pain. Her mind was focused on the information appearing on her display. The *Princess Cecile* began to accelerate at the highest rate possible with the High Drive alone.

"Launching one," Daniel announced. A jet of steam, expanding so quickly that it rang like a hammer blow, shoved the missile out of its launch tube. The High Drive motor didn't light until it was in vacuum, where the corrosive exhaust would not damage the *Sissie*'s fabric.

"Launching two," and another *clang!* that rocked the ship and startled anyone who wasn't familiar with the sequence of events.

Cranes had shifted missiles from the two magazines onto roller tracks. They had started rumbling toward the launch tubes even before the first salvo had left the ship. Because the missiles were so heavy, every stage of the process made the hull tremble as much as the straining High Drive motors did.

Pistons shoved the missiles into the corvette's pair of

tubes. The *Princess Cecile*'s rate of fire was only half that of a destroyer and a tiny fraction of what a battleship could launch in a single salvo. Still, a well-aimed missile from the *Sissie* would finish any target.

Vesey had the conn, so Daniel must consider the attack to be the critical part of his plan. Chief Missileer Chazanoff was very able, or he wouldn't have been a member of the *Sissie*'s crew. He wouldn't publically object to Captain Leary pushing him out of his job, but it would offend him. Daniel treated his officers with as much consideration as possible, so he must not have thought he had time to explain the situation to Chazanoff and leave the execution in his hands.

"Launching three," Daniel said. *"Launching four."*

The ringing launches followed his calmly spaced words. It was possible for a missile's track to perturb that of another launched at the same time, so Daniel was providing a two-second delay. He sounded as though he had nothing more on his mind than the question of what to have for lunch.

Because Adele had been considering Chazanoff's reaction, she echoed his display for a moment. She didn't expect to make any sense of it—it was an attack board, as she had expected—but though the columns of numbers were meaningless, the schematics seemed clear enough.

The Chief Missileer's screen was identical to Daniel's, except that in addition to the pale blue missile tracks, there were four—

"Launching five," said Daniel's voice. *"Launching six."*

—now six additional white tracks leaving the *Princess Cecile*. Chazanoff was predicting that the *Estremadura* would appear at a slightly different location from the one which Daniel was targeting. At the speeds and distances involved in a space battle, the choice was of critical significance.

The High Drive shut off. *"Preparing to insert,"* Vesey announced as the corvette drifted.

The precursors of a ship extracting from the Matrix pulsed in the miniature PPI Adele had retained as a sidebar. Adele imported the new data to her echo of Chazanoff's attack board.

Chazanoff had been correct: the *Estremadura* was appearing where he, not Daniel, had predicted. The cruiser's gunners wouldn't burn out their cannon bores by firing at missiles which did not endanger their ship.

"Inserting!" Vesey said. The *Princess Cecile* slid from the sidereal universe into the realm of infinite possibility.

Daniel was breathing hard, both in response to the past half hour and to what was certainly going to happen when they extracted again in approximately ninety seconds. Even if things went as well as he could hope, the *Sissie* was in for a bad time. The possibilities ranged downward from there, and perhaps a long way downward.

"Command," he said, keying the system. He had considered using the general push since he liked to keep all the ship's personnel informed about what was going on, but present matters were really for the command group alone. He didn't want his officers to feel that they were being judged in front of an audience of their juniors.

"Missileers, as soon as we've extracted, launch at maximum

rate toward what you predict as the position at which the *Estremadura* will extract. Continue launching after the enemy appears, until and unless I countermand these orders."

All he could hope from missiles launched on this extraction was to attract the *Estremadura*'s attention, but that was an extremely valuable asset. It was certainly more valuable than retaining the missiles in the *Sissie*'s magazine to add to the value of the loot she would offer to her captors.

"Gunners," Daniel continued, "you may open fire as soon as your target appears. She'll be out of effective range, but what happens to your gun tubes is less important than making the enemy feel threatened."

Daniel had kept the missileers and gunners both on a short leash while preparing for this moment. That had been necessary, and he certainly didn't apologize for it: he was the captain and he would have been shirking his duties if he *hadn't* given the commands he felt were necessary.

Nonetheless, it pleased him to know how thrilled Chazanoff and Sun—as well as their mates, if the chiefs were willing to give them a piece of it—were allowed to do their jobs however they pleased. Even aboard a ship that saw as much action as the *Princess Cecile* did, the gunner and missileers spent almost all their time running simulations.

"Bosun, all your riggers should be within the hull," Daniel said. "*Are* they all inside, respond please, over?"

"*Aye, they are,*" said Woetjans in a growl of frustrated anger. "*We ought to have a squad on the hull, though, even if you are Six, out.*"

Simply the fact that the bosun spoke proved to Daniel that

she had obeyed his orders. Woetjans would never have ordered her riggers onto dangerous duty without joining them herself.

Woetjans didn't have to agree with Daniel's assessment, she just had to obey it. In the present case, his assessment was that it wouldn't be dangerous to have riggers on the hull when the *Princess Cecile* extracted this time: it would be suicidal.

Daniel would spend his spacers if he had to. He was the captain of a warship, and that meant sometimes having to send personnel to their deaths. He wasn't going to throw his Sissies' lives away for nothing, though.

Aloud he said, "Bosun, I'm going to need your people badly when we repair our rigging after we've defeated the *Estremadura*. I have no intention of putting them outside now to be fried."

He looked at the clock counting down on his screen. "I am taking the conn," he said. "Break. Ship, we are extracting."

Daniel thumbed the toggle. He didn't have vernier control at this station as he did on the command console, but the simple electronic in/out was the correct choice this time.

The *Princess Cecile* dropped into normal space and the certainty of battle.

"*Launching one!*" said Chazanoff. The *clang!* of his release blurred the final syllable.

"*Launching two!*" said Fiducia, a little quicker off the mark than would have ideally been the case. Still, the corvette's tubes were on opposite sides of the hull, so the missiles themselves wouldn't affect one another. The danger was that the hull, flexing as it expelled a five-ton projectile, would bind the second missile in its tube.

That was unlikely at any time. Under the present circumstances, the possibility could scarcely be said to increase the *Sissie*'s danger at all.

Rocker made a minute adjustment to the ventral gun turret. Like the chief missileer, Sun was sharing the duties with his subordinate. It was probable that the *Princess Cecile* would be taking damage very shortly, and splitting control between the bridge and the BDC from the beginning would make for a smoother handoff if one or the other specialist were incapacitated.

Were maimed. Killed. Completely obliterated.

Daniel grinned. *Or not, of course.*

"Launching three!" Followed by, *"Launching four!"*

Even over the intercom, Daniel could hear the excitement in the missileers' voices. Well, excitement and the strain of acceleration.

He had considered getting the rig in before the *Sissie* extracted this time, but the antennas and sails would go some way toward protecting their hull against the punishment of the *Estremadura*'s guns. The anti-pirate cruiser's 10-centimeter weapons were actually less affected by the sails than heavier cannon would have been, because their high rate of fire allowed them to clear fabric with one bolt and follow it quickly with another bolt and many after that.

"Launching five!" said Chazanoff.

"Launching six!" echoed Rocker.

A ship began to congeal out of the Matrix some 23,000 miles from the *Princess Cecile*. The missileers' predictions had been quite good: at least three of the recent launches were tracking toward the target, and the other three would inhibit the *Estremadura*'s opportunities to maneuver—if the cruiser bothered to maneuver, which it would not.

The corvette's four plasma cannon began to fire, but at their low rate, fifteen rounds per minute per tube, rather than the high rate of double that. The *Estremadura* was still out of range, and Sun knew that high rate would erode the bores logarithmically faster than a rhythm which permitted the bores to clear and cool between shots.

Sun was a skilled expert. A sleet of ions, even if it was too dispersed to do real damage, would make the recipients nervous and might cause them to make mistakes. He was doing his best to keep his tubes functional for when the range closed to where 4-inch bolts were effective on a ship's hull. Given the cruiser's proper velocity, that would be very soon.

The *Estremadura* snapped into normal space; a box on Daniel's attack board read EST and would expand to full particulars if he highlighted it. He grinned, because the expression was natural to him. He didn't need to check the data bank to know what they were facing.

The cruiser began firing very quickly. There was always a delay while personnel recovered from the transition, and for the *Estremadura,* as well as for her quarry, the quickly repeated in-and-out would have been wearing.

The complements of both vessels were used to the experience. That didn't make a repetition less painful, but it taught them to function despite the pain.

The *Sissie*'s missileers knew where their target would appear. Likewise, the *Estremadura*'s gunners knew where to lay their cannon before they extracted.

The three missiles which Daniel had considered dangerous tumbled from their courses one after another. The cruiser carried its cannon in individual mountings, but they appeared to be salvoed in groups of four or even all six—the other two did not bear on the target from this angle—at a time.

Then, for good measure, the other three missiles ruptured and spun hopelessly off course. A missile's body was merely a thin tube. Most of the mass was concentrated in the solid frontal portion. A plasma bolt flash-heated the reaction mass to steam, which thrust the missile in the opposite direction.

"Launching seven! Launching eight!" said the missileers. They were RCN. You don't stop trying simply because you know that you'll fail.

The *Princess Cecile* shuddered as though she were entering a planetary atmosphere. This buffeting was from the *Estremadura*'s guns, which had switched their aim to the corvette. Sail fabric vanished; steel masts and yards sublimed into balls of gas which rattled nearby tubes and slapped the hull itself. The noise deafened anyone aboard without sound-cancelling headgear.

Some bolts hammered the hull directly, but the range was still too great for a single round to penetrate. The range was closing quickly.

The *Sissie*'s guns were now firing on high rate, but the recoil that would have been wracking by itself was lost in the cacophony of the incoming bolts. The dorsal turret halted, then resumed with single shots. Either the *Estremadura* had hit the turret, or a gun had failed from the stress of action.

"Launching—" Chazanoff began.

A segment of missile moving at .007 light speed passed ahead of the *Estremadura* at a quartering angle. The separation was too close for the *Princess Cecile*'s sensors to determine without processing, but it was certainly less than a hundred feet and might have been within the thickness of a coat of paint.

"What the bloody hell!" Chazanoff screamed.

A second projectile hit the Alliance cruiser at the base of a dorsal antenna. At the combined velocity, tons of steel expanded as a ball of white-hot gas, throwing the *Estremadura* into a cartwheel and stripping off all but the ventral antennas on her aft four rings.

"Ship," said Daniel. He had almost forgotten his duties in his sudden delight. "Cease fire, I repeat, cease fire. They're done, Sissies! We've won!"

Her hull probably hasn't been penetrated, Daniel thought, *but the whipping from a punch like that must have started every seam.*

Another segment passed through the gas ball, swirling eddies into the glowing steel. This projectile would have hit the *Estremadura* amidships if the previous glancing blow hadn't shoved her out of the way.

I doubt any of the crew will thank me if we happen to meet in the future, though, Daniel thought.

The *Sissie*'s ventral turret fired five more rounds before responding to the cease-fire order. Daniel could have locked the gunnery and missile consoles if he had wanted to, but a few unnecessary rounds into a beaten enemy weren't the worst thing that could happen in wartime.

He hadn't been at all sure that the *Estremadura* would have given quarter to the corvette's crew if the battle had gone the other way. From Adele's description of how the cruiser's corporate masters had fared on the other end of the *Sissie*'s guns, they at least would have been pleased to learn there were no survivors.

Daniel let out a deep breath. Then, grinning like a happy cherub, he said, "Ship! Up Cinnabar! Up the RCN!"

Then he closed his eyes for a moment and let the cheers roll over him.

Adele put the battle, starting with the appearance of the *Estremadura*, on a loop as soon as she had cleaned it up. None of the lenses had taken a direct hit, but side-scatter from the cruiser's bolts had degraded the exterior sensors. Adele's software reduced the blurring, though she had been careful not to let it give the imagery the gloss that screamed "Fake!" to a viewer.

She had then made a shorter loop of the climax: the *Estremadura* suddenly silhouetted against the white flare that scoured her aft hull as bare as a rock in the desert. That was the scene that the spacers would watch over and over again when they returned from cleaning up the damage and getting a rig of some sort back on what remained of the *Sissie*'s antennas and yards.

Adele was probably the only person aboard the *Princess Cecile* who was unhappy; angry, even. Oh, they were all alive, and they had defeated a more powerful enemy vessel by a masterstroke; that was certainly good.

But Officer Mundy had watched the whole thing take place, and she *still* did not understand what had happened. She was angry with herself.

Pursing her lips, Adele got up and walked the two steps across the bridge to stand beside the astrogation console. "Lieutenant Cory?" she said. "Do you have time to explain to me what happened to the *Estremadura*?"

Adele had checked what Cory was doing before she spoke, of course. He was the watch officer, since Daniel was out on the hull clearing damage and Vesey had used her rank to insist that she be permitted to go out also. She wasn't as physically strong as Cory, and brute force was what the present job needed; but Vesey didn't want the reputation of a clever officer who was unfortunately too frail for hard work.

Cory looked up in surprise. He was going over course plots to Tattersall, comparing his own with the proposals Vesey and Daniel had filed. Cory wasn't vain; he was probably determining where he had gone wrong so as to do a better job the next time.

"Mistress?" he said, pleasantly surprised. "Why, yes. Won't you—"

He looked nonplussed for a moment.

"—ah, well, sit down?" He gestured toward the training seat of his console; then, diffidently, hooked his thumb toward the signals console and added, "Unless you . . . ?"

Adele folded down the jumpseat and sat primly, facing Cory. Using her data unit, she expanded the console's active sound cancellation to include both of them. Otherwise the buzz of the High Drive combined with the metallic shrieks and hammering from the hull would require that that shout unless they wanted to use the intercom.

"Thank you, Cory," Adele said, meeting the young officer's eyes directly. He had shrunk his display when she accepted his offer. "I'm punishing myself for not being able to figure the business out by myself."

Cory blinked to hear that. He didn't protest that she shouldn't feel that way or any of the other nonsense with which people tended to respond to the blunt truth. If he didn't understand Adele, he at least understood how she reacted to what she considered to be failures.

"Well, it *was* a slick piece of work," Cory said, grinning slowly. "Even for Six, ma'am. And I'll bet the cruiser's officers still don't know what hit them. The ones that're still around to wonder, I mean."

He brought up an attack board. Adele frowned. It was not the layout of the battle just over but rather that of the first exchange with the *Estremadura*, when the corvette fled as soon as the cruiser extracted.

"You see," Cory said, "the problem was that the Alliance pilot was extracting too close for missiles to be effective. Not on top of us, but out just far enough that they could gut our missiles as quick as we launched."

"Yes, I see that," Adele said. She frowned again. Cory was overlaying missile tracks, but they were Chazanoff's preferred—and more accurate—plots, not the actual launches Daniel had made.

"But what Six did was *this*," Cory said enthusiastically, adding the real tracks of Daniel's missiles. "Which are far enough off that the *Estremadura* wasn't going to bother about them, but they look like they're aimed to hit, right? So her captain doesn't think anything about them, and the Matrix pilot they've got out on the hull doesn't even know they've been launched. You see?"

"Daniel—" she said but caught herself. She began again, stating rather than asking, "Captain Leary aimed at the point where the target would extract after the next insertion, not the current extraction. The missiles had broken into segments, and they were at terminal velocity when they hit the *Estremadura*. The *Estremadura*'s crew wasn't expecting attack from that angle anyway."

She smiled faintly and added, "I understand now, Cory. Thank you."

"It wouldn't have worked without the Alliance pilot being so bloody good," Cory said, shaking his head at the recollection. "Say, I wonder if he was a Palmyrene? Do you think so?"

"I can check the information from Cremona and possibly find an answer," Adele said with a shrug. "If he was on the hull when the missile hit, I suppose he's dead now."

"I bloody well hope so!" Cory said with unexpected venom. "He just about turned *my* hair white, I'll tell you."

The airlock in the rotunda cycled open. Daniel stamped in, holding his helmet, with a lock-full of riggers and technicians behind him. The *Estremadura*'s gunfire had damaged the propulsion system as well as the rigging, though Adele had the impression that it wouldn't affect them too badly.

"It'll take a dockyard to get us back to where we want to be," Daniel said cheerfully, unlatching his hard suit as he entered the bridge, "but in ten minutes we should be ready to insert. I think we can make Tattersall in five days, and just possibly we might be a little luckier than that."

Adele rose, but she waited for Daniel to get out of his suit. Under ordinary circumstances he would have stripped it off in the rotunda, but he had obviously wanted to get back to where he belonged after fighting the recent battle from the BDC.

A rigger gathered up the sections of Daniel's suit and went off to stow them. Adele crossed to her proper station, and Daniel settled onto the command console with a sigh of relief.

He opened his eyes and grinned broadly. "By all that's holy!" he said. "There's never been a better crew than my Sissies. Never!"

Yes, Daniel, Adele thought as she reviewed the imagery of the Alliance cruiser flaring into impotent ruin. *The* Princess Cecile *has exactly the kind of crew that its captain deserves.*

Chapter Twenty-six

ABOVE TATTERSALL

Ordinarily Adele allowed herself a little time following extraction—a very little time, a few heartbeats or so—to savor the fact that she was back in the sidereal universe. All thought of relaxation vanished when a challenge came from the battleship *Warhol* even before both her eyes were able to focus on the same point. It was like trying to act after being sliced through the middle vertically and glued back together a few millimeters off the correct registration.

Though Adele hadn't been able to process the words of the signal, she responded by rote. "RCS *Princess Cecile* requesting landing permission from Tattersall Control, over."

She felt a flash of anger. The battleship must have begun signalling as soon as it picked up the precursor effects of the *Sissie*'s extraction. *Nobody* could be expected to react instantly after transition, and to back up the challenge with pointed guns and missile tubes unshuttered—she had a clear image of the *Warhol* on her display now—was stupidly insulting.

"Princess Cecile, *this is RCS* Warhol!" snarled the communications officer on the other end of the microwave transmission. "*You have extracted in the hundred thousand mile restriction zone without obtaining clearance. You're bloody lucky that you haven't been blown to atoms already. Do you understand, over?*"

The transition hadn't left Adele in a good humor to begin with. Her temper was not being improved by this lecture from a lieutenant—or possibly lieutenant commander—who had been posted to the frontier on a ship that was too old to be useful in a real war. She thought of passing her duties up to Daniel or Vesey, then decided not to.

She must have been smiling. Tovera, who had stood up when the corvette extracted, suddenly smiled back at her.

Do I look like that? I suppose I do.

"Lieutenant Stefalou," Adele said, reading the name from the *Warhol*'s complement. That was one of the files she had downloaded at Macotta Base against possible need; the need had arisen. "This is the corvette RCS *Princess Cecile*, five days out from Sunbright and making our first return to sidereal space since we lifted from Hester 27514CH."

Daniel had paused in what he was doing—plotting the descent to Flounder Harbor on Tattersall—and was grinning at her. Adele supposed that meant he was authorizing her to proceed; but neither he nor she thought she needed authorization.

"Because our officers are RCN trained," Adele continued, "we extracted a proper thirty thousand miles above Tattersall. Now that we know about the restriction zone, I suppose we could leave the system and let our bosun bring us back to deliver the time-sensitive material which Admiral Cox sent us to gather. Though even our bosun might be too competent an astrogator to meet the apparent standards of the Macotta Squadron. What are your instructions, over?"

Stefalou was listed as the deputy communications officer; his superior—a lieutenant commander—was female, so Adele was comfortable enough with the identification to chance her hand. An appearance of magical omniscience could prove usefully unsettling.

There was blank silence for fifteen seconds. Stefalou— it must be him—clearly didn't know what he'd caught, but he was apparently smart enough to realize that he had been pulled out of his depth.

"Princess Cecile, *this is Commander Lowestoff, acting Tattersall Control,*" a deeper, older male voice said. *"State your business, over."*

A quick check showed that Lowestoff was first lieutenant of the *Warhol* under normal circumstances. Apparently the battleship—or perhaps this battleship in rotation with the *Schelling* in harbor below—was acting as gatekeeper and orbital defense for Tattersall. The planet was too insignificant to have an automatic defense array, a field of nuclear mines in interlocking orbits.

"Tattersall Control," Adele said. "RCS *Princess Cecile* requests permission to land in Flounder Harbor with urgent material requested by Admiral Cox. Over."

Flounder Harbor was a large, natural embayment. Though there was plenty of surface area in the harbor for the ships now present, the port facilities were certainly strained.

According to the *Sailing Directions*, Flounder Harbor was ordinarily a sleepy place for which the arrival of three moderate-sizcd freighters—root vegetables were the main export—would be a busy day. Now it held seventeen ships of the Macotta Squadron in addition to the *Warhol* and a pair of destroyers in orbit, and twenty-one other vessels. The latter included ships from Rides and Cobbet, the associated worlds of the Alliance which had been planning the coup against Tattersall; and the Alliance heavy cruiser *Marie*, which bore the flag of Admiral Jeletsky, commander of the Forty Star Squadron.

The *Marie* had two escorting destroyers, but Jeletsky's other three cruisers were not present; he hadn't come to fight. That left the question of why he had come at all, however.

"Princess Cecile," Lowestoff said, *"you are cleared to land following the vessel currently making its approach. Course and berth data are being sent to you—now."*

An icon indicating the arrival of a packet of information appeared on Adele's right sidebar.

"We will inform Macotta Command of your arrival," Lowestoff concluded. *"Control out."*

"Princess Cecile out," said Adele. She found that she followed commo protocol perfectly so long as it was part of her playacting. It was only then that she concentrated on what she personally felt was nonsense.

"Command," said Daniel, keying the net. *"Officer Mundy, there's an Alliance cruiser below, I think either the* Marie *or the* Chloe *from the Forty Stars Squadron. Please explain the situation to your fellow officers, myself very much included. Over."*

Cazelet would be a better choice to explain, Adele thought.

While she had been jumping through bureaucratic hoops with the makeshift Tattersall Control, Cory and the midshipman had sucked data from the ships in harbor, RCN and Alliance both. Cazelet had laid out the necessary information in a neat, tabular fashion which Adele could expand into a left sidebar, though, so she didn't have to pass Daniel's question to him.

She smiled again. *A good officer.*

"Instead of simply proceeding in force to Tattersall, as we expected when we left Kronstadt," Adele said, "Admiral Cox called a regional meeting on Tattersall with a strongly worded hope that Rides, Cobbet, and the governor of the Forty Stars would attend. Deputy Quinley came in place of the sector administrator, but Admiral Jeletsky is here."

She pursed her lips for a moment before adding, "Jeletsky won't admit anything, of course, but this is a very public warning for him and for the rulers of Rides and Cobbet."

After a pause, Adele said, "We, the *Princess Cecile*, were sent here to warn Macotta Headquarters of the plot against Tattersall and to prevent a resumption of war between ourselves and the Alliance. I believe we have carried out that mission."

She wasn't sure what Daniel had intended her to say. Admiral Cox should reasonably release the *Sissie* immediately; but then, Cox should not have shipped them off to Sunbright on what was certainly meant to be a wild-goose chase. Adele could only hope that the admiral would be as glad to see them lift for Cinnabar as they would be to do so.

"Thank you, Mundy," Daniel said. *"Officers, prepare for landing. Six out."*

Other officers certainly would have continued the discussion had not Daniel closed it so abruptly. Adele was puzzled only for a moment, because Daniel continued on a two-way link, *"Adele, what can you tell me about the ship that's landing just ahead of us, the* Feursnot, *over?"*

Adele checked the only available data, the clearance form the *Feursnot* had filed with the *Warhol* before braking to land. The lack of corroboration from the ship's log was puzzling; Cory, who had taken the Alliance ships as his province while Cazelet examined the friendly vessels, should have been able to enter the database of a freighter easily.

"The *Feursnot* is a fast freighter under contract to the Alliance diocesan headquarters at Port Sanlouis," she said. "That's the headquarters which oversees the Funnel Sector *and* the Forty Stars Sector—and several others—for the Alliance. The ship is bringing—it claims to be bringing—foreign ministry personnel to the conference, which would be reasonable."

"You've obviously got your doubts," Daniel said. *"My doubt is this: Port Sanlouis is seven days from Kronstadt by the fastest ship that was in Harbor Holm when we arrived there. If Admiral Cox sent an invitation to the diocesan officials immediately, and if those officials reacted immediately, the* Feursnot *could not have arrived here in the available time unless her crew is better than ours. Much better than ours. I would hate to think that the Alliance has spacers that good, and a captain so much better than I am."*

His image grinned at Adele. *"Over."*

Ah, thought Adele. And that also explained why the freighter's electronic security was so good.

Aloud she said, "Daniel, I believe that the *Feursnot* may have come in response to information which I provided to Alliance intelligence officials on Madison and which those officials would have passed on to their superiors on Port Sanlouis. That is, the *Feursnot* has not come to Tattersall at the request of Admiral Cox."

"Alliance intelligence officials?" Daniel said, frowning. *"Do you mean Commander Doerries of Fleet Intelligence? Because I suspect..."*

He let his voice trail off as he remembered who he was talking to. *"Over,"* he said.

"I do not mean Commander Doerries," Adele said flatly. "I think that if there are foreign ministry officials on the *Feursnot*, they are present as cover for officers of the Fifth Bureau."

"Is that a problem, Adele?" Daniel said.

"No, Daniel," Adele said, letting her smile show itself on her lips. "Quite the contrary. That is, not a problem for *us*."

LEELBURG ON TATTERSALL

"All I can say about this," said Hogg, looking around the circular room. The walls between the radiating hallways were decorated with children's watercolors and flat-plate displays, which for the moment were blank instead of listing schedules and room assignments. "Is that Cox seems to have found the place where he belongs."

"Perhaps," said Daniel, smiling despite himself. "But we won't need to broadcast our opinion too widely, I hope."

The arrival of the Macotta Squadron along with representatives of local powers would have stretched the facilities of a more developed world than Tattersall. Admiral Cox had taken the Leelburg Primary School for his headquarters.

Only senior officers and officials were billeted in permanent facilities. For the most part, the others remained aboard the ships that brought them; the nightly storms that blew in from the sea did not encourage sleeping rough.

One of the three ratings within the central secretarial station looked up, nodded to someone on the other end of the signal on her commo helmet, and called, "Captain Leary? Commander Ruffin will see you now."

She pointed. "The door marked Deputy Master."

Daniel started to say, "I'd hoped to see Admiral Cox," but that would be pointless and *particularly* pointless to say to a Clerk 2. Cox knew Daniel wanted to see him; Ruffin knew that Daniel wanted to see Cox; and Daniel had known before he arrived that what Captain Leary wanted was of no concern to the leaders of the Macotta Squadron.

"Roger," he said with a smile. He stepped jauntily toward the indicated door, a vaguely pinkish panel of extruded plastic with ventilation slots in the bottom.

Not very long ago I was being shot at by people who had a good chance of killing me. I think I can accept insulting behavior from the likes of Admiral Cox with equanimity.

Daniel rapped with his knuckles on the plastic door. It made a sort of not-quite-right sound that seemed to fit the color. *At least I'm not being asked to eat it.*

"Come in and close it behind you!" Ruffin said.

Daniel obeyed. He stood at parade rest and said, "I'm here to report to Admiral Cox about our mission, Commander."

"Well, you're not going to see the admiral," said Ruffin, typing industriously. Her eyes were on the display of the portable console which had been installed on a desk of pressed metal. The only places to sit, besides her chair, were three stools low enough for an eight-year-old's feet to touch the floor. "He's far too busy, of course."

She finally looked up at Daniel. He wished Adele were here. He suspected that the commander wasn't actually working at the console but was simply making her disdain clear, and Adele would know whether he was right.

"It's just as well for you that Admiral Cox *is* busy," she said. "You were given clear instructions to leave for the Funnel Region, but instead you turn up on Tattersall. I don't suppose it's really important, since we've already sorted the business here, but I suggest you take yourself back to Cinnabar as quickly as your little yacht can manage. Otherwise, the admiral's mind may turn to questions of insubordination and disobedience to orders. Understood, Leary?"

"No, Commander, I don't understand," Daniel said. He wasn't on the verge of losing his temper, but he was finding it increasingly difficult to keep an internal smile about the situation. "I have, my crew and I have, carried out the admiral's instructions: we've removed from Sunbright the former rebel who called himself Freedom."

Ruffin stared at him in blank anger for a moment. Then she said, "You *what*?"

"We carried out our instructions, Commander," Daniel

said, cheerful again. "In this instance, the rumors were true: Freedom, so called, really is a Cinnabar citizen, though he's been resident in the Alliance for most of his life. We'll take him back to Cinnabar with us and repatriate him."

"You'll do nothing of the sort!" Ruffin said. "This is the business of the Macotta Region. I'm sure the admiral will want to take charge of the prisoner!"

Daniel stepped forward and placed his splayed fingertips on the desktop. He leaned his weight onto them.

"May I remind you, *Commander* Ruffin," he said in a pointedly calm voice, "that I am here under the orders of the Navy Board? I was to cooperate with the Macotta regional command in the solution of the Tattersall situation. You have assured me that you've 'sorted the business.' I believe that was your phrasing? *Do* you understand?"

Ruffin was ten years Daniel's senior, and she obviously spoke for Admiral Cox. That must have given her a presumption of power even when dealing with the senior captains of the Macotta Squadron.

Now she flushed, then grew pale and edged back in her chair. "Sorry, Captain, if I seemed to have spoken out of line," she mumbled. "The fact is that Sunbright is in the Macotta Region, so it's for the Macotta Squadron to deal with in the first instance."

Daniel straightened, but he didn't retreat from where he stood. Smiling, he said, "There are people on Pleasaunce who would argue about how much authority Admiral Cox has over Sunbright, don't you think? In any case, that's a matter for our External Affairs and their foreign ministry to argue about."

He shrugged and turned to the door, then paused and looked over his shoulder. "Commander, I was perfectly willing to explain the situation to Admiral Cox. I came here to do so, in fact. But my main purpose in reporting was to inform Macotta headquarters that my mission here has been completed. The *Princess Cecile* will return to Cinnabar immediately, in obedience to my orders from the Navy Board."

"Captain," Ruffin said, rising from her chair with an anguished look. She had obviously been considering how her handling of the situation was going to look to Admiral Cox and those above him in the Navy House bureaucracy. "Please. What do you intend to do with this rebel leader?"

"Ex-rebel," Daniel said. "But as for your question, Commander—I'll do the same as I'd do for any distressed Cinnabar citizen if it was practical: I'll take him home."

He closed the door gently behind him. Commander Ruffin didn't try to call him back. Maybe she had realized that she would be wasting her breath.

Chapter Twenty-seven

LEELBURG ON TATTERSALL

Tovera drove the vehicle Hogg had found for them. It was a clumsy thing whose wheels were splayed out from the body on long struts. It was suitable for the broken terrain they had to cross along the bay to where the *Feursnot* was berthed, but that considerably increased the jouncing unpleasantness.

Adele had never learned to drive: she had been born in Xenos, and her tastes were entirely urban. Occasionally, as now, it occurred to her that the bucket seat for the driver would be less uncomfortable than the bin in back in which she rode; but learning to drive would require effort which she preferred to spend on other forms of education. Besides, comfort had never been a high priority with her.

"The boat's coming over," Tovera said as she wrenched hard on the steering wheel. "It's about time. They've probably been watching us ever since we started."

Tovera was in a bad mood. She had originally tried to drive through patches of a local beach plant with thick, glossy leaves.

After backing out when they had almost bogged on the sticky coating, she had circled onto outcrops where the plants' roots didn't find purchase. Despite her slim, colorless appearance, Tovera had nothing of subtlety in her nature; it frustrated her to be unable to tear through whatever was in front of her.

"I certainly hope Master Storn is competent enough to keep us under observation, Tovera," Adele said as she took out her data unit. Using it while the vehicle was moving had its problems, but the practice could be useful in the future. "And to time his arrival to match ours is simply common sense."

She began searching for information on the beach plant. It interested her only as a scrap of information—but that was sufficient.

Normally Adele would be looking up something like this for Daniel. Doing so now brought Daniel closer, which was also an inducement to her search.

The vehicle which left the *Feursnot* operated as a boat at present, but it had large tires as well. It didn't openly mount weapons, but it certainly seemed more military than civilian in appearance. It was painted the gray-green of Fleet uniforms.

The difficult ground cover was called gray plantain. It required iodine and therefore was rarely found at any distance from the sea. The sticky covering was a tool of predation rather than defense, and it was responsible for the plantain's remarkable success anywhere the conditions were favorable. The leaves not only caught and absorbed insectoids which landed on them, they also smothered plants which tried to share the same territory.

Daniel will be interested. I must remember to tell him.

Tovera pulled around in a half turn on the shoreline before she stopped, so that the vehicle was positioned to drive away without hesitation. Adele's smile barely touched her lips: there was very little chance that the *Feursnot* did not carry marksmen as skillful as Hogg with a stocked impeller. Nonetheless, the principle was sound.

The Alliance vehicle rolled up beyond the surf line on its broad tires and stopped twenty feet from Adele and Tovera. A man of about fifty got out of the cab. As soon as he was clear, the driver—his only visible companion, though the body of the vehicle would hold a squad of twelve—began backing around also. Adele wondered if the fellow had been in the same class as Tovera during Fifth Bureau training.

Adele climbed out of the borrowed car. The bin where she rode was generally used to haul a surf fisherman's catch, but Adele's present drab black clothing—cut like RCN utilities but without the mottled pattern—was intended for hard service. She walked toward the Alliance official with Tovera—unexpectedly—following a pace behind and to the left.

"Lady Mundy?" the official said. His civilian suit was a single shade of brown, but a subtle pattern of gloss and matte varied the surface. "I am Adolf Storn, who left the message for you. I'm glad you could meet me at this short notice."

"I'm Mundy," Adele said, letting her fingertips rest on the data unit in its thigh pocket. "How do you wish to proceed?"

She consciously kept her left hand at the small of her back lest it absently stroke her pistol. Reflexes had saved her life a number of times, but there were times that they could be fatal because they sent the wrong signal.

"The briefing materials told me not to expect small talk," Storn said with a faint smile. "I'm glad to see that our information is accurate."

Without any change in tone, he continued, "There are various ways of handling this matter, Lady Mundy. I would prefer to do so informally, avoiding discussions between Pleasaunce and Xenos. Is that possible?"

"It should be," said Adele. "Go on."

The Leelburg Docks could service no more than ten moderate-sized ships at a time. The Macotta Squadron frequently operated from harbors no more developed than those here, so they were prepared. A construction crew had laid mooring buoys and floating quays along the bayfront to the south of the permanent facilities. The seafront in that direction was sloping and easily accessible.

The *Feursnot* had landed a mile to the north. The beach wasn't a great deal worse than that in the other direction, but there was a steep escarpment just north of the docks and settlement, making it inaccessible at high tide—except by sea or to vehicles like the one Hogg had found for Tovera.

There could be no privacy in Leelburg, packed with outsiders as it was, and Storn didn't want Adele and her data unit within his ship any more than she wanted to be there. Their beach was a good location for the meeting, as well as being the only location possible.

"If you don't mind handling the matter quietly," Storn said, "then...can we expect your republic's navy to remain neutral?"

"This is in the interests of both nations," Adele said. "The RCN will provide support if you request it."

She considered for moment, then added, "It will take me a little time to make arrangements. A few hours, perhaps."

"Thank you, Your Ladyship," Storn said with a smile as faint as Adele's own when she considered the sort of matter which he was probably planning now. "I don't believe additional personnel will be necessary except for traffic control, but I appreciate the thought."

"Very well," said Adele. "I'll get back to the *Princess Cecile* and change uniform, then take care of the RCN part of the arrangements."

Storn dipped his head to her in acknowledgment, then looked at Tovera. "Did you know," he said lightly, "that there's a price on your head?"

"Do you plan to collect it?" Tovera said. Her tone was politely interested.

Storn chuckled. "Not now," he said. "Another time, perhaps."

Tovera followed Adele to the vehicle at the same proper distance, then got into the saddle. She closed and latched her attaché case, then hooked it to the steering column at her feet.

The Alliance vehicle was already snorting into the water. Adele watched it for a moment and said, "I'm glad Hogg didn't put us in a boat. Things are working out rather well, I believe."

"My brother's a poor missionary," Hogg croaked. *"He saves fallen women from sin."*

His voice was a sort of bass growl, even though he'd had enough of the local brandy to really lubricate it. Daniel had drunk a tumbler or two as well. He probably shouldn't have, and he certainly shouldn't have while still wearing his Whites, but it had worked out all right.

"He'll save you a blonde for a florin," Hogg sang.

As Daniel left squadron headquarters, he had run into his Academy classmate Pennyroyal—now Lieutenant Pennyroyal, first officer of the destroyer *Montrose*. Because her ship was part of the flotilla based on Tattersall, she had her own car and had offered to carry Daniel and Hogg back to the *Sissie*.

Since the ride would save them so much time over what they would have spent waiting for the Fleet-commandeered trucks acting as trams, she suggested they stop at a club where Lieutenant Ames, a mutual friend, was already waiting. Hogg had really wanted a drink—

And Hogg's master had felt like celebrating too, since he'd delivered his report and thus ended his association with the Macotta Squadron. Daniel didn't hold grudges, and Admiral Cox appeared to have handled his duties on Tattersall well. Nonetheless, Daniel would be very pleased to see the last of the region and of the commander of its RCN squadron.

"My God, how the money rolls in!"

"Steady on, Hogg," Daniel said, pausing at the base of the floating gangplank. Hogg swam like a fish and, indeed, a bath in the chilly harbor might do him some good; but the splash was likely to wet Daniel's only first-class uniform.

"Want us to give him a hand, sir?" asked Riley, the senior spacer of the entry watch. He was smiling indulgently.

"I could walk up that gangplank on my hands if I chose to!" said Hogg, striking a regal pose. He relaxed and continued,

"However, I do not choose to do so. You may assist me, Technician Three Riley!"

"Captain Leary," called the *Sissie*'s external speakers in what sounded like Adele's voice. *"Report to the bridge at once, if you please."*

The tone caused Daniel to brace to attention and sobered him more effectively than any of the cures he had attempted at one time or another. "Roger!" he muttered, though of course Adele couldn't hear him.

He trotted up the gangplank and through the entry hold to the up companionway. He didn't know what had gone wrong, but nobody was going to say that Daniel Leary took his time when duty called. The fact that it called in Adele's voice was an added inducement.

The off-duty spacers in the hold nodded, but nobody spoke to Daniel as he passed. Either they knew what was up—or at least that something was—or they had made the same assessment of Officer Mundy's summons as he had himself.

Daniel climbed the companionway at a swift, steady pace; drunk or sober, it was always the same. Trying to sprint the whole way didn't work, would never have worked, but neither did he waste time.

He crossed the rotunda to the bridge where Adele waited. She was wearing a civilian suit of cream on off-white. Instead of being alone—well, alone except for Tovera, her poisonous reptile—as Daniel had expected, Vesey was at the command console. Each other station—save for the signals console—was occupied by the proper officer.

Witnesses. For my sake, Adele has arranged witnesses.

"Captain Leary," Adele said. She sounded as she normally did: coldly formal. "You are now under my command, by the authority of the Speaker of the Republic as delegated to the Permanent Secretary of the Senate. Would you care to see my authorization?"

Daniel frowned. "Would you lie to me, Your Ladyship?" he asked.

Adele considered for a moment. "No," she said. "I don't think I would."

Hogg entered the bridge. Daniel caught the movement from the corner of his eye, but Hogg was moving as silently as only an old poacher could. He too understood the situation.

Daniel smiled faintly. "Then I'm ready to go," he said, patting the blouse of his Whites. He wasn't feeling the brandy, for a blessing.

"No," said Adele unexpectedly. "While you're under my command, Captain, I want you in utilities and wearing a commo helmet. This is dismounted operation. Oh, and wear a sidearm."

"Ah," said Daniel, nonplussed. "Ah, Officer, *Lady* Mundy, that is, I'm not a good pistol shot. I could draw a submachine gun if you think ...?"

He stopped, embarrassed to be so completely at sea. Adele smiled—broadly, for Adele—and said, "Thank you, Captain. The pistol will send a signal to Admiral Cox. A submachine gun would send a different signal, which I hope won't be required."

"I trust her Ladyship will delegate any shooting to her household servant," said Tovera. She smiled also. "Since I enjoy it."

"Yes," said Adele, the humor gone from her face. "Tovera will accompany us and will drive the staff car which Squadron Headquarters is sending here. Hogg—"

She glanced at him, but she continued to address Daniel.

"—will *not* accompany us."

Hogg touched his forelock and bowed. "Yes, mum," he said. "I will go look for a sheep to dip or some other employment proper to a simple countryman."

"I'll get changed," Daniel said, turning to go to his quarters just forward of the Battle Direction Center. He was smiling.

But he was *very* glad that Hogg had understood this wasn't a time to argue with Lady Mundy.

Chapter Twenty-eight

LEELBURG ON TATTERSALL

Adele strode toward the entrance of the school with Daniel behind and to the left like a mottled gray shadow; Tovera balanced him to the right. The car sported the metal pennon of Squadron Headquarters. It remained in front. It had been dispatched in response to a signal coded to Admiral Cox. It was unlikely that anyone—else—on Tattersall would be able to trace to call's origination back to the *Princess Cecile*'s bridge.

Adele had reviewed the imagery of Daniel reporting to the temporary headquarters a few hours earlier. The sergeant commanding the Marine detachment on guard had saluted not Daniel, whom he hadn't known from Adam, but the RCN captain in Whites. Lady Mundy would have to work harder to breeze through.

She had never minded hard work.

The sergeant cupped his hand over his right ear as an order came through the bud. He shouted, "Atten-*shun!*"

As his squad stiffened and threw their weapons to their

shoulders, the sergeant snapped out a sharp salute, then pulled the door open. "Ma'am!" he said.

Adele nodded regally as she passed him. Inside the building, and muffled by the echoes of chattering and feet on concrete, Daniel said, "How did you do that, if I may ask?"

"Cory directed the guards to admit the Navy Board plenipotentiary and her aides," Adele said. "He's watching through your helmet."

Then—it might be considered bragging, but it was important to her to be accurate—she added, "I could have done it by keying a preset message as we approached, but I thought having a human in the loop was preferable in case anything went wrong."

They crossed the central rotunda. The enlisted clerks watched but didn't speak. The supervising lieutenant, who hadn't been present when Daniel arrived on his own, said, "Mistress? Mistress! You can't go through there!"

He lifted the gate in the circular counter. Daniel shifted to block him. He didn't raise his hands, but Adele had seen how quickly Daniel could move when he wanted to.

"Lieutenant!" said the senior clerk. From the urgency in her voice, she had predicted correctly what was going to happen if her superior tried to push Daniel out of the way. "They're authorized! The message just came through! They're from Xenos!"

That was true only in the most general sense, but Adele didn't feel obliged to correct the clerk on her way to the door marked HEADMASTER. Cox had taken that office and the associated meeting room for his temporary headquarters.

The lieutenant said, "What?" but he allowed the clerk to tug him back within the counter. Plaintively he added to no one in particular, "The admiral's in conference with Captain Butler, though."

Butler was regional head of Naval Intelligence. Well, that wasn't a problem.

Adele touched the door. It was locked. She felt a flash of cold fury and turned to Daniel.

"Ma'am?" the senior clerk said. "Please, I'll call through and—"

The latch plate clicked; the door not only unlocked, it slumped open a finger's breadth. Cory must have figured out how to shut down the lock system completely. Perhaps because it was a school, the doors had to open if the facility lost power in an emergency.

Her good humor restored, Adele strode into the suite. She must have been more on edge than she had realized to have turned immediately to the alternative of having Daniel kick the door down.

The office proper was empty, but the door to the adjoining conference room was open. Admiral Cox sat at a console which was part of the school's furnishings; Commander Ruffin and a portly captain who must be Butler sat to either side of him with their personal data units on the long table.

"What's this?" Cox said. "Who *are* you?"

Ruffin got to her feet with an angry expression. Captain Butler, by contrast, stared at his holographic display, scrolled down it, and looked at Adele in amazement. He said, "You're *Lady* Mundy, that's right?"

"Yes," said Adele. "Now get out."

She gestured to Commander Ruffin and added, "You too. My business is with Admiral Cox."

She smiled, more or less. "My aides will stay."

Butler rose, scooping up his data unit and dropping it into the briefcase beside him on the table. He closed but didn't bother to latch the case. Carrying it in both hands, he moved quickly around the table.

"Whoever you are," said Cox, "get out and get out now! We're discussing security matters!"

"Admiral?" Butler called over his shoulder. Daniel stepped to the side to leave a path to the door. "Check your console, sir. It's on your console too, I'm sure."

Which of course it was, thanks to Cory. Butler was proving quicker off the mark than Adele would have expected for someone filling a Naval Intelligence slot in the Macotta Region, but not infrequently a person who was smart but lacked influence ran into someone influential who wasn't smart. In Adele's experience, influence generally won.

Cox was staring at his display; Ruffin was staring at Cox. *Do they think they're posing for a wax tableau?*

Adele sat in the chair across from Cox—he and his aides had been in line on one side of the table—and took out her data unit. She said, "Captain Leary, put Ruffin out of the room, since she doesn't appear to understand words of one syllable."

She twitched her wands and cut the power to the console Cox was using. His eyes didn't focus on her at first.

"This way, Commander," Daniel said, reaching for Ruffin's elbow.

Tovera patted the aide's cheek and said, "It's better if he does it, sweetie. But my way will be quicker if you decide to make a problem."

"Get out of here, Ruffin!" Cox said hoarsely. He appeared to have realized that his aide was the only person present against whom it was safe to release his frightened anger. "Just get out!"

"Aye aye, sir," muttered Ruffin. She stepped back as if unaware of Daniel's hand and followed Butler out of the office. When she closed the outer door behind her, it latched and probably locked.

Cory continues to be a credit to his training.

"Admiral Cox," Adele said, raising her eyes to meet the admiral's. Daniel and Tovera remained standing to either side of her chair. "You chose not to deal with Captain Leary; therefore you're dealing with Mundy of Chatsworth. Do you have any questions about your present situation?"

"I don't know what's going on," Cox said. With a little more vigor he added, "I don't have *any* bloody idea!"

"Then let me rephrase that," Adele said. She thought of adding, "because you appear to be as thick as two short planks." She did not, because that was what Hogg would have said. Hogg was an estimable servant, but for Daniel rather than for her; and anyway, he was not a suitable role model for Lady Mundy.

"You have read my credentials from Admiral Hartsfeld, authorizing me to issue orders to naval personnel in the name of the Navy Board and to supersede any officer in the Macotta Region without recourse. Do you understand *that*?"

"But how?" Cox said. He sounded hurt rather than angry. "You came from nowhere and now you're giving me orders!"

Adele's tongue touched her lips in exasperation. After a moment's pause while she determined how to handle this, she said, "I'm sure that Admiral Hartsfeld hoped his own personnel would be able to handle the situation without need for the representative of the Senate to step in. I hoped that myself, to be honest. Unfortunately, Admiral, you and your staff have shown yourselves to be too parochial to be trusted with the safety of the Republic in a situation so delicate."

Cox flushed, then swallowed. He did not speak.

"Now," said Adele. "*Will* you accept my orders quickly and without cavil? Or shall I replace you with Captain Leary, here?"

She tilted her head slightly toward Daniel. She didn't gesture with her hands because she was holding the wands.

"I'm sure the captain could handle the job, but he would be bored sitting at a desk. I would prefer to spare him that."

She smiled, very slightly.

Cox flushed again. He glanced up at Daniel; recognition dawned. In the confusion, he had not appreciated who Adele's utility-clad escort really was. *He probably hasn't recognized me even now. And he won't.*

"What are your orders, Lady Mundy?" Cox growled, looking at the tabletop between them.

Adele stared at Cox for a moment before she decided to accept the surrender without forcing him to make it explicit. She would do whatever was necessary to gain her ends, but the admiral was now broken. Insulting him further would be cruel, not ruthless.

"All right," she said. "A party of Alliance officials has arrived to arrest some of their own citizens. I'm sure that the necessary paperwork will eventually arrive, but I've already informed the head of the mission that the RCN will accept it as complete as of now. I also said we'll offer assistance as required, though I doubt that will be necessary."

Cox touched his keyboard, then remembered that the console was dead. Adele thought of turning it back on, but she decided the dynamics were working in her favor at present.

Cox looked up and said, "Officials. You mean Alliance police?"

"Not exactly," Adele said without inflection.

Cox made a sour face. "All right," he said, "since it doesn't matter what I think anyway. What else do you want of me?"

"I have no other special instructions at present," Adele said. She switched on the console and got to her feet, then paused. "On second thought, I have one request."

She could have used a stronger term than "request," but she didn't think it would be necessary.

"When you open the conference this afternoon, I want you to have Captain Leary beside you. Tell people that he's your aide for the duration of the proceedings. Leary, you'll change back into your Whites."

"Yes, Your Ladyship," Daniel said. He dipped his head in further acknowledgment.

"Then I'll leave you to your business, Admiral," Adele said. "Captain Leary, I'll brief you more fully on our return to the *Princess Cecile*."

She strode out of the office with Daniel following. Tovera

was in the lead, implying that she thought that was the direction danger was most likely to come from.

Tovera was probably right, but Adele doubted there was much to fear in any direction. Not for anyone whom she regarded as being on her side, that is.

The driver who had delivered the staff car to the *Princess Cecile* was now carrying Admiral Cox and his aides to the conference in the same vehicle. Daniel and Cox sat on the leather cushions in back; Ruffin and Captain Butler faced them on the molded fiberglass seats across the enclosed passenger compartment.

Hogg was beside the driver in the open cab, which had only a canvas roof without even side-curtains. The men chatted in friendly fashion despite the rain pelting down. A countryman and hunter—well, poacher—like Hogg had plenty of experience being rained on, and it seemed likely that the admiral's driver did also.

"I'm hanged if I know why the Alliance wanted this bloody place," Cox said as they splashed toward the conference site: West House, though it must be south of Leelburg proper. "*I* certainly could have done without ever visiting Tattersall in my life."

Shrugging, he added, "We couldn't let the Alliance take it, of course. But that's the only reason I can think of for the Republic to care—and it's one more than I can find for Guarantor Porra giving a toss."

"I don't believe Porra actually cares, sir," Daniel said. He'd read Adele's briefing, which as usual was thorough. "I believe this has all been arranged by the head of Fleet Intelligence on

Madison, a fellow named Doerries. He was clever; but a bit too clever, it seems. He was posted to the Forty Stars because of some problems at his previous posting."

"Ah!" said the admiral, nodding wisely. "The secret accounts, I suppose?"

Cox was being much more human—friendly, even—since he picked up Daniel at the *Sissie* on the way to West House. The change was pleasant, but it was also unexplained. A spacer learned quickly that inexplicable good fortune is likely to turn sour once you learn what's really going on. Pigs being fattened aren't really in luck.

"Surprisingly, no," said Daniel. "It appeared that the squadron commander had a serious gambling problem which Doerries knew about. He was blackmailing the admiral to get glowing efficiency reports—which came out in the investigation after the admiral shot himself, you see. Not because of anything Doerries did, but the admiral's journal described the whole business."

"How would arranging a coup on Tattersall have helped him, Leary?" said Butler, leaning forward in his seat. Adele had spoken well of the intelligence officer. "Surely he didn't hope to be made Resident? And even if it did, governor of Tattersall is scarcely a career for an—"

He gestured toward the side window without looking away from Daniel. They were passing a rambling processing plant. Narrow channels crossing the road surface carried effluent toward the harbor. The stench of vegetable decay lay heavy on the wet atmosphere.

"—ambitious officer."

Daniel cleared his throat, wondering how much to explain. His normal reaction was to be completely open. That was probably the correct response here, at least if he limited his comments to what he had deduced on his own.

"Ah, sir?" Daniel said, speaking to the admiral although the aide had asked the question. The choice was as much for Butler's sake as for his own. "You were aware that the Macotta Squadron had been on high alert for several weeks now?"

"Right," said Cox, nodding toward his intelligence chief. "Rab there told me all about it. Said they'd been alerted because of that trouble I sent you to Sunbright about, though. Not so?"

"Yes and no," said Daniel, aware that Butler was watching with tension under his pleasant smile. "Pleasaunce had delivered a regional alert in case the Funnel Squadron requested help on Sunbright, but Doerries was responsible for the revolt on Sunbright also. Not the initial trouble, but the fact that it built to the level it did. He did that to have an excuse for keeping the Forty Stars Squadron at high readiness. That way they could react immediately when Rides and Cobbet landed on Tattersall and their puppet government called for Alliance help."

The road curved slightly. Daniel hadn't been able to see anything forward, but the side window was clear. He glimpsed an ornate, turreted house at least three stories high, painted pink with green trim, in the direction they were going.

"The Forty Stars Squadron?" Cox said in an amazement that was building toward anger. "Look, Leary, you may not think much of us here in the Macotta Region, but I'll bloody well tell you that we could see off four cruisers not much younger than the *Warhol*. And any support the Funnel Squadron sent besides. They're all anti-pirate gunboats anyway."

"They couldn't hold Tattersall a day after we arrived!" Ruffin said forcefully. Either she felt even more insulted than Cox had, or she was trying to convince her superior that she was.

"I agree," Daniel said. "There would be a short battle. The Forty Stars Squadron would retreat, probably with damage or even after ships had been destroyed. What would happen then?"

"What?" said the admiral. "We'd land, clear out the foreigners, and arrest the locals who were in league with them. Much as we've done now, in fact, when we arrived ahead of them."

"By the great gods," said Captain Butler. "Doerries was trying to start a war! That's it, isn't it, Leary? He thought he was too able to waste in a crisis. He believed that he'd be moved out of this backwater if the war resumed full-force."

"I believe so, yes," Daniel said. "And there's the further possibility that because of how he was treated, Doerries is as angry with his own people as he is with Cinnabar. Perhaps more so, in fact."

Cox scowled fiercely—in the direction of his two aides, but probably at something unseen outside his own mind. "Well," he growled, "I suppose that's for others than ourselves to worry about. So long as it's handled, the likes of you and me don't need to know the details, eh, Leary?"

Daniel thought about Tovera, who had no human feelings, and about his friend Adele, who *did* have feelings but who acted as though she did not. Adele regularly awoke in the dark hours of the morning with an expression like that of a prisoner about to be hanged.

"Yes, sir," he said. "We space officers have our duties, and those are certainly enough for me."

The car paused on the driveway to the grounds of the garish house Daniel had noticed. The estate was surrounded by recently erected chain-link fencing. Though Admiral Cox was the highest authority in the Macotta Region to the Marines guarding the entrance, the vehicles ahead of his staff car physically blocked the entrance until they could be moved; either inside the fencing after they had been checked and approved, or out of the way.

Unlike the Marines, vehicles ahead were not occupied by people junior to the admiral in a chain of command. The all-terrain command car directly in front bore Fleet markings. It seemed that Admiral Jeletsky had found a way to stow it aboard a heavy cruiser, though Daniel would have liked to know how. Perhaps the vehicle had taken the place of several missiles from a magazine.

The line of vehicles whined or blatted—the command car's twin diesels were unmuffled—forward a car's length. Cox grimaced and turned to Daniel.

"I've heard you've worked with this Lady Mundy before, Leary," he said. "Is she always the ballbuster she was today?"

That's why he's turned friendly toward me! We're two honest spacers who're being ordered around by a civilian from some dirty nook of the spy services!

Daniel cleared his throat. "Well, sir," he said carefully, "she has days and, well, other days. I swore to do my duty when I received my commission, and I accept the orders which my superiors give me."

"Good man," Cox growled. Perhaps if there had been more room, he would have clapped Daniel on the shoulder.

Across from them, Ruffin appeared to be taking Daniel's statement at face value. Captain Butler's expression was the careful neutral of someone who has no intention of speaking his mind but who certainly has an opinion. Given that Butler had presumably been the source of everything the admiral knew about Adele, the intelligence officer wasn't likely to correct his superior's misunderstanding.

The line moved forward again and stopped. The Fleet command car was being examined now.

The roar of a ship descending smothered other sounds even this far from the harbor. Daniel didn't have goggles to filter the UV of the plasma exhaust, but because they were in an RCN staff car, the windows would automatically block actinics.

The harbor was behind them, but the rain had stopped. Daniel swung open the rear-hinged door, stepped out, and hunched so that he could look through the glass. To his surprise—though perhaps it shouldn't have been—Cox slid out to join him.

There was no question but that the descending vessel was naval rather than civilian: the heavy sparring which required a crew too large to be commercially viable proved that. But though the ship's hull had the lines of a light cruiser, her overall length had been reduced by removing several frames and resetting the antennas to fit the full sail-plan onto the shortened hull. With a trained crew, she would be very fast indeed.

"That isn't a cruiser," Daniel said in surprise. "That's an RCN courier!"

His first cruise following graduation from the Academy had been as a supernumerary about the RCS *Aglaia*, also a courier vessel. Couriers were hard postings because they carried high officials to whom the ship's officers, especially the junior officers, were peons. But the *Aggie* had been Lieutenant Daniel Leary's first ship, and she would always have a place in his heart.

"She's the *Themis*, straight from Harbor Three," said Commander Ruffin from inside the car.

"I suppose she's bringing another high muckymuck to deal with whatever in blazes is going on," said Cox, squatting at Daniel's side. "Nobody's told me, of course. Just requested landing permission in the tone of voice you'd use when you told your servant how you wanted your eggs this morning."

"I don't see how she"—Daniel thumbed toward the *Themis*—"could have anything to do with our mission," he said. "The voyage can't have taken her less than fifteen days, so she had to have lifted before you called the conference. But I don't believe it's a coincidence, either. I suppose we'll learn what it's all about eventually."

He stood. The courier was below the horizon now, so the glare of its exhaust was concealed. "Or not," he concluded with a lopsided grin toward the admiral.

Cox doesn't know what's going on, Daniel realized. *He's treating me as a friend not for what I know, but because I'm puzzled also. Two spacers, left in the dark by faceless bureaucrats.*

The Alliance vehicle grunted loudly, then started forward. The staff car's driver was looking back at his passengers, and the Marines at the entrance had braced to attention.

"Duty calls," the admiral said without enthusiasm as he got back into the car. They started forward as soon as Daniel had closed the door. The major commanding the guard detachment saluted, but nobody wasted time trying to check the squadron commander's credentials.

"You know," Cox said as the car swung toward the front of the commandeered house, "I thought we had things sorted out pretty well here, pretty *bloody* well. We've rounded up the chancers on Tattersall—that's right, isn't it, Butler?"

"Yes, sir," said the intelligence officer. "I'm satisfied that we have."

He looked at Daniel and added apologetically, "They weren't very sophisticated. It doesn't appear to have crossed their minds that their plans would fail."

"I don't see what call there was to bring in this Mundy spook," Cox said in an aggrieved tone. "We'd taken care of it. And now the *Themis*, carrying somebody from Navy House or External Affairs or for all I know the Senate itself! Because they don't trust us to handle a little piss-pot revolution on a little piss-pot world. It's not right!"

He looked at Daniel and added, "I'm not blaming you, Leary. You're following orders just the same as I am or Captain Gillian on the *Themis*. I just wish our lords and masters trusted us, you see?"

The staff car stopped again. The Alliance vehicle was being shunted into the parking area without being permitted to drop off its passengers first. Marines in second-class uniforms—the same gray as those of RCN spacers, but with red instead of black piping—backed up the woman giving directions, but she wore utilities and carried her pistol in a shoulder holster. She had no rank or unit insignia.

Lieutenant Commander Vondrian, a friend whom Daniel planned to get together with if he had a moment before the *Princess Cecile* lifted from Tattersall, stood to the side. He too was in utilities and was watching the discussion—argument—between the woman giving directions and the driver. Better, the driver's protest and the woman's implacably calm disinterest.

Vondrian was well-born and wealthy. He was normally a pleasant, sophisticated fellow, but at the moment he looked as grim as if he were commanding a firing squad.

"I think," said Daniel, "that the Alliance involvement was the problem. Even though Pleasaunce isn't involved, the central government *could* be if things went wrong. It's a complicated mess all going back to Doerries and Forty Stars headquarters, not only the Sunbright rebellion but also much of the blockade running and even the private-venture cruiser that was *catching* blockade runners, the *Estremadura*. Though he had partners on Cremona for the cruiser."

"Was this Doerries out of his mind?" said Ruffin. "Why was he working against himself? And against his government, if it comes to that?"

"The blockade running and the *Estremadura* were both to make money to keep the Sunbright rebellion going," Daniel said. "He was letting cargoes he'd backed go through and capturing ships sent by rival syndicates. And as for the Sunbright business itself, well, that's complicated. Too complicated for—"

He looked from Ruffin to the admiral.

"—a spacer like me."

"What's going on up there?" said Cox, cocking his head to see past his aides on the facing seats. That didn't show him as much as he wanted to see, so he started to get out of the vehicle on his side.

As he did so, the Alliance vehicle finally pulled away with a snarl of exhaust. The RCN driver checked to see that Cox was still inside, then moved smoothly to the drop-off point. Marines in Grays opened the four doors of the passenger compartment. Hogg lifted himself feet-first out of the open cab and dropped to the ground. Perhaps the cab door didn't open.

The Macotta Squadron had raised a marquee of sail fabric supported by spars. The thin film was translucent, blurring but not concealing the pink-with-blue/green upperworks of the ornate building.

Ruffin followed Daniel's eyes. "It's the best we could find here," she muttered in a defensive tone. "A resident factory manager built it three generations ago. There's nothing else bigger than four rooms and a low ceiling in Leelburg, unless we hold the conference in a packing plant."

Admiral Cox instead was looking toward the parking area across the lawn of dark, broad-leafed ground cover. The staff car drove away, but Marines blocked the approach of the next vehicle, a locally hired utility van with a flag Daniel didn't recognize dangling in soggy state from a magnetic mount on the fender. It was probably the delegation from one of the semi-independent worlds of the cluster.

"Leary?" the admiral said. "That's Mundy over there, isn't it? Did those people with her come on your ship too?"

Daniel peered. He could see the command car—its bulk

stood out among the ordinary passenger vehicles—but Cox was taller than he was. All Daniel could see was a wall of bulky people in drab—but not military—clothing. Even so, he could answer the more important of the admiral's questions.

"They didn't come on the *Princess Cecile*, sir," Daniel said. "I think they may be the foreign officials that Lady Mundy mentioned."

"I'm going to see what's happening," Cox said. He stepped off, ignoring the wet ground cover and the resuming drizzle.

"Sir—" said Daniel, and paused, though no one outside his head would have realized it. He wasn't sure how to continue.

Adele had ordered him to accompany the admiral closely. She had not, however, told Daniel to prevent Admiral Cox from performing his duties—and the admiral's expressed intention to sort out the trouble here in the parking lot was certainly part of the duty of the admiral commanding the Macotta Squadron.

Daniel *could* provide information and perhaps a buffer, however. He caught up with Cox and said, "If you don't mind, sir, I suggest your other aides remain under the marquee."

And out of the way. Nothing about Ruffin's past behavior made Daniel want to trust her if things got rough, and Butler seemed even less of a man of action than the commander did.

"Roger," said Cox. He turned his head and snapped, "You two, stay on the porch!"

I'm as glad not to be on the squadron staff, Daniel thought. On the other hand, it was scarcely unusual for a senior officer to behave like an arrogant bastard some of the time, and Cox was at least competent.

Passengers were getting out of the back of the command car. There would be room for twelve soldiers in battle dress if the extra communications and sensing electronics were stripped out, as they must have been in this case, since half a dozen had disembarked already and more were stepping onto the steep ramp.

Fleet dress uniforms weren't quite as bulky as the body armor, pack, and shoulder weapons that combat troops wore, but the difference was one of degree rather than kind. The garments were the same gray-green—Field Gray—color as Fleet utilities, but they were of glossy fabric—silk for those who could afford it—with peaked saucer hats, flaring shoulder boards, and the fittings in gold rather than silver or black.

Adele, in a dark business suit, stood facing the vehicle's rear hatch. Her hands were before her and empty, but crooked elbows put her hands near her tunic pockets.

To Adele's left was Tovera, as was to be expected. The man on Adele's right was a stranger to Daniel. He was of moderate height and build. Like Adele he wore civilian clothing, and he looked almost as insignificant from a distance as she did.

The officers who had gotten out of the command car intended to wait near the base of the ramp for Admiral Jeletsky. Instead, RCN Marines in second-class uniforms were easing them back, as gently as possible but firmly nonetheless. The Marines were under the command of a lieutenant colonel who looked just as stern as Vondrian had at the drop-off point in front of the house.

"That's LaSalle from the *Schelling*," Cox said. "*I* didn't give him orders to do this."

I wouldn't bet on that, Daniel thought. If orders were to be transmitted electronically, Adele generally preferred to do it herself under the proper codes and protocols rather than bother with the formality of requesting action by the person whose responsibility it was.

Three men and a woman, all in nondescript clothing, waited at the sides of the ramp. The woman was watching the man beside Adele. He hooked his left index finger, a motion as slight as what was required to pull a trigger.

The woman faced around and nodded. The next man out of the vehicle was a commander, well built and apparently fit. He had a pencil moustache and a small goatee. He gave the Marine officer a look of guarded concern.

The woman at the base of the ramp touched his wrist said, "If you'll come with me, please, Commander Doerries."

Doerries jerked away from her. While his attention was concentrated on the woman, a man in back of him took the wrist in his left hand and twisted it behind Doerries' neck. Doerries tried to turn into the grip to loosen it, but a man on the other side had his free hand. He appeared to hold Doerries gently, but from the commander's choked scream his thumb and fingers were on the verge of being dislocated.

Stumbling, sobbing, Doerries allowed himself to be walked toward the Alliance assault boat which loomed over the vehicles at the rear of the parking area. The trail its floatation tires left in the soggy ground was clearly visible now that Daniel had walked near. Not only had the boat been in place before the conference attendees started to arrive, it had come straight in from the bay three miles north.

Doerries' arrest had startled the Alliance staff officers into gabbling like a rookery of large birds awakened in the night. Admiral Jeletsky, portly but solid looking, pushed aside the captain who had frozen in the command car's hatch and stepped out.

"Wait a bloody minute!" Jeletsky shouted. "You can't arrest my officers! This is an act of war! Cox! Where are you, Cox?"

He thinks Doerries has been arrested by Cinnabar personnel, Daniel realized.

The man beside Adele tapped his finger again. Seeing what was about to happen—the scene clarified the way battle plans did, all the swirling possibilities suddenly freezing into one crystal certainty—Daniel started forward.

"Stop right bloody now or—"

"If you'll come with me, please, Admiral Jeletsky," the woman said. She took Jeletsky's wrist.

The admiral looked at her in sudden realization. He screamed like a nose-clamped hog about to be butchered and pulled himself away. The remaining man took Jeletsky's left wrist and elbow and began to raise them.

"Help me!" Jeletsky cried. "Help me!"

A trim-looking Fleet lieutenant unsnapped her holster. The pistol was small, part of her uniform rather than a real weapon, but it would probably work. The gods knew that Adele's pistol did, and it was smaller yet.

Daniel took her hand in his. "Excuse me, Lieutenant," he said, "but I'd rather that you not do that. This is my only set of Dress Whites, and I'd prefer not get them spattered with your blood."

The staff lieutenant looked around wild-eyed. Tovera and the hulking minder beside Adele's companion had submachine guns pointed at her. She stopped pulling against Daniel's grip and her knees began to shake.

The Fifth Bureau operatives walked Admiral Jeletsky into the assault boat. The people guarding that vehicle were either Fleet Marines in civilian clothes or the Bureau's own muscle.

Daniel returned to the side of Admiral Cox. "Sir," he said. "I think you have brought the Tattersall operation to a satisfactory conclusion."

Chapter Twenty-nine

LEELBURG ON TATTERSALL

Adele let out a deep breath as the hatch of the assault boat closed behind Master Storn. Doerries and Jeletsky were already on board. She didn't relax, but she noticed that she felt less tense.

The closest Adele came to relaxation occurred when she was deep in research with all the resources she needed and nothing standing between her and the answer except the limits of her own abilities. Thus far, she had not reached any such limits.

The boat—should she call it a truck or bus since it was on land now?—wallowed off in the direction of Flounder Harbor. It was quite possible that it would be driven straight into the hold of the *Feursnot*. If so, there was a good chance that Tattersall's wet grayness had been the last open sky Doerries and Jeletsky would ever see.

Daniel and Admiral Cox remained together, talking with animation. Cox turned toward the house, then turned back to look directly at Adele. She stood straight, her face set. *I will listen to whatever the admiral chooses to say; then I will decide whether I will respond or not respond.*

Cox bowed at the waist. It was what he would have done if, at a formal affair, Admiral Cox in uniform met Lady Mundy in civilian garb.

Adele curtseyed. Her mother's training brought the correct response out by reflex. She watched Daniel and Cox walk side by side toward the building's entrance.

I didn't expect him to draw his pistol and try to shoot me, but I wouldn't have been surprised. That *surprised me.*

Tovera coughed minusculely. *Tovera never coughs.*

Adele kept her left hand out of her tunic pocket, but she turned very quickly. Mistress Sand stood at Tovera's elbow. She shielded a snuffbox—a lovely thing, carved from burl—in her upturned palm, but she didn't attempt to use it in the drizzle. Her tweed suit and circular hat of matching fabric were close-woven.

Adele felt humor that didn't reach her lips. These were exactly the conditions for which Sand's outfit was intended. The older woman was in truth as well as appearance a squire from Cinnabar's central uplands. She was considerably more than that also.

And she was most unexpectedly here on Tattersall.

"I wonder if I might have a word, Mundy?" Mistress Sand said. She phrased it as a question; Adele was one of the few people who might not accept a direct order from Mistress Sand.

"Yes, of course," Adele said. She gave the older woman her equivalent of a broad smile and added, "I'm glad to see you; but even if I weren't, I would be glad to grant so courteous a request."

To a degree, Adele regretted choosing to to wave her independence in Mistress Sand's face in that fashion. On the other hand, if Mistress Sand ever forgot that she was dealing with Mundy of Chatsworth, she might try to behave as a superior in fact rather than on an organizational chart. Adele's reaction to that might go beyond what could be swept under the table in the future. Since Adele wanted to continue the relationship, it was better not to take the risk.

Sand thrust her hands into her jacket pockets. She eyed the house into which the last of the conference attendees were filtering and said, "I doubt we'd find much privacy there, and I'd prefer to give that place a wide berth anyway. It looks like a carnival funhouse."

Glancing sidelong at Adele, she added, "Shall we go somewhere in my car?"

An aircar waited at the edge of the parking lot. It was a comment on how focused Adele had been on the drama which the Alliance visitors had just acted that she hadn't noticed the sound. No matter how well tuned an aircar's fans were, the intake rush couldn't be completely muffled.

Adele looked beyond the car. "Let's just walk on the other side of the road," she said. "The ground there is firmer, I believe. I think it will be as private as anywhere on the planet."

After a moment's thought, she added, "It's possible that we'll be overheard by some burrowing animal or the like, but I haven't seen any myself."

I wonder if Daniel would know the answer to that?

Sand looked startled, then laughed. "I forget you have a sense of humor, Mundy," she said. In a wistful tone she said,

"Sometimes I forget I do myself. Yes, let's walk."

The Marines who had been directing traffic relaxed now that vehicles had stopped coming up the drive. There might be a few latecomers, but the senior officers were inside by now, which took the pressure off the junior personnel who remained.

By becoming a Sissie, a member of the crew of the *Princess Cecile*, Adele had found herself forced to observe human behavior with her own eyes. She had become fairly skilled at the business, though she still would have preferred to gain her information through recordings and the reports of third parties.

She wondered if she had ever seen, let alone entered, a carnival funhouse. It wasn't the sort of thing which would have interested Senator Lucas Mundy's bookish daughter. Immediately after the Proscriptions, Adele could not afford anything nonessential; since then, Signals Officer Mundy had not had the time.

Daniel might know about funhouses; Hogg certainly would. She would ask Hogg to arrange for her to see one at the next opportunity. It would be part of her education in her new role to see a funhouse—and to do so in her own person rather than through video imagery.

"Did you perchance request that I come out here, Mundy?" Mistress Sand said. They had crossed the road and were continuing on toward the forest a mile or so away.

Adele frowned. "Of course not," she said. "I didn't realize how serious the business was until the *Princess Cecile* reached Madison. Not till the end of our stay there, as a matter of fact. I didn't have any way of sending a priority message to Xenos from an Alliance world, and even if I had, the round trip would be at least thirty days. By then the matter would have ended one way or another."

She shrugged. "I sent a report," she said. "I would have built an altar and prayed to the great gods before I did anything as foolish as trying to summon you. I would have consulted you if you'd been present, but the Navy Board authorization you provided when we met on Cinnabar was all that I needed to deal with the matter. Matters."

The vegetation here was knee-high. Adele's trouser legs were being soaked, but her RCN boots were waterproof. She'd walked in the rain before, and slept under culverts when it rained, come to that.

"I began reviewing information on the Macotta Region after I sent you—" Sand said. She stopped when she saw Adele's almost smile.

"I misstated," Sand said. "When I signed off on *your* plan to go to Kronstadt with a warning about the coming trouble on Tattersall. Which is my excuse for not having read into the region sooner and thus having missed the clues that something was badly amiss."

What Adele had thought were flowers among the plants were actually star-shaped patches of white on the dark green leaves. Though . . . the patches swelled from the leaf surfaces, and creatures no more than a tenth of an inch long crawled on and about them. Perhaps they *were* flowers, or anyway served the purposes of flowers.

She looked up again. Mistress Sand was waiting patiently for her to choose her answer.

"I had no idea of the ramifications either until we arrived

in the region," Adele said. "I don't see why you fault yourself for not seeing them."

"Because it's my job," Sand said. "Not yours."

She looked at the sky and apparently decided that the mist had stopped falling. She spilled a quantity of snuff into the cup between her closed left thumb and the back of her hand. From the tickle in Adele's nose, the tobacco was mixed with cinnamon.

Sand knuckled her right nostril shut, snorted half the charge, then repeated the process through her right nostril. Facing away from Adele she sneezed loudly, sneezed again, and finally sneezed a third time with transporting violence.

She wiped her lower face with a large handkerchief printed in the same pattern as her tweeds, then smiled at Adele. Her cheeks were flushed.

"Filthy habit, I know," Sand said. "Still, it settles me, and I've decided it's a better choice than my flask—"

She tapped her tweed jacket; the dull thump located the flat metal container.

"—when I'm talking to you. I have enough trouble keeping up when I'm not buzzed."

Sand's expression tightened. "I should have known," she said, "because it's my job to keep in touch with what's going on in all regions. I have access to more data than you do. As soon as I looked at the Sunbright situation, I saw that elements in the Alliance itself were behind the rebellion, and that they were trying to blame it on us. On Cinnabar."

"Sunbright is an Alliance world," Adele said. "There was no reason for you be concerned about what was going on there."

She smiled wryly. "For that matter," she said, "though the Alliance authorities *did* have reason for concern, they didn't get very far without our help."

"I had the advantage of knowing that Cinnabar wasn't backing the revolt," Sand said. "Even if the support was unofficial, weaponry at that level would have left traces moving through RCN accounts. No doubt the Fifth Bureau could have found it also, if they'd been looking in that direction."

The horizontal leaves of a plant a little taller than most of those around it dangled lines covered with what Adele thought were flowers. As her next step brought her closer, the "flowers" drifted away in discrete masses, leaving the tendrils white and bare.

Plant and animal behavior can be interesting if I imagine that I'm viewing holographic images, Adele thought. Human behavior became interesting that way too.

"*Your* advantage over the Fifth Bureau...," Sand said. "Because obviously you'd already learned the things I rushed from Xenos to tell you. Was that you're a magician."

Adele sniffed. "Scarcely that," she said. "I located the information specialist who was supplying Doerries with particulars on the blockade runners. The specialist's database had a record of the whole operation. He was perforce inside Doerries' firewall; and he gathered information as I do, not for any reason of Doerries. I think a clerk in Macotta Headquarters could have done what I did. Though the clerk would have taken longer to sift out the important elements."

Mistress Sand looked at her. Adele was suddenly afraid that the older woman was going to ask how she had gotten access to Platt's databases. Adele wouldn't lie; but neither, she decided, would she answer fully.

Sand wouldn't be happier to know the truth. Neither was Adele herself. Platt had been a loathsome beast whose death made the human universe marginally better...but despite that, Adele had dreamed of his moonlike face and his one accusing eye every night since she killed him.

"I came to the region to bring you information, Mundy," Mistress Sand said, changing the subject. "I would have left the execution in your hands, because I've never met anyone with better tactical appreciation of matters of this kind. I trust your judgment implicitly."

She didn't change the subject after all. She heard about what happened on Madison and has drawn the correct conclusions about who was responsible.

"I'll credit myself with making sure that you left Cinnabar with plenipotentiary authority from Admiral Hartsfeld," Sand said. Her smile grew. "On the other hand, I don't think you would have found it difficult to create that authorization yourself. Would you have, Mundy?"

Adele considered the question. "Creating documents that would pass scrutiny in the Macotta Region," she said neutrally, "would be easier than creating something that would be examined on Xenos, that's true."

"Would you have hesitated to forge them if I hadn't been so farsighted?" Sand said, this time with the edge of real challenge.

"Would I have hesitated to do my duty, mistress?" Adele said in the same tone. "No, I would not."

"I'm glad to hear that," said Sand. "Because I may not always be as sharp as I was when you and I last met on Cinnabar."

She laughed and turned. "Let's go back," she directed. "I thought I was going to have to soothe the ruffled feathers of the regional commander about the cavalier way my department usurped his authority. From the look on Cox's face as he went into his conference, it seems that your friend Leary has already done that. I wonder how?"

Adele really smiled. "I don't know," she said. "But I think you *do* know a better tactician than I am."

"Hogg," Daniel said. "Stay here with Tovera and protect the jeep against car thieves."

Turning to Adele he said, "Wait a moment," to stop her from trying to clamber out of the air-cushion vehicle. He walked around to her side and offered his arm as a brace.

Adele's foot had slipped on the wide bulge of the plenum chamber when she got into the vehicle. Tripping while getting out would at best be an embarrassment in front of the Alliance official whose assault boat was approaching the shore. If she managed to break her neck—and it could happen—the loss to Cinnabar would be great, and the loss to Daniel Leary personally would be incalculable.

Daniel had borrowed the jeep from the Macotta Squadron; it was part of the *Warhol*'s regular equipment. Admiral Cox was being very helpful. His behavior toward the *Princess Cecile* and her complement was averaging out to the pleasant neutrality Daniel had expected of the squadron commander before they arrived on Kronstadt.

Tovera had been driving. She started to get out to follow. Adele looked at her servant and said, "I believe Captain Leary and I can handle matters, Tovera. I'll summon you if your presence is required."

Tovera looked as though she intended to protest. Instead, she gave a curt nod and slid back behind the car's control column.

"I think we'll wait midway between our vehicle and where Master Storn lands," Adele said, walking north along the beach. "Which I expect will be where he landed when we met yesterday."

The assault boat raised a bow wave out of proportion to the modest speed at which it was approaching the shore. The wheels and wheel wells ruined any hope of streamlining, but they allowed the big vehicle to drive through shallows and up the beach without the hesitation a hull better adapted to water would have.

"If you can tell me...," Daniel said, standing with his hands crossed behind his back. "Was Admiral Jeletsky actually involved in the plot, or were the authorities—"

He didn't like referring directly to the Fifth Bureau. He knew the organization existed, just as he knew cancer existed. Naming a thing sometimes seems too close to calling it up.

"—just blaming him for poor oversight?"

He and Adele wore utilities, in his case with a commo helmet. Adele didn't like helmets and instead stood bareheaded, which violated uniform regulations. Her commanding officer had better things to do with his time than to train the most brilliant signals officer in the RCN to follow nitpicky rules.

Adele shrugged. "While I can't speak for my Alliance counterpart," she said, smiling faintly, "Jeletsky had to have known about the plot to take Tattersall. The Sunbright revolt provided him with an excuse for holding his squadron at high readiness, but it didn't require him to do so. Doerries offered Jeletsky a coup that would put sparkle on his service record, and Jeletsky was too limited to see the wider implications."

"Guarantor Porra doesn't like high officers who think in broad policy terms," Daniel said. "Commander Doerries would have learned this if he'd risen to flag rank himself, I suspect."

It struck him suddenly that the RCN's greatest strength may have been that it was nonpolitical. The Senate and the Republic itself had factions whose differences might burst into mutual violence; the RCN remained above the struggle, shielding the Republic regardless of which person or party or class ruled the body politic.

"Doerries wasn't a strategic thinker," Adele said coldly. "He thought of everything in tactical terms."

The assault boat grunted onto the beach and began to turn around. Only the driver and a single passenger were visible, though any number might be hunching out of sight below the gunwales.

"Daniel," Adele said, turning her head toward him. "Could you make yourself sole ruler of the Republic? In, say, fifteen years?"

She didn't ask if I would. This is Adele, whose words mean exactly what they mean—and no more.

The question involved too many variables to have a real

answer. Still, if from this moment he directed all his efforts to that end, he would have a real possibility; one in three, perhaps. Except—

The Alliance vehicle stopped. The passenger, the man in brown who had overseen the arrests of Doerries and Jeletsky, got down from the cab and started toward them.

Daniel looked at Adele and grinned. "I couldn't succeed without perverting the RCN from its traditional role," he said. "In effect I would have to destroy it. I wouldn't do that."

"Your answer," said Adele, straight-faced, "demonstrates *real* strategic thinking."

The Alliance official stopped a polite six feet away. She nodded to him and said, "Master Storn. I'm glad you could meet me here."

"The least I could do, Your Ladyship," Storn said with a polite bow.

"Allow me to introduce my colleague, Captain Leary," Adele said. "Captain, Master Storn is an official in the government of the Alliance."

Storn switched his attention to Daniel. *When his eyes focus on you, he isn't nondescript.* He said, "Captain Leary, you demonstrated great presence of mind when Admiral Jeletsky was being taken into custody. Thank you for helping avoid public awkwardness."

"Lieutenant Bazaine was showing courage and loyalty to her superior officer in an unclear situation," Daniel said. He'd learned the lieutenant's name with the help of a directory of the Forty Stars Squadron; he hadn't caught her name tag when it was all happening. "I hope her actions won't negatively affect her future career."

Storn looked at Daniel with the expression he might have given a strange dog; a potentially dangerous dog. He said, "All right, I'll see to it."

Adele looked from one man to the other. She smiled minusculely and said, "Daniel—"

Using his given name rather than his rank was a signal as clear as if she had fired a shot in the air.

"—perhaps you would explain to Master Storn why you're concerned that the Fleet not remove a junior officer who has shown herself willing to risk her life and career in a crisis?"

Daniel chuckled. "Well, since you put it that way," he said. He met Storn's eyes. "I suppose I'm a spacer first and an enemy of the Alliance only second," he said. "At least while we're at peace."

"Then let us all hope that our nations remain at peace," Storn said mildly. His smile was as slight as Adele's and was as hard to interpret. To Adele he added, "Which will be longer than would have been the case without your intervention, Lady Mundy. My superiors thank you for your assistance. As for me personally—"

He turned his hand outward, palm up, in a deprecatory gesture.

"—such help as I can provide consonant with my duties is yours for the asking. I am not without influence even beyond the boundaries of my diocese."

"I would expect that anything I asked from you," said Adele, "would be of mutual benefit to our nations . . . as this recent matter was. May I say that while I expected your bureau to dispose of the business in a thorough fashion—"

She smiled. Storn smiled back. Love Adele though he did, Daniel felt as though he were watching a pair of cobras meeting.

"—I *am* impressed by the speed with which you did so."

The driver of the assault boat was the same bruiser who had backed Storn during the arrests. His hands weren't visible as he watched the conference from the cab, but the only question in Daniel's mind was what kind of weapon the fellow held ready. *Though I'd put my money on Tovera if it came down to cases.*

"My bureau's station on Madison will have some questions to answer about how Fleet Intelligence was able to mount so extensive an operation without being noticed," Storn said. "The station forwarded to me in a very expeditious fashion the material you provided them, however. Therefore the questions will be asked in a—"

He paused to consider his words. "In more survivable fashion," he resumed, "than might otherwise have been the case."

Storn repeated the gesture with his left hand. "You called this meeting, Lady Mundy," he said. "I assume you have a request for me?"

"I have information for you," Adele said. "Daniel, please give Master Storn the chip I asked you to carry."

Daniel reached into his right cargo pocket. He paused and burst into laughter as he finally understood the reason Adele had given him the chip case.

"Oh, my goodness!" he said. "Captain Leary, the harmless beast of burden who can stick his hand into his pocket without risking a resumption of war! Here you are, Master Storn—

documents which my good friend Lady Mundy thought would interest you."

Storn wore a chip reader pinned to the outside of his breast pocket. He inserted the chip from Adele's case, looking somewhat embarrassed.

"I'm sorry, Daniel," Adele said, sounding ill at ease. "I meant no reflection on your..."

She doesn't know how to go on.

Grinning at both spies, Daniel said, "If you meant that I'm a terrible pistol shot, then you're right and I don't feel in the least insulted. Quite a practical solution to the problem of trust, I would say."

"I told Olafsen," Storn said, tilting his head slightly to the assault boat to indicate the driver, "that even if I were killed in front of him, he should return to the *Feursnot* and inform my superiors instead of reacting himself. I'm not, however, certain that he would obey my orders."

His eyes were focused on the holographic image blurring the air in front of him. His twitching left little finger was presumably controlling the data flow.

"I have the same concerns about Tovera," Adele said. "Though of course it won't matter to me under those circumstances."

She and Storn exchanged smiles again.

Storn switched off his chip reader and met Adele's eyes. "So," he said. "Another case where it's uncertain which of us is doing the other the favor. If your information is correct—"

Daniel chuckled.

Storn looked at him and said, "Yes, I have a tendency to be overcautious with my phrasing. Habit, of course. If your information is correct, Lady Mundy, then my government will find another position for Governor Blaskett. As fertilizer, for example."

"I leave the matter in your capable hands," Adele said. The hint of approval in her voice suggested that she wasn't being ironic. "Then I believe our business here is finished."

"Yes," Storn said. He bowed again to Adele. Then he faced Daniel and saluted. Daniel returned the salute in awkward amazement.

"The personnel of Master Storn's bureau hold military rank, Daniel," Adele said. "I believe he is the equivalent of a lieutenant general."

"General of the Army, Lady Mundy," Storn called over his shoulder as he mounted the step into his vehicle. "It has been a pleasure to meet you both. It gives me faces to put to the reports I've been reading."

The assault boat drove into the low surf. It proceeded in a relatively sedate fashion until it was far enough out that spray from the water jets didn't splash Daniel and Adele.

Daniel let out his breath. "We should get back to the *Sissie*," he said. "When the *Feursnot* lifts, it won't be dangerous on the beach, but it won't be very comfortable, either. And besides—"

He grinned at Adele. *We've won!*

"—I'll be *really* glad to be back on Cinnabar!"

"Yes," said Adele. "But we've got a little time, Daniel. I want to show you the beach vegetation I noticed when I came here the first time. It's called gray plantain."

ACKNOWLEDGMENTS

Dan Breen continues as my first reader. Thank goodness.

Dan, Dorothy Day, and my webmaster, Karen Zimmerman, archive my texts. I copy them to three machines of my own, but given my track record with computers I feel a lot happier having the texts spread around.

Though for a wonder, I didn't kill (or even badly bruise) any computers on this book. The last time that happened, I lost two computers and a separate keyboard in the course of writing the next one. I am prepared!

Dorothy, Karen, and Evan Ladouceur help with research and continuity problems. Basically, I say, "What was the name of…?" or "Where the dickens did X take place?" and an answer appears in my inbox. My focus is on story, not continuity, and I'm sure it shows; but the situation would be much worse without the help of my friends.

Indeed, life would be much worse without the help of my friends. That's another matter, but it seems proper to make public acknowledgment of that too.

My wife, Jo, continues to run the house and coddle me while I'm writing. Which I do most of my waking life, so it isn't a small or an easy task.

I could not write as I do without the help of those named and of many others. Thank you all. I know how lucky I am.

—Dave Drake

ABOUT THE AUTHOR

David Drake was attending Duke University Law School when he was drafted. He served the next two years in the Army, spending 1970 as an enlisted interrogator with the 11th Armored Cavalry in Vietnam and Cambodia. Upon return he completed his law degree at Duke and was for eight years Assistant Town Attorney for Chapel Hill, North Carolina. He has been a full-time freelance writer since 1981. His books include the genre-defining and bestselling Hammer's Slammers series, and the nationally bestselling RCN series including *What Distant Deeps*, *The Road of Danger*, and *The Sea without a Shore*.

THE GENESIS FLEET

JACK CAMPBELL

VANGUARD
ASCENDANT
TRIUMPHANT (*May 2019*)

Earth is no longer the centre of the universe. After the invention of
the faster-than-light jump drive, humanity is rapidly establishing
new colonies. But the vast distances of space mean that the
protection of Earth's laws no longer exists. When a nearby world
attacks, the new colony of Glenlyon turns to Robert Geary, a former
junior fleet officer, and Mele Darcy, once an enlisted Marine. They
must face down warships with nothing but improvised weapons and
a few volunteers – or die trying.

The only hope for lasting peace lies with Carmen Ochoa, a
"Red" from anarchic Mars, and Lochan Nakamura, a failed
politician, and their plan for a mutual alliance. But if their efforts
don't succeed, space could become a battlefield between the first
interstellar Empires...

"Campbell's skilfully constructed tale keeps a riveting pace"
Publishers Weekly

"This book has the whole package"
Elizabeth Moon, bestselling author of the *Vatta's War series*

TITANBOOKS.COM

For more fantastic fiction, author events, exclusive excerpts,
competitions, limited editions and more

VISIT OUR WEBSITE

titanbooks.com

LIKE US ON FACEBOOK

facebook.com/titanbooks

FOLLOW US ON TWITTER

@TitanBooks

EMAIL US

readerfeedback@titanemail.com